THE GLOBAL CONSPIRACY EXPOSED

Collusion of the World Government, the Elite, and Agenda 21 and the Veracity of the Fallen Angels and UFOs

THE WHISTLEBLOWER

PAGE PUBLISHING, INC.
Conneaut Lake, PA

First originally published by Page Publishing 2021

ISBN 978-1-6624-0445-0 (pbk)
ISBN 978-1-6624-6405-8 (hc)
ISBN 978-1-6624-0446-7 (digital)

Printed in the United States of America

CONTENTS

Author's Note

This book asks an important question: Who really wields power in America and around the world today? This very question is widely debated in government, the media, and the general public. I am adding my own voice to that public conversation.

You will find some strong opinions in this book. Needless to say, I do not claim or suggest any endorsement by or affiliation with the individuals and organizations that are mentioned or quoted in these pages. The opinions you find here are my own.

Acknowledgements

A good portion of the material in this book has been reprinted with permission from the original authors because these authors are highly educated on the subject matter and have articulated it in way that will captivate readers. This material is available for all to see on the internet, but most people have no knowledge of its existence or the authors who created it. That irritates me because the material presented by these great patriots is intended to save our republic. Thus, the intent of this book is to draw attention to these valuable people, who are largely unknown and should have a wider audience.

Tom DeWeese at the American Policy Center at http://
    americanpolicy.org
Stephen Lendman at http://stephenlendman.org
Eileen DeRolf at http://agenda21course.com
Dane Wigington at http://geoengineeringwatch.org
Minister Irvin Baxter at http://endtime.com
Global Research at http://globalreseach.ca
The History Channel's *Ancient Aliens* series
Daniel Estulin, author

Chapter 1
The World Government Conspiracy

World Government: Conspiracy Theory or Conspiracy Fact?

This book offers compelling evidence that the world government is a conspiracy fact and is about to become a reality.

The following article is a review of Daniel Estulin's book *The True Story of the Bilderberg Group*. The article was written by Stephen Lendman and has been reprinted here with permission.

The article has been split into two parts, comprising chapters 1 and 2 of this book.

> "Fifty men have run America and that's a high number."
> —Joseph Kennedy, father of JFK, from the *New York Times*, July 26, 1936

* * *

The True Story of the Bilderberg Group and What They May Be Planning Now (Part One)

By Stephen Lendman

Daniel Estulin has investigated and researched the Bilderberg Group's far-reaching influence on business and finance, global politics, war and peace, and control of the world's resources and its money.

His book, *The True Story of the Bilderberg Group*, was published in 2005 and is now updated in a new 2009 edition. He states that in 1954, "the most powerful men in the world met for the first time" in Oosterbeek, the Netherlands, "debated the future of the world," and decided to meet annually in secret. They called themselves the Bilderberg Group with a membership representing a who's who of world power elites, mostly from America, Canada, and Western Europe, with familiar names like David Rockefeller, Henry Kissinger, Bill Clinton, Gordon Brown, Angela Merkel, Alan Greenspan, Ben Bernanke, Larry Summers, Tim Geithner, Lloyd Blankfein, George Soros, Donald Rumsfeld, Rupert Murdoch, and other heads of state, influential senators, congressmen and parliamentarians, Pentagon and NATO brass, members of European royalty, selected media figures, and others—some invited quietly by some accounts, like Barrack Obama and many of his top officials.

Always well represented are top figures from the Council on Foreign Relations (CFR), International Monetary Fund (IMF), World Bank, Trilateral Commission (TC), European Union (EU), and powerful central bankers from the Federal Reserve, the European Central Bank's Jean Claude Trichet, and Bank of England's Mervyn King.

For over half a century, no agenda or discussion topics became public nor is any press coverage allowed. The few invited fourth-estate attendees and their bosses are sworn to secrecy. Nonetheless, Estulin undertook "an investigative journey" that became his life's work. He states, "Slowly, one by one, I have penetrated the layers of secrecy surrounding the Bilderberg Group, but I could not have done this without help of 'conscientious objectors' from inside, as well as outside, the group's membership." As a result, he keeps their names confidential.

Whatever its early mission, the group is now "a world shadow government…threaten[ing] to take away our right to direct our own destinies [by creating] a disturbing reality," very much harming the public's welfare. In short, Bilderbergers want to supplant individual nation-state sovereignty with an all-powerful global government, corporate controlled, and checkmated by militarized enforcement.

"Imagine a private club where presidents, prime ministers, international generals, and bankers rub shoulders, where gracious royal chaperones ensure everyone gets along, and where the people running the wars, markets, and Europe (and America) say what they never dare to say in public."

Early in its history, Bilderbergers decided "to create an 'Aristocracy of purpose' between Europe and the United States [to reach consensus to rule the world on matters of] policy, economics, and [overall] strategy." NATO was essential for their plans—to ensure "perpetual war [and] nuclear blackmail" to be used as necessary. Then proceed to loot the planet, achieve fabulous wealth and power, and crush all challengers to keep it. Along with military dominance, controlling the world's money is crucial, for with it comes absolute control, as the powerful nineteenth-century Rothschild family understood. As the patriarch Amschel Rothschild once said, "Give me control of a nation's money and I care not who makes its laws."

Bilderbergers comprise the world's most exclusive club. No one buys their way in. Only the group's Steering Committee decides whom to invite, and in all cases, participants are adherents to One World Order governance run by top-power elites.

According to Steering Committee rules,

> The invited guests must come alone; no wives, girlfriends, husbands or boyfriends, personal assistants [meaning security, bodyguards, CIA or other secret service protectors] cannot attend the conference and must eat in a separate hall. [Also] The guests are explicitly forbidden from giving interviews to journalists" or divulge anything that goes on in the meetings.
>
> Host governments provide overall security to keep away outsiders. One third of attendees are political figures. The others are from industry, finance, academia, labor, and communications.

11

Meeting procedure is by Chatham House rules letting attendees freely express their views in a relaxed atmosphere knowing nothing said will be quoted or revealed to the public. Meetings "are always frank, but do not always conclude with consensus.

Membership consists of annual attendees (around eighty of the world's most powerful) and others only invited occasionally because of their knowledge or involvement in relevant topics. Those most valued are asked back, and some first-timers are chosen for their possible later usefulness.

Arkansas Governor Bill Clinton, for example, attended in 1991. "There, David Rockefeller told [him] why the North American Free Trade Agreement...was a Bilderberg priority and that the group needed him to support it. The next year, Clinton was elected president," and on January 1, 1994 NAFTA took effect. Numerous other examples are similar, including who gets chosen for powerful government, military, and other key positions.

Bilderberg Objectives

The group's grand design is for a one-world government (world company) with a single, global marketplace, policed by one world army, and financially regulated by one world (central) bank, using one global currency. Their "wish list" includes the following:

- One international identity observing one set of universal values
- Centralized control of world populations by "mind control"—in other words, controlling world public opinion
- A New World Order with no middle class, only rulers and servants (serfs), and of course, no democracy
- A zero-growth society, without prosperity or progress, only greater wealth and power for the rulers
- Manufactured crises and perpetual wars

- Absolute control of education to program the public mind and train those chosen for various roles
- Centralized control of all foreign and domestic policies—one size fits all globally
- Using the UN as a de facto world government, imposing a UN tax on world citizens
- Expanding NAFTA and WTO globally
- Making NATO a world military
- Imposing a universal legal system
- A global "welfare state where obedient slaves will be rewarded and non-conformists targeted for extermination"

Secret Bilderberg Partners

In the US, the Council on Foreign Relations (CFR) is dominant. One of its 1921 founders, Edward Mandell House, was Woodrow Wilson's chief advisor and rumored at the time to be the nation's real power from 1913 to 1921. On his watch, the Federal Reserve Act passed in December 1913, giving money creation power to bankers, and the Sixteenth Amendment was ratified in February, creating the federal income tax to provide a revenue stream to pay for government debt service.

From its beginnings, CFR was committed to "a one-world government based on a centralized global financing system." Today, CFR has thousands of influential members (including important ones in the corporate media) but keeps a low public profile, especially regarding its real agenda. Historian Arthur Schlesinger Jr. called it a "front organization [for] the heart of the American establishment." It meets privately and only publishes what it wishes the public to know. Its members are only Americans.

The Trilateral Commission (discussed below) is a similar group that "brings together global power brokers." It was founded by David Rockefeller, and he's also a leading Bilderberger and CFR chairman emeritus; these are organizations he continues to finance and support.

Their past and current members reflect their power:

- Nearly all presidential candidates of both parties
- Leading senators and congressmen
- Key members of the fourth estate and their bosses
- Top officials of the FBI, CIA, NSA, defense establishment, and other leading government agencies, including state, commerce, judiciary, and treasury

For its part, "CFR has served as a virtual employment agency for the federal government under both Democrats and Republicans." Whoever occupies the White House, "CFR's power and agenda have been unchanged since its 1921 founding."

It advocates a global super-state with America and other nations sacrificing their sovereignty to a central power. CFR founder Paul Warburg was a member of Roosevelt's "brain trust." In 1950, his son, James, told the Senate Foreign Relations Committee, "We shall have world government whether or not you like it—by conquest or consent."

Later, at the 1992 Bilderberg meeting, Henry Kissinger said,

> Today, Americans would be outraged if UN troops entered Los Angeles to restore order; tomorrow, they will be grateful. This is especially true if they were told there was an outside threat from beyond, whether real or promulgated, that threatened our very existence. It is then that all people of the world will plead with world leaders to deliver them from this evil... Individual-rights will be willingly relinquished for the guarantee of their well-being granted to them by their world government.

CFR planned a New World Order before 1942, and the "UN began with a group of CFR members called the Informal Agenda Group." They drafted the original UN proposal, presenting it to

Franklin Roosevelt, who announced it publicly the next day. At its 1945 founding, CFR members comprised over forty of the US delegates.

According to Professor G. William Domhoff, author of *Who Rules America,* the CFR operates in "small groups of about twenty-five, who bring together leaders from the six conspirator categories (industrialists, financers, ideologues, military, professional specialists—lawyers, medical doctors, etc.—and organized labor) for detailed discussions of specific topics in the area of foreign affairs." Domhoff added, "The Council on Foreign Relations, while not financed by the government, works so closely with it that it is difficult to distinguish Council action stimulated by government from autonomous actions. [Its] most important sources of income are leading corporations and major foundations." The Rockefeller, Carnegie, and Ford Foundations, to name three, and they are directed by key corporate officials.

Dominant Media Partners

Former CBS News president Richard Salant (1961–1964 and 1966–1979) explained the major media's role: "Our job is to give people not what they want, but what we decide they ought to have."

CBS and other media giants control everything we see, hear, and read through television, radio, newspapers, magazines, books, films, and large portions of the internet. Their top officials and some journalists attend Bilderberg meetings—on a condition that they report nothing.

The Rockefeller family wields enormous power, even though its reigning patriarch, David, will be ninety-four on June 12 and surely near the end of his dominance. However, for years "the Rockefellers [led by David] gained great influence over the media. [With it] the family gained sway over public opinion. With the pulse of public opinion, they gained deep influence in politics. And with this politics of subtle corruption, they are taking control of the nation" and now aim for total world domination.

The Bilderberg-Rockefeller scheme is to make their views so appealing (by camouflaging them) that they become public policy and can pressure world leaders into submitting to the needs of the masters of the universe. "The free world press" is their instrument to disseminate "agreed-upon propaganda."

CFR Cabinet Control

"The National Security Act of 1947 established the office of Secretary of Defense." Since then, fourteen DOD secretaries have been CFR members. Since 1940, every Secretary of state, except James Bymes, has been a CFR member or Trilateral Commission (TC) member.

For the past eighty years, virtually every key US national security and foreign policy advisor has been a CFR member.

Nearly all top generals and admirals have been CFR members.

Many presidential candidates were/are CFR members, including Herbert Hoover, Adlai Stevenson, Dwight Eisenhower, John Kennedy, Richard Nixon, Gerald Ford, Jimmy Carter (also a charter TC member), G. H. W. Bush, Bill Clinton, John Kerry, and John McCain.

Numerous CIA directors were/are CFR members, including Richard Helms, James Schlesinger, William Casey, William Webster, Robert Gates, James Woolsey, John Deutsch, George Tenet, Porter Goss, Michael Hayden, and Leon Panetta.

Many treasury secretaries were/are CFR members, including Douglas Dillion, George Schultz, William Simon, James Baker, Nicholas Brady, Lloyd Bentsen, Robert Rubin, Henry Paulson, and Tim Geithner.

When presidents nominate Supreme Court candidates, the CFR's "Special Group, Secret Team" or advisors, vet them for acceptability. Presidents, in fact, are told who to appoint, including designees to the high court and most lower ones.

Programming the Public Mind

According to sociologist Hadley Cantril in his 1967 book, *The Human Dimension—Experiences in Policy Research*, government "psycho-political operations are propaganda campaigns designed to create perpetual tension and to manipulate different groups of people to accept the particular climate of opinion the CFR seeks to achieve in the world."

Canadian writer Ken Adachi (1929–1989) added, "What most Americans believe to be 'public opinion' is in reality carefully crafted and scripted propaganda designed to elicit a desired behavioral response from the public."

And noted Australian academic and activist Alex Carey (1922–1988) explained the three most important twentieth century developments: "The growth of democracy, the growth of corporate power, and the growth of corporate propaganda as a means of protecting corporate power against democracy."

Web of Control

Numerous think tanks, foundations, the major media, and other key organizations are staffed with CFR members. Most of its life-members also belong to the Trilateral Commission (TC) and the Bilderberg Group, operate secretly, and wield enormous power over US and world affairs.

The Rockefeller-Founded Trilateral Commission (TC)

On page 405 of his *Memoirs*, David Rockefeller wrote,

> Some even believe we are part of a secret cabal working against the best interests of the United States characterizing my family and me as "internationalists" and conspiring with others around the world to build a more integrated global, political, and economic structure—one world, if

you will. If that's the charge, I stand guilty, and I am proud of it.

In alliance with Bilderbergers, the TC also "plays a vital role in the New World Order's scheme to use wealth, concentrated in the hands of the few, to exert world control." TC members share common views and all relate to total, unchallengeable global dominance.

Founded in 1973 and headquartered in Washington, its powerful US, EU, and East Asian members seek its operative founding goal—a "New International Economic Order," now simply a "New World Order" run by global elites from these three parts of the world with lesser members admitted from other countries.

According to TC's website, "each regional group has a chairman and deputy chairman, who all together constitute the leadership of the Committee. The Executive Committee draws together a further thirty-six individuals from the wider membership," proportionately representing the US, EU, and East Asia in its early years, now engaged to be broadly global.

Committee members meet several times annually to discuss and coordinate their work. The executive committee chooses members, and at any time around 350 belong for a three-year renewable period. Everyone is a consummate insider with expertise in business, finance, politics, the military, or the media, including past presidents, secretaries of state, international bankers, think tank and foundation executives, university presidents and selected academics, and former senators and congressmen among others. Although its annual reports are available for purchase, its inner workings, current goals, and operations are secret—with good reason. Its objectives harm the public, so they mustn't be revealed. *Trilaterals over Washington* author, Anthony Sutton, wrote, "This group of private citizens is precisely organized in a manner that ensures its collective views have significant impact on public policy."

In her book, *Trilateralism: The Trilateral Commission and Elite* *r World Management,* Holly Sklar wrote, "Powerful figerica, Europe, and East Asia let "the rich…safeguard the Western capitalism in an explosive world—probably by discouraging protectionism, nationalism, or any response that would pit the elites of one against the elites of another," in their common quest for global dominance."

Trilateralist Zbigniew Brzezinski (TC's cofounder) wrote in his *Between Two Ages: America's Role in the Technetronic Era*, "People, governments and economies of all nations must serve the needs of multinational banks and corporations. [The Constitution is] inadequate…the old framework of international politics, with their sphere and influence…the fiction of sovereignty…is clearly no longer compatible with reality."

TC today is now global with members from countries as diverse as Argentina, Ukraine, Israel, Jordan, Brazil, Turkey, China, and Russia. In his *Trilaterals Over America*, Anthony Sutton believes that TC's aim is to collaborate with Bilderbergers and CFR in "establishing public policy objectives to be implemented by governments worldwide." He added that "Trilateralists have rejected the US Constitution and the democratic political process." In fact, TC was established to counter a "crisis in democracy"—too much of it that had to be contained.

An official TC report was fearful about "the increased popular participation in and control over established social, political, and economic institutions and especially a reaction against the concentration of power of Congress and of state and local government."

To address this, media control was essential to exert "restraint on what newspapers may publish [and TV and radio broadcasts]." Then, according to Richard Gardner in the July 1974 issue of *Foreign Affairs* (a CFR publication), CFR's leadership must make "an end run around national sovereignty, eroding it piece by piece" until the very notion disappears from the public discourse.

Bilderberg/CFR/Trilateralist success depends on finding "a way to get us to surrender our liberties in the name of some common threat or crisis. The foundations, educational institutions, and research think tanks supported by [these organizations] oblige by financing so-called 'studies,' which are then used to justify their every excess. The excuses vary, but the target is always individual liberty, our liberty," and much more.

Bilderbergers, Trilateralists, and CFR members want, "an all-encompassing monopoly"—over government, money, industry, and property that's "self-perpetuating and eternal." In *Confessions of a Monopolist* (1906), Frederick C. Howe explained its workings in practice:

> The rules of big business: Get a monopoly; let Society work for you. So long as we see all international revolutionaries and all international capitalists as implacable enemies of one another, then we miss a crucial point…a partnership between international monopoly capitalism and international revolutionary socialism is for their mutual benefit.

In *The Rockefeller File*, Gary Allen wrote, "By the late nineteenth century, the inner sanctums of Wall Street understood that the most efficient way to gain a monopoly was to say it was for the 'public good' and 'public interest.'"

David Rockefeller learned the same thing from his father, John D. Jr., who learned it from his father, John D. Sr. They hated competition and relentlessly strove to eliminate it—for David on a global scale through a New World Order.

In the 1970s and 1980s, Trilateralists and CFR members collaborated on the latter's 1980 Project, the largest-ever CFR initiative to steer world events toward a particular desirable future outcome involving the utter disintegration of the economy. "Why so?" is the question.

Because by the 1950s and 1960s, worldwide industrial growth meant more competition. It was also a model to be followed and had to be "strangled in the cradle" or at least greatly contained. In America as well, beginning in the 1980s. The result has been a transfer of wealth from the poor to the rich, shrinkage of the middle class, and plan for its eventual demise.

* * *

Key Quotes from the First Part of Mr. Lendman's Review Article

The following has been quoted from the first part of Mr. Lendman's review article "The True Story of the Bilderberg Group and What They May be Planning Now," which is reprinted in this chapter.

Whatever its early mission, the group is now "a shadow world government...threaten[ing] to take away our right to direct our own destinies [by creating] a disturbing reality" very much harming the public's welfare. In short, Bilderbergers want to supplant individual nation-state sovereignty with an all-powerful global government, corporate controlled, and checkmated by militarized enforcement.

Imagine a private club where presidents, prime ministers, international bankers and generals rub shoulders, where gracious royal chaperones ensure everyone gets along, and where the people running the wars, markets, and Europe [and America] say what they never dare say in public.

Early in its history, Bilderbergers decided "to create an 'aristocracy of purpose' between Europe and the United States [to reach consensus to rule the world on matters of] policy, economics, and [overall] strategy." NATO was essential for their plans—to ensure "perpetual war [and] nuclear blackmail" to be used as necessary. Then proceed to loot the planet, achieve fabulous wealth and power, and crush all challengers to keep it.

Bilderbergers comprise the world's most exclusive club. No one buys their way in. Only the group's Steering Committee decides whom to invite, and in all cases, participants are adherents to One World Order governance run by top-power elites.

According to the Sterling Committee Rules, "Host governments provide overall security to keep away outsiders. One-third of attendees are political figures. The others are from industry, finance, academia, labor, and communications."

Membership consists of annual attendees (around eighty of the world's most powerful) and others only invited occasionally because of their knowledge or involvement in relevant topics. Those most valued are asked back, and some first-timers are chosen for their possible later usefulness.

Arkansas Governor Bill Clinton, for example, attended in 1991. "There, David Rockefeller told [him] why the North American Free Trade Agreement…was a Bilderberg priority and that the group needed him to support it. The next year, Clinton was elected president," and on January 1, 1994 NAFTA took effect. Numerous other examples are similar, including who gets chosen for powerful government, military, and other key positions.

Bilderberg Objectives

The Group's grand design is for a one-world government (world company) with a single, global marketplace, policed by one world army, and financially regulated by one world (central) bank, using one global currency. Their "wish list" includes the following:

- One international identity observing one set of universal values
- Centralized control of world populations by "mind control"—in other words, controlling world public opinion
- A New World Order with no middle class, only rulers and servants (serfs), and of course, no democracy
- A zero-growth society, without prosperity or progress, only greater wealth and power for the rulers
- Manufactured crises and perpetual wars
- Absolute control of education to program the public mind and train those chosen for various roles
- Centralized control of all foreign and domestic policies— one size fits all globally
- Using the UN as a de facto world government, imposing a UN tax on world citizens
- Expanding NAFTA and WTO globally
- Making NATO a world military
- Imposing a universal legal system
- A global "welfare state where obedient slaves will be rewarded and non-conformists targeted for extermination"

Secret Bilderberg Partners

In the US, the Council on Foreign Relations (CFR) is dominant. One of its 1921 founders, Edward Mandell House, was Woodrow Wilson's chief advisor and rumored at the time to be the nation's
real power from 1913 to 1921. On his watch, the Federal Reserve Act
passed in December 1913, giving money creation power to bankers,
and the Sixteenth Amendment was ratified in February, creating the
federal income tax to provide a revenue stream to pay for government
debt service.

From its beginnings, CFR was committed to "a one-world
government based on a centralized global financing system." Today,
CFR has thousands of influential members (including important
ones in the corporate media) but keeps a low public profile, especially regarding its real agenda."

For its part, "CFR has served as a virtual employment agency
for the federal government under both Democrats and Republicans."
Whoever occupies the White House, "CFR's power and agenda have
been unchanged since its 1921 founding."

It advocates a global super-state with America and other nations
sacrificing their sovereignty to a central power. CFR founder Paul
Warburg was a member of Roosevelt's "brain trust." In 1950, his
son, James, told the Senate Foreign Relations Committee, "We shall
have world government whether or not you like it—by conquest or
consent."

CFR planned a New World Order before 1942, and the "UN
began with a group of CFR members called the Informal Agenda
Group." They drafted the original UN proposal, presenting it to
Franklin Roosevelt, who announced it publicly the next day. At
its 1945 founding, CFR members comprised over forty of the US
delegates.

According to Professor G. William Domhoff, author of *Who
Rules America,* the CFR operates in "small groups of about twenty-five, who bring together leaders from the six conspirator categories (industrialists, financiers, ideologues, military, professional specialists—lawyers, medical doctors, etc.—and organized labor) for

detailed discussions of specific topics in the area of foreign affairs."
Domhoff added, "The Council on Foreign Relations, while not
financed by the government, works so closely with it that it is difficult to distinguish Council action stimulated by government from
autonomous actions. [Its] most important sources of income are
leading corporations and major foundations." The Rockefeller, Carnegie, and Ford Foundations, to name three, and they are directed by
key corporate officials.

Dominant Media Partners

Former CBS News president Richard Salant (1961–1964 and
1966–1979) explained the major media's role: "Our job is to give
people not what they want, but what we decide they ought to have."

CBS and other media giants control everything we see, hear,
and read through television, radio, newspapers, magazines, books,
films, and large portions of the internet. Their top officials and some
journalists attend Bilderberg meetings—on a condition that they
report nothing.

CFR Cabinet Control

For the past 80 years, "Virtually every key US national security
and foreign policy advisor has been a CFR member."

Nearly all top generals and admirals have been CFR members.

Many presidential candidates were/are CFR members, includ-
ing Herbert Hoover, Adlai Stevenson, Dwight Eisenhower, John
Kennedy, Richard Nixon, Gerald Ford, Jimmy Carter (also a charter
TC member), George H. W. Bush, Bill Clinton, John Kerry, and
John McCain.

Numerous CIA directors were/are CFR members, including
Richard Helmes, James Schlesinger, William Casey, William Webster, Robert Gates, James Woolsey, John Deutsch, George Tenet, Porter Goss, Michael Hayden, and Leon Panetta.

Many treasury secretaries were/are CFR members, including Douglas Dillon, George Schultz, William Simon, James Baker,

Nicholas Brady, Lloyd Bentsen, Robert Rubin, Henry Paulson, and Tim Geithner.

When presidents nominate Supreme Court candidates, the CFR's "Special Group, Secret Team" or advisors, vet them for acceptability. Presidents, in fact, are told who to appoint, including designees to the high court and most lower ones.

Programing the Public Mind

According to sociologist Hadley Cantril in his 1967 book, *The Human Dimension—Experiences in Policy Research*, government "psycho-political operations are propaganda campaigns designed to create perpetual tension and to manipulate different groups of people to accept the particular climate of opinion the CFR seeks to achieve in the world."

Canadian writer Ken Adachi (1929–1989) added, "What most Americans believe to be 'public opinion' is in reality carefully crafted and scripted propaganda designed to elicit a desired behavioral response from the public."

And noted Australian academic and activist Alex Carey (1922–1988) explained the three most important twentieth century developments: "The growth of democracy, the growth of corporate power, and the growth of corporate propaganda as a means of protecting corporate power against democracy."

Web of Control

In alliance with Bilderbergers, the TC also "plays a vital role in the New World Order's scheme to use wealth, concentrated in the hands of the few, to exert world control." TC members share common views and all relate to total, unchallengeable global dominance.

Founded in 1973 and headquartered in Washington, its powerful US, EU, and East Asian members seek its operative founding goal—a "New International Economic Order," now simply a "New World Order" run by global elites from these three parts of the world with lesser members admitted from other countries.

TC today is now global with members from countries as diverse as Argentina, Ukraine, Israel, Jordan, Brazil, Turkey, China, and Russia. In his *Trilaterals Over America,* Anthony Sutton believes that TC's aim is to collaborate with Bilderbergers and CFR in "establishing public policy objectives to be implemented by governments worldwide." He added that "Trilateralists have rejected the US Constitution and the democratic political process." In fact, TC was established to counter a "crisis in democracy"—too much of it that had to be contained.

Bilderberg/CFR/Trilateralist success depends on finding "a way to get us to surrender our liberties in the name of some common threat or crisis. The foundations, educational institutions, and research think tanks supported by [these organizations] oblige by financing so-called 'studies,' which are then used to justify their every excess. The excuses vary, but the target is always individual liberty, our liberty," and much more.

CHAPTER 2
The North American Union Agenda

The True Story of the Bilderberg Group and What They May Be Planning Now (Part Two)

By Stephen Lendman

The North American Union (NAU)

The idea emerged during the Reagan administration in the early 1980s. David Rockefeller, George Schultz, and Paul Volker told the president that Canada and America could be politically and economically merged over the next fifteen years except for one problem—French-speaking Quebec. Their solution was to elect a Bilderberg-friendly prime minister, separate Quebec from the other provinces, then make Canada America's fifty-first state. It almost worked, but not quite when a 1995 secession referendum was defeated, 50.56 percent to 49.44 percent, but not the idea of a merger.

At a March 23, 2005, Waco, Texas, meeting attended by George Bush, Mexico's Vincente Fox and Canada's Paul Martin, the Security and Prosperity Partnership (SPP) was launched, also known as the North American Union (NAU). It was a secretive Independent Task Force of North America agreement, a group organized by a Canadian Council of Chief Executives (CCCE), the Mexican Council on Foreign Relations, and the CFR with the following aims:

- Circumventing the legislatures of three countries and their constitutions

- Suppressing public knowledge or consideration
- Proposing greater US, Canadian, and Mexican economic, political, social, and security integration with secretive working groups formed to devise non-debatable, not voted on agreements to be binding and unchangeable

In short, a corporate coup d'état against the sovereignty of three nations enforced by hardline militarization to suppress opposition.

If enacted, it will create a borderless North America, corporate controlled, without barriers to trade or capital flows for business giants, mainly US ones, and much more—America's access to vital resources, especially oil and Canada's fresh water.

Secretly, over three hundred SPP initiatives were crafted to harmonize the continent's policies on energy, food, drugs, security, immigration, manufacturing, the environment, and public health along with militarizing three nations for enforcement.

SPP represents another step toward the Bilderberg/Trilateralist/CFR goal for world government, taking it one step at a time. A "united Europe" was another, the result of various treaties and economic agreements:

- The December 1951 six-nation European Coal and Steel Community (ECSC)
- The March 1957 six-nation Treaty of Rome establishing the Economic Community (EEC); also, the European Atomic Energy Commission (EAEC) by a second Treaty of Rome
- The October 1957 European Court of Justice to settle regional trade disputes
- The May 1960 seven-nation European Free Trade Association (EFTA)
- The July 1967 European Economic Community (EEC) merging the ECSC, EAEC, and EEC together in one organization
- The 1968 European Customs Union to abolish duties and establish uniform imports taxing among EEC members

- The 1978 European Currency Unit (ECU)
- The February 1986 Single European Act revision of the 1957 Treaty of Rome, establishing the objective of forming a Common Market by December 31, 1992
- The February 1992 Maastricht Treaty, creating the EU on November 1, 1993
- The name *euro,* adopted in December 1995, was introduced in January 1999, replacing the European Currency Unit (ECU); euros began circulating on January 2002 and are now the official currency of sixteen of the twenty-seven EU states

Over half a century, the above steps cost EU members their sovereignty "as some 70 to 80 percent of the laws passed in Europe involve just rubber stamping of regulations already written by nameless bureaucrats in 'working groups' in Brussels or Luxembourg."

The EU and NAU share common features:

- Advocacy from an influential spokesperson
- An economic and later political union
- Hard line security, and for Europe, ending wars on the continent between EU member states
- Establishment of collective consciousness in place of nationalism
- The blurring of borders and creation of a "supra-government," a super-state
- Secretive arrangements to mask real objectives
- The creation of a common currency and eventual global one

Steps Toward a North American Union

- The October 4, 1988 Free Trade Agreement (FTA) between the US and Canada, finalized the previous year
- At the 1991 Bilderberg meeting, David Rockefeller got Governor Bill Clinton's support for NAFTA if he became president

- On January 1, 1994, with no debate under "fast-track" rules, Congress approved WTO legislation.
- In December 1994, at the first Summit of the Americas, thirty-four hemispheric leaders committed their nations to a Free Trade Area of the Americas (FTAA) by 2005—so far unachieved.
- In July 2000, Mexican president Vincente Fox called for a North American common market in twenty years.
- In February 2001, the White House published a joint statement from George Bush and Vincente Fox called the Guanajuato Proposal; it was for a US-Canada-Mexico prosperity partnership (a.k.a. the North American Union).
- In September 2001, Bush and Fox agreed to the Partnership for Prosperity initiative.
- The September 11, 2001 attack gave cover to including "security" as part of a future partnership.
- On October 7, 2001, a CFA meeting highlighted the future of North American integration in the wake of terrorist attacks; for the first time, "security" became part of a future "partnership for prosperity"; also, Canada was to be included in a North American agreement.
- In 2002, the North American Forum on Integration (NAF) was established in Montreal "to address the issues raised by North American integration as well as identify new ideas and strategies to reinforce the North American Region."
- In January 2003, the Canadian Council of Chief Executives (CCCE, composed of 150 top CEOs) launched the North American Security and Prosperity Partnership of North America, calling for continental integration.
- In April 2004, Canadian Prime Minister Paul Martin announced the nation's first-ever national security policy called Securing an Open Society.
- On October 15, 2004, CFR established an Independent Task Force on the Future of North America—for a future continental union.

- In March 2005, a CFR report titled *Creating a North American Community* called for continental integration by 2010 "to enhance, prosperity, and opportunity for all North Americans."
- On March 23, 2005, in Waco, Texas, American, Canadian and Mexican leaders launched the Security and Prosperity Partnership (SPP)—a.k.a. the North American Union (NAU).

Secretive negotiations continue. Legislative debate is excluded, and public inclusion and debate are off the table. In May 2005, the CFR Independent Task Force on the Future of North America published a follow-up report titled *Building a North American Community*, proposing a borderless three-nation union by 2010.

In June and July 2005, the Dominican Republic-Central America Free Trade Agreement (DR-CAFTA) passed the Senate and the House, establishing corporate-approved trade rules to further impoverish the region and move a step closer to continental integration.

In March 2006, the North American Competitive Council (NACC) was created at the second SPP summit in Cancun, Mexico. Composed of 30 top North American CEOs, it serves as an official trilateral SPP working group.

Secret business and government meetings continue, so there's no way to confirm SPP's current status or if Barack Obama is seamlessly continuing George Bush's agenda. In an earlier article, this writer said that SPP efforts paused during the Bush to Obama transition, but "deep-integration plans" remain. Canada's Fraser Institute proposed renaming the initiative the North American Standards and Regulatory Area (NASRA) to distinguish its real purpose. It said the "SPP brand" is tarnished so rebranding is essential—to fool the public until it is too late to matter.

Bilderbergers, Trilateralists, and CFR leaders back it as another step toward global integration and won't "stop until the entire world is unified under the auspices and the political umbrella of a one-world company, a nightmarish borderless world run by the world's most powerful clique" comprised of key elitist members of these dominant organizations.

In April 2007, the Transatlantic Economic Council was established between America and the EU to

- create an official international governmental body by executive fiat;
- harmonize economic and regulatory objectives;
- move towards a Transatlantic Common Market; and
- step closer to one-world government run by the world's most powerful corporate interests.

* * *

Key Quotes from the Second Part of Mr. Lendman's Review Article

The following has been quoted from the second part of Mr. Lendman's review article "The True Story of the Bilderberg Group and What They May be Planning Now," which is reprinted in this chapter.

The North American Union (NAU)

At a March 23, 2005, Waco, Texas, meeting attended by George Bush, Mexico's Vincente Fox and Canada's Paul Martin, the Security and Prosperity Partnership (SPP) was launched, also known as the North American Union (NAU). It was a secretive Independent Task Force of North America agreement, a group organized by a Canadian Council of Chief Executives (CCCE), the Mexican Council on Foreign Relations, and the CFR with the following aims:

- Circumventing the legislatures of three countries and their constitutions
- Suppressing public knowledge or consideration
- Proposing greater US, Canadian, and Mexican economic, political, social, and security integration with secretive

32

working groups formed to devise non-debatable, not voted
on agreements to be binding and unchangeable

In short, a corporate coup d'état against the sovereignty of three
nations enforced by hardline militarization to suppress opposition.

If enacted, it will create a borderless North America, corporate
controlled, without barriers to trade or capital flows for business
giants, mainly US ones, and much more—America's access to vital
resources, especially oil and Canada's fresh water.

- At the 1991 Bilderberg meeting, David Rockefeller got
  Governor Bill Clinton's support for NAFTA if he became
  president
- On October 7, 2001, a CFA meeting highlighted the
  future of North American integration in the wake of terrorist attacks; for the first time, "security" became part of a
  future "partnership for prosperity"; also, Canada was to be
  included in a North American agreement.
- On October 15, 2004, CFR established an Independent
  Task Force on the Future of North America—for a future
  continental union.
- On March 23, 2005, in Waco, Texas, American, Canadian
  and Mexican leaders launched the Security and Prosperity
  Partnership (SPP)—a.k.a. the North American Union.

Secretive negotiations continue. Legislative debate is excluded,
and public inclusion and debate are off the table. In May 2005, the
CFR Independent Task Force on the Future of North America published a follow-up report titled *Building a North American Community*, proposing a borderless three-nation union by 2010.

In June and July 2005, the Dominican Republic-Central America Free Trade Agreement (DR-CAFTA) passed the Senate and the
House, establishing corporate-approved trade rules to further impoverish the region and move a step closer to continental integration.

Secret business and government meetings continue, so there's no way to confirm SPP's current status or if Barack Obama is seamlessly continuing George Bush's agenda. In an earlier article, this writer said that SPP efforts paused during the Bush to Obama transition, but "deep-integration plans" remain. Canada's Fraser Institute proposed renaming the initiative the North American Standards and Regulatory Area (NASRA) to distinguish its real purpose. It said the "SPP brand" is tarnished so rebranding is essential—to fool the public until it's too late to matter.

Bilderbergers, Trilateralists, and CFR leaders back it as another step toward global integration and won't "stop until the entire world is unified under the auspices and the political umbrella of a one-world company, a nightmarish borderless world run by the world's most powerful clique" comprised of key elitist members of these dominant organizations.

* * *

A Final Note

Before making one last addition to the arguments offered, by Estulin and Lendman, I want to thank Mr. Lendman again for his work and the use of his materials.

One of the many topics included at the 2009 Bilderberg Group annual meeting in Vouliagmeni, Greece during May 4–17 included **exploiting the swine flu scare** to create a WHO global department of health and the overall goal of a global government and the end of national sovereignty.

One of the aforementioned quotes bears repeating and should infuriate everyone concerned by the influx of migrants at our southern border because it reveals that **our legislators manufactured the crises**. Can you say "conspiracy"? Again, from Lendman: "In June and July 2005, the Dominican Republic-Central America Free Trade Agreement (DR-CAFTA) passed the Senate and the House, establishing corporate-approved trade rules to further impoverish the region and move a step closer to continental integration."

G. W. Bush has warned, on numerous occasions, that we should not buy into conspiracy theories. But his attendance at the March 23, 2005 meeting in Waco, Texas could indicate that he was and is aware of a conspiracy that he actually is or was a participant in, along with what appears to be the majority of our elected representatives from both parties.

CHAPTER 3
Incriminating Quotes and Events

The following quotes have been retrieved from multiple sources. All bolding and capitalization are my own; all italics are my notes and comments.

Slobodan Milosevic served as the Serbian president of the Federal Republic of Yugoslavia from 1997–2000. He didn't want to be integrated into the "United States of Europe," so **Clinton agitated for his removal.** The US and NATO led a military attack on Slobodan Milosevic, and ultimately, he was removed from power. The United States then demanded that he be placed on trial at the **World Court.** The Yugoslavian government issued an executive order approving his extradition to the **World Court** in Holland, but the Yugoslavian Supreme Court ruled it an unconstitutional order and stopped it. **That evening, helicopters swooped in and hauled him away.**

> —Rev. Irvin Baxter, founder and president of Endtime Ministries from his video "World Government Forming Now"

In 1910, there was a secret meeting at the Jekyll Island Resort (off the coast of Georgia) that laid the foundations for the Federal Reserve system. The attendees were Nelson Aldrich, A. Piatt

Andrew, Henry Davison, Arthur Shelton, Frank Vanderlip, and **Paul Warburg.** The intention of the meeting was to write a plan to reform the nation's banking system. The meeting and its purpose were closely guarded secrets, and the participants did not admit that the meeting occurred until the 1930s. But the plan written on Jekyll Island laid the foundation for what would eventually be the Federal Reserve system. **The purpose of the Federal Reserve Act**, which became law on December 23, 1913, was to **place control of Americas money into the hands of private bankers.** They set interest rates and determine the amount of money in circulation, which was **previously the job of our elected Congress** as per the Constitution.

—Rev. Irvin Baxter, from his video "Master Plan of the Dragon, Part 1"

The **world government plan** was launched between 1913–1921 with the creation of these three institutions:

- 1913, the Federal Reserve Bank
- 1916, the Brookings Institute (it's a **world government,** liberal think tank)
- 1921**, the Council on Foreign Relations (they establish the policies that are leading us into the one-world government system).**

—Rev. Irvin Baxter, "Master Plan of the Dragon, Part 1"

The CFR was kept a secret for many years because **50 percent of all cabinet members (both parties) over the last 50 years were members.**

—Rev. Irvin Baxter, "Master Plan of the Dragon: Part 2"

Special advisor for the Clinton administration, Strobe Talbott, authored a book titled *The Great Experiment,* **which is a blatant endorsement for a one-world government.**
—Rev. Irvin Baxter, "Master Plan of the Dragon: Part 2"

Globalization [a deceptive alternative phrase for world government] is the process of moving from the nation-state structure of the world to a **one-world global government structure.**
—Rev. Irvin Baxter, "Master Plan of the Dragon: Part 3"

The Libya invasion: **Obama bypassed our elected Congress** and instead **opted to go directly to the UN Security Council for approval to invade a sovereign nation.** With their approval, we sent our troops in and paid the bill. The UN has given itself authority to overthrow a sovereign nation's government if they deem it necessary and attempt to justify their actions via the **Responsibility to Protect Act.**
—Rev. Irvin Baxter, "Master Plan of the Dragon: Part 3"

As long as a child breathes the poisoned air of nationalism, education in world-mindedness can produce only precarious results. As we have pointed out, it is frequently the family that infects the child with extreme nationalism. The schools should therefore…**combat family attitudes that favor nationalism.** We shall see presently recognized in nationalism the major obstacle to the development of world-mindedness. We are at the beginning of a long process of **breaking down**

the walls of national sovereignty. UNESCO [United Nations Educational Scientific and Cultural Organization] must be the pioneer.
—William Benton, US assistant secretary of state for public affairs (1945–1947)

The tectonic era involves the gradual appearance of a more controlled society. **Such a society would be dominated by an elite unrestrained from traditional values.** Soon it will be possible to assert almost continuous surveillance over every citizen and maintain up-to-date complete files containing even the most personal information about the citizen. These files will be subject to instantaneous retrieval by the authorities.
—Zbigniew Brezinski, President Carter's national security advisor (1977–1981)

Perhaps the **world order of the future** will truly be a family of nations.
—G. H. W. Bush, US president (1989–1993)

We have before us the opportunity to forge for ourselves and for future generations a new world order... When we are successful, and we will be, we have a real chance at this **new world order**, an order in which a credible United Nations can use its peacekeeping role to fulfill the promise and visions of the UN founders.
—G. H. W. Bush

What is at stake is more than one small country; it is a big idea—**a new world order.**
—G. H. W. Bush

It's not the US against Iraq but Iraq against the world. The world can therefore seize the opportunity to fulfill the long-held promise of a **new world order** where diverse nations are drawn together in common cause to achieve the universal aspirations of mankind.

—G. H. W. Bush, after his decision to invade Iraq in 1990

G. W. Bush, US president (2001–2009), in 2006 signed into law the US Military Commissions Act, also known as HR-6166. It allows the US government to confine citizens without charges to be transported to foreign torture camps and be secretly executed.

In March 1915, the J.P. Morgan interests, the steel, shipbuilding, and powder interests and their subsidiary organizations, got together 12 men high up in the newspaper world and employed them to select the most influential newspapers in the United States and sufficient numbers of them **to control generally the policy of the daily press**... They found it was only necessary to **purchase the control** of 25 of the greatest papers. An agreement was reached; **the policy of the papers was bought,** to be paid for by the month; an editor was furnished for each paper to properly supervise and edit information regarding the questions of the preparedness, militarism, financial policies, and other things of national and international nature **considered vital to the interests of their purchasers.**

—Oscar Callaway, US congressman representing Texas (1911–1917)

We've become, now, an oligarchy [a form of government run by a small number of people, such as the very wealthy or the military] **instead of a democracy.** I think that's been the worst damage to the basic moral and ethical standards to the American political system that I've seen in my life.

—Jimmy Carter, US president (1977–1981)

Whatever starts in California unfortunately has an inclination to spread.

—Jimmy Carter

The plan is for the United States to rule the world. The overt theme is unilateralism, but it is ultimately a story of domination. It calls for the United Stated to maintain its overwhelming superiority and prevent new rivals from rising up to challenge it on the world stage. **It calls for dominion over friends and enemies alike.** It says not that the United States must be more powerful, but that it must be absolutely powerful.

—Dick Cheney, former US vice president, from a lecture at West Point in June 2002

Before the century ends, **we should establish a permanent international court** to prosecute the most serious violations of humanitarian law.

—Bill Clinton, US president (1993–2001) speaking at the UN General Assembly on September 22, 1997

On July 17, 1998, the International Criminal Court of Rome was established. To this day, any US citizen could be taken before that court and put on trial without the protection of the US Constitution or the Bill of Rights.

It seems to many of us that if we are to avoid the eventual catastrophic world conflict, we must strengthen the United Nations as a first step toward a world government patterned after our own government with a legislative, executive, and judiciary, and police to enforce its international laws and keep peace. To do that, of course, **we Americans will have to yield up some of our sovereignty.** That would be a bitter pill. It would take a lot of courage, a lot of faith in the new order. But the American colonies did it once and brought forth one of the nearly perfect unions the word has ever seen.

—Walter Cronkite, American broadcast journalist, in an acceptance speech before the UN in 200. He was accepting the Norman Cousins Award, which is given by the World Federalist Organization (now Citizens for Global Solutions) to the person that contributed the most toward advancing world government.

For a long time, I felt that FDR had many thoughts and ideas that were his own to benefit this country, the United States. **But he didn't.** Most of his thoughts, his political ammunition, as it were, **were carefully manufactured for him in advance by the Council on Foreign Relations-One World Money Group.** Brilliantly, with great gusto, like a fine piece of artillery, he exploded that prepared "ammunition" in the middle of an unsuspecting target, the American people, **and thus paid off and returned his internationalist political support.**

—Curtis Dall, Franklin Delano Roosevelt's son-in-law, in *F. D. R.: My Exploited Father-in-Law*

The UN is but a long range, international banking apparatus clearly set up for financial and economic profit by a small group of powerful One-World revolutionaries, hungry for profit and power.

—Curtis Dall

The depression was the calculated shearing of the public by the world money powers, triggered by the planned sudden shortage of call money in the New York money market... **The one-world government leaders** and **their ever-close bankers** have now acquired full control of the money and credit machinery of the US via the creation of the **Federal Reserve Bank.**

—Curtis Dall

As my beautiful wife puts it, elected officials only ostensibly run the visible government, as outlined in Civics 101. She says they are merely Muppets who do the bidding of the **Deep State,** the people **George W. Bush** referred to as **"the deciders"**—a fascinating phrase from a former president who was twice elected by voters who naively assumed that **Mr. Bush** would be the **"decider"** so long as he inhabited the Oval Office.

—James Dale Davidson, *The Breaking Point: Profit from the Coming Money Cataclysm*, pp. 236–237

The governments of the present day have to deal not merely with other governments, with emperors, kings, and ministers, but also with secret societies which have everywhere their unscrupulous agents, and can at the last moment upset all the government's plans.

—Benjamin Disraeli, British prime minister (1874–1880)

Israel has a security concern involving geography. But geography does not have the same value it had in 1967.

—Rahm Emanuel, Clinton advisor (1993–1999), mayor of Chicago (2011–2019)

Republicans can go fuck themselves.

—Rahm Emanuel

The United Nations is a dictatorship from which nothing good comes because they find a million ways to prevent anything from happening… Within the Security Council, there are five countries that have veto power. But without a doubt, the most influential country in the United Nations is the United States. And it's really amazing that **the most warmongering country in the history of mankind** is put there in charge to make sure that there is peace… The United Nations Charter tells you how you can proceed to reform it. They say you have to call a general conference, and how you have to call it, and the approval that you have to have from the Security Council. But at the end, when it's all said and done, when you have decided what reforms you want to make, they have a veto power over it. **So, it's a farce. It's a fraud… The United Nations is beyond reform.** It's beyond patchwork. It's the most important organization in the world to help

THE GLOBAL CONSPIRACY EXPOSED

save the human species and Mother Earth, but it has to be reinvented.

—Miguel d'Escoto, former UN General Assembly president

The Bilderberg Group has been meeting secretly behind closed doors once or twice each year since its formation. **Its purpose is to remove independence from all countries** and permit the atrocities to have **tyrannical rule from behind the military might of the United Nations.**

—Daniel Estulin, in *The True Story of the Bilderberg Group*

The idea was that those who direct the overall conspiracy could use the differences in those so-called ideologies [Marxism, fascism, socialism vs. democracy, capitalism] to enable them [the Illuminati] **to divide larger and larger portions of the human race into opposing camps so that they could be armed and then brain washed into fighting and destroying each other.**

—Myron Fagan, ardent anti-communist theorist and author

A taste of the ideas making the rounds in Obama circles is offered by a recent report from the Managing Global Insecurity (MGI) project, whose small US advisory group includes John Podesta, the man heading Obama's transition team, and Strobe Talbott, the president of the Brookings Institute, from which Ms. Rice has just emerged.

The MGI report argues for the creation of a UN high commissioner for counter-terrorist activity, **a legally binding climate-change agreement negotiated under the auspices of the**

UN and the creation of a fifty-thousand-strong UN peace keeping force. Once countries have pledged troops to this reserve army, **the UN will have first call upon them.**

> —The *Financial Times*, "And Now for a World Government," December 8, 2008

The real rulers in Washington are invisible and exercise power from behind the scenes.

> —Felix Frankfurter, associate justice of the US Supreme Court (1939–1962)

The UN is but a long-range, international banking apparatus clearly set up for financial and economic profit set up by a **small group of powerful one-world revolutionaries,** hungry for profit and power.

> —Felix Frankfurter

The **new world order** will have to be built from the bottom up rather from the top down...**an end-run around national sovereignty, eroding it piece by piece will accomplish much more than the old-fashioned frontal assault.**

> —Richard Gardner, Council on Foreign Relations member, in the 1974 issue of the CFR's *Foreign Affairs* magazine

If you tell a lie long enough and keep repeating it, people will eventually come to believe it. The lie can be maintained only for such time as **the State** can shield the people from the political, economic and/or military consequences of the lie. It thus becomes vitally important for the state to use all of its powers to repress dissent, for the truth is the mortal enemy of the lie, and thus

46

by extension, **the truth is the greatest enemy of the State.**

> —Joseph Goebbels, Adolf Hitler's close associate and devoted follower

If you repeat a lie often enough, it becomes the truth.

> —Joseph Goebbels

The bigger the lie, the more it will be believed.

> —Joseph Goebbels

The truth is the greatest enemy of the State.

> —Joseph Goebbels

Not every item of news should be published. Rather must those who control the news policies endeavor **to make every item of news serve a certain purpose.**

> —Joseph Goebbels

The Trilateral Commission is intended to be the vehicle for the multinational consolidation of the commercial and banking **interest by seizing control of the political government of the United States.** The Trilateral Commission represents a skillful, coordinated effort to seize control and consolidate the four centers of power—political, monetary, intellectual, and ecclesiastical. What the Trilateral Commission intends to do is to create a worldwide economic power superior to the political power of the nation-states involved. As managers and creators of the system, they will rule the future.

> —Barry Goldwater, US senator representing Arizona (1953–1965, 1969–1987), in *No Apologies*

We are turning toward **a new world order, the world of communism.** We shall never turn off that road.

> —Mikhail Gorbachev, general secretary of the Communist Party of the Soviet Union (1985–1991)

The five veto powers and permanent members of the Security Council have corrupted the UN Charter. And corrupted the work of the UN. Applying double-standards and disregard for law—they have made the organization primarily serve their best interests rather than serve its mandate. The five most dangerous member states together manufacture and sell some 85 percent of military arms, including nuclear weapons and so-called weapons of mass destruction. This is the UN of the arms dealers—the most disreputable and yet profitable business on earth. And tragically and quite bizarrely, the arms dealers are the same member states that the UN Charter entrusts with maintaining peace and security around the world! I trust you see the disconnect? The incompatibility? The mind-boggling reality of nuclear powers and weapons salesmen being responsible for peaceful co-existence?! It's madness!

> —Denis Halliday, former UN humanitarian coordinator in Iraq, lecturing in Canada in 2009

The most powerful clique in these **Council on Foreign Relations** groups have one thing in common—**they want to bring about the surrender of the sovereignty and the national independence of the United States. They want to end national boundaries** and racial and ethnic loyalties supposedly to increase business and

ensure world peace. What they strive for would inevitably lead to dictatorship and a loss of freedoms by the people. The **Council on Foreign Relations** was founded for the purpose of promoting disarmament and national independence into an all-powerful, **one-world government.**
—*Harper's Magazine*, July 1958

How fortunate for leaders that men do not think.
—Adolf Hitler, führer of Germany (1934–1945)

The real menace of our republic is the **invisible government,** which like a giant octopus sprawls its slimy legs over our cities, states, and nation. To depart from mere generalizations, let me say that at the head of this octopus are the **Rockefeller** Standard Oil interests and a small group of powerful banking houses generally referred to as international bankers. **The little coterie of powerful international bankers virally run the United States government for their own selfish purposes. They practically control both parties,** write political platforms, make catspaws [a person used unwittingly or unwillingly by another to accomplish the other's own purpose] of party leaders, use the leading men of private organizations, and resort to every device to place in nomination for high public office only such candidates as will be amenable to the dictates of corrupt big business. **These international bankers and the Rockefeller Standard Oil interests control the majority of the newspapers and magazines in this country,** they use columns of these papers to club into submission or drive out of office public officials who refuse to do the bidding of the powerful corrupt cliques which compose **the invisible government.** It operates under cover of a self-created screen and seizes our executive officers, legislative bodies, schools, courts, newspapers, and every agency created for the public protection.

—John Francis Hylan, New York City mayor (1918–1925), in a speech in 1922

There exists a shadowy government with its own Air Force, its own Navy, its own fundraising mechanism, and the ability to pursue its own ideas of the national interests, free from all checks and balances, and free from the law itself.

—Daniel Inouye, US senator representing Hawaii (1963–2012)

A great nation betrayed the principles which have made it great, and thereby became hostage to hostage-takers.

—Daniel Inouye

Today the path of total dictatorship can be laid by strictly legal means, unseen and unheard by the Congress, the president, or the people. Outwardly we have a constitutional government. **We have operating within our government and political system another body representing another form of government—a bureaucratic elite.**

—William Jenner, state senator representing Indiana (1934–1942)

We have the opportunity to move not only toward the rich society and the powerful society but upward to the Great Society.

—Lyndon Baines Johnson, US
president (1963–1969)

I am Roosevelt New Dealer… Kennedy was a little too conservative to suit my taste.

—Lyndon Baines Johnson

Fifty men have run America, and that's a high number.

—Joseph Kennedy, JFK's father, the
New York Times, July 26, 1936

Who controls the food supply controls the people; who controls energy controls whole continents; who controls the money controls the world.

—Henry Kissinger, US secretary of state
under Richard Nixon (1973–1977)

Today, America would be outraged if UN troops entered Los Angeles to restore order [referring to the 1991 LA riots]. Tomorrow they will be grateful! This is especially true if they were told that there was an outside threat from beyond, whether rear or promulgated, that threatened our very existence. It is then that all peoples of the world will plead to deliver them from this evil. The one thing every man fears is the unknown. **When presented with this scenario, individual rights will be willingly relinquished** for the guarantee of their well-being granted to them by the **world government.**

—Henry Kissinger

My country's history, Mr. President, tells us that it is possible to fashion unity while cherishing diversity, that common action is possible despite the variety of races, interests, and beliefs we see here in this chamber. So, we say to all peoples and governments: Let us fashion together a **new world order.**

—Henry Kissinger, in an address before the General Assembly of the UN, October 1975

The New World Order under the UN will reduce everything to one common denominator. The system will be made up of a single currency, single centrally financed government, single tax system, single world court of justice, single state religion... Each person will have a registered number without which he will not be allowed to buy or sell; and there will be one universal world church. Anyone who refuses to take part in the universal system will have no right to exist.

—Dr. Kurk E. Koch, Protestant theologian and writer

By 2020, there will be a **one-world government.**

—Ray Kurzweil, author, inventor, and futurist

In June and July 2005, the Dominican Republic-Central America Free Trade Agreement (DR-CAFTA) passed the Senate and the House, establishing corporate-approved trade rules to further impoverish the region and move a step closer to continental integration.

—Stephen Lendman, in his review of Daniel Estulin's book *The True Story of the Bilderberg Group*

**Our job is to give people not what they want,
but what we decide they ought to have.**
—Richard Salant, CBS News president (1961–1964 and 1966–1979)

CBS and other media giants control everything we see, hear, and read through television, radio, newspapers, magazines, books, films, and large portions of the internet. Their top officials and some journalists attend Bilderberg meetings—on a condition that they report nothing.
—Stephen Lendman, in his review
of Daniel Estulin's book *The True
Story of the Bilderberg Group*

I have here in my hand a list of two hundred and five people that were known to the **secretary of state** as being members of the Communist Party and who nevertheless are still working and shaping the policy of the **State Department.**
—Joseph McCarthy, US senator representing Wisconsin (1947–1957), speaking before a Republican women's group in 1950

Wall Street executive investment banker Senator Prescott Sheldon Bush (G. H. W. Bush's father) and his allies mocked and ridiculed Senator McCarthy for his accusations. He was made out to be a paranoid lunatic, but I believe that he was nothing less than a loyal American who detected that people in **the State Department** *were implementing policy that was/is intended to erode the sovereignty of the United States. These people were obviously* **CFR-embedded puppets** *who he assumed had to be communists, and he was probably right. The CFR had so many of their people embedded by that time that his attempts to expose and purge the communists from our government and institutions were a hopeless cause.*

The drive of the **Rockefellers** and their allies is to create a **one-world government** combining super capitalism and **communism** under the same tent, all under their control... **Do I mean conspiracy? Yes, I do. I am convinced there is such a plot, international in scope, generations old in planning, and incredibly evil in intent.**
—Larry P. McDonald, US congressman representing Georgia (1975–1983)

It was a carefully contrived occurrence. **International bankers** sought to bring about a condition of despair so that they might emerge the **rulers of us all.**
—Louis McFadden, US congressman representing Pennsylvania (1915–1935), commenting on the stock market crash of 1929

COVID-19 has created a condition of despair, and that is working out pretty well for the elite—just as the stock market crash of 1929 did!

The press is the enemy.
—Richard Nixon, US president (1969–1974)

The cold war isn't thawing; it's burning with a deadly heat. **Communism isn't sleeping;** it is, as always, plotting scheming, working, and fighting.
—Richard Nixon

The Rothschild cabal have infiltrated your government, your media, your banking institutions. They are no longer content with committing atrocities in the Middle East; they are now doing it on their own soil [Europe], desperate to complete the plan for a one-world government, world army, complete with a world central bank.

> —Vladimir Putin, Russian president, comment made to a Kremlin tour group in 2017

The Council on Foreign Relations is the establishment. Not only does it have influence and power in key decision-making positions at the highest of government to apply pressure from above, but it also announces and uses individuals and groups to bring pressure from below, to justify the high-level decisions for **converting the United States from a sovereign constitutional republic into a servile member of a ONE-WORLD DICTATORSHIP.**

> —John Rarick, US congressman representing Louisiana (1967–1975)

We are grateful to **the *Washington Post*, the *New York Times*, *Time* magazine** and other great publications whose directors have attended our meetings [Bilderberg Group, the Council on Foreign Relations, the Trilateral Commission, etc.] and respected their promises of discretion for almost forty years. It would have been impossible for us to develop **"our plan for the world"** if we had been subject to the bright lights of publicity during those years. But the work is now much more sophisticated and prepared to march towards a world government. **The supranational sovereignty of an intellectual elite and world bankers is surely preferable to the national autodetermination practiced in past centuries.**

> —David Rockefeller, chairman and chief executive of Chase Manhattan Bank (1969–1980), in 1992 quote

For more than a century, ideological extremists at either end of the political spectrum have seized upon well-publicized incidents, such as my encounter with Castro, to attack the Rockefeller family for the inordinate influence they claim we yield over American political and economic institutions. Some even believe we are part of a secret cabal working against the best interests of the United States by characterizing my family and me as 'internationalists' and of conspiracy with others around the world to build a more integrated global, political, and economic structure—one world, if you will. If that's the charge, I stand guilty as charged and am proud of it.

—David Rockefeller, *Memoirs* (p. 405)

This present window of opportunity, during which a truly peaceful and interdependent world order might be built, will not be open for too long. We are on the verge of a global transformation. **All we need now is the right major crisis, and the nations will accept the New World Order.**

—David Rockefeller

Whatever the price of the Chinese Revolution, it has obviously succeeded not only in producing more efficient and dedicated administration, but also in fostering high morale and community of purpose. The social experiment in China under Chairman Mao's leadership is one of the most important and successful in history.

—David Rockefeller, *New York Times*, August 10, 1973

Obviously, the Bilderberg Group and those aligned with them consider **communist China to be the model for the one-world government.**

Franklin Delano Roosevelt, US president (1933–1945) **was the driving force behind the creation of the United Nations in 1945.**

Give me control of a nations money and I care not who makes her laws.
—Amschel Mayer Rothschild, German banker

Diet, injections, and injunctions from a very early age, to produce the sort of character and **the sort of beliefs that the authorities consider desirable.** And any serious criticism of the powers that be, will become psychologically impossible.
—Bernard Russell, political activist and author, in *The Impact of Science on Society*

No one will enter the New World Order unless he or she will make a pledge to worship Lucifer. No one will enter the New Age unless he will take a Luciferian initiation.
—David Spangler, Director of Planetary Initiative for the United Nations

In the twenty-first century, national sovereignty would cease to exist; that we would all answer to a single global authority.
—Strobe Talbott, deputy secretary of state under Bill Clinton (1994–2001), *Time* magazine journalist, president of the Brookings Institute (2002–2017), and CFR member

In the next century, nations as we know it will be obsolete; **all states will recognize a single global authority.**
—Strobe Talbott, *Time* magazine, July 20, 1992

The American people will never knowingly adopt socialism. But under the name of **"liberalism"** they will adopt every fragment of the socialist program, until one day America will be a socialist nation, without knowing how it happened.
—Norman Thomas, six-time US presidential candidate for the Socialist Party of America (1928–1948)

We are at present working discreetly with all our might to wrest this mysterious force called sovereignty out of the clutches of the local nation states of the world. All the time we are denying with our lips what we are doing with our hands.
—Professor Arnold Toynbee, British historian, philosopher of history, and author, in his address before the Institute for the Study of International Affairs in Copenhagen, June 1931

I think that we declare our willingness to participate in some sort of world organization capable of enacting, administering, interpreting and enforcing **world law,** whether you call it a federation, a government or **world order. We will have a world government whether you like it or not. The only question is whether that government will be achieved by conquest or consent.**
—James Paul Warburg, German-born American banker and financial advisor to FDR, son of Paul Warburg (father of the Federal Reserve

system), speaking before the US Senate Committee on Foreign Relations, February 17, 1950

In essence, Warburg, while speaking on behalf of the international bankers (now referred to as the Bilderberg Group), made **a direct threat against America when he stated that we will have a world government, whether you like it or not, by conquest or consent.** *His comment illustrates the total contempt that the Bilderberg Group and their public base, the Council on Foreign Relations, have for America and strongly suggests they have methodically contrived all of the anarchy (via multiple mechanisms but mainly the media) that has been occurring all across America.* **China, ISIS, Al-Qaeda, the Bilderberg Group, and the Council on Foreign Relations all have one common desire—to destroy America.** *Why is it that* **our government officials go to great lengths to publicize the threat presented by China, ISIS, and Al-Qaeda but NEVER DARE MENTION the GREATEST threat to America: the Bilderberg Group and the Council on Foreign Relations.** *Does that not make our government officials, who have sworn to serve and protect America, lying, deceitful, American-hating* **traitors** *themselves?*

The main purpose of the Council on Foreign Relations is promoting the disarmament of US sovereignty and national independence, and submergence into an all-powerful one-world government. In the entire CFR lexicon, there is no term of revulsion carrying a meaning so deep as "America first."
> —Admiral Chester Ward, former judge advocate for the US Navy and CFR member (an organization he became one of the most vocal critics of)

Countless people…will hate the new world order…and will die protesting against it.
> —H. G. Wells, English writer and outspoken socialist who, in his 1940 book *The*

New World Order, advocated that such a
new order be formed to unite the nations

I am a most unhappy man. I have unwittingly
ruined my country. A great industrial nation is
controlled by its system of credit. Our system of
credit is concentrated. The growth of the nation,
therefore, and all our activities are in the hands
of a few men. **We have come to be one of the
worst ruled, one of the most completely controlled and dominant governments in the civ-
ilized world. No longer a government by free
opinion, no longer a government by conviction and the vote of the majority, but a government by the opinion and duress of a small
group of dominant men.**

—Woodrow Wilson, US president
(1913–1921), referencing the Federal
Reserve Act of 1913 that he introduced,
signed into law, and later regretted

The term internationalism has been popularized
in recent years to cover an interlocking financial, political, and economic world force for the
purpose of establishing a World Government.
Today internationalism is heralded from pulpit
and platform as a League of Nations or a Federal
Union to which **the United States must surrender a definite part of its National Sovereignty.
The World Government plan** is being advocated under such alluring names as the "International Order," **"The New World Order,"**
"World Union Now," "World Commonwealth
of Nations," "World Community," etc... All the
terms have the same objective; however, the line

of approach may be religious or political, according to the taste or training of the individual.

—Excerpt from a memorial to be addressed to
the House of Bishops and the House of Clerical
and Lay Deputies of the Protestant Episcopal
Church in General Convention, October 1940

The final act of the Uruguay Round, marking the
conclusion of the most ambitious trade negotiations of our century, will give birth in Morocco
to **the World Trade Organization,** the third
pillar of the **New World Order** along with **the
United Nations and the International Monetary Fund.**

—Part of a full-page advertisement
by the government of Morocco in
the *New York Times*, April 1994

CHAPTER 4
The United Nations Agenda for the Twenty First Century, Detailed via Eileen DeRolf's Agenda 21 Course

The United Nations Agenda for the twenty-first century is the elite's master plan for the creation of a one-world, corporate-controlled, unelected government.

The elite and their loyal allies use many titles for the agenda and change them on occasion to distract from what the titles really represent, but they all represent the same international agenda. Agenda 21, Agenda 2030, the President's Council on Sustainable Development, and the Green New Deal are all just alternate titles for the same thing.

The Green New Deal actually became the law of the land in 1993 with Executive Order 12852. **President Bill Clinton DAMNED the United States** in June 1993 when he officially created the **President's Council on Sustainable Development,** and from that time forward, the United Nations agenda for the twenty-first century policies have been and continue to be put into law all across America.

The material presented in this chapter and chapters 5–13 have been reprinted (with permission) from Eileen DeRolf's Agenda 21 Course (http://agenda21course.com).

Agenda 21 Course

Understanding Sustainable Development and How it Affects You

Lesson 1: Introduction to Agenda 21

This is the first lesson in a series of ten lessons on Agenda 21, commonly known as sustainable development. Today we will learn the...

Definition of Agenda 21, a short history, and the three E's.

So, what is Agenda 21, also referred to as sustainable development? It is <u>NOT</u> an environmental movement, it <u>IS</u> a political movement which seeks to control the world's economy, dictates its development, captures and redistributes the world's wealth on a national, state, and local level.

The process locks away land and resources from use by citizens and plans a central economy while controlling industry, transportation, food production, water, and the growth, size, and location of the population.

In short, Agenda 21 is one of several global plans of action designed to create a coalition of government, business, and nongovernmental organizations (NGOs) under the auspices of the United Nations. When fully operational, this system of Global Governance, will command a one-world court, a one-world army, a one-world media, etc., all working in lockstep to gain control over all human activity and all of the earth's wealth.

It is hard to believe that something so sinister could be happening right under our noses. However, it is easier to understand when you learn how Agenda 21 has slowly and steadily been implemented for many decades.

Through the second half of the twentieth century, the powers that be in the United Nations were crafting documents and treaties to position themselves to implement Agenda 21. These early efforts in 1992 led to the introduction of five key documents at the United Nations Summit in Rio de Janeiro.

The five documents were

- The **Convention on Climate Change**, the precursor to the Kyoto Climate Change Protocol, later adopted in 1997.
- The second document was the **Biodiversity Treaty**, which would declare that massive amounts of land should be off-limits to human development
- The third document was called the **Rio Declaration**, which called for the eradication of poverty throughout the world by the redistribution of wealth.
- The fourth document was the **Convention on Forest Principles**, calling for the international management of the world's forests, essentially shutting down or severely regulating the timber industry.
- The fifth document was **Agenda for the 21ˢᵗ century**, now commonly called Agenda 21.

Agenda 21 is a 300-page document that contains forty chapters which address virtually every facet of human life and contain great detail as to how the concept of sustainable development should be implemented through every level of government. Agenda 21 is the "how to" document for sustainable development.

It was at the Rio Summit that George H. W. Bush, along with 178 heads of state, signed agreement to Agenda 21.

One year later, newly elected President Bill Clinton signed Executive Order 12852 to create the President's Council on Sustainable Development. This council contained twelve cabinet secretaries. Six of them belonged to the Nature Conservancy, the Sierra Club, the World Resources Institute, or the National Wildlife Federation.

These same groups, called nongovernmental organizations (NGOs), worked directly with the United Nations to craft Agenda 21, and now were in a key position to put Agenda 21 policies into every single agency in the US federal government. This means every federal agency, the Department of Education, the Department of Homeland Security, the EPA, are all currently using your tax dollars to undercut our sovereignty and steal our property rights bit by bit.

The United Nations and the non-governmental organizations that do the "heavy lifting" for the UN have been very clever in the ways they have chosen to get people around the world and in the US to accept "sustainable development policies."

First, the United Nations created the **three E's: social equity, economic justice,** and **environmental justice.**

By selecting the three terms used for the three E's, the sustainablists were very clever. You see, sustainablists are very good at selecting terms whose meaning seems self-explanatory and sound very positive. Social equity, economic justice, and environmental justice are three examples of this. Most people who hear these terms for the first time think they understand what they mean, and with words like "equity" and "justice" in them, think that they are probably good thing. The reality is quite different for several reasons.

First, the terms themselves vary. Sometimes social equity is called social justice. The same is true of the other two terms. The swapping out of terms is very confusing.

Secondly, just finding agreed-upon definitions is very challenging. Of the three, only for the definition of social equity is there some degree of agreement, and even then, when you find a definition of economic justice, the examples cited sound like the examples given for social justice. This is done by design. Precise use of words allows everyone to know their true meaning. Agenda 21 is a stealth effort. The less the average citizen knows and understands, the better.

So, how do we know the real definitions for the three E's? By working backwards! First, you must find examples of the three E's. Remember, "Actions speak louder than words."

* * *

Examples of social **in**justice, according to the sustainablists, occur when…

> …a person cannot move freely to meet his needs (i.e., no access to transportation or borders preventing immigration to another country).

...a person has ill-health, so cannot meet their needs.

...a person does not have access to good housing.

...a person does not have access to quality food.

Using those examples, **social equity** can be defined as the right and opportunity of all people "to benefit equally" from the resources afforded us by society and the environment.

Looking at all four examples, it is not hard to see why solutions like mass transit, open borders, Obamacare, low-income housing, food stamps, and free lunch programs in the schools are all part of the sustainable development equation because they create "social justice."

* * *

Examples of economic **in**justice occurs when...

...a person's gender, ethnicity, religious affiliation or a handicap places a limitation on their chances of success in the workplace.

...a person's social economic status prevents them from receiving higher education.

...a person's social economic status prevents them from moving up in the workplace.

...certain countries, through a wealth of natural resources, prosper over other less fortunate countries.

Using these examples, **economic justice** can be defined as the equal ability of the individual or countries to gain wealth.

Again, you can see why quotes in the workplace, college scholarships for the low-income student, and redistribution of wealth from the wealthier countries to the poorer countries, sometimes through outright monetary "gifts" and sometimes through treaties and agreements that work to the US's disadvantage, are part of the formula of sustainable development because they create "economic justice."

* * *

Examples of environmental **in**justice are when...

> ...man pollutes the air, land, or water.
> ...man fills in a swamp.
> ...man causes the climate to warm, or change, whichever
> claim the environmentalists are making this week.

From these examples, it is not hard to create the definition of Environmental Injustice.

Environmental justice says that man is responsible for all of nature's woes. The presence of man on this planet is an environmental **in**justice. Consequently, it is critical that all of man's activities be severely controlled, of course, by the government, in order to protect the environment.

Or as stated by the Club of Rome (the premier environmental think-tank consultants to the United Nations),

> The common enemy of humanity is man. In searching for a new enemy to unite us, we came up with the idea that pollution, the threat of global warming, water shortages, famine, and the like would fit the bill. All of these dangers are caused by human intervention, and it is only through changed attitudes and behavior that they can be overcome. The real enemy is humanity itself.

Further, since Americans value the environment, it allows the sustainablists to use environmental justice to effectively convince Americans that in order to save their planet, they must give up their individual rights for those of the collective.

In other words, the three E's are a way to be sure no one has any more than anyone else (unless you are a member of the elite), even if you are smarter, worked harder, took more risks, made all the right decisions, and sacrificed. Your very success is a social injustice. Further, God may have given Man dominion over the earth, but apparently big government feels it has veto power over God.

For a sustainablist a regulation, or sustainable development policy, that manages to create social equity, economic and environmental justice, all in one fell swoop, is the ideal regulation or policy. That regulation is said to have achieved the Triple Bottom Line (= sustainability).

If you look at the logo for Agenda 21, you will see three overlapping circles, where all three circles overlap, represents the Triple Bottom Line, and that also represents "sustainability."

It is the "precautionary principle" (Principle 15 of the Rio Declaration) that allows the government to use the environment as a hammer. This principle says that, if there is the slightest chance that an activity of man "MAY" harm the environment, then **that activity must be stopped**. The Keystone Pipeline is a perfect example of that.

You say this is just craziness! While you are certainly right, that does not mean millions of Americans don't believe this or are unwilling to go along with the three E's. So, how has sustainable development been swallowed by so many Americans you ask? As lesson two will show, it is done through indoctrination, regulation, intimidation, and the outright destruction of our culture.

CHAPTER 5
Agenda 21 Course

Lesson 2: Getting America to Buy the Scam Called Agenda 21

This is the second lesson in a series of ten lessons on Agenda 21, commonly known as sustainable development. Today you will learn how...

Indoctrination is used to soften up the American citizen to make them receptive to the transformation of a free world into a socialist, sustainable development world. Think of all the commercial and nature shows you have been seeing pushing the green agenda; think of all the articles our biased media create pushing the green agenda, even various churches push the three E's.

Let's not forget the schools and colleges that have curricula that have Agenda 21 ideas embedded that are designed to create good global citizens that are willing to give up their individual constitutional rights for the common good in order to protect the environment.

As you combine all of these strategies with the overly generous and trusting nature of most Americans, and the reality that many Americans are not paying any attention to politics, you can then understand why sustainable development policies, which on the surface seem harmless, have soaked into the fiber of American thinking.

The average American thinks that by buying into sustainable development ideas that they are protecting the environment for their children. They do not understand that the proponents of Agenda 21 have a whole different viewpoint. Maurice Strong (chairman of the 1992 Rio Summit) stated, "Isn't the only hope for the planet that the industrial nations collapse? Isn't it our responsibility to bring that about?"

Or the quote by Judi Bari of Earth First, "If we don't overthrow capitalism, we don't have a chance of saving the world ecologically. I think it is possible to have an ecologically sound society under socialism. I don't think it's possible under capitalism."

The proponents of Agenda 21 may or may not be concerned about the environment, but they all agree capitalism and the American Dream must be eliminated. Do you really think that the average American citizen believes that by going along with the policies that seem to benefit the environment, they are putting their very way of life and prosperity, and that of their children, in harm's way?

Once enough Americans are indoctrinated, it is much easier for the government to get these same Americans to accept the heavy regulatory burden that will be required to fully implement Agenda 21 policies. **The use of thousands of sustainable development regulations is proof that Agenda 21 cannot be implemented voluntarily.**

The written regulations began in 1993 when President Clinton created the Presidential Council on sustainable development. Through the recommendations of this council, sustainable development policies are put into every single federal agency.

Unfortunately, the efforts to control us now extend beyond the federal government. Grants from the federal government are helping to move sustainable development policies into the state and local governments. At this point in time, virtually every state or local governments has some type of sustainable development regulations on their books.

Amortization of nonconforming use is a particularly evil regulation. If new green home codes are adopted in a community and then applied to older homes (instead of allowing the older homes to be grandfathered), then the owners of the older homes must make the necessary upgrades to come into compliance. These improvements may create a home that, using today's term, is under water. Of course, there is always the possibility that the homeowner cannot afford the upgrades. In that case, the home may be confiscated.

An equally scary regulation is likely coming down the pike. It is one that will force homeowners to pay a tax based on the amount of impervious surface located on their property. This regulation is based on the idea that an impervious surface, like a roof or concrete driveway, is preventing rain water from absorbing into the ground. Using the Precautionary Principle discussed in lesson 1, just the possibility that preventing water from soaking into the ground might cause harm to the environment is enough of an excuse to create regulation to prevent it.

Making the situation even worse are the activist judges who are more than willing to uphold any challenges to these sustainable development policies.

Furthermore, our Constitution, culture, and religion have been under attack for a very long time. This is no accident. **Anything that weakens the moral fiber or the finances of America will contribute to her downfall and the advance of a One World Order.**

The Second Amendment gun rights debate is not just over our right to protect ourselves from individuals or a government that may want to harm us. It is also about destroying the Constitution. The same can even be said for political correctness. Political correctness is not about offending others. It is about restricting our First Amendment right to express our thought freely.

Religion and culture are entwined. Damage one—damage both, The United States is the only country where the Constitution is based on God-given rights; the fewer people who believe in God, the fewer people who will understand the importance of rights granted by God rather than man. If God gives us our rights, then only God can remove them. Also, if religion is eliminated from our culture—another hit to the Constitution—there will be no moral compass to guide our citizens. That makes it much more likely that citizens will look to their government for direction.

For example, many people today, by fighting harder to protect an endangered species of animals than protecting the life of an unborn human, prove that they have been indoctrinated to value animal life over human life, and that they have been conditioned to accept the guidance of a government that fights aggressively to keep the funding to Planned Parenthood flowing for abortion services rather than create policies that support intact families. To support the reality that human life has little if any value is this quote from Dave Foreman, co-founder of Earth First: "Among environmentalist sharing two or three beers, the notion is quite common that if only some calamity could wipe out the human race, other species might once again have a chance."

Now add to this, if the population has been educated in their schools to be good global citizens, who value diversity and the common good, instead of people who value individual rights and the free market system, then the population may go willingly into a socialist One World Order without a whimper.

Of course, **it is impossible to create a One World Order if borders are not eliminated**. You might ask yourself, are the European countries really sovereign anymore now that they have formed the European Union? After all, they all share the same currency, have a free flow of people across their borders, and share many of the same regulations and socialist policies.

Then there is the North American continent, where treaties like the North American Free Trade Agreement and our very open borders threaten the sovereignty of the US. You might ask yourself, if countries "voluntarily" combine with other countries to make a larger government entity, would that not make it much easier to combine those blocs into a one-world government?

However, we must not forget that the US's government was designed to be strongest at the local level. Federal policies have resulted in cash-starved local governments. That makes the local governments easily bribed with grant money—not just grant money from the states and federal government but also from regional governments.

Regional governments are cropping up at an amazing speed. Over time, might these regional governments, with their unelected boards, using our tax dollars, strip away the sovereignty of our city and county governments, and thereby undermine our 250-year-old political structure, consequently making it easier to ease the US into a global government system?

Still, you say, we are a strong country and we would never allow the loss of our local control or national sovereignty.

A country loses control of its destiny when it loses control of its finances. We, like Greece, must dance to the tune that others play, if we are allowed, or even pushed over the edge financially and cannot pay our debts to foreign countries, cannot maintain a strong military, cannot pay our enormous entitlements. Is it not conceivable that outside powers could force us to merge with them? Or perhaps our own people will willingly, in a belief that the United Nations is our friend, push for this solution.

So, in this second lesson, I have tried to explain how the American people have been made to "buy" the scam that is Agenda 21, through indoctrination and regulation, and the ongoing destruction of our value system, borders, economy, and Constitution, with the ultimate goal of creating a Global Governance System, where all human behavior and wealth will ultimately be under strict control.

In lesson 3 you will learn how sustainable development policies steal the rural lands from our citizens. Or, to quote the 1976 United Nations Conference report, "Private property ownership is also a principal instrument of accumulation and concentration of wealth and therefore contributes to social injustice… Public control of land use is therefore indispensable."

CHAPTER 6
Agenda 21 Course

Lesson 3: Wildlands Project

This is the third lesson in a series of ten lessons on Agenda 21, commonly known as sustainable development. Today you will learn...
   How Sustainable Development Policies Will Force Citizens Off of Rural Lands.

> Land, because of its unique nature and the crucial role it plays in human settlement, cannot be treated as an ordinary asset, controlled by individuals and subject to the pressures and inefficiencies of the market. Private land ownership is also a principal instrument of accumulation and concentration of wealth and therefore contributes to social injustice; if unchecked, it may become a major obstacle in the planning and implementation of development schemes. Social justice, urban renewal and development, the provision of decent dwellings, and healthy conditions for people can only be achieved if land is used in the interest of society as a whole.
>
> —The preamble to The Vancouver Action Plan approved at Habitat: United Nations Conference on Human Settlements (May 31st to June 11th 1976).

This quote is compelling evidence that the goal of the United Nations is to eliminate private property around the globe in order to use it for the "common good." The only thing different today, rather than forty years ago, is the rate at which land is being taken from the American citizen and the number of ways this is made to happen.

Through many venues, including but not limited to local, state, and federal regulations and programs, private property rights of rural land owners are incrementally taken—then stolen. This is in compliance with the Biodiversity Treaty, which is one of three treaties foisted on America at the Agenda 21 conference in Rio de Janeiro in 1992.

The treaty, while not fully ratified, is being implemented through the executive branch of government. This treaty spawned the Wildlands Project. The intent of the Wildlands Project is to gain control over, and then return at least 50 percent of the rural land in the US to the condition that predates Columbus's arrival.

The strategies used to remove the landowner from his land include, but are not limited to, the following:

Land is taken…

> …by denying water, and/or grazing rights to farmers and ranchers or limiting their use of pesticides and herbicides, which in turn will force the farmers and ranchers out of business, causing the land to possibly fall into the hands of the federal government.
> …when wilderness areas, parks, etc. are established. Not only the land is out of production, but the mineral resources underground or in the forest above can also be made off-limits for development.
> …by expanding the legal definition of a wetland. By making any trickle of water or puddle a wetland, the EPA can prevent the development of the land and all the land around it. This makes the land worthless and easy to acquire by sundry entities, including the government.

...when an endangered species is located within a forest. Then large areas around this area are made off-limits to development, and once again, the land loses its value and is easily acquired by the government.

...by the direct taking of land through eminent domain.

...when Road RIP, a nongovernmental organization, was created for the sole purpose of removing existing roads and preventing the construction of new roads into wilderness areas. Then humans are locked away from land that was once served by roadways.

...when urban boundaries are created around a town, beyond which development may not occur and/or utilities may not be provided. This will destroy the economic value of the rural lands around the town. Comprehensive land use plans in existence today and their policies are creating this scenario.

...when the government declares land part of a flood plain, then forces the homeowners to give up their homes. The homes are then destroyed and the land is not allowed to be developed. The government gets a twofer if the land is along a river. Then, not only is the land off limits to development, the government has total control of the river and the priceless water it contains.

...when a land trust purchases private property rights from a land owner to do certain environmentally friendly things. In return, the landowner and his heirs are then able to stay on this land in perpetuity.

Unfortunately, over time, the land trust may make more and more environmental demands on the landowner, until the landowner can no longer make a living off of the land. With all the restriction placed on the property, no one but the government may be willing to buy it. These agreements are called conservation easements.

President Obama has greatly advanced the locking down of rural America through Executive Order 13575 with its far-reaching consequences.

Executive Order 13575, which was signed in 2011, created the White House Rural Council. This council requires every federal agency in the US to oversee all the food, fiber, and energy needs for all the rural sustainable communities. Across the US, this executive order affects 16 percent of the population.

It is worth spending some time discussing some of the key plans of those who push the sustainablist agenda and what they have in mind for the vacated rural land.

In a very large area, usually at least five thousand acres, land can be freed of human activity, then a core area can be created there. This is where large predators, like wolves, cougars, grizzly bears, etc. have been or will be reintroduced.

The human-free land that connects the cores are called corridors. Around the corridors and cores are buffer zones, where…

"Only human activity compatible with protection of the core reserves and corridors would be allowed." (From the mission statement to the Wildlands Project).

As the carnivore population increases, it may become necessary to enlarge the core areas, and consequently also the buffer zones, to meet the increased range needed by the carnivores.

This process of relocating the human population in order to create habitat for the wildlife is called the Wildlands Project.

Planning for where to relocate humans in order to create the cores, corridors, and buffer zones began in the United States several decades ago. We know this because in 1994 the US Senate was scheduled to ratify the Biodiversity Treaty. During that year, Dr. Michael Coffman pounded the capital with emails and calls, and before ratifying the Biodiversity Treaty, Dr. Coffman presented a copy of the biodiversity map to his senator, who showed it to the Senate. The Senate majority leader took the treaty off of the calendar, and it was never ratified. Who says one person cannot make a difference!!

Nineteen ninety-four, the first year the Biodiversity Map was presented to the general public, was most of 20 years ago. Since then, the sustainablists have been very busy thinking and rethinking the best way to work around Congress to implement the unratified Biodiversity Treaty and to keep the Wildlands Project advancing. If you would like to see a possible recent version of the Wildlands Map, you might want to Google "America 2050 megaregions" and take a look at a possible updated version of the 1994 Michael Coffman map.

This kind of land acquisition is occurring all over the globe in order to prepare the world for, as Al Gore said, "the wrenching transformation of society" or stated more clearly by John Davis, editor of *Wild Earth* magazine…

"Does all the foregoing mean that *Wild Earth* and the Wildlands Project advocate the end of industrial civilization? Most assuredly."

In summary, since the founding of this country, it has been known that man cannot be free without the ability to own property.

George Washington said, "Property rights and freedom are inseparable."

John Adams said, "Property must be secure or liberty cannot exist."

The proponents of United Nations Agenda 21 understand very well that ownership of land provides wealth and security to those who control it. A government that denies land ownership of its citizens is knowingly reducing its citizenry to little more than serfs dependent on their government for their every need. **NEVER forget that Agenda 21 IS NOT an environmental movement. It is a political movement designed to control all of mankind's behaviors and that only by taking our property away from us can Agenda 21 be successful.**

The next lesson, lesson 4 in this series, will teach you what will happen to the folks who are forced off the rural lands and how the government will control where they live, how they provide for their own needs, how big their homes can be, how much energy they can use, how many children they can have—virtually every aspect of their lives.

Chapter 7
Agenda 21 Course

Lesson 4: Smart Growth

This is the fourth lesson in a series of ten lessons on the United Nations Agenda for the twenty-first century, commonly known as sustainable development. Today you will learn…
   How Smart Growth Strategies are Used to Control Human Behavior Within the Human Settlement.
   One of the goals of Agenda 21 is to re-wild over 50 percent (plus an additional 10 percent for buffer zones around the re-wilded areas) of the United States. Out of necessity, this will force the human population off the rural lands and into, using Agenda 21 language, "human settlements." Once there, the behavior of humans can be more easily monitored and controlled, thus creating "sustainability."
   Sustainability, as defined by the 1987 United Nations report is "development that meets the needs of today without compromising the ability of future generations to meet their own needs."
   Using the words of Maurice Strong, who was secretary of the 1992 UN Summit that was held in Rio de Janeiro (see lesson 1), "the consumption patterns of the affluent middle class-involving high meat intake, use of fossil fuels, appliances, home and work air conditioners, and suburban housing are not sustainable."
   In other words, for Agenda 21/sustainable development to be fully implemented, Americans must give up the American dream and embrace the life style foisted upon them by the radical leftist sustainablists.

To create sustainability in the "human settlements" there will be rules and regulations to control use of all resources; air, land, water, energy, and all resources underground. These rules are included under the heading of "smart growth."

Smart growth regulations fall primarily into three categories that are all designed to modify human behavior:

1. Regulations to discourage travel and ownership of automobiles
2. Regulations that discourage you from having children
3. Regulations that will discourage you from using water, land, energy, and the consumption of materials, whether it be toilet paper or materials to build a home

Here are some of the ways smart growth would control life and development in the human settlements. Note that all of these fall into one or more of the three categories discussed above and that all of the items listed below are impacted if energy resources are rationed.

Establishing boundaries around the city and preventing any development outside the perimeter is a smart growth tactic. This creates a situation where land inside the human settlement is at a premium, while land outside the boundary has little if any value. This in turn will cause land prices, land taxes, and congestion within the perimeter to increase but a decrease in the size of homes and number of children. Smaller homes and fewer children will also decrease energy usage.

Another smart growth strategy is to not expand the width or length of highways in an attempt to create congestion and an unpleasant driving experience. Allowing bikes to travel on these inadequate highway systems will further force the issue.

Creating rules to prevent the building of garages on new homes will discourage automobile ownership and save on building materials.

The installation of smart meters is a particularly contentious smart growth issue. Smart meters can monitor and/or remotely turn off home appliances when the utility company decides the consumer is using too much energy. Further, the radio frequencies given off by these smart meters are associated with a variety of health issues.

Restricting the mining, drilling, refining, and/or transporting of fossil fuels will increase the cost curve for electricity, gasoline, natural gas, etc., which will in turn force conservation by the users.

Growth regulations may eliminate from the marketplace all appliances except those that radically control energy and resources, like water and electricity. Everyone is familiar with low-flow toilets which, while they may save on water, often function poorly.

Sometimes when regulations cannot create the desired change, grants and subsidies are used instead. When the government steps in to drive change in this way, the free market is eliminated.

An example of this is how the government has, through subsidies, encouraged the development of alternative energies while applying onerous regulations on the fossil fuel industry. At some point, when the cost of fossil fuels increase enough, and the cost of alternative energy decreases enough, alternative energy will be cost competitive. However, at this point in time, the cost of all energy sources will be artificially high, forcing conservation by consumers.

Then again, expensive energy is seen by the proponents of Agenda 21 as a good thing, as shown by this quote from Amory Lovins of the Rocky Mountain Institute: "It would be little short of disastrous for us to discover a source of clean, cheap, abundant energy because of what we might do with it."

Smart growth policies are also being used to design new road projects. Many of the projects are driven by grants from the federal government, sometimes funneled down through regional government. One of these projects is called Complete Streets. Below is a paragraph, which can easily be found on the internet, from the Complete Streets Coalition. It reads,

> Creating "Complete Streets" means those transportation agencies must change their approach to community roads. By adopting a "Complete Streets" policy, communities direct their transportation planners and engineers to routinely

design and operate the entire right of way to enable safe access for all users, regardless of age, ability, or mode of transportation. This means that every transportation project will make the street network better and safer for drivers, transit users, pedestrians, and bicyclists—making your town a better place to live.

There are many things about this single paragraph that are concerning.

First, it says that "transportation planners MUST change their approach to community roads." Whatever happened to local government control? What happened? Grants happened! The federal government is using your tax dollars to entice the local government to build the infrastructure for future "human settlements" where walking, bicycling, and mass transit will be the primary modes of transportation. Further, while sidewalks and bicycles may make sense in a populated area, "Complete Streets" is pushing for sidewalks and bicycles paths in rural areas as well.

The local government may find that, by the time the cost of bicycle paths and sidewalks are figured against the added grant money, the grant money went mostly to build road features that were unnecessary for rural use, while in exchange the government sold its autonomy for a too-narrow road.

Add one final insult! By the time bike paths and sidewalks are added, even to a narrow road, the overall width of the roadbed will have increased, causing homeowners along the length of the project to lose parts of their front yards. This can have a negative impact on their property values.

Food and Fiber Sheds, Woodsheds, and False Choices

Since much of the land in the United States will be off-limits to humans, it will require that humans be limited to procuring that which they need to survive from the land near to the human settlements. But not to fear, the sustainablists have this all planned out.

Imagine a shooting target/bullseye with three consecutive smaller rings. The inner ring represents the area populated by humans. The ring that surrounds the inner ring is called the food-shed. That is where all the food and fiber for the human settlement should be procured, of course, only through strictly approved and monitored methods of sustainable farming. The outside ring is the woodshed, where certain environmentally friendly human activities can occur. Beyond that lies the re-wilded land containing the buffer zones, cores, and corridors. These are off limits to humans. Travelling from one human settlement to another may incur fines, as the human will have, by passing through an environmentally delicate area, caused some degree of harm to the environment.

The loss of the rural lands for traditional farming, coupled with the design of future high-density human settlements and the relatively small area of land around them for the raising of food, could create quite a dilemma for a human settlement that needs food to survive.

An idea being strongly forwarded by the proponents of Agenda 21 to replace traditional farming is vertical farming in multistoried greenhouses. The claim is that food could be grown year-round, isolated from disease and pests, and there would be a reduction in transportation costs.

If given a bit more critical scrutiny, one might ask how would a multistory greenhouse be immune to pests and diseases when anyone who has ever raised a house plant knows that, at times, the plants get mites even under the strictest conditions.

One might also wonder, because this technology is a long way from production, if a lot of folks might die of starvation unless the switch-over from traditional farming to vertical farming is done in an extremely gradual and thoughtful way. However, as population reduction is a major goal of the proponents of Agenda 21, it makes one wonder if a situation resulting in mass starvation is not considered, by them, as a good outcome.

And then there is the never-ending litany over greenhouse gas emissions. Let's take a look at the following quote:

> Buying local food within a foodshed can be seen as a means to combat the modern food system and the effects it has on the environment. It has been described as "a banner under which people attempt to counteract trends of economic concentration, social disempowerment and environmental degradation in the food and agricultural landscape."
>
> Agriculture production alone contributes to 14 percent of anthropogenic (= "manmade") greenhouse gas emissions. The food system's contribution of greenhouse gases contributes to the global issue of climate change. More attention is being paid to possibilities for reducing emissions through more efficient transport and different patterns of consumption, specifically, an increased reliance on local foodsheds. (Peters, 2008)

First, it is easy to see that, as usual, the environment, in this case global warming and climate change, is the supposed excuse for this radical reconfiguring of man's life style. Yet it remains to be seen if the globe is actually warming, and if so, whether man's activity is responsible for the warming. A lot of doubt is cast when you see quotes like this one from Timothy Wirth, president of the UN Foundation: "We've got to ride this global warming issue. Even if the theory of global warming is wrong, we will be doing the right thing in terms of economic and environmental policy."

The second thing worth noting is it is easy to see that Agenda 21's three E's, social, economic, and environmental justice, are all behind this effort to force a food-fiber-woodshed-human settlement model on mankind.

This is Agenda 21 social engineering at its best—or worst, depending on how you look at it. Simply put, the folks behind this (and you might want to Google "the Club of Rome") are retraining humans like we are lab rats.

In summary, while protecting the environment is a good thing, and if you CHOOSE to get your food close to home, recycle, or use a fuel-efficient car, that is fine. However, it is a false choice being offered here. It is NOT necessary to give up our freedom or our lifestyle and be forced into human settlements in order to protect the environment. It is NOT an either/or. We can live our lives in freedom and still protect the planet.

ALWAYS remember the END GAME that is being sought by folks pushing Agenda 21. The endgame is CONTROL, over humans and earth's resources, with the environment being used as an excuse.

Lesson 5 will explain how the vast wealth of the free market will be replaced by something called Corporatism, also called Crony Capitalism, which will allow the federal government to harness the wealth of big business for the good, not the people, but the government.

CHAPTER 8
Agenda 21 Course

Lesson 5: Public-Private Partnership

This is the fifth lesson in a series of ten lessons on the United Nations Agenda for the twenty-first century, commonly referred to as sustainable development. Today we will learn...

How Public-Private Partnerships Are Used by Government to Take Control of the Economy.

A public-private partnership is sometimes referred to as a PPP or a 3P.

The definition for a public-private partnership is an exclusive partnership between a public entity and a private entity that uses the financial resources of the private sector to carry out the legal activities or functions of the public sector.

Public-private partnerships do not work in a free-market way where competition decides who wins and who loses.

This is because a 3P company is granted special privileges by the government, such as the liberal use of eminent domain, tax breaks, subsidies, "front of the line" for permits, and freedom from certain regulations, etc. Hence the company accepting the "goodies" is the "private" part of the public-private partnership, while the government granting the "goodies" is the "public" part of the partnership.

These corporations force their competitors to play on an unlevel playing field. This is called corporatism, crony capitalism, or more commonly "choosing winners," and undermines the free market system on which our prosperity rests. This can over time cause the creation of government-sanctioned monopolies in selected segments of the economy.

The corporation, because of all the "goodies" it has received from the government, will have a stronger bottom line. In return the corporation will allow the government to tell it what to produce, for example let's say solar cells, wind turbines, mercury-laden light bulbs, etc. The corporation in return will have the job of promoting its government-approved products through its many advertisements. These advertisements not only increase the corporation's bottom line but serve as a vehicle for the indoctrination of the citizen to accept whatever the government is pushing. In this way, the company's bottom line benefits while the government watches the company do the government's bidding, and the public is limited to, or indoctrinated into, buying artificially expensive products that would not be successful in a free market system. Add to this, the corporation is most likely using **your** tax dollars, and if the corporation fails, the tax dollars disappear.

An infamous example of a 3P is Solyndra. The government provided huge amounts of money, which came out of the pockets of taxpayers, to "encourage" the corporation to produce solar cells. When the company went bankrupt, for lack of demand, it cost the public sector approximately $500 million in tax dollars.

These green sector jobs are especially worrisome because it appears that sustainable development policies are designed to destroy, through unreasonable regulations, certain existing industries, like the coal companies, which will then be replaced by new "green" industries created with federal subsidies paid for by the taxpayers.

A more complicated situation occurred in 2007 when the federal government passed legislation to begin phasing out certain of the "old fashioned" incandescent light bulbs by January 1, 2012. The major companies that manufactured these light bulbs. GE, Royal Phillips Electronics, and Siemens all lobbied for the passage of the 2007 bill to remove the incandescent light bulb from the marketplace for the simple reason that there was a greater profit margin in manufacturing the new halogen incandescent and compact fluorescent light bulbs. Late in 2011, the Republican Party managed to legislate a reprieve to the banning of the incandescent light bulb by preventing the Department of Energy from receiving any funds to force the change.

Before you sigh, a sigh of relief, the reality is that the reprieve came too late.

Joseph Higbee, a spokesman for the National Electrical Manufacturers Association, which represents 95 percent of US light bulb manufacturers, said even if the Department of Energy does not have the funding to enforce the energy efficiency standards, manufacturers are not going to retrofit their assembly lines to produce the less efficient traditional light bulb.

So, where does that leave us? First you need to realize that there are three key players in the mess: General Electric, the federal government, and we, the people. General Electric, the "private" in this public-private partnership, got a light bulb that provided the company with a much higher margin of profit, plus some very generous tax breaks from the federal government. The federal government, the "public" in this public-private partnership, got the energy-efficient light bulbs they wanted, undermined the free market, and by sending jobs overseas, created economic justice.

That just leaves, we, the people. What did we get? Oh, quite a lot. We got expensive, mercury-laden, slow-to-heat-up-in-the-cold light bulbs, a weaker free market, and fewer jobs and a weaker economy in America which is the natural result of the redistribution of wealth from a rich country to poorer countries.

This example goes back to what was said in the definition of Agenda 21 (refer to lesson 1).

Agenda 21 is **NOT AN ENVIRONMENTAL MOVEMENT!** If it was, the EPA would never allow this mercury-laden light bulb to be manufactured or used in the US nor allow the creation of windmill farms that are known to kill every year thousands of birds, including the bald eagle. As said previously, it is a political movement designed to control humans and their wealth.

Of course, it's not just American companies entering into PPPs with our government. Foreign companies are being met with open arms by local, state, and federal officials who see a way to use private corporations and their massive bank accounts to fund projects.

As the Associated Press reported on July 15, 2006, "On a single day in June [2006] an Austra-lian-Spanish partnership paid $3.6 billion to lease the Indiana Toll Road, an Australian company bought a ninety-nine-year lease on Virginia's Poca-hontas Parkway, and Texas officials decided to let a Spanish-American partnership build and run a toll road for fifty years." (Tom DeWeese of the American Policy Center from his *Agenda 21 & How to Stop It*)

Perhaps most worrisome of all are public-private partnerships that involve the infrastructure (roads, sewer systems, water supplies, water treatment facilities, etc.) of a community. Many communities are cash-strapped and are always looking for ways to raise money. With that in mind, communities may be tempted to sell and/or lease (often for very long periods of time) parts of their infrastructure. Not only do they get cash, but they are no longer required to maintain expensive infrastructure.

However, when government is in charge of a community's infrastructure, there is an implied responsibility to maintain it to an acceptable degree while at the same time minimizing the tax/ser-vice fee burden, if for no other reason than, if this does not happen, elected officials become unelected ex-officials.

If public infrastructure is sold off or leased to a private entity, the cost of service to the taxpayers is subservient to the corporation's need for profit. The private entity is not electable, so if rates soar, un-electing the heads of the corporation is not an option. Even more concerning is if, as mentioned previously, a foreign entity buys/leases the infrastructure, they are even less likely to have the best interest of the American taxpayer in mind. In addition, profits from these ventures are likely to leave the US.

Taking this one step further, it might be suggested, that when governments lose control of their infrastructure, they will lose control of their governing ability and will no longer remain accountable to their taxpayers. You might even say, as did President Clinton, that we are "reinventing government."

Speaking for myself, I kind of liked our "old government."

Another 3P concern with public-private partnerships is that, over time, due to the uneven playing field, fewer and fewer small businesses are able to survive. This works well for a government that is trying to destroy the free market. This type of government does not want competition. It wants control. The fewer companies that exist, and the more compliant to government demands they become, the greater is the control of the government over the marketplace.

Unfortunately for the economy, small business is the driver of the economic engine. Therefore, the citizens will have diminished opportunity for prosperity as the economy falters. The ultimate goal of a government that is implementing sustainable development is to lower the standard of living and diminish the consumption of goods by its citizens. Reducing the chance of success for our small businesses will certainly stall the economy, reduce the living standard of America, while advancing the United Nations Agenda for the twenty-first century goal of decreasing consumption habits in the US.

Public-private partnerships can exist on the highest level of our government, as shown by the North American Free Trade Agreement (NAFTA). NAFTA was touted as a way to make the US more competitive with Asia and Europe by combining the economic strength of the US with that of Canada and Mexico. Instead, NAFTA caused US jobs to go overseas, real wages in the US to drop, an increase in our trade deficit, and an enrichment of select corporations. In other words, NAFTA redistributed American wealth overseas. Further, it was designed to blur our national borders and weaken our sovereignty. Can you say "North American Union"?

Validation of this can be seen in this quote by Henry Kissinger in July 1993:

> [NAFTA] will represent the most creative step toward a new world order taken by any group of countries since the end of the Cold War, and the

> first step toward an even larger vision of the free-
> trade zone for the entire Western Hemisphere.
> [NAFTA] is not a conventional trade agree-
> ment, but the architecture of a new international
> system.

This brings us back, yet again, to the definition of Agenda 21 given in lesson 1 of this course where we learned that, in an Agenda 21/sustainable development world, the government seeks to control the world's economy, dictate its development, and capture and redistribute the world's wealth.

In summary, a corporation involved in a public-private partnership with the government must comply with the government or lose their strategic advantage. This makes the relationship between the government and business so entwined that it is difficult to determine where the government begins and the private sector ends.

The loser is the American citizen who can no longer vote with their dollars in the free market. The government instead uses the taxpayer's dollars to determine what products or services a corporation will produce and therefore what products and services the taxpayer will be allowed to purchase.

Further, if the American citizen's infrastructure is sold to the highest bidder, they will have no representative looking out for their best interests, and as the prices go up, they will have no recourse.

Last but not least, certain policies, like NAFTA, entered into by our federal government can damage the free market on a global level, weaken our sovereignty, and hasten a One World Order.

In the next lesson, lesson 6, you will learn how your tax dollars, through the use of grants, are used against you to destroy borders within the US and ultimately your representative form of government.

CHAPTER 9
Agenda 21 Course

Lesson 6: Grants are Used as a Major
Tool to Implement Agenda 21

This is the sixth lesson of a series of ten lesson on the United Nations Agenda for the twenty-first century, commonly known as sustainable development. Today we will learn how...

Grants are Used as a Major Tool to Implement Agenda 21.

As one looks at the financial crises in which one finds the United States, whether one sees this as a bad or a good thing depends on one's point of view. If the federal government wishes to create voluntary compliance at a local level with certain federal goals, would not making grants available to cash-starved local governmental entities, grants with strings attached, not be an effective way to create compliance? Making matters worse is that the grant money the government uses to create local compliance is your tax dollars.

The federal government has many grant programs. One of those programs is called the Sustainable Development Challenge Grant program.

If a citizen should go on the internet to *Federal Register* 45156, vol. 63, no. 163, August 24, 1998, in Notices, Environmental Protection Agency, a citizen could find some very interesting information—information, in this case, about the Sustainable Development Grants for the fiscal year 1998. In this document, it says,

> The Environmental Protection Agency (EPA) is
> soliciting proposals for the FY 1998 Sustainable

> Development Challenge Grant (SDCG) pro-
> gram, one of President Clinton's "high priority"
> actions described in the March 16, 1995 report,
> *Reinventing Environmental Regulation...* This
> program challenges communities to invest in a
> sustainable future that links environmental pro-
> tection, economic prosperity, and community
> well-being [a.k.a. social justice].

In other words, Sustainable Development Challenge Grants are being administered by the EPA, an environmental agency, as bribes by the federal government to institute actions that foster the three E's of sustainable development on a local level.

Continuing to quote from this document, "In keeping with this philosophy, the EPA will implement this program consistent with the principles of Executive Order 12898, 'Federal actions to Address Environmental Justice in Minority Populations and Low-Income Populations' (February 11, 1994)." The Sustainable Development Challenge Grant program is consistent with other community-based efforts the EPA has introduced, such as Brownfield's Initiative, the Environmental Justice Small Grants Program, Project XL, the President's American Heritage Rivers Initiative, Watershed Protections Approach...and many more that I will not mention here.

This section of the document makes two things very clear. First, that through the Challenge Grant program, the EPA has the federal government's full permission to redistribute wealth from the rich to the poor. Secondly, that there are many other federal grant programs administered by the EPA to forward, social, economic, and environmental justice on the taxpayer's dime, not just the Challenge Grant Program.

What makes this document so really, really important, though, is that it **provides irrefutable proof that the United States government** is forcing, through regulations and de facto bribery, **the implementation of Agenda 21.** The following quote from this document provides the smoking gun directly connecting the federal government to the implementation of Agenda 21.

"The Sustainable Development Challenge Grant program is also a step in implementing Agenda 21, the global plan of action on sustainable development signed by the United States at the Earth Summit in Rio de Janeiro in 1992."

This is important enough to repeat.

"The Sustainable Development Challenge Grant program is also a step in implementing Agenda 21, the global plan of action on sustainable development signed by the United States at the Earth Summit in Rio de Janeiro in 1992."

This one sentence makes two critical points. First, that sustainable development is the exact same thing as—a synonym for—Agenda 21. So, any time sustainable development is referenced, always remember that it is a substitute for the words "Agenda 21."

Secondly, through its own document, the federal government is admitting that it is indeed, through the Challenge Grant Program, implementing Agenda 21, a United Nations directive. Remember that Agenda 21 was a treaty that was never ratified by Congress. So, the implementation of Agenda 21 is in direct violation of Article 1 Section 10 of the Constitution of the United States, which says, **"No State shall without the Consent of the Congress...enter into any Agreement** or Compact with another state, or **with a foreign power**, or engage in Wars, unless actually invaded, or in such imminent Danger as will not admit of delay." That means that our federal government is implementing an illegal set of actions counter to our Constitution. (Also see Article IV, second paragraph of the US Constitution.)

The Challenge Grant Program proves that the federal government cannot further the three E's or implement Agenda 21 by regulations alone. It requires the use of grants to create compliance and the appearance that America is anxious and willing to sacrifice her freedom in order to save the environment and the collective. However, the true fact is that most state and local governments are simply so desperate to keep their roads paved and lights on, that they will not look too closely at the strings attached to the offered grants. The result is that the Agenda 21 train races down the track towards completion.

One final thought on grants. This lesson should make one wonder: If all the grant moneys currently being paid out were combined and then used to reduce the federal deficit, might not the federal deficit melt away? In other words, might the massive amount of money used for grants to encourage social justice and green programs not be the very reason our federal deficit is so large?

The next lesson, lesson 7, will allow you to learn how regional governments use grants to take the power away from our locally elected government.

CHAPTER 10
Agenda 21 Course

**Lesson 7: Regional Governments Will Destroy
Our Local Representative Government**

This is the seventh lesson in a series of ten lesson on Agenda 21, commonly known as sustainable development. Today we will learn...
   How Regional Governments Will Destroy Our Local Representative Government and Hasten a One World Order.
   It is impossible to create a One World Order unless borders are completely eliminated. Take the European Union as an example. All of the nations of the European Union share the same currency, have a free flow of people across their borders, have a central tax system with the means to enforce collections, and a common court system. That said, are they really sovereign anymore? After all, there is a reason they are called the European Union.
   Then there is the North American continent, where treaties like the North American Free Trade Agreement and our open borders threaten the sovereignty of the United States.
   Once borders become irrelevant, then for all intents and purposes, the affected countries have been combined into one larger political entity. At that point, would that not make it much easier to combine a number of these larger blocs of countries into a one-world government?
   There are also boundaries between local government entities, like cities, townships, and counties, and these boundaries, too, are under attack.
   To understand this, we must not forget that the United States government was designed by the founders to be strongest at the local

level. As has been discussed, because the local governments are desperate for cash, it is not difficult to make them accept grants with strings attached. It is not just grant money from the states and federal government that can tempt the local governments but also grants extended from regional governments. Regional governments are cropping up at an amazing speed.

Below is a list of regional governments in Ohio that belong to the National Association of Regional Councils (NARC).

> Akron Metropolitan Area Transportation Study
> Bel-O-Mar Regional Council and Interstate Planning Commission
> Brook-Hancock-Jefferson Metropolitan Planning Commission
> Brook-Hancock-Jefferson County Metropolitan Planning Organization
> Buckeye Hills-Hocking Valley
> Clark County-Springfield Transportation Coordinating Committee
> Eastgate Regional Council of Governments
> Erie Regional Planning Commission
> Lima-Allen County Regional Planning Commission
> Licking County Area Transport Study
> Miami Valley Regional Planning Commission
> Mid-Ohio Regional Planning Commission
> Northeast Ohio Areawide Coordinating Agency
> Ohio-Kentucky-Indiana (OKI) Regional Council of Governments
> Richland County Regional Planning Commission
> Toledo Metropolitan Area Council of Governments
> Southern Ohio Council of Governments
> Stark County Area Transportation

Below is the mission statement for NARC (National Association of Regional Councils).

As a national public interest organization, NARC works with and through its members to:

- Shape federal policy that recognizes the increased value of local intergovernmental cooperation;
- Advocate effectively for the role of regional councils in the coordination, planning and delivery of current and future federal programs;
- Provide research and analysis of key nation issues and developments that impact our members; and
- Offer high quality learning and networking opportunities for regional organization through events, training, and technical assistance.

When you read NARC's mission statement, it is easy to see that NARC is the "gatekeeper" for the information, money, and power that are being directed downward from the federal government to the regional governments who then decides how best to direct it to the local government.

In other words, the local government, which was meant from the founding of this country to be the "dog" and not the "tail," is now subservient to all layers of government above it through grants that the regional government offer to the local government. Put another way, just as presidential executive orders can make Congress irrelevant, so can regional governments make local governments irrelevant.

Regional governments can also be a threat to boundaries between states. Notice in the list of Ohio regional governments provided, one of them, OKI, straddles three state lines, Ohio, Kentucky, and Indiana. One would have to question how in the world a regional government could answer to three different states' regulations. Conversely, one would wonder how, if a legislator in one state passes a new law, that new law could be implemented and prosecuted in a different state. The answer…only if, at some point in time a One World Order makes the states' borders become irrelevant.

This quote from the UN Commission on Global Governance makes the case. It says, "**Regionalism must precede globalism. We** foresee a seamless system of governance from local communities, individual states, regional unions, and up through to the United Nations itself."

And then there is a new unholy alliance that has been created in recent years and enhanced by Executive Order 13602.

Executive Order 13602, signed by President Obama in March, 2012, gives the Department of Housing and Urban Development (HUD) the authority to engage in city, community, and regional planning to "augment their vision for stability and economic growth." This executive order ensures that "federal assistance is more efficiently provided and used." HUD now has the ability to create regulations to enforce local and regional planning that the government feels is beneficial to the fiscal stability of the US.

This executive order increases the likelihood that various federal agencies, working hand in hand with regional government, will create/make local government compliant to sustainable development policies. The series of steps goes like this: taxpayer dollars are given by the feds to the Department of Transportation (DOT) or the EPA, who directs them to HUD, who directs them down to the regional governments, who dangle them with sustainable development in front of the faces of local governments to create compliance by the local governments to the sustainable development policies of the feds.

An example of how this alliance works and will forward the building of the human settlements (see lesson 4) is seen by looking at the Consolidated Appropriations Act, 2010 (Public Law 111-117), where a total of $150 million was provided to HUD for a sustainable communities initiative.

HUD, then, established grant programs to improve regional planning efforts that integrate housing and transportation decisions, and to increase the capacity of municipal, regional, and state government to change land use and zoning practices. Of that total ($150 million), $100 million was made available for the Sustainable Communities Regional Planning Grant program, $40 million for Challenge Planning Grants, $8.5 million for a joint HUD and DOT research and evaluation effort, and up to $1.5 million for HUD's transformation.

In plain terms, what HUD is doing, once the money is funneled down to it, is to funnel the money down to the unelected boards of the regional governments, who in turn will provide grants to local governments to create "equitable" high density housing complete with sidewalks and bike paths., likely using the Complete Streets design (see lesson 4), near public transit lines. In this way, once humans are forced off of the rural lands by the Wildlands Project (see Lesson 3) the human settlement infrastructure will be in place (see lesson 4) and social, economic, and environmental justice will have been achieved (see lesson 1).

Further, once humans arrive in these newly designed human settlements, their need for cars will be minimized or eliminated because of the bike paths, sidewalks, and nearby transit lines. The high density of humans will also allow for excellent surveillance and control by the government.

In summary, by funneling grant money through regional governments, the power of the local government is eliminated along with the relevance of borders between the countries, states, or local governmental entities. Once borders are eliminated and our local governments with their elected officials are replaced by unelected bureaucrats serving on regional governments, a One World Order cannot be far behind.

The only thing still required is for the government to maintain control of the human population until enough time has passed for citizens to forget that there was ever a time when the citizen, through their vote, actually had a voice in their government. After all, in the New World Order...

"Individual rights have to take a back seat to the collective." (Harvey Ruvin, vice chairman, ICLEI, the Wildlands Project)

The next lesson, lesson 8, will allow you to learn that through indoctrination and the dumbing down of the curricula in the classroom, our children are learning that their God-given constitutional rights must take a back seat to the common good.

||||||||||||||||||||||||||||||||||||||||||||||||||||||||||||||||||||||||||||

CHAPTER 11
Agenda 21 Course

Lesson 8: Education and Sustainable Development

This is the eighth of ten lessons on Agenda 21, commonly known as sustainable development. Today you will learn...

How, Through Education, the American Citizen is being Dumbed Down and Trained to be a Cog in the Centralized Industrial Machine of a One-World Government.

I doubt that many people today believe that in America we have a strong, successful educational system. Yes, most would agree that there are many places where we could improve the system.

The question you should ask yourself during this lesson is, "Has the federal government manufactured the crisis in education so that, at the appropriate time, the it could ride to the rescue and create the solution—a nationalized education system from birth to career, used to indoctrinate our children to be good global citizens with the appropriate skills to meet, not their needs, but those of the centralized government?"

Keep in mind during this lesson that there are many things outside of the classroom that can affect a child's chances of learning, such as the destruction of our families, Constitution, and Christian faith. Many of these have been, if not caused by the government, exacerbated by the government. These ideas that were discussed in lesson 1 deserve to be revisited in that they have a significant role to play in their negative effect on a child's ability to learn.

Today, the family structure is too often in disarray. Without a stable home life, it is difficult for the child to focus on his learning and further, if there is only one parent in the home, supervision of the child's behavior and homework is especially challenging.

Do you remember in 1992 when Dan Quayle was excoriated by the left for suggesting that two parents are better than one? Have you seen how the role of women in society today has been elevated until the perception is that women can and should do it all? It might be asked: Do women really want that much responsibility, and does the family benefit when it is implied that men have little importance either at home or in the workplace?

This elevation of women in the workplace has nothing to do with women and everything to do with Agenda 21. Agenda 21 states that educated women tend to have fewer children. So, if sustainable development policies can increase the socioeconomic status of women, who then will produce fewer children, causing the population to decease, the sustainablists will have achieved their primary goal. If the family is destroyed in the process, and children are too distracted to pay attention in school, that is simply the price that must be paid to advance sustainable development policies.

Add to the destruction of the family unit, Christianity is under attack. Christianity teaches many key lessons that give society a value-driven citizen. Christianity teaches to not lie or steal.

The author of this article was a science teacher for thirty years. As those years passed, it became increasingly clear that the students were lying and cheating with abandon—lying to avoid taking responsibility for their actions and cheating to avoid doing the necessary work to earn the good grade. The result was a student who lacked the knowledge, skills, and values necessary to be an asset to themselves or society.

Furthermore, our Constitution and the brave men that worked so hard to create that amazing document are now being relegated to the back seat on the history bus. These fine men believed in limited government, the importance of owning property, and the value of self-relance. By ignoring the contributions of these men to society, our children are prevented from using them as positive role models and learning the lessons they taught. This makes it much easier for our educational system today to teach instead that private property must be given up for the good of the collective and that dependance on the government is desirable.

Towards the end of the twentieth century, the stage was set. The crisis in education was evident enough to the public that big government felt it could receive a mandate to make reforms in education. Congress passed three educational laws during the Clinton presidency; they were the Goals 2000: Educate America Act, the School-To-Work Opportunities Act, and the Improving America's Schools Act of 1994.

Those were followed by the passage in 2001 of George W. Bush's No Child Left Behind Act. Bush, while signing the No Child Left Behind Act (NCLB), openly agreed to work with the United Nations Educational, Scientific, and Cultural Organization (UNESCO), the education arm of the United Nations, to work towards common goals in education. In other words, as directed by Chapter 36 of Agenda for the twenty-first century (Agenda 21), Bush was promising that the United States was fully on board with integrating sustainable development ideas into the classrooms of America.

Through a myriad number of rules, NCLB attempted to force the schools and teachers to accept the responsibility for students' performances. There were many rules about what would happen if schools did not improve the required amount in any given year. The pressure on the schools to improve the students' performances was huge. While scores often improved, in the case of Ohio, the improvement was so great that it looked suspicious. It came, then, as no surprise that in 2012, a group of Ohio school districts, including the Columbus School District, began to be investigated for fudging their numbers.

No Child Left Behind did not require that states participate; however, the federal funds were withheld if the states did not. At least NCLB did not attempt to force a nationalized educational system. It left at least some of the decisions to the states.

It is important for citizens to remember that the founders wanted education to be a state issue. In that way, each state could decide what was best for their citizens. It also allowed a citizen who was dissatisfied with the way their state handled education to move to another state to be serviced. Keep this in mind as we move on to discussing the...

Common Core Curriculum

In 2007, the efforts to create a nationalized educational system called the Common Core (CC) began.

Common Core Standards were written with the help of a $100 million dollar donation from the Bill & Melinda Gates Foundation along with other grant money provided by our tax dollars that were passed out by the federal government via the US Department of Education.

Two separate sets of states combined efforts to either participate in the Smarter Balanced Assessment approach or the Partners for Assessment of Colleges and Careers (PARCC). Ohio is a member of PARCC, which is being pushed by Linda Darling Hammond, a colleague and friend of the infamous Bill Ayers. Secretary of Education Arne Duncan has also been an active player in the push for Common Core.

He is quoted at the Sustainability Summit in 2010, as saying,

> **Today I promise you that the Department of Education will be a committed partner in the national effort to build a more environmentally literate and responsible society. We must advance the sustainability movement through education... Education and sustainability are the keys to our economic and our ecological future.**

Wow, and I thought education was about learning to read, write, and do arithmetic. Apparently not anymore!

Just because a state, like Ohio, is part of the Consortium, does not mean it is automatically signed up to adopt these standards. That requires that the government do what it does best, use our tax dollars to entice the states to adopt this new set of standards. So, $4.35 million dollars from the 2009 Stimulus Bill was used to create the Race to the Top Competition (RTTT).

To enter the competition, to **possibly** earn money and waivers to some of the No Child Left Behind mandates, a state must accept the Common Core Standards, in this case SIGHT UNSEEN, as the standards had not yet been written.

One of the most successful government strategies for implementing new ideas with minimum backlash is to do it as quickly as possible before opposition can be rallied. This ploy was used very effectively in the case of Common Core.

The states were rushed to judgement when the Race to the Top applications became available in November of 2009 but were due back by January 2010. During this time, few state legislators were open for business, so the state officials, if they chose to sign on, would have to do so without the approval of their state legislators.

It was not until two months later, in March 2010, that the draft standards for Common Core were available for reading. The final Common Core Standards came out three months later, in June. The states had two more months to make their final commitments by August of 2010 as to whether they wished to abide by requirements of the CC standards.

It is important to point out that standards are not curriculum; however, standards drive the curriculum. Standards are a little like the frame of a house. The frame of the house decides what the house will look like. In that same way, standards decide what the curriculum will look like and what kinds of things will appear on the tests. Standards drive the educational experience for the student and, ultimately, how well or poorly the student will be prepared for his career and life.

Just because the government was heavy-handed in the development and acceptance of the Common Core, that does not necessarily mean it is going to turn out badly, does it? An inventory of the concerns about Common Core should serve to provide that answer.

Once a state adopts Common Core, the state and parents have control over only 15 percent of the curriculum., although they will pay for 100 percent of the expense. **In essence, the state and the**

parents have lost virtually all control over the education of the students in their state. This goes against the Tenth Amendment to our US Constitution, which gives control of education to the states. Further, CC violates three federal statutes: the General Education Provisions Act, the Dept. of Education Organizational Act, and the Elementary and Secondary Education Act of 1965.

The tests that will go along with CC standards will be very expensive, as the students must take them on computers. The purchase and maintenance of all this technology makes the donation by the Gates Foundation look like an example of crony capitalism (see lesson 5). The expense of this program will increase even more because all of the tests are to be graded by hand. All these people will have to be hired, trained, and paid for their service.

Possibly more worrisome is that the current administration is constantly pushing social equity. Couple this with the fact that each student will be identified by any number of non-educational markers, like ethnicity, religion, and gender. **Might those, who are hired to grade these tests, be tempted or encouraged to add to or subtract from the test scores to balance out for any social inequalities?**

You might also wonder if this administration, which is equally interested in achieving economic justice, **might not use the data like ethnicity, gender, religion, etc. that is being compiled and stored on each student to decide at the end of the student's education whether that student should or should not be eligible for higher-paying jobs?**

And compiling and storing data on our children they are! Whether it is legal or not is somewhat questionable. In the past, sharing of student personal information with the federal government was illegal. However, both consortiums, Smarter Balanced Assessment and Partners for Assessment of Colleges and Careers, are both contractually obligated by the federal government to give this information to the Department of Education, Department of Labor, and Department of Health and Human Services. Additionally, now that the Family Educational Rights and Privacy Act has been gutted, many of those records are being funneled by the states directly to the feds, which somehow makes this OK.

There are significant concerns about the height of the hoop through which our students using CC will be expected to jump. CC, at this point, only applies to a school's math, language arts, and English curricula. It is expected that, later, all areas of the curriculum will be affected. While proponents say the standards are rigorous, some say the harshest critics were those who were on the validation committees for math, language arts, and English.

Dr. James Milgram of Stanford University, the only math person on the validation committee, said that our kids will be two years behind when they graduate, compared to most successful countries, and that it would be unlikely that they would be ready for university-level math after completing Common Core.

Dr. Sandra Stotsky, who served on the English validation committee, refused to sign off on the English standards, saying that they will not prepare the students for college, and that she thought that the highest reading level was on about a seventh-grade level.

Assumptions would be that most students upon high school graduation would be able to attempt a two-year college using these standards. One of the major concerns is that there will be 50 percent less classical literature in English classes and no British literature, except for a small amount of Shakespeare. In its place will be nonfiction informational text, like manuals, brochures, and even menus. In addition, teachers are being discouraged to give historical context and/or to encourage passionate readings of great historical works like the Gettysburg Address. This is likely to cause the best teachers to quit and the lesser teachers who remain to be retrained to teach the nonfictional material.

If you remember from previous lessons, the founders knew it was critical for the states to maintain their individuality and sovereignty. You also learned that making borders irrelevant is a requirement of a one-world government. If Common Core proponents succeed, by nationalizing the curriculum, while creating uniform mediocrity across state lines, then there will be no recourse for the citizen. There will be no opportunity to move to another state to acquire a better education for their child. **If there is a total uniformity, and the education is mediocre in all states, then students**

will have no choice but to participate in a uniformly mediocre educational experience.

Not even homeschoolers or private schools will be exempt from the CC standards. The ultimate irony is that those that are pushing the hardest for CC are the same folks who criticize anyone who does not embrace diversity. Yet CC's whole strategy is to eliminate diversity in the classroom. The only way for a state to sidestep CC is if their legislature never adopts it or if they repeal it.

If the main reason for creating CC was to create uniformity across state lines—for which there is no data showing it works for large countries like the US—and to create a more rigorous academic curriculum, which there is no reason to believe is the case, then why is there such a push to implement CC by the school year 2014–2015? The answer, as with most of our problems today, comes back to sustainable development/Agenda 21.

Those who were once called socialists but are now called progressives have long attempted to replace the free market with a managed economy where educational and job opportunities are under the strict control of a centralized economy. In that way, the government can ensure, that social, economic, and environmental justice is always achieved so that ethnicity, gender, and religious, inequalities can be redressed, perhaps through advantageous job opportunities. Thus, today's youth will be tomorrows cogs in the industrial machine controlled by big government and at the mercy of social, economic, and environmental justice.

So, going back to the question that was posed at the beginning of this lesson: "Has the federal government manufactured this crisis in education so that, at this point in time, the federal government could ride to the rescue and create the solution—a nationalized education system from birth to career, used to indoctrinate our children to be good global citizens with the appropriate skills to meet, not their needs, but those of the centralized government?" Only time will tell—unless you are willing to make stopping Common Core a priority right now.

In lesson 9 you will learn how sustainable development policies will create a One World Order that will be unresponsive to the citizen and run by big government, big business, and nongovernmental organizations.

CHAPTER 12
Agenda 21 Course

Lesson 9: Nongovernmental Organizations and the Delphi Method

This is the ninth lesson in a series of ten lessons on Agenda 21, commonly known as sustainable development. Today we will learn the...

Role of Nongovernmental Organizations and How City Planners Make Dupes of Citizens Through the Delphi Method and in so Doing Undermine our Representative Government.

There are two types of non-governmental organizations (NGOs):

- **Operational NGOs** are community based and can work on an international or national level. The Red Cross is an example of an international NGO.
- **Advocacy NGOs** promote a specific political agenda by lobbying, using news media, organizing activist political events, etc.

In this lesson, we will only learn about advocacy NGOs, as they are the type of NGO that is forwarding Agenda 21 policies around the globe.

So, what is an advocacy NGO?

They are groups of people with specific political agendas, who want to get the government to force YOU to do whatever they wish. To be an NGO for the United Nations, the organization must complete paperwork with the United Nations to become officially sanctioned by the UN.

- The largest NGO is Amnesty International, with a membership of 1.8 million members.
- The 3 NGOs with the greatest impact on the United Nations Environmental Program (UNEP), the arm of the UN that deals with environmental policy are the World Wildlife Fund for Nature (WWF), the World Resources Institute (WRI), and the International Union for Conservation and Nature (IUCN).

And then there is the infamous NGO called the International Council for Local Environmental Initiatives (ICLEI), whose main function is to design ways to force sustainable development into local government policies. There will be more information on ICLEI in lesson 10.

The list provided below lists some of the more familiar nongovernmental organizations.

National Audubon Society
The Nature Conservancy
National Wildlife Federation
Zero Population Growth
Planned Parenthood
The Sierra Club
The National Education Association
The Environmental Defense Fund

NGOs are the "worker bees" for the UN. Without the NGOs, it is doubtful that Agenda 21 could have been implemented around the world.

Here are some of the things the NGOs, in their worker-bee function, do for the United Nations.

1. Working closely with United Nations Environmental Program, the NGOs write policies that combine their political agenda with that of the UN Agenda 21. For example, an NGO like Zero Population Growth would have no problem writing policy for the United Nations Environmental Program that would go right along with Agenda 21's desire to control population, as that is also the goal of the NGO called Zero Population Growth.

2. The NGOs work to get the policy adopted by one or more UN organization for consideration at a regional conference.

3. The NGOs convince the delegates at the regional conference to adopt the policy.

4. The NGO writes a legally drawn up policy statement on the issue. This document is called a "convention."

5. The NGOs lobby to get the delegates at the conference to adopt the convention.

6. The convention is sent to national governments to be ratified.

7. Once the convention is ratified, it becomes international law.

8. Then the NGOs go into full swing lobbying, in our case to Congress, to write national laws that comply with the treaty. It is not uncommon for key leaders of these radical NGOs to be appointed to presidential councils, creating a direct, official connection between the UN and our federal government, and an even greater likelihood that the policy will be written into law. This was the case with Clinton's Presidential Conference on Sustainable Development in 1992 (see lesson 1).

9. Once national laws are created and passed, the NGOs go to state governments and lobby them to pass state laws that comply with the national laws.

However, since the federal government is prohibited by the Tenth Amendment from writing laws that dictate local policy, the NGOs must take a different tack when trying to force Agenda 21 ideas into local government.

So, to "encourage" local governments to comply with Agenda 21 policies, NGOs lobby Congress to include special grants (see lesson 6) to help states and communities fund Agenda 21 policies.

In this way, your federal tax dollars are funneled down to the local level to help implement Agenda 21/sustainable development policies, which are designed to

- Steal your private property rights (lesson 3)
- Control all human behavior (lesson 4)
- Control the business sector (lesson 5)
- Destroy our representative republic (lesson 7 and lesson 9)
- Indoctrinate our children in order to create good global citizens (lesson 8)
- Create social, economic, and environmental justice (lessons 1–9)

Should a community or state refuse to participate "voluntarily," local chapters of the NGOs are trained to go into action. They begin to pressure city councils or county commissioners to accept the grants and implement the policies. Should they meet resistance, the NGO begins to issue news releases telling the community their elected officials are losing millions of dollars for the community. The pressure continues until the grant is finally taken and the policy becomes local law.

It is now easy to see why the NGOs can be compared to worker bees. The NGOs do the heavy lifting required to implement Agenda 21 throughout the globe.

Understanding the Delphi Method and How It is Used to Dupe the Citizen and Undermine the Power of the Local Government

It may not be necessary for an NGO to send anyone to your city or county to create compliance to sustainable development policy—not if your city or county has hired one or more city planners who have been exposed to the American Planning Association's (APA) *Growing Smart Legislative Guidebook.*

The American Planning Association's guidebook was paid for by the Department of Housing and Urban Development and other federal agencies, using your tax dollars. This massive 1500-page compilation of boilerplate legislation and planning practices guides planners on ways to implement the principles of United Nations Agenda 21 in your local communities.

There are over sixteen thousand certified planners in the United States. The APA helps planners learn what some many consider a manipulative method of reaching consensus about community concerns. This method goes by a number of names, including **the Delphi method, consensus planning, or visioning.**

A planner runs this process in such a way as to allow citizens to think that they are giving input into their communities—input that will help lead the community to an acceptable solution to a community problem. Whereas, in reality, the data the citizen is providing is minimized in such a way as to allow the predetermined outcome that the planners desired all along to be realized. In this way, citizens will be made to believe that green space, bicycle paths, and walking trails were the top concerns of the community because the data will have been manipulated by the planners to create the sustainable development-desired outcome.

This explains why, around the country, small towns and large, are adopting plans for their communities that have similar sounding names, like Vision 2020, and that are following very similar sustainable development plans. Columbus, Ohio has the Columbus 2050 plan. Here is an excerpt from a journalist's account:

> **If there's one reoccurring theme throughout the entirety of the Columbus 2050 document, it's sustainability.** It's a word that gets thrown around a lot, and the definition can vary wildly, but the local leadership at the Urban Land Insti-

tute sees it primarily as a call to personal and community responsibility.

"At its most basic, sustainability means living within your means and can be applied to individuals, businesses, and governments," says Reidy. **"For individuals, it can be living closer to the workplace or community centers, eating locally raised foods, consciously minimizing energy use—at work, home, and in modes of transportation."**

While the Columbus 2050 document may lack the visions of flying cars and Jetsons-like fashion, it does provide a solid foundation for **smart growth** and the building blocks that can potentially shape Central Ohio to be globally competitive for decades to come.

How is it possible that a country with such diverse communities could achieve such uniformity in terminology, strategy, and future community planning unless "the fix is in"—unless city planners schooled by the American Planning Association's influence are not "guiding" the process to create a predetermined outcome.

This process makes a mockery of our representative government. Through the use of the Delphi method, only an **illusion of a functional representative government exists.** In reality, decisions that should be reserved for the citizen are stolen by unelected city planners. This in turn destroys the power of our local representative government and instead places the power into the hands of the unelected city planners.

In summary, put in simple street language, the procedure really amounts to a collection of NGOs, bureaucrats, and government officials, all working together toward a predetermined outcome. They have met together in meetings, written policy statements based on international agreements, which they helped to create and now they are about to impose laws and regulations that will have dire effect on people's lives and national economies.

Yet with barely a twinge of conscience, they move forward with the policy, saying nothing. No one objects. It is understood. Everyone goes along because this is a barbaric procedure that ensures their desired outcome without the ugliness of bloodshed or even a debate. It is the procedure used to advance the radical, global environmental agenda: Agenda 21. (Tom DeWeese, the American Policy Center, from the *Agenda 21 & How to Stop It Tool Kit*)

I am going to make an exception here and directly discuss the supplemental materials for lesson 9. There is a series of videos by Henry Lamb called "Confronting Agenda 21." These videos are a "must" if you are to truly understand how the Delphi method is carried out. For your convenience, notes to go along with the three videos can also be printed from this website. Please make the effort to watch these videos, especially if you are going to attend any kind of visioning/consensus meeting.

In the first nine lessons of this series, the goal has been to educate. It is often said that "knowledge is power." I beg to differ. Knowledge has NO power—unless it is used. The goal, then, of the last lesson, lesson 10, is to teach you how you can take what you learned and put it to use to save our precious representative republic and your children's liberty by stopping Agenda 21.

CHAPTER 13
Agenda 21 Course

Lesson 10: Stopping Agenda 21

This is the last lesson in a series of ten lessons on Agenda 21, commonly known as sustainable development. Today we will learn the...
Strategies that Will Help You Stop Agenda 21 from Destroying our Representative Republic.

We can hope that the politicians, with no push from the people, will on their own find out, learn about, and address sustainable development through appropriate legislation. If hoping for something worked, we would all have won million-dollar lotteries by now. No, unfortunately, hope is not the answer. Only if enough Americans are educated to understand what Agenda 21 is, how it has been implemented, and then choose to engage our politicians in order to create enough "pressure" to force the politicians to stop passing sustainable development policies and to instead sponsor anti-Agenda 21 legislation, will we be able to throw off the shackles that are currently being created for the American people.

Pressure from the educated citizens can be applied on every level of government: local, state, and national. This will not be an easy task nor a quick task, but if we as a nation wish freedom for ourselves and the generations to come, we must accept this challenge. But for this challenge to be successful, we must be smart about how we go about tackling Agenda 21 because if we make mistakes, we will at the least miss an opportunity to create positive change.

In order to make my point, I am going to reprint, with permission from the American Policy Center, headed by long time Agenda

21 activist Tom DeWeese, an article titled "New Strategies in the Fight to Stop Agenda 21." Remember, I am using Tom DeWeese's words.

* * *

I hear from an ever-growing list of activists working in their communities to stop Agenda 21. A revolution is certainly underway across the country.

However, as we are gaining success, we are also beginning to face stiffer resistance from the proponents of Agenda 21 and sustainable development. More than ever, we are hearing their charges of "conspiracy theories," "fringe nuts," and "extremism." It's to be expected. We are openly challenging them, and they are feeling the heat. That means, as we move forward, it's vitally important that anti-Agenda 21 activist be very careful with how they approach local government to express their opposition.

I'm finding that there is a bit of a misconception in regard to one of the main proponents of Agenda 21, and it is hurting our ability to make progress in the fight. It is vitally important that we all get the following facts right when launching our attacks against ICLEI. Please listen carefully. The International Council for Local Environmental Initiatives (ICLEI) has been a main target by the anti-Agenda 21 forces. We targeted ICLEI because it has a clear United Nations connection, making it easier for us to make our case to elected officials about the UN connection to Agenda 21 and sustainable development policy. However, some have misunderstood the ICLEI role and have misrepresented who it is and what it does. The result, in some cases, is that our legitimate arguments have been ignored and even laughed at.

What ICLEI Is, and What ICLEI Does

Let me try to set the record straight and provide some ideas on how to deal with the ICLEI situation. First, the following facts are certainly true and need to be understood by all anti-Agenda 21 activists: ICLEI is a UN NGO organization that helped write Agenda 21 for the 1992 Earth Summit and then set, as its mission, to bring Agenda 21 policy to every city in the world. It does this by meeting with local officials, signing contracts with them to set standards for energy and water use, building and development codes, farming policy, etc. It brings in training for city hall staff; software to manage the programs; guidelines for legislation; networking with other communities, other NGO and Stakeholder groups, and other agencies of state and federal government. They reach out to other public officials in the communities, including newspaper editors, school superintendents, local college presidents, and chamber of commerce leaders— all designed to assure everyone who helps make decisions and policy in the community are on board. And of course, ICLEI leads the officials to the most important ingredient to impose Agenda 21— money—grant money that comes with specific strings to guarantee that Agenda 21 is enforced.

That grant money is like heroin in the veins. Once there, the addiction and dependence is in force. Once ICLEI has done its job, the community is hooked, and an entirely new attitude and community atmosphere of top-down control is enforced by the government. ICLEI's influence basically creates an entirely new culture in the community where it becomes natural and basically unquestioned to expect local government to be involved in every aspect of your property, job, family, and your whole life.

What to Do and Not Do When Dealing with ICLEI

Now, that is what ICLEI does, why we targeted it, and why it is so dangerous. However, the manner in which we expose and oppose ICLEI is very important, and I have heard some enthusiastic activists go about it in a damaging and ineffective way. First, ICLEI is NOT the United Nations, as I have heard some charge before city councils. It is a private organization with its own agenda—of course it is promoting Agenda 21. But to say the city council is paying dues to the UN is just not accurate.

Another misconception is that ICLEI **IS** Agenda 21, and if the community stops paying dues and ends their contract with ICLEI, the battle is over. I am receiving messages from people who are dismayed to learn their community is still moving forward with sustainable development programs even after they ended the contract with ICLEI. The fact is, ending the contract with ICLEI is just the first punch. From there you must be active in an effort to undo any programs ICLEI helped put in place. That includes...

>...changing the very culture of city hall and its ICLEI-trained staff.

>...an active campaign to dismantle nonelected boards and councils that are the prime source for enforcement of policy.

>...removing your community from regional government councils.

>...electing new officials who oppose the Agenda 21 policy and have the ability and courage to stand up to an assault by federal and state agencies who will not be happy that you are rejecting their agenda. And through all of that you will have to be prepared to counter the attacks from the entrenched NGOs and the lackeys down at the local paper. Withdrawal from the drug of Agenda 21 can be deadly.

Outsmart the Opposition by Employing Common Sense

Finally, I believe there is a more effective way to attack Agenda 21/sustainable development polices in your community, at least initially. You may be fired up about the UN, but others are not. As I wrote a few months ago in my article "How to Fight Back Against Sustainable Development," rather than rushing into city hall and immediately start accusing them of implementing a UN program, take some time to research the policy being proposed or implemented. Determine the effect it will have on the community or your property. Who else will be affected and how? These are the victims of the policy and the most likely to support your efforts to stop it. In that way, you will recruit new people to the cause. You will find it much more effective than sounding like a rabid bear growling about the UN.

For example, smart meters or energy audits affect everyone in town. What is the problem: Government is dictating your energy use that you are paying for. It is a violation of your right to choose how much energy you are willing to buy. It denies you the right to determine how warm or cool your house will be. It denies you the choice of taking a hot shower or not. It even affects your health if you can't get warm enough—or if you are denied access to hot water, allowing germs to grow.

I believe such an argument will gain more support for your cause across the city and across party and philosophical lines than rushing to bring up the UN. Yes, the policy certainly did originate in the bowels of the UN. But why are we opposed to it? Because of what it does to us. And that is the place to start to oppose it. As people come to your side, if they want to know more, then will be the time to teach them the rest of the story about Agenda 21 and its UN origins.

So, focus on the victims and the impact the policy will have on the well-being of the community and you. Question how they intend to enforce the policy (such as having government agents come into your home). Make your officials explain that. They won't want to. This will show the heavy hand of control required to make the policy work. Put the officials on the defensive over their enforcement efforts and watch them retreat as it's exposed.

The same approach can be used effectively in dealing with plans to put meters on private wells, or in dealing with plans for historic preservation schemes that suddenly disallow private property owners to change or improve anything on their house because "Robert E. Lee didn't see that change." (You have to live in Virginia to understand that reference.)

Ask your county commissioners this question: "Name one thing I can do on my property without your permission." To answer that question honestly will force them to admit that under these policies there is no private property. The important message here is to keep your fight local to stop their global agenda.

Agenda 21 is a vast, complicated structure. The organizations promoting it number in the thousands and include nongovernmental organizations (NGOs), public policy groups, federal, state, and local agencies, self-proclaimed "stakeholders," Congress, the White House, 50 statehouses, and your local officials. You can't fight them all individually. Instead, fight the policy and watch them come out of the woodwork to challenge you. By attacking the policy, you have made them defend it and you will have shaped the debate. Then we'll see who is really wearing the tinfoil hats.

* * *

Tom DeWeese gave some really excellent information and advice in this article—advice that will now be elaborated upon. First, ICLEI has done what is typical for those pushing Agenda 21; it changed its name once people started questioning its actions. ICLEI originally stood for International Council for Environmental Initiatives, but while keeping its acronym, it changed the name to Local Governments for Sustainability. This is worth mentioning because it is quite confusing. If you want to know if your town is a member of ICLEI, there is information available in the lesson 10 supplemental materials to help you do that.

Regardless of whether you are trying to remove your town from membership in ICLEI or trying to stop your town from taking grants from regional governments, you must determine a strategy for success. It would be great if there was one way to move forward to fix this mess, and that way forward would guarantee success. Sadly, that is not the case. Every town and every issue will require careful thought on how to move through it to success. It will, in most situations, be easier if you can round up the troops. If you can create a coalition of people from businesses, as well as average citizens, and the more the better, you can more easily delegate the work, have a greater pool of resources, and be able to create a greater show of force. This is the ideal situation. However, in a situation in which you find that there is not an ability to gather a larger group, a small group can make a big difference. It will require greater work on the part of each individual, and there will be no "show of force," but there are still possibilities. A smaller group is indeed less intimidating. That may keep the officials from going on the defense—not a bad thing. It also forces the small group to create "relationships" with those in "power." If you can keep cool, and argue using logic and facts, you may create key alliances with these folks. Once you have one or two of them on your side, they then become allies in influencing the remaining "non-believers." Further, you are a "lean, mean, fighting machine." These situations can change on a dime, and if there are only a few of you engaged in stopping Agenda 21 policies in your community, you can make decisions and adjustments rapidly.

Regardless, before you can employ any strategies, you need to be educated on the structure of your government and the key players in your government. For example, in my city of about fifteen thousand citizens, there is a mayor, city council, city administrator, full-time planning and zoning director, a planning and zoning board, a planning and zoning appeals board, a parks and recreation board, a water and sewer board, blah, blah, blah. You get the idea—lots of layers of government. You will need to decide which of these pieces-parts of the government you wish to monitor and effect.

You will be sitting in a lot of meetings while you try to decide how to respond to the drama that plays out—and drama it is. I would say from personal experience there is more drama in politics than any soap opera you have ever watched. Also, it is really important to stay for the WHOLE meeting. Just because nothing of importance seems to be going on early in the meeting does NOT mean that a "big" event will not occur later in the meeting! If nothing else, those in charge of the meeting respect the citizen that "hangs in" for the whole meeting, which in turn allows the citizen to more easily build the required relationship with the officials in charge of community decisions.

One last point on local government. Do not forget your school system. Everything said so far applies to trying to put our school boards on notice. Lesson 8 on Education should have brought home the dire situation in which our children, through no fault of their own, find themselves. It is just as important, and it could be argued that it is more important, that we reform our schools. There is a saying that says, "Our children are our future." If that is the case, our future is about to be determined by the decisions we make—or don't make—to save our children today from a corrupt educational system.

In summary, think about where, education or government, you wish to put your time and resources. Then study their pieces and parts to decide a more specific target. Begin to go to meetings, talk to anyone who knows anything, and begin to build alliances and strategies to save our precious republic. When you get discouraged, know, if George Washington and his men were able to survive through the winter in Valley Forge to eventually create the greatest free nation on earth, that we can do no less.

Congratulations! You have made it through all ten lessons—no small achievement. Please give yourself a pat on the back!

* * *

We all owe Ms. DeRolf a great debt of gratitude for revealing the elite's America-destroying agenda in such great detail.

Chapter 14
Live-Time Agenda 21

The following articles have been reprinted (with permission) from the American Policy Center website (http://americanpolicy.org).

The purpose of the American Policy Center is to inform an unaware public of the elite's America-destroying agenda and educate them on how to counter their attacks. Please donate if you can.

The Growing Assault on Private Property— Are Single-Family Homes "Racist"?

By Tom DeWeese

One of the main indicators used by economists to measure the health of the nation's economy is housing starts—the number of private homes being built around the nation. In 2018, housing starts fell in all four regions of the nation, representing the biggest drop since 2016.

While many economists point to issues such as higher material costs as a reason for the drop in housing starts, a much more ominous reason may be emerging. Across the nation, city councils and state legislatures are beginning to remove zoning protections for single-family neighborhoods, claiming they are racist discrimination designed to keep certain minorities out of such neighborhoods. In response to these charges, some government officials are calling for the end of single-family homes in favor of multiple-family apartments.

- Minneapolis, Minnesota: The city council is moving to remove zoning that protects single-family neighborhoods, instead planning to add apartment buildings in the mix. The mayor actually said such zoning was "devised as a legal way to keep black Americans and other minorities from moving into certain neighborhoods." Racist, social injustices are the charges.

- Chicago, Illinois: So-called "affordable housing" advocates have filed a federal complaint against the longtime tradition of allowing city aldermen veto power over most development proposals in their wards, charging that it promotes discrimination by keeping low-income minorities from moving into affluent white neighborhoods. Essentially, the complaint seeks to remove the aldermen's ability to represent their own constituents.

- Baltimore, Maryland: The NAACP filed a suit against the city charging that Section 8 public housing causes ghettos because they are all put into the same areas of town. They won the suit, and now the city must spend millions of dollars to move such housing into more affluent neighborhoods. In addition, landlords are no longer permitted to ask potential tenants if they can afford the rent on their properties.

- Oregon: Speaker of the Oregon House of Representatives Tina Kotek (D-Portland) is drafting legislation that would end single-family zoning in cities of ten thousand or more. She claims there is a housing shortage crisis and that economic and racial segregation are caused by zoning restrictions.

Such identical policies don't just simultaneously spring up across the country by accident. There is a force behind it. The root of these actions is found in "fair housing" policies dictated by the federal Department of Housing and Urban Development (HUD). The affected communities have all taken HUD grants. There is very specific language in those grants that suggest single-family homes are a cause of discrimination. Specifically, through the HUD program called Affirmatively Furthering Fair Housing (AFFH), the agency is taking legal action against communities that use "discriminating zoning ordinances that discourage the development of affordable, multi-family housing." The suits are becoming a widely used enforcement tool for the agency.

To enforce its social engineering policies, HUD demands the following from communities that have applied for or taken HUD grants:

- First, HUD forces the community to complete an "Assessment of Fair Housing" to identify all "contributing factors" to discrimination. These include a complete breakdown of race, income levels, religion, and national origin of every single person living there. They use this information to determine if the neighborhood meets a preset "balance," determined by HUD.

- Second, HUD demands a detailed plan showing how the community intends to eliminate the "contributing factors" to this "imbalance."

- Once the plan is prepared, then the community is required to sign an agreement to take no actions that are "materially inconsistent with its obligation to affirmatively further fair housing."

Americans who have grown up experiencing private home ownership as the root to personal prosperity must quickly learn of the threat of the HUD/AFFH program. They must fully understand why cities like Chicago, Minneapolis, and Baltimore and states like Oregon have suddenly announced actions to eliminate single-family home zoning. These cities have already taken the grant poison and must now comply. The ultimate government game is to reorganize our cities into massive urban areas where single-family neighborhoods are replaced by the sustainable/smart growth model of "stack and pack," wall-to-wall apartment buildings.

To the frustration of those sustainablists determined to change our entire economic system, the legal protection of private property rights and ownership have proven to be a roadblock for implementation. New York Mayor William DeBlasio best expressed the frustration of those driving to control community development when he was quoted in *New York* magazine, saying, "What's been hardest is the way our legal system is structured to favor private property. I think people all over this city, of every background, would like to have the city government be able to determine which building goes where, how high it will be, who gets to live in it, and what the rent will be."

Most importantly, HUD and its social engineering advocates have sold these so-called sustainable policies using the well-worn excuse that such programs are simply to help lower income families to succeed. In fact, these programs are actually at the very root of why many of them are NOT succeeding.

The immediate result of eliminating single-family homes and in turn destroying private property rights is to degrade the property values of the homes so many have worked to build. It used to be called the American dream. Now it's labeled racism, discrimination, and social injustice.

Eradicating poverty is the most popular excuse for the expansion of government power. Yet it's interesting to note that not a single government program, from the federal to the local level, offers any plan for eradicating poverty except the well-worn and unworkable scheme of wealth redistribution. After decades of following such a failed policy, the only result is that we have more poor.

Today, as demonstrated in Oregon, Minneapolis, Baltimore and Chicago, we hear the claims that there is a "housing crisis," and so government must take a dramatic step to solve the very crisis it has created. As economist Thomas Sowell has said, "The first lesson of economics is scarcity: There is never enough of anything to fully satisfy all those who want it. The first lesson of politics is to disregard the first lesson of economics."

It is interesting to note that, as private property ownership shrinks under these misguided policies, so too does the nation's wealth. Sustainable policies are at the root of nearly every local, state, and federal program. Each step diminishes individual freedom, personal and national prosperity, and the destruction of the hopes and dreams of every American. The American Policy Center is determined to lead the fight to end this misnamed and disastrous "sustainable" course for our country.

Growing Drive to Destroy the Beef Industry

By Tom DeWeese

The American beef industry has long been a tasty target of the environmentalists and their allies in the animal rights movement. To understand the reason is to know that protecting the environment is not the goal, rather the excuse in a determined drive for global power. Their selected tactic is to control the land, water, energy, and population of the earth. To achieve these ends requires, among other things, the destruction of private property rights and elimination of every individual's ability to make personal lifestyle choices, including personal diet.

Of course, no totalitarian-bound movement would ever put their purpose in such direct terms. That's where the environmental protection excuse comes in. Instead, American cattle producers are simply assured that no one wants to harm their industry, just make it safer for the environment. The gun industry might recognize that such assurance sounds a bit familiar. Same source, same tactics, same goals.

So, the offered solution to "fix" the beef industry is "sustainable certification." All the cattle growers have to do, they are assured, is follow a few simple rules and all will be fine, peaceful and profitable. Enter the players: the World Wildlife Fund (WWF), the Global Roundtable for Sustainable Beef (GRSB), and the US Department of Agriculture.

First, let's reveal the sustainablists' stated problems with the beef industry. What's not sustainable about raising beef? According to the environmental "experts," there are ten reasons why the meat industry does not meet sustainable standards:

1. Deforestation—The claim is that farm animals require considerably more land than crops to produce food. The

World Hunger Program calculated that if the land was used to grow grain and soy instead of cattle the land could provide a *vegan* diet to 6 billion people. Do you get that—a vegan diet! The fact is, most grazing land in the US cannot be used for growing food crops because the soil wouldn't sustain crops.

2. Fresh water—They claim that the America diet requires 4,200 gallons of water per day, including animal drinking water, irrigation of crops, processing, washing, etc., whereas a *vegan* diet only requires 300 gallons per day. Apparently, they don't plan to irrigate the land to grow wheat or to wash the vegetables.

3. Waste disposal—Factory farms house hundreds of thousands of animals that produce waste. They claim these giant livestock farms produce more than 130 times the amount of waste humans do. The interesting thing about this detail is that the actual sustainable policies they are enforcing to fix this problem destroy the small family farms in favor of the very giant corporate factory farms they profess to oppose. In addition, those global corporations that join the Green cabal have the ability to ignore many of the "sustainable" restrictions, unlike the small, family farms that are much better at protecting the environment on their own.

4. Energy consumption—For the steak to end up on your plate, say the Greens, the cow has to consume massive amounts of energy along the way as the cattle are transported thousands of miles to slaughter, market, and refrigerate. And let's not forget, the meat must then be cooked! Well, this transportation argument is a direct result of the existence of a limited few packing companies in cahoots with the Green Lords that dictate the market as they work against a more decentralized, local industry. Meanwhile, last time I checked, Tofurkey—made from soy—also has to be cooked!

5. Food productivity—Say the Greens, food productivity of farmland is falling behind the population, and the only

option, besides cutting the population, is to cut back on meat consumption and convert grazing lands to food crops. As noted in point 1, most grazing land cannot be converted. Everything dealing with the sustainable argument is based on some unseen crisis. Yet we do not have a worldwide food shortage or pending famine. In fact, the media is persistently reporting "price-depressing crop surpluses." The only places where such shortages may exist are in totalitarian societies where government is controlling food production and supplies—kind of like the Greens' plan for sustainable beef.

6. Global warming—Here we go! Say the Greens, global warming is driven by energy consumption, and cows are energy guzzlers. But there's more to the story. Cow flatulence! A single dairy cow, they claim, produces an average of 75 kilos of methane annually. Meanwhile, environmentalists want to return the rangelands to historic species, including buffalo. And a buffalo, grazing on the same grass on the same lands, would emit about the same amount of methane. It's a nonissue.

7. Loss of biodiversity—What are some of the examples the Greens give for loss of biodiversity? Poaching and black-market sale of bushmeat including everything from elephants and chimpanzees to birds??? Please explain what this has to do with the American cattle industry—other than a pure hatred of anyone who eats meat of any kind. And that, of course, is the argument from the animal rights/vegan wing of the Green movement that is leading the assault on cattle.

8. Grassland destruction—Apparently, this is based on the Green premise that domesticated animals like cows replaced bison and antelope, which, in turn, caused a loss of biodiversity of species. I've got two pieces of news for you. First, the Native Americans, so revered by the Greens, hunted bison before the white man arrived. Take a trip to Bozeman, Montana and see the cliff where they used to run entire herds to their death, not just selectively choosing

a few to eat. Second, the Greens, not the cattle ranchers, forced the reintroduction of wolves, and that has caused a near annihilation of the antelope and elk herds.

9. Soil erosion—The Greens claim that US pastureland is overgrazed, causing soil erosion. In truth, a great many of today's cattlemen are third and fourth generation on their land. Those ranches could not have existed for over a hundred years if they were so careless in taking care of the land. It is vital to their survival to assure the land stays in good shape. Of course, an environmentalist who has never worked a ranch or farm and rarely comes out of his New York high-rise might not know that.

10. Lifestyle disease—This is my favorite of the reasons why beef is supposedly unsustainable. In short, it's because of stupid people! This one is blamed on "excessive" consumption of meat, combined with environmental pollution and "lack of exercise" leading to strokes, cancer, diabetes and heart attacks. So, it's the beef industry's fault that people eat too much and refuse to exercise. The solution—ban meat consumption. Yet doctors are now realizing that meat eating is not the problem, carbs are.

So, these are the ten main reasons why it's charged that beef is unsustainable and must be ruled, regulated and frankly, eliminated. These are charges brought by anti-beef vegans who want all beef consumption stopped. In cahoots are global sustainablists who seek to stop the private ownership and use of land, all hiding under the blanket excuse of environmental protection.

To bring the cattle industry into line with this worldview, the National Cattlemen's Beef Association has accepted the imposition of the Global Roundtable for Sustainable Beef, which is heavily influenced, if not controlled, by the World Wildlife Fund, one of the top three most powerful environmental organizations in the world and a leader in the United Nations Environmental Program (UNEP), which basically sets the rules for global environmental policy. This is the same World Wildlife Fund that issued a report saying, "Meat consumption is devastating some of the world's most valuable and vulnerable regions, due to the vast amount of land needed to produce animal feed." The report went on to say that, to save the earth, it was vital that we change human consumption habits away from meat. As pointed out earlier, the fact is most land used for grazing isn't capable of growing crops for food. Further, to have the WWF involved in any part of the beef industry is simply suicidal.

It's interesting to note that the "Principles for Sustainable Beef Farming," issued for the Global Roundtable for Sustainable Beef by the Sustainable Agriculture Initiative Working Group (SAI), follow the exact guidelines originally presented in the United Nations' Agenda 21/sustainable development blueprint. Agenda 21 divided these into three categories including social equity, economic prosperity, and ecological integrity. Using almost identical terms, the SAI plan for sustainable beef uses the following headings for each section of its plan: economic sustainability, social sustainability, and environmental sustainability.

under social sustainability are such items as human rights, worker environment, business integrity, and worker competence (that means that workers are required to have the proper, acceptable sustainable attitudes and beliefs). Under the heading environmental sustainability are climate change, waste, and biodiversity, for the reasons already discussed.

Regulations using these principles impose a political agenda that ignores the fact that smaller, independent cattle growers have proven to be the best stewards of their own land and that for decades have produced the highest grade of beef product in the world. Instead, to continue to produce, they will be required to submit to centralized control by regulations that will never end and will always increase in costs and needless waste of manpower.

To follow the sustainable rules and be officially certified, the cattle growers must agree to have much of the use of their land reduced to provide for wildlife habitat. There are strict controls over water use and grazing areas. This forces the growers to have smaller herds, making the process more expensive and economically unviable for the industry. In addition, there is a new layer of industry and government inspectors, creating a massive bureaucratic overreach, causing yet more costs for the growers.

The roundtable rules are now enforced through the packing companies. You see, the cattlemen actually have no direct market. Instead, they first bring their product to feedlots for final preparation. The feedlots then sell the cattle to the packers. The packers are the ones who then have direct contact with stores, restaurants, and other entities that actually buy the beef. The packers are a major force in the Roundtable, working side by side with the WWF, and so dictate the rules to the feedlots to comply with sustainable certification for the cattle they will buy from the growers. If the beef they obtain isn't grown according to the sustainable beef principles, then the packers refuse to buy it. That has quickly put smaller feedlots out of business. Consequently, it also destroys the cattle growers who rely on the feedlots to take their product.

There are only four main packing companies in the United States. These are Cargill, Tysons, JBS, and Marfrig. These packers have already successfully taken control of the hog and poultry industries. JBS and Marfrig are both from Brazil. It's interesting to note that one of their first tactics was to remove the country of origin (COO) labeling from the packaging so that consumers have no idea where their product is coming from. So, as the packers force their expensive, unnecessary, and unworkable sustainable certification on American cattlemen, they are systematically bringing in cheaper product from other countries that don't necessarily adhere to the strict, sanitary, safe production American producers are known for. As a result, there is a noticeable rise in news reports of recalls of diseased chicken and beef in American grocery stores.

Some cattle growers have tried to fight back by creating new packing companies to compete and provide an honest market. However, the costs to do so are huge, as high as $50 million. One such company called Northern Beef Packers was formed, using all the latest state of the art, high-grade processing. The four established packers reacted by drastically reducing their prices to the grocers, thereby destroying any hope of establishing a market for the new packing company.

This then is the situation that is threatening the American beef industry. If one reads the documents and statements from the World Wildlife Fund, the United Nations Environment Program, and others involved, it is not hard to realize that the true goal is not to produce a better grade of beef but to ban it altogether. The question must then be asked: Why is the National Cattlemen's Beef Association allowing this to happen, and indeed, is joining with the Sustainable Beef Roundtable to force these policies on their members?

The answer is actually quite tragic. American ranchers, farmers, and livestock growers have been targets of the environmental and animal rights movements for years. They are beaten down. Like the rest of us they just want to be left alone to work their farms and herds like their forefathers have done for more than a century. But the pressure is growing day by day. So, they have come to believe that if they just go along—put the sustainable label on their product—then this pressure will stop. In short, they see it as a pressure valve.

The reality is it's not going to go away because the goal is not environmental protection, rather the destruction of their industry and control through what the UN calls the reorganization of human society. The attack has now grown to major proportions with the Green New Deal. Beef eaters have no place in the sustainable paradise of city apartment dwellers who accept government controls to choose for them what they are permitted to eat.

There are efforts to fight back. A group of cattlemen has organized under the banner of R-CALF (Ranchers-Cattlemen Action Legal Fund), and they have managed to slow the Sustainable capture of the industry. But the packers' control of the industry is a major roadblock if the cattlemen can't reach their market. R-CALF has filed abuse of conduct suits to shed light on the antitrust activities of the monopoly tactics of the packers.

However, the beef industry cannot recover on its own. There must be outrage from the consumers who are facing higher prices, possible inferior meat, and the danger of disease because of this sustainable tyranny. If you want the right to your own food choices instead of the dictatorship of radical Greens, then get mad. Demand that country of origin labels be put on all beef products so you know where your food comes from. Demand that the Department of Agriculture rejects this sustainable myth and protects the American free market that has always provided superior products.

The so-called sustainable policy is not a free market. It is a government-sanctioned monopoly that is just short of a criminal enterprise. Stand with American farmers and cattlemen. If Americans don't fight back now, we will lose the freedom to our own dinner plates in the name of sustainable lies.

Green New Deal Reveals the Naked Truth of Agenda 21

By Tom DeWeese

Sometimes, if you fight hard enough and refuse to back down, no matter the odds, your truth is vindicated and prevails!

For twenty years I have been labeled a conspiracy theorist, scaremonger, extremist, dangerous, nut case. I've been denied access to stages and major news programs and awarded tinfoil hats. All because I have worked to expose Agenda 21 and its policy of sustainable development as a danger to our property rights, economic system, and culture of freedom.

From its inception in 1992 at the United Nation's Earth Summit, fifty thousand delegates, heads of state, diplomats and nongovernmental organizations (NGOs) hailed Agenda 21 as the "comprehensive blueprint for the reorganization of human society." The 350-page, 40-chapter Agenda 21 document was quite detailed and explicit in its purpose and goals. They warned us that the reorganization would be dictated through all-encompassing policies affecting every aspect of our lives, using environmental protection simply as the excuse to pull at our emotions and get us to voluntarily surrender our liberties.

Section I details "Social and Economic Dimensions" of the plan, including redistribution of wealth to eradicate poverty, maintenance of health through vaccinations and modern medicine, and population control.

To introduce the plan, the Earth Summit Chairman Maurice Strong boldly proclaimed, "Current lifestyles and consumption patterns of the affluent middle class—involving meat intake, use of fossil fuels, appliances, air-conditioning, and suburban housing—are not sustainable." Of course, according to the plan, if it's not "sustainable," it must be stopped.

In support of the plan, David Brower of the Sierra Club (one of the NGO authors of the Agenda) said, "Childbearing should be a punishable crime against society, unless the parents hold a government license." Leading environmental groups advocated that the earth could only support a maximum of one billion people, leading famed Dr. Jacques Cousteau to declare, "In order to stabilize world populations, we must eliminate 350,000 people per day."

Section II provides the "Conservation and Management of Resources for Development" by outlining how environmental protection was to be the main weapon, including global protection of the atmosphere, land, mountains, oceans, and fresh waters—all under the control of the United Nations.

To achieve such global control to save the planet, it is necessary to eliminate national sovereignty and independent nations. Eliminating national borders quickly led to the excuse for openly allowing the "natural migration" of peoples. The UN Commission on Global Governance clearly outlined the goal for global control stating, "The concept of national sovereignty has been immutable, indeed a sacred principle of international relations. It is a principle which will yield only slowly and reluctantly to the new imperatives of global environmental cooperation." That pretty much explains why the supporters of such a goal go a little off the rails when a presidential candidate makes his campaign slogan "Make America Great Again."

The main weapon for the Agenda was the threat of environmental Armageddon, particularly manifested through the charge of man-made global warming, later to conveniently become "climate change." It didn't matter if true science refused to cooperate in this scheme, as actual global temperatures really are not rising and there continues to be no evidence of any man-made effect on the climate. Truth hasn't been important to the scaremongers. Timothy Wirth, president of the UN Foundation said, "We've got to ride this global warming issue. Even if the theory of global warming is wrong, we will be doing the right thing in terms of economic and environmental policy." To further drive home their complete lack of concern for truth, Paul Watson of Green Peace declared, "It doesn't matter what is true, it only matters what people believe is true."

So, in their zealotry to enforce the grand agenda, social justice became the "moral force" over the rule of law as free enterprise, private property, rural communities, and individual consumption habits became the targets, labeled as racist and a social injustice. Such established institutions and free-market economics were seen as obstructions to the plan as were traditional family units, religion, and those who were able to live independently in rural areas.

Finally, Agenda 21 was summed up in supporting documents this way:

> Effective execution of Agenda 21 will require a profound reorientation of all human society, unlike anything the world has ever experienced. It requires a major shift in the priorities of both governments and individuals, and an unprecedented redeployment of human and financial resources. This shift will demand that a concern for the environmental consequences of every human action be integrated into individual and collective decision-making at every level.

Of course, such harsh terms had to be hidden from the American people if the plan was to be successfully imposed. They called it a "suggestion" for "voluntary" action—just in case a nation or community wanted to do something positive for mankind! However, while using such innocent-sounding language, the Agenda 21 shock troops lost no time pushing it into government policy. In 1992, just after its introduction at the Earth Summit, Nancy Pelosi introduced a resolution of support for the plan into Congress. It's interesting to note that she boldly called it a "comprehensive blueprint for the reorganization of human society." In 1993, new President Bill Clinton ordered the establishment of the President's Council for Sustainable Development, with the express purpose of enforcing the Agenda 21 blueprint into nearly every agency of the federal government to assure it became the law of the land. Then the American Planning Association (APA) issued a newsletter in 1994, supporting Agenda 21's ideas as a "comprehensive blueprint" for local planning. So much for a voluntary idea!

However, as we, the opponents started to gain some ground in exposing its true purpose and citizens began to storm city halls protesting local implementation, suddenly the once-proud proponents lost their collective memories about Agenda 21. Never heard of it! "There are no blue-helmeted troops at city hall," said one proponent, meaning policies being used to impose it were not UN driven, but just "local, local, local." "Oh, you mean that innocuous twenty-year-old document that has no enforcement capability? This isn't that!" These were the excuses that rained down on us from the planners, NGOs, and government agents as they scrambled to hide their true intentions.

I was attacked on the front page of the *New York Times* Sunday paper under the headline "Activists Fight Green Projects, Seeing UN Plot." The Southern Poverty Law Center (SPLC) produced four separate reports on my efforts to stop it, calling our efforts an "Antigovernment Right-Wing Conspiracy Theory." *The Atlantic* magazine ran a story entitled "Is the UN Using Bike Paths to Achieve World Domination?" Attack articles appeared in the *Washington Post, Esquire* magazine, *Wingnut Watch, Mother Jones,* and *Treehugger* to name a few. All focused on labeling our opposition as tin-foil-hat-wearing nut jobs. Meanwhile, an alarmed American Planning Association created an "Agenda 21: Myths and Facts" page on its website to supposedly counter our claims. APA then organized a "Boot Camp" to retrain its planners to deal with us, using a "Glossary for the Public," teaching them new ways to talk about planning. Said the opening line of the glossary, "Given the heightened scrutiny of planners by some members of the public, what is said—or not said—is especially important in building support for planning." The glossary went on to list words not to use, like "public visioning," "stakeholders," "density," and "smart growth" because such words make the "critics see red."

Local elected officials, backed by NGO groups and planners, began to deride local activists—sometimes denying them access to speak at public meetings, telling them that Agenda 21 conspiracy theory has "been debunked." Most recently, an irate city councilman answered a citizen who claimed local planning was part of Agenda 21 by saying, "This is what's 'trending.'" So, of course, if everyone is doing it, it must be right!

Such has been our fight to stop this assault on our culture and constitutional rights.

Over the years, since the introduction of Agenda 21 in 1992, the United Nations has created several companion updates to the original documents. This practice serves two purposes. One is to provide more detail on how the plan is to be implemented. The second is to excite its global activists with a new rallying cry. In 2000, the UN held the Millennium Summit, launching the Millennium Project, featuring eight goals for global sustainability to be reached by 2015. Then, when those goals were not achieved, the UN held another summit in New York City in September of 2015, this time outlining seventeen goals to be reached by 2030. This document became known as the 2030 Agenda, containing the exact same goals as were first outlined in Agenda 21 in 1992 and then again in 2000, only with each new incarnation offering more explicit direction for completion.

Enter the Green New Deal, representing the boldest tactic yet. The origins and the purpose of the Green New Deal couldn't be more transparent. The forces behind Agenda 21 and its goal of reorganizing human society have become both impatient and scared. Impatient that 27 years after Agenda 21 was introduced, and after hundreds of meetings, planning sessions, massive propaganda, and billions of dollars spent, the plan still is not fully in place. Scared because people around the world are starting to learn its true purpose and opposition is beginning to grow.

So, the forces behind the Agenda have boldly thrown off their cloaking devices and their innocent-sounding arguments that they just want to protect the environment and make a better life for us all. Instead, they are now openly revealing that their goal is socialism and global control, just as I've been warning about for these past twenty years. Now they are determined to take congressional action to finally make it the law of the land.

Take a good look, those of you who have heard my warnings about Agenda 21 over the years. Do you see the plan I have warned about being fully in place in this Green New Deal?

- I warned that Agenda 21 would control every aspect of our lives, including how and we're we live, the jobs we have, the mode of transportation available to us, and even what we eat. The Green New Deal is a tax on everything we do, make, wear, eat, drink, drive, import, export, and even breathe.

- In opposing smart growth plans in your local community, I said the main goal was to eliminate cars, to be replaced with bikes, walking, and light rail trains. The Green New Deal calls for the elimination of the internal combustion engine. Stay alert. The next step will be to put a ban on the sale of new combustion engines by a specific date and then limit the number of new vehicles to be sold. Bans on commercial truck shipping will follow. Then they will turn to airplanes, reducing their use. Always higher and higher taxes will be used to get the public to "voluntarily" reduce their use of such personal transportation choices. That's how it works, slowly but steadily towards the goal.

- I warned that under smart growth programs now taking over every city in the nation that single-family homes are a target for elimination, to be replaced by high-rise, stack-and-pack apartments in the name of reducing energy use. That will include curfews on carbon heating systems, mandating they be turned off during certain hours. Heating-oil devices will become illegal. Gradually, energy use of any kind will be continually reduced. The Green New Deal calls for government control of every single home, office, and factory to tear down or retrofit them to comply with massive environmental energy regulations.

- I warned that Agenda 21 sustainable policy sought to drive those in rural areas off the farms and into the cities where they could be better controlled. Those in the cities will be ordered to convert their gardens into food producers. Most recently I warned that the beef industry is a direct target for elimination. It will start with mandatory decreases in meat consumption until it disappears form our daily diet. The consumption of dairy will follow. Since the revelation of the Green New Deal, the national debate is now over cattle emissions of methane and the drive to eliminate them from the planet. Controlling what we eat is a major part of the Green New Deal.

- I warned that part of the plan for Agenda 2030 was "zero economic growth." The Green New Deal calls for a massive welfare plan where no one earns more than anyone else. Incentive to get ahead is dead. New inventions would disrupt their plan for a well-organized, controlled society. So, where will jobs come from after we have banned most manufacturing, shut down most stores, stopped single-family home construction, closed the airline industry, and severely regulated farms and the entire food industry? This is their answer to the hated free markets and individual choice.

The Green New Deal will destroy the very concept of our constitutional republic, eliminating private property, locally elected representative government, free markets, and individual freedom. All decisions in our lives will be made for us by the government—just to protect the environment of course. They haven't forgotten how well that scheme works to keep the masses under control.

Though the label "Green New Deal" has been passing around globalist circles for a while, it's interesting that its leaders have now handed it to a naïve, inexperienced little girl from New York who

141

suddenly found herself rise from bartending to a national media sensation almost overnight. That doesn't just happen, and there is no miracle here. Alexandria Ocasio-Cortez is a created product. They probably needed her inexperienced enthusiasm to deliver the Green New Deal because no established politician would touch it. Now that it's been introduced, and she is set up to take the heat, the gates have swung open, allowing forty-five members of Congress to co-sponsor it in the House of Representatives as established Senator Ed Markey (D-MA) has sponsored it in the Senate. That doesn't just happen either. Nothing has been left to chance.

Behind the sudden excitement and rush to support it are three radical groups, each having direct ties to George Soros, including the Sunrise Movement—which markets itself as an "army of young people" seeking to make climate change a major priority. Justice Democrats—which finds and recruits progressive candidate—and New Consensus organized to change how we think about issues. Leaders of these groups have connections with other Soros-backed movements, including Black Lives Matter and Occupy Wall Street. According to *The New Yorker* magazine, the plan was written over a single weekend in December 2018. Ocasio-Cortez was included in the effort, chosen to introduce it. This may be the single reason why she was able to appear out of nowhere to become the new darling of the radical left.

So, there you have it—Agenda 21, the Millennium Project, Agenda 2030, the Green New Deal. Progress in the world of progressives! They warned us from the beginning that their plan was the "comprehensive blueprint for the reorganization of human society." And so, it is to be the total destruction of our way of life.

To all of those elected officials, local, state, and federal, who have smirked at we who have tried to sound the alarm, look around you now, hot shots! You have denied, ignored, and yet, helped put these very plans into place. Are you prepared to accept what you have done? Will you allow your own homes and offices to be torn down—or will you be exempt as part of the elite or just useful idiots? Will you have to give up your car and ride your bike to work? Or is that just for we peasants?

Over these years, you have listened to the Sierra Club, the Nature Conservancy, the World Wildlife Fund, ICLEI, the American Planning Association, and many more, as they assured you their plans were just environmental protection, just good policy for future generations. They have been lying to you to fulfill their own agenda! Well, now the truth is right in front of you. There is no question of who and what is behind this. And no doubt as to what the final result will be.

Now, our elected leaders have to ask real questions. As the Green New Deal is implemented, and all energy except worthless, unworkable wind and solar are put into place, are you ready for the energy curfews that you will be forced to impose, perhaps each night as the sun fades, forcing factories, restaurants, hospitals, and stores to close at dusk? How about all those folks forced to live in the stack-and-pack high-rises when the elevators don't operate? What if they have an emergency?

How much energy will it take to rebuild those buildings that must be destroyed or retrofitted to make them environmentally correct for your brave new world? Where will it come from after you have banned and destroyed all the workable sources of real energy? What are you counting on to provide you with food, shelter, and the ability to travel so you can continue to push this poison? Because this is what's trending now! And how is it going to be financed when the entire economy crashes under its weight? Is it really the future you want for you, your family, and your constituents who elected you?

Every industry under attack by this lunacy should now join our efforts to stop it. Cattlemen, farmers, airlines, the auto industry, realtors, the tourist industry, and many more all will be put out of business—all should now take bold action to immediately kill this plan before it kills your industry. Stomp it so deeply into the ground that no politician will ever dare think about resurrecting it.

For years I've watched politicians smirk, roll their eyes, and sigh whenever the words Agenda 21 were uttered. As George Orwell said, "The further a society drifts from the truth, the more it will hate those who speak it." Today, I stand vindicated in my warnings of where Agenda 21 was truly headed because it's no longer me having to reveal the threat. They are telling you themselves. Here's the naked truth—socialism is for the stupid. The Green New Deal is pure socialism. How far its perpetrators get in enforcing it depends entirely on how hard you are willing to fight for freedom. Kill it now or watch freedom die.

American Policy Center—New Voices and Growing!

By Tom DeWeese

I'm excited to report that the American Policy Center (APC) is growing as our impact and influence are having more of an effect on the nation's political debate than any time in our thirty-one-year history. Through a huge presence in radio programs, issue papers, and public appearances, APC has almost single-handedly made the issue of Agenda 21 one of the most discussed subjects in the nation.

In January 2018, APC plans to roll out its biggest project ever, intended to make the assault on private property rights a central issue at all levels of government. It will begin with the launching of a new book entitled *Sustainable: The War on Free Enterprise, Private Property and Individuals*. To follow the book's release will be the establishment of a new property rights network of organizations, elected officials, and individual activists. Each will be promoting solutions and strategies for positive approaches to influence and change public policy for property rights protection, from the inner cities to the Great Plains. The launch will include regular training webinars featuring some of the nation's leading experts and most effective activists, who will share their experiences in fighting Agenda 21 policy.

Obviously, a project of this magnitude will create an even larger demand than ever for APC spokesmen to travel the country and address organizations, elected officials and radio audiences. To meet that need, I am pleased to announce that new APC leaders and expert voices are stepping forward.

First, Kathleen Marquardt, who has served as APC's Vice President since 2000, is stepping up her APC action and leadership role. In addition to her regular duties in writing the APC online *News*

Wire, Kathleen will now take to the speaking circuit to address local and state groups about Agenda 21 and its assault on property rights.

Kathleen is well qualified for this effort. Before joining the American Policy Center, she was founder and president of Putting People First, one of the original groups to expose the dangers of the radical animal rights movement. She is author of the best-selling book *Animal Scam*. Through that effort, she was one of the leaders of the Wise Use movement. It was the first coalition to take on the fight against the radical environmental movement as it was destroying western farms, ranches, and the timber industry—even before Agenda 21 was created. She's a dedicated veteran of the Eco Wars. Kathleen resides in Tennessee and will primarily cover speaking invitations in southern and western areas of the nation.

Second, I am excited to announce that well-known activist Hal Shurtleff is joining with APC as one of our expert speakers. Hal is the cofounder and director of Camp Constitution. He was born and raised in Boston, where he currently resides. He is a US Army veteran who served a tour of duty with the US Airborne. Since 2011, he has conducted over 300 presentations on Agenda 21, from Ft. Kent, Maine, to Valparaiso, Indiana. Hal has visited towns and city halls, documenting evidence of Agenda 21. He has appeared on hundreds of radio and TV shows and is currently host of Camp Constitution Radio. He and his wife homeschool his five children. Hal will primarily over speaking invitations in North East areas of the nation.

These two outstanding representatives will allow APC's voice to spread like never before. I, of course, will also continue to travel the nation, speaking and appearing on radio and TV as I have done for the past thirty years. But their assistance will also allow me to devote more time to writing and producing APC papers and activist tools for the coming fights.

Finally, I am pleased to announce a new member to the American Policy Center Board of Directors. My long-time right hand, CJ, has agreed to fill the position on the APC Board as secretary, to fill the vacancy caused by the passing of my wife, Carolyn DeWeese. CJ is a master at marketing. He is my technical rock who keeps APC programs operating efficiently and effectively. As a member of the board, he will join with me and Kathleen, along with fellow board members, John Meredith and Dr. Bonner Cohen.

Both John and Bonner have been with APC from the very beginning. Both started as APC employees. John served as our Capitol Hill director, meeting with congressional members and staff, representing our positions. Last year, he was named one of the top one-hundred most influential black Republicans. Bonner was the creator and editor of an early APC publication called EPA Watch. It was the first publication to ever tackle the massive overreach of the EPA. Today, Bonner serves in positions with several major Capitol Hill groups, plus he writes, appears on radio, and attends many UN international meetings, helping to report the truth from those gatherings. Each of these men will take major roles in the upcoming APC projects.

This, then, is the stronger and growing American Policy Center. I am honored to have all of these incredible leaders working with me as we move forward. To contact us, book speakers, and to learn more about APC's upcoming projects, contact us.

American Policy Center
53 Main Street
Box 3640
Warrenton, VA 20188-3640
844-287-3640
americanpolicy.org

Agenda 21 or Agenda 2030: There Is No Difference

By Tom DeWeese

Editor's Note

Many times in the past year, when I have continued to use the term Agenda 21, people will rush in to correct me—"It's Agenda 2030 now!" Well, yes and no. This is what the UN does—it changes names and titles like a judo move—but the plan is the same. Remember, that's just what ICLEI did a few years ago when they changed their name. They were originally named the International Council for Local Environmental Initiative. But when we started to reveal that they were part of a global movement to change our way of life by inserting themselves into local policymaking, they quickly moved to drop the "international" from their name. Now they are simply known as "ICLEI—Local Governments for Sustainability." That's how these cockroaches seek to hide when a bright light is shone on them. The name changes, but the game is the same.

*The 2030 Agenda is nothing more than a reboot of Agenda 21. The UN uses such updates of plans to keep their people excited and involved. The 2030 Agenda simply goes into more detail as to how and what they intend to do. Remember, Agenda 21 was introduced as the "comprehensive blueprint for the reorganization of human society." The 2030 Agenda gives more detail on how that is to be done along with providing a more specific date for its full implementation. In reality, there's nothing new here. **It's still Agenda 21!***

So, I wanted to reissue an article I wrote in 2015 about Agenda 2030, when it was first announced, to help build understanding of its threat, but to also assure you that Agenda 21 and its goal to restructure the world is still very much alive. As I say in the article, now we should better understand what we are fighting because they are clearly telling us. Please pass this on and help others to understand the threat. It's very real.

Tom DeWeese

It's 1992 All Over Again.

A New Agenda 21 Threatens Our Way of Life

by Tom DeWeese

If you had a time machine and could travel back to 1992 as the UN's Earth Summit was underway, your efforts to abort this subversive policy would be aided by all you had experienced in the Orwellian world of "sustainable living." You wouldn't have to wonder what the NGOs who created it had in mind. You wouldn't have to trust the news media to provide the details. You would know because you would have lived it. You would know that Nancy Pelosi's open claim that Agenda 21 is a "comprehensive blueprint" for the reorganization of human society was true. And what's more, you don't like it!

We were told, without hesitation, that Agenda 21 was aimed at destroying free enterprise. That it is was a clarion call for humans to live on less and that the earth could no longer sustain the consumptive appetite of the United States of America. They told us, but so many weren't listening. It took over fifteen years for many to finally understand the agenda of Agenda 21. By then it was firmly entrenched in every government agency, every community plan, and every school curriculum. So much so that many now say it is impossible to combat. That it's a done deal.

Well, guess what, Agenda 21 is not a done deal and one of the main forces to recognize that fact is the UN itself, along with a mob of enabling nongovernmental organizations (NGOs). And because it is not a done deal, they are all planning a new, massive gathering to reboot Agenda 21 and force it across the finish line.

Over the weekend of September 25–27, 2015, at the United Nations Headquarters in New York City, thousands of delegates, UN diplomats, representatives of nongovernmental organizations, heads of state, and the Pope will converge to present a new fifteen-year plan, entitled *Transforming Our World: the 2030 Agenda for Sustainable Development*.

Just as in 1992, they are openly telling us what the plan includes and how they intend to put it in force. The preamble to the plan says, "All countries and all stakeholders, acting in collaborative partnership, **WILL** implement this plan." It goes on to say, "We are determined to take the bold and transformative steps which are urgently needed to shift the world onto a sustainable and resilient path. As we embark on this collective journey, we pledge that no one will be left behind." When I read these words, I don't glow with anticipation, I bristle with dread.

That, my friends, is a direct challenge and a threat to anyone who dares to disagree with the plan or stand in their way. They promise us that they "WILL" do it and it will be forced on everyone. Our experience with Agenda 21 over the past twenty-three years tells us what to expect.

Here are the seventeen goals to be presented and what they really mean:

Goal 1. End poverty in all its forms everywhere. The only answer the plan offers for eliminating poverty is redistribution of wealth. The document calls for "equal rights to economic resources." That means government is claiming an absolute power to take away anything that belongs to you to give to whomever it deems more deserving. That is government-sanctioned theft. These are only Band-Aids that solve nothing. Tomorrow, those on the bread lines will still need more. There is not a single idea in these plans to give the poor a way to earn their own wealth so they no longer need government handouts. The final result: a never-ending cycle of poverty that will consume the middle class.

Goal 2. End hunger, achieve food security, and improve nutrition and promote sustainable agriculture. UN documents go into great detail on controlling food supplies. They detail enforcing "sustainable farming tactics," which have been proven to force up the cost of food production while decreasing yield. It is basically the old Soviet practice of farm control that turned the breadbasket of the world into nonproductive wasteland. The document details the use of government-controlled seed and plant banks "to ensure access to and fair and equitable sharing of benefits arising from the utilization of genetic resources and associated traditional knowledge as internationally agreed." In other words, our future food sources will be put into the hands of politically connected bureaucrats who have never been on a farm. Starvation on a massive scale will trim the population to more sustainable levels.

Goal 3. Ensure healthy lives and promote well-being of all at all ages. This means cradle to grave control over how and where we live and what we are permitted to eat. The healthy lives they promote means basically forcing us out of our cars and into walking and riding bikes as we are relocated into controlled high-rise apartment buildings sanctioned by government. Meat will be out of the question, as raising herds is not considered to be "sustainable." But don't worry. Obamacare for all will deal with the predictable decline in health that is sure to follow.

Goal 4. Ensure inclusive and equitable quality education and promote lifelong learning opportunities for all. We have long known that lifelong learning is the means to continually apply behavior modification practices to assure we maintain the desired attitudes, values, and beliefs to live in a global village.

Goal 5. Achieve gender equality and empower all women and girls. The rainbow flag flies as we ignore Shariah law and its war on women.

Goal 6. Ensure availability and sustainable management of water and sanitation. Ask California how sustainable water control is working for them as these policies have torn down water systems and dams to "free the rivers." The original pioneers found the land to be a desert. They built a sophisticated water control system that resulted in an emerald-green paradise. Now, as sustainable policies are being enforced, they are witnessing the return of the desert, destroying productive land. Meanwhile, across the nation, the EPA is moving to take control of all the water in the United States. Control the water, control the population.

Goal 7. Ensure access to affordable, reliable, sustainable, and modern energy for all. Seriously? Their solution is to ban oil and enforce wind and solar power. Every study across the nation and around the world has proven that these "modern" energy sources are unreliable and force up the cost of energy. Some report health problems related to life under the turbines. Moreover, the carnage of the birds and bats that are being chopped up and fried by these "sustainable" energy practices goes against everything environmentalists told us about protecting species.

Goal 8. Promote sustained, inclusive and sustainable economic growth, full, and productive employment and decent work for all. One thing our twenty-three years of Agenda 21 have proven—there is no economic growth. European nations that implemented sustainable energy and water controls guidelines are now dumping those programs as fast as they can to save their economies. And who decides what is "productive" or "decent" work? Do we leave it to the bureaucrats to decide?

Goal 9. Build resilient infrastructure, promote inclusive and sustainable industrialization, and foster innovation. Oh, come now. Sustainable industrialization means destroyed industry. No real industry can remain in business under a government-managed economy with its shifting rules and constant increase in taxes. Government does not create industry or prosperity. Our government's real job is to provide protection of the marketplace so real innovators are free to create new ideas, industries, and opportunities. Government itself is a job killer when it gets in the way.

Goal 10. Reduce inequality within and among countries. This is another form of redistribution of wealth that forces industries from first world to third world nations. By using oppressive sustainable policies to drive up production costs, companies are forced to take their factories to the poorer nations. The second trick is to exempt those poorer nations from the very environmental rules and regulations that caused the factories to move in the first place. Can anyone explain how this helps the environment? It does not. It simply makes everyone equally poor. This is also an assault on national sovereignty.

Goal 11. Make cities and human settlements inclusive, safe, resilient, and sustainable. This is smart growth, which promises a utopia of families and neighbors playing and working together, riding bikes, walking to work in stress free communities. It really means the end of private property rights and single-family homes, and stack-and-pack high-rises where residents are over taxed, over regulated, rents are high, and individual thoughts and actions are viewed as a threat to the "well-ordered society." And, by the way, the American Planning Association did a study to see if their smart growth plans worked and their own report concluded that smart growth does not work.

Goal 12. Ensure sustainable consumption and production patterns. What more is there to say? Control from the top down.

Goal 13. Take urgent action to combat climate change and its impacts. Here it is! The root of the entire plan. Climate change. How many scientific reports do real scientists have to present to show this is the greatest scam ever devised to create a reason for government to control every aspect of our lives? Well, here, let the global warming scaremongers tell you their true purpose in their own words:

"No matter if the science of global warming is all phony— climate change provides the greatest opportunity to bring about justice and equality in the world." Christine Stewart (former Canadian minister of the environment). Justice built on a lie? And here is another quote to make it clear. **"We've got to ride this global warming issue. Even if the theory of global warming is wrong, we will be doing the right thing in terms of economic and environmental policy."** Timothy Wirth (president, UN Foundation). The end justifies the means! Notice that Mr. Wirth is as concerned with the economy as he is with the environment.

Goal 14. Conserve and sustainably use the oceans, seas, and marine resources for sustainable development. Control the water, control society. This one is really aimed at destroying the oil industry in order to enforce wind and solar power. This is the UN pounding its chest to become the central global government it has always sought to be. It has no more right to the seas than it does to the air we breathe or the surface of the moon.

Goal 15. Protect, restore, and promote sustainable use of terrestrial ecosystems, sustainably manage forests, combat desertification, and halt and reverse land degradation and halt

biodiversity loss. Have you been watching the news as the greatest fires in history are destroying millions of acres of forests? Why is this happening? Because of sustainable forest management that refuses to allow the removal of dead trees from the forest floor. This creates a density of combustible-material to fuel massively hot and unmanageable fires. If you want to save a forest, send an environmentalist back to his high rise in New York City where he belongs.

Goal 16. Promote peaceful and inclusive societies for sustainable development, provide access to justice for all, and build effective, accountable, and inclusive institutions at all levels. This is social justice, which really means social engineering. Have you ever once witnessed an "effective" or "accountable" institution coming out of the United Nations? By its very nature, the UN is unaccountable. Who would be the entity to oversee that accountability? Every one of these programs outlined in the 2030 Agenda creates money, power, and unaccountability at every level of government. That is why government is now running out of control and people are feeling so hopeless in trying to deal with their governments. Goal 16 should be named the "foxes running the henhouse" goal.

Goal 17. Strengthen the means of implementation and revitalize the global partnership for sustainable development. This means the reboot of Agenda 21 because that was the original "global partnership." This goal is a call for all of the treaties, plans, and schemes devised in the massive UN meetings to be made the law of the globe. It is total global government, and it is a sure highway to misery, destruction of human society, individual thought, motivation, and dreams.

In 1992, they told us that Agenda 21 was just a suggestion. Today, after experiencing the "wrenching transformation" of our society that Al Gore called for, we know it was much more than that. And we have suffered the consequences as our economy has plummeted, as the middle class is disappearing, jobs are nonexistent, and the world is in turmoil.

Now, the power elite that prey on the poor and helpless are determined to finish the job. They are fast moving toward the goal of eliminating individual nation-states, controlling individual actions, and wiping private property ownership from the face of the earth. Their goal is to make us all "equal" in the same chains to assure none of us can disrupt their well-ordered utopian nightmare.

Well, now our time machine has brought us back from 1992 to the present. As we disembark, one voice should be ringing in our ears. In clear and concise words, we were warned of what Agenda 21 was designed to do. **"Isn't the only hope for the planet that the industrialized nations collapse? Isn't it out responsibility to bring that about?"** The voice belonged to Maurice Strong, secretary general of the UN Earth Summit as he delivered an official statement.

But here in 2015, the same forces are about to introduce the 2030 Agenda. We have the advantage of knowing what is intended. The 2030 Agenda to "transform the world" is to be built on the ruins and desolation of a thousand such schemes for control over human life. Each time they have failed to achieve their lofty goals but have brought about a slow decline in liberty and self-sufficiency. And each time they have come back with a new "plan." The 2030 Agenda is Agenda 21 rebooted. But this time, you and I don't have an excuse to ignore it. We know what it is from the start. Now we have a new opportunity and the obligation to stop it dead in its tracks. We've been given a second chance. Let's not waste it.

This Happens If Trump Fails to Rein in HUD

By John Anthony

If you want to know what will happen to your hometown if Trump allows the Department of Housing and Urban Development to continue its devastating control of local rule, look at Whitehall Township, Pennsylvania. It is the latest community to surrender to HUD's aggressive tactics.

Much of the chaos we see in America today is designed to stop President Trump from dismantling the federal system of rampant waste, dishonesty, and bullying. The largest "swamp" he must drain is the embedded federal bureaucracy.

In theory, at least, we can "fire" politicians every two, four, and six years. But federal agency employees can linger for decades, beneath the radar, issuing guidance documents on little-understood regulations that are now devastating our communities and property rights.

That is why the administration must work closely with Congress to pass the House and Senate bill titled the Local Zoning Decisions Protection Act of 2017. Once signed by the president, the new law will outlaw HUD's worst offenders, its Affirmatively Furthering Fair Housing (AFFH) regulation.

AFFH uses legal actions against communities that accept popular HUD grants to force them into a bizarre, centrally managed program of regionalism and forced socioeconomic integration. AFFH use of litigation threats is becoming a widespread enforcement tool for the agency.

Whitehall Township is the most recent victim of HUD's new legal intimidation. The community, located in the heart of the Lehigh Valley, ninety miles north of Philadelphia, has its own home-rule charter. They have their own mayor, township commissioners, and planning commission.

That autonomy and the voice of their voters mean little to HUD.

In February 2014, PathStone, a regional affordable housing developer from the Philadelphia area, proposed purchasing a parcel of land in the township and constructing fifty-two (later reduced to forty-nine) affordable housing units in the Loft Project. By May, the planning commission rejected the proposal.

Rather than accept the commission's decision and find another location to build, in April 2015, PathStone hired a civil rights law firm who filed a complaint with HUD requesting they investigate Whitehall for a "discriminatory zoning ordinance that discourages the development of affordable, multifamily housing in high-opportunity areas."

The suit claimed, "The Zoning Hearing Board denied zoning relief…on the basis of the race, color, national origin, familial status, and disability status of the prospective residents of the housing."

HUD was involved because the Township had received $395,000 in Community Development Block Grants (CDBG) since 2009. But how were the attorneys and HUD able to interpret the board's decision as discriminatory?

The planning commission argued that PathStone's proposal only allowed for one parking space per unit, in violation of zoning laws that called for two. In addition, citizens raised concerns over reduced property values and increased crime.

PathStone's attorneys countered that the commission had previously approved similar zoning relief for the same parcel for a senior citizen's home. Therefore, they reasoned, any rejection for affordable housing is clearly the result of discrimination.

Their rationale was limited to selective portions of the voters' issues. Rather than address the community's worries about crime, attorneys and HUD dismissed that issue as racist.

But safety and racism are different topics, and the citizens' fears were legitimate. While senior citizen housing rarely raises crime rates, a detailed block-by-block study shows that high density, low-income housing does attract larger numbers of homicides, no matter who lives there. This should be a real concern for any community.

Whitehall's citizens were outraged at PathStone's and HUD's heavy-handed tactics and continued to voice their objections to the Lofts, even in the face of threatened lawsuits.

It was a losing fight. In HUD's view, resistance to affordable housing is in itself discriminatory and bore the threat of even greater charges.

By June of 2016, Whitehall finally caved to the federal government's pressure. They altered their zoning laws to meet HUD's demands and agreed to sign a voluntary compliance agreement allowing the project to advance. As Commissioner Philip Ginder, caught between signing an oppressive agreement that voters did not want and facing mounting lawsuit threats, said before voting, "This is one of the hardest 'yes' votes I've ever made in my life.

Among other stipulations, Whitehall "voluntarily" agreed to defend their zoning changes from third-party challenges and "extend its full cooperation throughout the remainder of the planning, application, and approval processes relevant to development of The Lofts, and throughout the infrastructure development, building permit process, construction, and initial rent-up phases of The Lofts."

Whitehall had to "actively promote the Lofts by endorsing the development."

In the biggest sting of all, HUD ordered the township, "No later than December 28, 2016, to remit the amount of Three Hundred Seventy-Five Thousand Dollars ($375,000.00) to Complainant PathStone."

The payment was in satisfaction for

> PathStone's claims for monetary compensation, additional carrying costs, out-of-pocket expenses, and additional staff time related to development of The Lofts from the time of the May 20, 2014 denial by Respondent Zoning Hearing Board, as well as additional payments to the current owner of subject property to reserve PathStone's purchase rights, the expense of reapplication for PHFA funding in 2015, additional interest on the predevelopment loan for The Lofts, and attorneys' fees and costs.

What happened in Whitehall Township can happen in any community that has zoning laws and accepts federal money for fair housing or urban development. Even if AFFH is overturned, as the Whitehall case shows, the agency can claim discrimination for a host of reasons that may or may not be fair to communities. This is why communities must protect their local autonomy and their right to control zoning and land use.

Community members must stay informed and involved. Learn about HUD and how their grant requirements can alter your town, city, or county. Study the effects of regional sustainable development on local jurisdictional authority, on taxes, and on lifestyles. Then work with local officials to protect your neighborhoods for now and for future generations.

* * *

Some of Mr. DeWeese's recent efforts include participating in the pro-Second Amendment rallies and stopping the COVID-19 TRACE Act.

Please donate to the American Policy Center if you can.

Mr. DeWeese can be contacted at
American Policy Center
53 Main Street
Box 3640
Warrenton, VA 20188-3640
844-287-3640
americanpolicy.org

CHAPTER 15
The Council on Foreign Relations and Political Factions

Is the Council on Foreign Relations Our De Facto Government?

The following quotes have been retrieved from multiple sources. All bolding and capitalization are my own; all italics are my notes and comments.

The Council on Foreign Relations was established in 1921. **They establish the policies that are leading us into a one-world government system.**
>—Rev. Irvin Baxter, from his video "Master Plan of the Dragon: Part 1"

The purpose of the CFR is to influence American foreign policy **and to prepare its members for key positions in the government.**
>—Rev. Irvin Baxter, "Master Plan of the Dragon: Part 2"

For a long time, I felt that FDR had many thoughts and ideas that were his own to benefit this country, the United States. But he didn't. Most of his thoughts, his political ammunition, as it were, were carefully manufactured for him

in advance by the **Council on Foreign Relations-One World Money Group.**
—Curtis Dall, Franklin Delano Roosevelt's son-
in-law, in *F. D. R.: My Exploited Father-in-Law*

The Bilderberg Group has been meeting behind
closed doors once or twice each year since its formation. **Its purpose is to remove independence
from all countries and permit the aristocracies
to have tyrannical rule from behind the military might of the United Nations.**
—Daniel Estulin, in *The True
Story of the Bilderberg Group*

The real rulers in Washington are invisible and
exercise power from behind the scenes.
—Felix Frankfurter, associate justice of
the US Supreme Court (1939–1962)

The UN is but a long-range, **international
banking apparatus** clearly set up for financial
and economic profit, set up by a small group of
powerful **One World Revolutionaries, hungry
for profit and power.**
—Felix Frankfurter

The **New World Order** will have to be built from
the bottom up rather from the top down...**an
end-run around national sovereignty,** eroding
it piece by piece will accomplish much more than
the old-fashioned frontal assault.
—Richard Gardner, Council on Foreign Relations member, in CFR's *Foreign Affairs* magazine, 1974

The most powerful clique in these Council on Foreign Relations groups have one thing in common—they want to **bring about the surrender of the sovereignty and the independence of the United States.** They want to end national boundaries and racial and ethnic loyalties supposedly to increase business and ensure world peace. What they strive for would inevitably lead to dictatorship and a loss of freedoms by the people. **The Council on Foreign Relations was founded for the purpose of promoting disarmament and national independence into an all-powerful, one-world-government.**

—*Harper's Magazine*, July 1958

There exists a shadowy government with its own air force, its own navy, its own fundraising mechanism, and the ability to pursue its own ideas of the national interests, **free from all the checks and balances,** and free from the law itself.

—Daniel Inouye, US senator representing Hawaii (1963–2012):

Fifty men have ruled this country, and that's a high number.

—Joseph Kennedy, the *New York Times*, July 26, 1936

A threat from JFK to expose the elite and their agenda may be the reason he was killed.

I have here in my hand a list of two hundred and five people that were known to the secretary of state as being members of the **Communist Party** and who nevertheless are still working and shaping the policy of the State Department.

> —Joseph McCarthy, US senator representing Wisconsin (1947–1957), speaking before a Republican women's group in 1950

I included the McCarthy quote because I believe Mr. McCarthy recognized that many working and shaping the policy of the State Department were devising policies that threaten our sovereignty and circumvent our Constitution. Senator McCarthy was mocked and ridiculed by Senator Prescott Sheldon Bush (father of G. H. W. Bush) and his allies for revealing that communists embedded in our government were determining the policy of the State Department. Now, bear in mind that the Council on Foreign Relations vet those considered for every position in our government.

The drive of the Rockefellers and their allies is to create a **one-world government** combining super-capitalism and **communism** under the same tent, all under their control... **Do I mean conspiracy? YES, I DO.** I am convinced there is such a plot, international in scope, generations old in planning, and **incredibly evil in intent.**

> —Larry P. McDonald, congressman representing Georgia (1975–1983)

The **Council on Foreign Relations is the establishment.** Not only does it have influence and power in key decision-making positions at the highest level of government to apply pressure from above, but it also announces and uses individuals and groups to bring pressure from below, to justify the high-level decisions for **converting the United States from a sovereign consti-**

THE GLOBAL CONSPIRACY EXPOSED

tutional republic into a servile member of a one-world-government dictatorship.
> —John Rarick, congressman representing Louisiana (1967–1975)

The Rothschild cabal have infiltrated your government, your media, your banking institutions. They are no longer content with committing atrocities in the Middle East; they are now doing it on their own soil [Europe], desperate to complete the plan for a one-world government, world army, complete with a world central bank.
> —Vladimir Putin, Russian president, comment made to a Kremlin tour group in 2017

In the twenty-first century, national sovereignty would cease to exist; that we would all answer to a single global authority.
> —Strobe Talbott, deputy secretary of state under Bill Clinton (1994–2001), *Time* magazine journalist, president of the Brookings Institute (2002–2017), and CFR member

I think that we declare our willingness to participate in some sort of world organization capable of enacting, administering, interpreting and enforcing **world law,** whether you call it a federation, a government or **world order. We will have a world government whether you like it or not. The only question is whether that government will be achieved by conquest or consent.**
> —James Paul Warburg, German-born American banker and financial advisor to FDR, son of Paul Warburg (father of the Federal Reserve system), speaking before the US Senate Committee on Foreign Relations, February 17, 1950

In essence, Warburg, while speaking on behalf of the international bankers (now referred to as the Bilderberg Group), made **a direct threat against America when he stated that we will have a world government, whether you like it or not, by conquest or consent.** *His comment illustrates the total contempt that the Bilderberg Group and their public base, the Council on Foreign Relations, have for America and strongly suggests they have methodically contrived all of the anarchy (via multiple mechanisms but mainly the media) that has been occurring all across America.* **China, ISIS, Al-Qaeda, the Bilderberg Group, and the Council on Foreign Relations all have one common desire— to destroy America.** *Why is it that* **our government officials go to great lengths to publicize the threat presented by China, ISIS, and Al-Qaeda but NEVER DARE MENTION the GREATEST threat to America: the Bilderberg Group and the Council on Foreign Relations.** *Does that not make our government officials, who have sworn to serve and protect America, lying, deceitful, American-hating* **traitors** *themselves?*

"**The main purpose of the Council on Foreign Relations is promoting the disarmament of US sovereignty and national independence, and submergence into an all-powerful one-world government.** In the entire CFR lexicon, there is no term of revulsion carrying a meaning so deep as 'America first.'"

—Admiral Chester Ward, former judge advocate for the US Navy and CFR member (an organization he became one of the most vocal critics of)

What More Needs to Be Said?

The Council on Foreign Relations (CFR), the establishment, the deep state, and the shadow government are all one and the same, and those serving them are referred to as "the swamp."

THE GLOBAL CONSPIRACY EXPOSED

Did We Lose Our Representative Republic in 1921? Are Our US Representatives Only Figureheads?

The following is posted on the Council on Foreign Relations' website:

> In 1921 a group of **diplomats, financiers, generals, and lawyers** concluded that Americans needed to be better prepared for significant responsibilities and decision making in world affairs. With this in mind, they founded the **Council on Foreign Relations**.

In essence, a group of power-hungry diplomats, international bankers, generals, and lawyers created their own government in 1921. That is just ASTOUNDING! A democracy is a government by the people and for the people—that is, *elected* by and for the people. So, how is it that a group of elites were and are being allowed by our *elected* representatives to decide foreign policy for American citizens who did not give them that authority? And, I would add, **they are instituting communist foreign policy**!

Consider these words from Woodrow Wilson, a former president who served during this key period, lamenting the state of affairs:

> I am a most unhappy man. I have unwittingly ruined my country. A great industrial nation is controlled by its system of credit. Our system of credit is concentrated. The growth of the nation, therefore, and all our activities are in the hands of a few men. We have come to be one of the worst ruled, one of the most completely controlled and dominant governments in the civilized world. No longer a government by free opinion, no longer a government by conviction and the vote of the majority, but a government by the opinion and duress of a small group of dominant men.

**What the Hell Has Happened to America? Chapters
1–3 Answer That Question. The Council on Foreign
Relations Is What Has Happened to America!**

> As my beautiful wife puts it, **elected officials
> only ostensibly run the visible government,** as
> outlined in Civics 101. She says **they are merely
> Muppets who do the bidding of the Deep
> State,** the people **George W. Bush referred to as
> the deciders**—a fascinating phrase from a former
> president who was twice elected by **voters who
> naively assumed that Mr. Bush would be the
> decider** so long as he inhabited the Oval Office.
> —James Dale Davidson

It appears as if all of our representatives are concealing a one-hundred-year-old secret that is so spectacular that revealing it to the American public would shock them to their bones! Was President John F. Kennedy threatening such a revelation? In my opinion, the Council on Foreign Relations has done more damage to America and presents more of a threat to America than all other communist organizations combined. And yet our representatives are still embracing them with open arms. That is comparable to parents welcoming pedophiles into their homes, allowing them to have their way with their children, and then telling them that everything is going to be just fine.

The Wilson quote above, revealing his deep regret in creating the Federal Reserve, suggests to me that his administration surrendered control of America to a small group of dominant men in 1913 who then went on to create the Council on Foreign Relations in 1921. This amounted to the creation of an unelected government designed to circumvent our elected representatives and operate behind the scenes as our primary government to this very day.

Everything mentioned thus far reveals that **the communist invasion of America began in 1921 with the creation of the Coun-**

cil on Foreign Relations. The Bilderberg Group and the CFR work hand in hand.

Consider the following:

- The Bilderberg Group wants to strip all nations of their sovereignty and replace their governments with an all-powerful, one-world government ruled by the group.
- The CFR is the establishment and was created by the Bilderberg Group to serve the Bilderberg Group.
- Many elected and appointed government officials are products of the CFR.
- The Bilderberg Group and UN created the European Union to serve as the first bloc of their one-world government. On November 1, 1993, the leaders of twenty-eight European nations traded their sovereignty for the prospect of creating a better economic environment for their nations.
- The CFR and the Bilderberg Group want to create the North American Union, which would be the second bloc of their one-world government. The Democrat-revised version of the United States-Mexico-Canada Agreement (USMCA) is the equivalent of what the twenty-eight European leaders agreed to in 1993. The document, as originally presented to Trump, was great and would have created an economic boon for the United States, Canada, and Mexico. **But the Democrat-revised version binds the three nations to common law. Can you say "North American Union"?**
- In 2004, our US Congress created the Dominican Republic-Central America Free Trade Agreement (CAFTA-DR), which destroyed the economies of the Central American nations, and *that is why their citizens are flocking to our southern border.* Can you say "CONSPIRACY"?
- No sincere attempts to change our ridiculous immigration laws have been made by either party. Trump requests it but gets no help!

- No sincere attempts have been made by either party to fully secure our southern border. The Republican Party leaders and their allies ignored the Trump agenda while controlling both chambers.
- The Bilderberg Group need a common threat or threats that can be used as a means to unite all the nations of the world **under one common government**, that is, a New World Order. The human-created climate change hoax was not producing the elites' desired objective fast enough, so they had to create something that would—enter COVID-19.

At this juncture, it should be crystal clear to readers that the majority of our legislatures are serving the communist elite. The CFR has stacked the deck! Their indebted puppets have been embedded in every branch and every level of our government. Judges, city council members, mayors, governors, congressmen, senators, diplomats, ambassadors, the CIA, the State Department, the FBI—you name it, they have got it covered. (Keep in mind that Senators Thom Tillis, Martha Mc Sally, Susan Collins, and Ron Johnson attempted to save Ambassador Sondland's job.) As they say, birds of a feather flock together!

Why have so many betrayed their nation? Answer: Because they are serving the communist elite! During the late 1800s, the international bankers concocted and put in motion a bloodless and methodical coup to take control of our republic, and that coup continues to this very day.

They understand that a submissive society—that is, a communist society—is required in order for them to obtain their objective. So, the Council on Foreign Relations has been loading our government with anyone willing to **betray the United States of America** and instead pledge allegiance directly to them. And that has been occurring since the CFR's creation in 1921. The CFR-embedded puppets have taken control of our government.

So, what do we do? Most importantly, *never* vote for a Democrat, as they are *all* serving the elite. We must also never support any Republicans associated with the "Never Trump" crusade. All those defying Trump and his base are serving the communist elite. Establishment Republicans claiming to align themselves with Trump never really have and never actually will! **Once establishment, always establishment!** They are only humoring his base to acquire votes for themselves.

We have to identify, expose, and attempt to primary out all establishment Republicans and replace them with anti-communist, loyal American Republicans (that is, patriots), but the NRCC, NRSC, and RNC make that a challenge. During the primaries, more often than not, they trash the antiestablishment challengers while glorifying and funding the establishment incumbents, which is an indication that they are also under the influence of the Council on Foreign Relations. The 2020 US Senate primary in Kansas is a good example. Mitch McConnell and company used every weapon at their disposal to keep antiestablishment (that is, anti-communist) candidate Kris Kobach from winning the primary. Examples like this are why I no longer donate to any of these kinds of politicians.

The Republican Party has no base without Trump. Their refusal to help overturn a rigged election reveals that **their loyalty to the communist elite supersedes their loyalty to America.** The Republican and Democratic Parties have united under one common cause: COMMUNISM! Both parties have a communist majority and desire a Communist president; thus, Donald Trump had to go. **It is all a charade, and it is quite obvious that the Republican Party has become just another front for the communists.** Both parties desire to have a communist occupying the White House and do not care if that communist identifies as a Republican or a Democrat.

Trump has had little support from Republicans. If not for Trump being the warrior he is, next to nothing would have been accomplished. The Republicans' refusal to help him make America great again has forced him to use executive orders over and over again. But that has only been wasted effort because the communists have taken control of our courts. **The communist-filled courts no longer allow DUE PROCESS and APPELLATE RIGHTS to anyone daring to challenge the communist elite, who are now in charge of our nation.** The pro-elite Republicans have got to be primaried out and replaced with American-serving, anti-elite Republicans, but we the people cannot do that because the communist elite choose the candidates. The NRCC, NRSC, and RNC use our donations to fund and elect the candidates preferred by the communist elite. And that elite have now assured that ONLY their candidates will be elected via rigged elections. Our votes have become nothing more than a suggestion, and our donations are wasted money.

The following quotation from Stephen Lendman's review of Daniel Estulin's book *The True Story of the Bilderberg Group* explains why the courts are constantly overriding the president of the United States of America and any efforts to expose **an election rigged against him**:

> When presidents nominate Supreme Court candidates, the CFR's Special Group, Secret Team or advisors vet them for acceptability. Presidents, in fact, are told who to appoint, including designees to the high court and most lower ones.

Damn, the America-hating CFR vets our judges, from the lower courts all the way to SCOTUS, for what they determine to be acceptable to them. That is a very disturbing revelation!

The following article, posted on the American Policy Center website, has been reprinted with permission from Tom DeWeese. This article reveals that the Republican Party has chosen the communist elite over we the people.

Growing Government Tyranny—Democrats Empower It. Republicans Are Clueless.

By Tom DeWeese

Where is the Republican Party? As insanity spews out of the Democrat Party, the longtime overseer of limited government, free enterprise, and individual liberty has no response, no unified plan to counter the Democrats, and, indeed, seems confused by the socialist antics. The only part of the long-lost Republican cause that seems to be functioning is their near-hysterics over the massive funds the Democrats are raising. Said a recent such Republican fund letter, "I'm hoping you have the courage and determination to fight for what we believe in."

Of course, if the Republicans had the courage and determination to fight over the past two years for "what we believe in," their fundraising would be soaring. Instead, they run candidates with nothing to say, seemingly clueless to the massive assault on our liberties. Now they wonder why they are being ignored in the elections.

Earlier this year, I addressed the leadership of the Constitution Party. I presented them with the real agenda of the Democrats and I asked this question: "Do you want to be the majority party?" They answered with a resounding YES! I then gave them a strategy to win. It occurs to me that all freedom-loving Americas, no matter what party, can benefit from this strategy and use it in their own local elections.

So, here is the speech I presented to the Constitution Party. Now, understand your true enemy, take these ideas, drain the swamp in your city or state, and take America back!

My address to the Constitution Party leadership.

> There has always been some kind of force loose in the world seeking domination over others. They built armies to invade, break things, and kill people in order to grab resources, build wealth and power, enslave people, and conquer.
>
> We've lived through such threats from megalomaniacs like Napoleon, Hitler, and Stalin. Secret societies have plotted to gain power in different ways.
>
> In every case, the efforts have failed. No one has ever managed to rule the entire world. In some cases, they just pushed too far, too fast. Or they miscalculated the weather conditions in

the lands they intended to control. It's incredible to note that both Napoleon and Hitler failed to remember that Russia has a severe winter, which ultimately led to their downfall and defeat.

However, what if such powermongers could find a way to keep their aggression under wraps and out of sight from those they intended to conquer—until it was too late?

Better yet, what if they could actually get their targeted victims to help them achieve control over them? No armies. No shots fired. Instead, the victims quietly pull in the Trojan horse and celebrate its arrival!

What if there was a way for a small, dedicated group to rule the world by simply organizing under a single unifying plan, accepted by everyone as fact and necessary?

Acceptance of the plan would see every nation voluntarily surrendering its independence and sovereignty to the aggressors!

What could possibly be such a powerful message that some of the world's oldest and proudest nations would do that? What could get the world's strongest religions to turn their back on their most fundamental beliefs? What would get the freest nation on earth to join in and agree?

How about the threat of environmental Armageddon! Who could oppose saving the planet? Only selfish zealots who refuse to give up their creature comforts would oppose efforts to save Mother Earth! It doesn't matter how many rights you think you have if you don't have a planet to stand on.

The truth is that's exactly the force you and I are facing today as it drives, almost unopposed, to change our lifestyle, economic system, and system of government.

The Club of Rome, one of the main forces behind this hidden plan to rule the world openly, explained their tactic and goal, saying, "The common enemy of humanity is man. In searching for a new enemy to unite us, we came up with the idea that pollution, the threat of global warming, water shortages, famine, and the like would fit the bill. All of these dangers are caused by human intervention, and it is only through changed attitudes and behavior that they can be overcome. The real enemy, then, is humanity itself." Diabolical! Turn man against himself so that he voluntarily submits to subjugation. The threat of global warming became the weapon of choice.

And it doesn't matter if true science refuses to cooperate in this scheme, as actual global temperatures really are not rising, and there continues to be no evidence of any man-made effect on the climate. Truth hasn't been important to the scaremongers.

Timothy Wirth, president of the UN Foundation said, "We've got to ride this global warming issue. Even if the theory of global warming is wrong, we will be doing the right thing in terms of economic and environmental policy."

To further drive home their complete lack of concern for truth, Paul Watson of Green Peace declared, "It doesn't matter what is true, it only matters what people believe is true."

Christiana Figueres, the executive secretary of the UN Framework Convention on Climate Change told us outright what the real goal of the threat of environmental Armageddon truly is:

"This is the first time in the history of mankind that we are setting ourselves the task of intentionally, within a defined period of time, to change the economic development model that has been reigning for at least 150 years, since the industrial revolution." Of course, she means free enterprise.

The blueprint for the implementation of this grand plan was revealed in 1992 at the UN's Earth Summit. It was called the Agenda for the twenty-first century—or just Agenda 21.

From its inception in 1992 at the United Nation's Earth Summit, fifty thousand delegates, heads of state, diplomats, and nongovernmental organizations (NGOs) hailed Agenda 21 as the "comprehensive blueprint for the reorganization of human society."

The 350-page, 40-chapter Agenda 21 document was quite detailed and explicit in its purpose and goals. They warned us that the reorganization would be dictated through all-encompassing policies affecting every aspect of our lives, using environmental protection simply as the excuse to pull at our emotions and get us to voluntarily surrender our liberties.

So, in their zealotry to enforce the grand agenda, social justice became the "moral force" over the rule of law as free enterprise, private property, rural communities, and individual consumption habits became the targets, labeled as racist and a social injustice.

Such established institutions and free market economics were seen as obstructions to the plan, as were traditional family units, religion, and those who were able to live independently in rural areas.

Finally, Agenda 21 was summed up in supporting documents this way: "Effective execution of Agenda 21 will require a profound reorientation of all human society, unlike anything the world has ever experienced. It requires a major shift in the priorities of both governments and individuals, and an unprecedented redeployment of human and financial resources. This shift will demand that a concern for the environmental consequences of every human action be integrated into individual and collective decision-making at every level."

The policy of Agenda 21 is called sustainable development. You hear the term used in every part of our society, from community development to production of our food supplies, to manufacturing of nearly every product.

While sold as a means to secure a happy, healthy future of equality for all as it protects the environment, sustainable development policy, as it is enforced in every single community in the nation, has proven to be a direct attack on free enterprise, private property, and individual choice in our lives. It is the epitome of tyrannical, out of control government.

Ironically, its perpetrators were quite open and honest in their plans. We just didn't want to listen.

The official report from the UN's Habitat 1 Conference explained the reasons for the attack on private property. It said, "Land...cannot be treated as an ordinary asset, controlled by individuals and subjected to the pressures and inefficiencies of the market. Private land ownership is also a principle instrument of accumulation and concentration of wealth, therefore contributes

175

to social injustice." That is a direct attack on the entire American economic system.

But it gets even clearer. Peter Berle of the National Audubon Society said, "We reject the idea of private property."

Thomas Lovejoy, science advisor to the Department of Interior admitted, "We will map the whole nation…determine development for the whole nation, and regulate it all."

Harvey Ruvin, the vice chairman of ICLEI, said, "Individual rights will have to take a back seat to the collective."

That is Agenda 21!

For over twenty years, I have been labeled a conspiracy theorist, scaremonger, extremist, dangerous, nut case. I've been denied access to stages, major news programs, and awarded tinfoil hats. All because I have worked to expose Agenda 21 and its policy of sustainable development as a danger to our property rights, economic system, and culture of freedom.

Now, the sustainable forces have taken their plans to the ultimate, inevitable point. No longer are they trying to hide its true goal—global domination. Now we have the Green New Deal.

I warned that Agenda 21 would control every aspect of our lives, including how and where we live, the jobs we have, the mode of transportation available to us, and even what we eat. The Green New Deal is a tax on everything we do, make, wear, eat, drink, drive, import, export, and even breathe.

In opposing smart growth plans in your local community, I said the main goal was to eliminate cars, to be replaced with bikes, walking, and light rail trains. The Green New Deal calls for the elimination of the internal combustion engine. Always higher and higher taxes will be used to get the public to "voluntarily" reduce their use of such personal transportation choices. That's how it works, slowly but steadily towards the goal.

I warned that under smart growth programs now taking over every city in the nation that single-family homes are a target for elimination, to be replaced by high-rise, stack-and-pack apartments in the name of reducing energy use. That will include curfews on energy use, mandating power be turned off during certain hours. Gradually, energy use of any kind will be continually reduced. The Green New Deal calls for government control of every single home, office, and factory to tear down or retrofit them to comply with massive environmental energy regulations.

I warned that Agenda 21 Sustainable policy sought to drive those in rural areas off the farms and into the cities where they could be better controlled. Most recently I warned that the beef industry is a direct target for elimination. It will start with mandatory decreases in meat consumption until it disappears form our daily diet. The consumption of dairy will follow. Since the revelation of the Green New Deal the national debate is now over cattle emissions of methane and the drive to eliminate them from the planet. Controlling what we eat is a major part of the Green New Deal.

I warned that part of the plan for Agenda 2030 was "zero economic growth." The Green New Deal calls for a massive welfare plan where no one earns more than anyone else. Incentive to get ahead is dead. New inventions would disrupt their plan for a well-organized, controlled society. So, where will jobs come from after we have banned most manufacturing, shut down most stores, stopped single-family home construction, closed the airline industry, and severely regulated farms and the entire food industry? This is their answer to the hated free markets and individual choice.

In short, the Green New Deal represents the largest step ever taken by the socialists/sustainablists forces that have been pushing Agenda 21 for twenty-seven years.

But just as I was met with scoffing and charges of being a conspiracy scaremonger, the Green New Deal has now been met with scoffing and lack of concern. When I said the Green New Deal was the most radical step to enforce Agenda 21, many of my own supporters sent me snarky emails laughingly telling me, "This is too nuts to ever be made into law!" Ha Ha!!!!

Then the laughing really started when the Republican-controlled Senate brought the Green New Deal up for a vote and the tally was 57-0. They didn't even vote for it themselves, went the joke. Such a silly, stupid little girl, they said with great hilarity!

Leaders of many establishment conservative organizations in Washington, DC laughed too.

Well, the fools are the Republicans and the establishment conservative movement in Washington, DC, which have failed to understand the determination of these forces behind that "silly little girl." They set a trap, and the Republicans marched right into it.

What really occurred is that this: The Green New Deal pushes the radical agenda way beyond anything ever imagined by Republicans and conservative leadership. In short, the socialist Democrats made a classic negotiating tactic. They came to the table and delivered the most radical, complete, all-inclusive agenda for the total takedown of the American republic, our free enterprise system, our property rights, and our way of life.

The Republicans were completely unprepared for it. Since they have ignored my warnings for twenty-seven years, the Green New Deal sounded too nuts. Too far out. No one would fall for it. They laughed and dismissed it without a thought. The Senate vote showed them!

But watch what has happened since the Senate vote and the laughing began. One hundred Democrat members of Congress have signed on to the House bill. Almost every one of the twenty-plus Democrat presidential candidates is talking about it. The news media is filled with stories on pieces and parts of the Green New Deal. The discussion is growing.

But here's the kicker—here's where the laughing stops as the Republicans fall into the trap!!! Florida Republican Representative Matt Gaetz announced that he is working on the Green REAL Deal!!! Says Gaetz—his bill will be more *reasonable.* In the Senate, Tennessee Senator Lamar Alexander is countering with his "Manhattan Project for Clean Energy." The difference? Almost nothing! Senator Lindsey Graham said, "We owe it to the country to have an alternative to the Green New Deal." He said he was frustrated because large parts of the Republican Party still resist the idea of climate change legislation.

Sen. Graham and other faltering Republicans seem to not understand that any attempt to provide "an alternative to the Green New Deal" means an automatic endorsement of the radical and wrong-headed leftist environmental movement.

This is exactly what the Democrats where counting on. They made an outrageously radical proposal that moves the agenda miles down the road and then—to be more "reasonable"—the stupid Republicans join right in with just a little smaller proposal. That's how we lose our nation—by being *"reasonable"* to tyrants.

The fact is, almost 50 percent of the Green New Deal is already in the works. California has set a deadline to force homeowners to install wind and solar power as traditional energy sources of oil and gas will be phased out within ten years.

In Minneapolis, Minnesota, the city council is moving to eliminate zoning protections for single-family homes, calling such protections "racist." That same attack on single-family homes is taking place in the Oregon state legislature, the Chicago City Council, and the Baltimore City Council, to name just a few. This marks the drive to abolish private property rights.

Smart growth programs are in every city in the nation—targeting the elimination of private cars for transportation, in favor of public buses, trains, and bikes—just as called for in the Green New Deal.

Landlords are being targeted, as the drive is on for rent controls—even as government is piling on the costs through higher taxes and more and more controls on energy use. How long can the landlords hold out?

And now comes this news. As Congress, news media, and presidential candidates debate the "good ideas" of the Green New Deal, New York City Mayor William De Blasio has rushed to introduce his own version. It's a bundle of ten bills designed to meet the massive reduction of energy use called for in the UN's Paris Agreement on climate, which President Trump refused to join. Among its provisions are a ban on glass skyscrapers, hot dogs, and massive cutbacks in energy use. Just as called for in the Green New Deal, the legislation seeks to eliminate more than one million cars from the road.

State by state, city by city, the radical provisions of the Green New Deal are being put into force—or at least openly considered. Controls on what we eat, how we live, and how we move about. Call it Agenda 21 or the Green New Deal—it's a disaster to our economy and our way of life. It's happening at a rapid rate. So, who is laughing now?

The challenge to us is what do we do about it? The fact is, every political party is talking about taxes, healthcare, immigration, and gun control. But no party is addressing the pain of the ranchers who are under siege of the federal government that is taking their land and their water.

No political party is talking about the attack on our food supply, such as the World Wildlife Fund's takeover of the beef industry. Yet we are getting reports daily now of dangers found in diseased beef.

No political party is talking about the over-taxing and destruction of single-family homes and neighborhoods.

No political party is even discussing the destruction of our local system of government through the establishment of nonelected regional councils. These councils are eliminating political boundaries and the power of locally-elected representatives. The American system is disappearing in silence.

No political party is talking about the massive influence and control of the private, nongovernmental organizations and planners that have invaded every single level of government, pushing these insane policies we now recognize in the Green New Deal.

NGOs are deeply entrenched in Congress, every state legislature, and every county commission and city council. There they lobby, push, demand, and intimidate to get your elected officials to make their private agendas law. The fact is, they are not government agencies, and they have no power unless your elected officials give it to them. And they have no intention of giving up their power.

The only way we can toss them into the street is to elect people who understand their tyrannical agenda and will take strong action to remove them from the halls of government.

Democrats empower them. Republicans are clueless. Libertarians are pathetically confused by the whole process, continuing to believe that public-private partnerships are free enterprise.

The Constitution Party is the only party that understands what needs to be done. You've never had a better opportunity to grow and change things and achieve your mission to restore the Constitution.

Do you, as a political party, want to get the attention of millions of Americans who are suffering from this government overreach? Do you want to defeat the socialist Democrats and the "me-too" Republicans? Do you want to restore the American republic?

Then get mad and be the party that takes on these issues. Thousands of victims are desperate to hear any elected official, any party even mention these policies that are overrunning every single city, county, and state.

They are losing everything. They have been shut out of the American dream. And if they hear you take on these issues in upcoming campaigns at every level of government—they will flock to you. Americans are starting to wake up to these dangers and they desperately want a new voice that stands for freedom!

Run candidates for city council, county commission, and the state legislatures who will articulate these issues. Make it your mission to run these enemies of freedom out of town on a rail.

Speak to these victims, these desperate Americans. Name the names of the NGOs— challenge them. Challenge their policies and their funding sources. Show the pubic what a danger they are. And then challenge your opponents as to why they are giving these NGOs such power and influence.

Elected officials keep referring to these NGOs and planners who live off the federal grants as "stakeholders." They are not stakeholders! You are the stakeholders. They are carpetbaggers—there to grab everything they can.

Paint a clear picture as to what life in American will be like under these policies. Will every choice Americans make in their lives be like a visit to the DMV? Make your opponents responsible for their own policies. Put their names to them. Make them defend their plans.

Help the people see the truth! That's how you drain the swamp and restore the United States of America!

* * *

That was a great but disturbing article from Tom DeWeese. If you vote Republican and **want the Green New Deal, then definitely vote for Lindsey Graham, Lamar Alexander, and Matt Gaetz.** If you live in Minneapolis, Minnesota, and want the Green New Deal, then definitely support the incumbent city council members.

The Republican Party cannot get rid of Trump fast enough and are surely already grooming a Council on Foreign Relations puppet to replace him in 2024.

Trump's Staff Is Loaded with CFR Members and Bilderberg Attendees

Trump's staff is loaded with traitors, but it is not of his doing. **His trusted advisors were tasked with filling key positions with people who would serve President Trump and America, but the advisors betrayed him by filling many of the positions with Council on Foreign Relations members.** Elaine Chao (McConnell's wife), Mark T. Esper, Lisa Gordan Hagerty, Larry Kudlow, Robert Lighthizer, and Steve Mnuchin are just six of the sixty (give or take) CFR members embedded in the Trump administration. And Wilbur Ross, Lindsey Graham, James H. Baker, and Jared Kushner have attended Bilderberg conferences. CFR member Lisa Gordan Hagerty also attended a Bilderberg conference. It appears obvious to me that the CFR-embedded puppets are only concerned with the Richard N. Haass agenda, which is clearly indicated by the passage of the Bilderberg Group's USMCA.

The only chance of draining the swamp is to eliminate the self-created government, the CFR, operating within our elected government.

Hate Crimes and Circumventing Our Constitution

The Republicans elected by and entrusted by the Trump base *did not* give the duly elected president the respect and support that he and his base were expecting. Why? Because he presents a threat to the communist elite that they serve, he is also a threat to them. Trump loves our sovereign nation and our Constitution, while the establishment only view them as obstacles that must go away. The communist elite despise the Constitution and use their **embedded traitors** to create laws that circumvent it. **Hate crime** laws are prime examples, as they **absolutely** circumvent the First Amendment and are designed to limit and punish free speech.

Hate crimes generally refer to criminal acts that are understood to be motivated by bias against one or more social groups or race. These crimes are considered by liberals and the communist elite to be more serious than others. One person assaulting another out of a bias against that particular person or group will be punished more severely than someone being violent out of anger over some event or just because that is what they do. However, in my view, an assault is an assault, and the reason for the assault (excluding self-defense) should have no bearing on the level of punishment for the assault.

In June 2019, **a man stole a gay pride banner hanging at Ames United Church of Christ** in Iowa and burned it in the street outside the Dangerous Curves Gentleman's Club in Iowa. Story County Attorney Jessica Reynolds said hate crime charges were added since the accused is suspected of criminal mischief against someone's property because of *what that property represents as far as sexual orientation.* Jessica Reynolds also went on to say, "The hard reality is there are people who target individuals and commit crimes against individuals because of their race, sexual orientation, and when that happens, it is so important that as a society we stand up and people have severe consequences for those actions." **The accused was sentenced to fif-**

teen years in prison for doing nothing more than burning a piece of cloth advocating homosexuality.

All *sane* people should be absolutely terrified by the court's ruling in this case because what happened to this man could happen to any of us **now that the CFR-embedded puppets are controlling our government.** The sentence is truly bizarre! A sentence forcing the accused to pay retribution to the Ames United Church of Christ and barring him from the property would be appropriate—but **fifteen years in prison?** There was no physical altercation, no verbal altercation, and no property damage to the church. All the man did was burn a banner.

But the **CFR-embedded puppets** running our government are okay with hate toward some people or things. **They are fine with anyone publicly displaying hatred for the United States of America.** Had the man burned an American flag, the punishment would have been minimal, if any at all, and the elite-owned and elite-controlled media would be glorifying him and his hatred for America.

Of course, there is a Bilderberg Group motive here. They hate our Constitution and consider it to be an obstacle that must go away. It is disturbing that hate-crime laws were ever created. The only reason they exist is to circumvent the US Constitution, which is exactly what they have done. **Can you say "conspiracy"?**

Governing Beyond Our Republic

CFR/Bilderberg Group agents deeply embedded in every branch and every level of our government have been and are now surrendering our republic by legislating a policy that is nullifying our Constitution and stripping away our rights, freedoms, liberties, and sovereignty. And yet, even the **representatives that seem to be on our side do nothing.** They put more effort into representing citizens of sovereign nations than they do their own, which just provides more proof that they are pushing to govern outside of their jurisdiction. It seems obvious to me that the Bilderberg Group is using their CFR-embedded puppets to force smaller and poorer nations to fall in line with what **Bilderberger-extraordinaire David Rockefel-**

ler described as **their "plan for the world."** Other nations have no choice but to fall in line or the United States will cripple their economy with sanctions. **Can you say "extortion"?**

The US government is now considering enforcing sanctions on the Philippines because they are detaining a top government critic, Senator Leila de Lima. Democrat senators Dick Durbin and Patrick Leahy are seeking to deny entry to the United States by any Philippines officials involved in the incarceration of Senator de Lima. Durbin and his liberal allies have a problem with the way Philippines President Rodrigo Duterte is handling the drug epidemic in his country. They insist on a more humane approach and threaten economic warfare if their demands are not met. Why are Senators Durbin and Leahy concerning themselves with a sovereign nation's affairs that have *nothing* to do with the United States? *It is none of their goddamn business!* Duterte is doing what he is doing because he is an intelligent man and realizes that a drug-addicted society is a dangerous and uncivilized society! The Philippines is sovereign and has *its own* representatives. Not one Filipino citizen cast a vote for Durbin, Leahy, or any other US representative.

Examples like this indicate that many of our elected representatives despise the word "sovereign" and view the United States as the world-governing authority. It is reasonable to suspect a motive here. Why are US senators representing drug users and dealers from any country?

The United States government has become the *most intrusive* government in the entire world! Its leaders never stop scheming and plotting. They consistently attempt to justify their unwelcome intrusions by claiming that our national security is at risk or that they must intervene out of concern for human rights. Although that sometimes may actually be the case, it does not appear to be so more often than not.

Democrats

I have already discussed the establishment and antiestablishment Republicans, so here's the gist on **the third and most repulsive faction, the Democrats:**

- Borders should be open and unprotected.
- Taxpayer-funded government handouts should be available for anyone requesting them (citizenship not required).
- No one should be allowed to own a firearm.
- One-world government should be imposed.
- Undocumented immigrants and illegal aliens should be considered citizens by the US census.
- The fossil-fuel industry should be destroyed along with millions of well-paying jobs.
- Politically correct speech, a.k.a. Marxism, should be mandated.
- White males are to be considered the evil of the land.
- Law enforcement officials are to be villainized, and criminals are to be thought of as victims.
- Fast food employees should earn the same as a brain surgeon.
- We should all be forced to drive an electric-powered vehicle.
- Women should be allowed to have a human life growing in their bodies destroyed (that is, murdered) because the child is considered an inconvenience.
- Endangered species should be given priority over an unborn child still in its mother's womb.
- There should be government mandates forcing privately owned companies to hire people they may not desire, and unproductive or incompetent employees' jobs should be protected.
- There should be no due process allowed for a male if the accuser of the alleged crime is a female.

- If our duly elected president disagrees with socialism or communism, then he should be mocked and ridiculed. (These idiots even encourage their children to participate.)
- We should not stand for our national anthem, and all should wear certain apparel to show that we agree with the liberals that law enforcement officials are our enemies and that those committing the crimes are victims.
- A minority should never be accused of a crime even when there is overwhelming evidence indicating that they did commit a crime because that would be prejudicial and discriminatory.
- Gays are not just equal; they are to be thought of as very special people and should be given exclusive rights. (I am not anti-gay; I am just against the government advocating for homosexuality).
- The United States should be a sanctuary and source of entitlements for the entire world.
- Bicycles should be allowed on public roadways designed for licensed motorized vehicles, and the inconveniences and hazards created by bicyclists for those driving licensed motorized vehicles are to be accepted with smiling faces. (This is actually a good segue into the President's Council on Sustainable Development, as it restricts our modes of transportation.)
- Seeing a president's tax returns supersedes EVERYTHING! No other issue in America could possibly be more important than seeing the president's tax returns; nothing even comes close. Of course, that only applies if the president is anti-elite.

I wouldn't vote for a Democrat if I had a gun to my head! I honestly believe that people that think like they do belong in mental institutions. **We have to vote Republican**—even though members of both parties are quite obviously conspiring with the communist elite. **At least we have hope with the antiestablishment Republi-**

cans. It will take time, but we can root out the traitors. And many are gone already, courtesy of **Donald J. Trump and his loyal base.**

And here's a tip for normal people engaging in a conversation with a liberal: Start the conversation with an apology, apologize throughout the conversation, and end the conversation with an apology. They will surely find fault with everything that you say, but they will appreciate that you offered an apology for being an American.

CHAPTER 16
Censorship, Liberal Lunacy, and the Subjugation of America

> Diet, injections, and injunctions will combine, from a very early age, to produce the sort of character and the sort of beliefs that the authorities consider desirable, and any serious criticism of the powers that be will become psychologically impossible.
>
> —Bertrand Russell, philosopher, activist, and author, in *The Impact of Science on Society*

I am concerned, shocked, amazed, and appalled by what our nation has become. Since its creation in 1921, the Bilderberg Group and their public base, the Council on Foreign Relations, have been systemically working to transform American citizens into **United Nations world government citizens**, that is, communists. Americans have been brainwashed. America is no longer America. It has been transformed into a nation of people who cannot even think for themselves! Wrong has become right, and right has become wrong. The following are some examples of just how sick our nation and society have become:

- A retailer was recently chastised by the **elite-created, dumbed-down citizens** and the black community for keeping the beauty products preferred by black women locked behind glass displays. The retailer did this because a large portion of the beauty products preferred by black women were being stolen. This was not true for the products preferred by white women, so those products were not locked away. The black community and the elite's dumbed-down citizens are crying discrimination, but it is not. It is just a company doing what is *necessary* to protect themselves and their profits. Sadly, pressure forced the retailer to cave, and they no longer lock up the products. They know that the products will continue to be stolen, but they decided that it is better to accept the loss than to alienate the **United Nations world-government citizens** that are a large portion of their customers.

- Common sense does not exist anymore! American citizens have been transformed—many are now submissive and obedient communists who no longer possess any thoughts of their own. Their thoughts are Chris Cuomo's, Jim Acosta's, and Rachel Maddow's. It just amazes me that the elite's brainwashing techniques have been so effective.

- Select movies and songs (Christmas songs, for example) are no longer seen or heard by the elite-owned and elite-controlled broadcasters because they do not align with the elite's narrative. And, of course, the **United Nations world government citizens** find them offensive. Then again, what don't they find offensive?

- Corporations are controlling what we are allowed to hear by removing select advertising from any media outlet broadcasting anything considered to be a threat to the elite's America-destroying plan. In essence, any media outlet broadcasting material considered unacceptable to the elite is forced to remove the material and replace it with something that is considered acceptable. Otherwise, they lose revenue as a result of losing advertisers.

- Disney, Papa John's, T-Mobile, and Poshmark all recently pulled their advertising from the Fox News program *Tucker Carlson Tonight* because he questions the real intent of the Black Lives Matter movement. Also, a training slide was recently shown to employees at a Goodyear Tire Company facility in Topeka, Kansas, which threatened zero tolerance for employees wearing Trump, White Lives Matter, or any pro-police apparel. But Black Lives Matter and LBGT gear is allowed. **Can you say "discrimination"? Corporations are trying to influence how we think and perceive things**; they want their thoughts and desires to be our own. Why? Because the unelected one-world government will be **corporate controlled!**

America is no longer America. It has become a crazy and disturbing place where right is now considered wrong, and wrong is considered right. Conservatives blame the liberals, progressives, and socialists for all the dissention and lunacy in America, but these groups are just the simple-minded soldiers. The Bilderberg Group and their public base, the Council on Foreign Relations, are the generals and the planners. Our representatives know damn good and well who bears responsibility for America's demise. Yet not one of them will reveal it. They commonly speak of the deep state, the shadow government, and the establishment, but the common citizen really has no idea who or what those titles actually refer to. They are all contained in one neatly wrapped package—the **Council on Foreign Relations.**

The Communist Elite Have SUBJUGATED America!

The definition of subjugation is to "bring under domination or control, especially by conquest, and the act of defeating people or a country in a way that allows them no freedom."

Words related to subjugation include invasion, attack, conquest, serfdom, enslavement, bondage, labor, servitude, captivity, hit, advantage, achievement, sweep, defeat, and triumph.

James Paul Warburg was a German-born American banker and financial advisor to FDR. His father, Paul Warburg, was also the father of the Federal Reserve system. Speaking before the US Senate Committee on Foreign Relations on February 17, 1950, he said, "We will have a world government whether you like it or not. The only question is whether that government will be achieved by conquest or consent."

Our treasonous representatives have concealed the identity of those responsible for the **subjugation of America** for a reason. Revealing the enemy would prompt loyal Americans to confront them—and those serving them do not want that. In the following pages, I will engage in a discussion of a number of topics that expose some of the insanity and anarchy being used and created by the Bilderberg Group, a.k.a. the communist elite, and the Council on Foreign Relations to **conquer America**.

Feminists/Activists/Anarchists

In my opinion, feminists are truly pathetic creatures. Even those possessing great wealth are hate-consumed bitches. Just thinking about all the wealthy (beyond our wildest dreams) celebrities attending these communist, anti-male rallies makes me want to puke. For some reason, these women are just miserable. They probably do not even know why but want to pin the blame on something, so they have chosen men. As the saying goes, "Misery loves company," so they are on a mission to influence as many as possible to jump on their man-hating train. Sadly, many women have allowed themselves to be influenced by these hatemongers, and that is creating a strain on our relationships and in society in general. Wives, girlfriends, daughters, mothers, grandmothers, and nieces are developing attitudes. They do not desire equal rights; **they desire special rights,** and those behind the world government agenda are convincing them that they are entitled to them.

My guess is that the majority of the women attending these contemptuous rallies have never been assaulted or denied a deserving, earned, or legitimate opportunity to advance in their careers but will seize the opportunity to attempt, not to level the playing field, but to tip it in their favor. And if you have been paying attention, that is exactly what they have done. The candidates many women vote for only need to fulfill two criteria. First and foremost, they must be women or at least men expressing sympathy or a willingness to support their agenda. Sadly, the *girl power* agenda is the only agenda that matters to them. Open borders, able-bodied leeches receiving taxpayer-funded government handouts, illegal immigrants receiving taxpayer-funded government handouts, socialized healthcare, censored media, foreign nations gouging the US on trade, "elected" US representatives, and appointees in every branch of government working covertly to implement the unelected shadow government's agenda while ignoring the *elected* US president's agenda, **educators indoctrinating our children to embrace communism** and so much more are all irrelevant to these idiots. They are women and they want women representing them, and to hell with the rest of it. **for them, it is women first, not America first.**

Any *sane* person observing the behavior of the newly elected Democratic congresswomen while watching Trump's amazing State of the Union Address on February 5, 2019 should be extremely concerned. They all wore white to show *female solidarity.* Female solidarity? What the hell? They were elected to represent Americans, not just women. And on top of that, they behaved like disrespectful children at the event. Alexandria Ocasio Cortez and Nancy Pelosi appeared disgusted and pissed off during the whole address (maybe they were just constipated) as did the majority of the others. Trump was advocating nationalism, a sovereign United States, secure borders, and fair trade, and he rightfully ignored the activists' desire for **special rights**. Thus, the Democratic congresswomen, a.k.a. activists/crazy bitches, were disgusted by everything the man was saying.

These activists have been elected by like-minded liberal idiots to make suggestions and decisions and possibly get legislation passed will negatively impact the future of our nation! It has all become insanity. Women run for public office to represent women, blacks run to represent blacks, Muslims run to represent Muslims, gays run to represent gays, Latinos run to represent Latinos, and so on. They do not seem to care that their position obligates them to represent *all Americans* (even men); they are only concerned with representing a specific group that they belong to.

Men are being attacked by multiple sources. **The Gillette razor company has an advertising campaign advocating against what they refer to as toxic masculinity.** Damn, guys, I guess we should all swing by the boutique and pick up some pretty ribbons for our hair! It is as if they desire the two sexes to be merged into one.

I would like to know just what the hell all these radical groups are bitching about. Sexual harassment? If working for a company, a woman or a man, or even a not-sure, of any nationality or skin color—simply anyone with a concern can seek help from the human resources department; they will surely take the appropriate actions. Equal pay? Company supervisors should have the right to determine a person's skill level and judge them on their job performance, hence determining their wage. This is the case even when two people or multiple people are tasked with the same job. If a male is performing better than a female, then he should receive a higher wage and vice versa. But feminists and other similar activists have no common sense; they are of the opinion "same job, same pay," end of discussion. And if these radical-thinking idiots continue to win elections, white men are screwed along with the rest of America! In their perfect world, white men are not to be given the privilege of due process; that only applies to everyone else. If a male is accused of a crime against a female, in their opinion, he is already guilty. The Kavanaugh hearings have shown that our feminist/activist representatives have absolutely no interest in hearing the male side of any argument. The feminists' desires to have like-minded elected officials running our government will always guarantee that they vote Democrat. Well, that is not entirely true. All levels of our government are loaded with liberal, like-minded Republicans.

And then there are the celebrity activists/feminists. They may not openly identify as feminists, but their attendance at the 2017 and 2018 women's rallies as well as their public comments would indicate that they probably are. Obviously, these are not happy women! These very successful and wealthy-beyond-our-wildest-dreams women petitioning for equality. And some give foaming-at-the-mouth radical speeches at the events as an attempt to somehow identify themselves with common people who have next to nothing. Many attending the events dress like militants. What the hell is that all about?

The following, partial list includes the names of female celebrities who have attended these anti-male rallies and their approximate net worth, according to a recent internet search.

Adele: $200 million
Patricia Arquette: $24 million
Drew Barrymore: $125 million
Maria Bello: $8 million
Ashley Benson: $6 million
Jessica Biel: $18 million
Sophia Bush: $9 million
Jessica Chastain: $20 million
Miley Cyrus: $200 million
Laura Dern: $20 million
Cameron Diaz: $140 million
Edie Falco: $40 million
Elle Fanning: $5 million
America Ferrara: $16 million
Jane Fonda: $300 million
Whoopie Goldberg: $45 million
Mariska Hargitay: $50 million
Katie Holmes: $25 million
Felicity Huffman: $20 million
Paris Jackson: $100 million
Scarlett Johansson: $140 million
Ashley Judd: $22 million

Alicia Keys: $100 million
Zoe Kravitz: $8 million
Mila Kunis: $65 million
Padma Lakshmi: $30 million
Jennifer Lawrence: $130 million
Juliette Lewis: $24 million
Blake Lively: $16 million
Eva Longoria: $35 million
Jennifer Lopez: $400 million
Madonna: $590 million
Debra Messing: $20 million
Alyssa Milano: $12 million
Chloë Grace Moretz: $12 million
Olivia Munn: $25 million
Piper Perabo: $10 million
Katy Perry: $330 million
Amy Schumer: $16 million
Mary Steenburgen: $12 million
Amber Tamblyn: $3 million
Chrissy Teigen: $26 million
Charlize Theron: $130 million
Marisa Tomei: $20 million

They give a variety of reasons for attending the event, one being a desire to show female solidarity. But that solidarity amounts to expressing their contempt for males, and they do not even seem to care that their contempt has alienated a large segment of their fanbase. One of the female celebrities will not allow her daughter to watch certain Disney films because males are portrayed as heroes. Damn! I wonder how a man could be married to such a hate-consumed bitch? Especially since this is a bitch that is obsessed with turning her young daughter into a hate-consumed bitch. Sick, twisted communist minds are destroying our society.

These women put a lot of effort into advocating for contempt. Just think of what these talented women could accomplish if they switched off their contempt and focused their efforts toward helping the handicapped children we see during the Shriners and Saint Jude's Children's Hospital commercials or the wounded warriors who have served our country. Maybe they could insist that any donations made from their efforts only go to female children and female wounded warriors.

Women Bear More Responsibility for America's Demise Than All the Other Groups Combined

I am wading into some more forbidden territory here, but what you are about to read will reveal why America has become the crazy, liberal, socialist/communist nation that it is today. Women envy men for a variety of reasons, including:

- On the whole, men are stronger than women.
- On the whole, men are more mechanically inclined than women.
- Women are cursed with their monthly cycle and envy that men do not have to go through this same inconvenience as well.

For these reasons, women feel cheated and desire a way to have control over those they believe to be privileged. Thus, many cast their votes only for other women for no other reason than viewing men as privileged due to the way nature has created the sexes and their differences. They have a grudge for the aforementioned reasons—a grudge that somehow needs to be satisfied. And it is satisfied by them securing public offices **only for their gender, ignoring the fact that many of the female candidates elected by them are just pawns for the America-hating communist elite.** They just do not care. The grudge kicks in and takes control when it is time for them to cast their votes, which is precisely why we see so many women all around the world in charge of governments. Women control the vote. It is simple math. And that is a disturbing reality because the grudge tells them that they *have to* vote only for women.

The elite prefer that women, gays, and blacks hold public office because so many of them have grudges. And we all know that people with grudges have the mentality of spoiled, disobedient children who will kick, scream, and holler until given their way. America is doomed! It is not that I believe women, gays, and blacks should not have those positions. That is simply not what I am saying. Rather, I am just saying that the majority of them have grudges, and when given authority, they will use it, not to help America, but to satisfy a desire for vengeance. These types of people are essential to the elite.

Many women put no more thought into their vote than what gender the candidate is. If it is a woman, then that is who they will vote for. That is a real issue given that women comprise a bit over 50 percent of America's population. **Men are the tiebreakers,** in a sense, which is working out well for the elite because they have targeted more than just women to be **dumbed down.** Gays, Hispanics, and blacks have also fallen hook, line, and sinker for the elite's brainwashing techniques. Trump and his base desire to **make America great again, but the grudge held by women against men has stacked the odds against that ever happening. Women have got to lose their attitudes** because those attitudes have brought America to the brink of its demise. **The communist elite could care less about women, blacks, Hispanics, and gays. They are only using them as pawns—useful but disposable.**

I hope that after reading this book, every American, regardless of race, color, creed, or status will have sense enough to realize that America has **been rolled by the communist elite** and fight to take it back. **Stop allowing these America-hating, enslaving, freedom-stealing, and greedy international bankers to get into your heads, and start thinking like Americans!** Is an unelected, corporate-controlled, one-world government really what you desire for you and your children? **Supporting any part of the communists' SUB-**

JUGATION of America is truly criminal. (Dear US Congress, are you getting this?) Our Founding Fathers are surely rolling in their graves.

Update: The activist/feminist congresswomen attending Trump's February 4, 2020 State of the Union all dressed in white again to show *female* solidarity. Their childish and contemptuous behavior was on full display once again.

Reparations for Slavery

Several members of the Democratic Party, including some presidential hopefuls, have suggested that the descendants of slaves should be given reparations or other compensation for their distant ancestors' bondage and suffering. Slavery was an absolutely heinous practice; I have trouble comprehending how human beings could do such a horrible thing to fellow human beings. This terrible reality began in 1619, and the Thirteenth Amendment to the US Constitution abolished it in 1865. Its lasted 246 years, which is absolutely ludicrous and strains the imagination.

Now, in 2019, 154 years after slavery was abolished, the Democrats are calling for some type of monetary compensation for people that were *never* a part of any of it. There are no living African Americans that were forced into slavery. So, what would this accomplish? An admission from the US government that it was wrong and that they regret that it ever happened? That *has* already happened, but the Democrats just will not let it die; they just keep stirring the pot, creating more and more racial divisions.

It would be a totally different story if there were any African Americans still living who were forced into slavery. In that case, I believe that compensation would be justified, but the distant relatives deserve nothing. It is just ridiculous! What's next? Are they going to suggest taxpayer-funded compensation for relatives of coal miners, factory workers, industrial workers, and all the others who were exposed to hostile working environments prior to government oversight? If I had a deceased grandfather that died of black lung from working in a coal mine, how and why in the world would that make me eligible for any type of compensation? He suffered, not me! In the same way, the slaves suffered, not their descendants! Furthermore, bear in mind that they are not suggesting some sort of a one-time payout. They want to put them on the government payroll. Oh yes, a paycheck from the government for the rest of their lives, which would be extended to every succeeding generation. Just another example of the type of lunacy the Democratic Party (and some Republicans) represent.

Reparations are actually already being distributed in the liberal, idiotic state of Illinois. The city of Evanston, (a northern suburb of Chicago) passed legislation on November 25, 2019 that will use the 3 percent tax revenue provided from the city's legal sales of recreational marijuana (which began on January 1, 2020) to provide **reparations** for blacks. November 25, 2019 was a glorious day for actor and activist Danny Glover and the black citizens of Evanston, Illinois.

I am certainly not supporting the passage of the law legalizing the sale of recreational marijuana, as it absolutely will create a dangerous environment on our roads by increasing the number of drivers under the influence, but I cannot help but wonder how the white users feel about being **forced** to contribute to **this ridiculous redistribution of wealth**, as they represent 77 percent of Evanston's population. And that is exactly what it is! **A redistribution of wealth.** The descendants of slaves deserve *absolutely* nothing—and so do the descendants of deceased coal miners or any other group subjected to hazards and hostile working environments prior to government oversight.

Black Lives Matter Is a Total Scam

The **communist elite's** success depends on its ability to create chaos in society, and all of the hate currently being generated in our nation is a result of their efforts. They have portrayed our Founding Fathers as villains and made a mockery out of the whole concept of America. Black Lives Matter is just one of the many schemes they have created and are using to destroy America. Consider the following:

- Around 7,881 blacks were murdered in 2016, and 6,576 whites were murdered during the same period. **The majority of the black homicides were committed by blacks.** Of those murders, only 243 blacks were killed by whites. Taking into consideration that, while only making up 13 percent of the total population, 1,305 more blacks were murdered than whites in 2016 and that the majority of the black homicides were committed by blacks **should be a wake-up call** to all those who have allowed themselves to be **brainwashed by the elite's DELUSIONAL propaganda.** Statistics reveal that, on a percentage basis, blacks represent a much greater threat to, not only themselves, but also society in general, than whites do. Some will consider what I am saying here to be racist and prejudicial, but it is not. All I am doing is revealing a forbidden truth.
- On a percentage basis, **far more white people have been killed by blacks** compared to black people being killed by whites.
- **In 2015, a police officer was 18.5 times more likely to be shot by a civilian black male than a civilian black male was to be killed by a police officer.**
- Around 233 blacks were killed by police in 2016, and of those, 217 were armed and dangerous.
- **Blacks, while consisting of only 13 percent of the total population, make up 42 percent of all the cop killers over the past ten years.**

Black Lives Matter Is Being Used as a Mechanism to Disarm the Police and Law-Abiding Citizens

The Black Lives Matter movement has absolutely nothing to do with the elite's phony deep concern for black lives (they could care less, in truth) and everything to do with disarming America. The elite are despicable and will do *anything* to implement their America-destroying agenda, including **making SACRIFICIAL LAMBS out of our PROTECTORS.**

The elite calculate every move that they make. They are portraying our protectors as villains to justify **disarming** them. Disarming a small group is much easier than disarming a large group, so they have launched an all-out assault against our protectors. Once they have managed to disarm them, taking all guns from law-abiding private citizens will be a top priority. **Welcome to the New World Order!** The elite-embedded government officials continue their **deliberate denial of the real problem** and are catering to the elite by pushing for **POLICE REFORM. Say what?** Are the police killing one another and civilians for sport? Are the police rioting, looting, raping, setting people on fire, and shutting down roads and highways? **It's all ass-backward! The police did not kill 7,383 blacks in 2016—blacks did!** Let's give credit where credit is due. There should be public outrage **WHENEVER** these simple-minded privileged idiots (anarchists) disrespect America, our protectors, and law-abiding citizens. But our dumbed-down citizens do not see it that way.

America has been turned upside down! People display support for the anarchists who only view the law as a nuisance and have contempt for the police, who are just trying to control them. The police are damned if they do and damned if they don't because the majority of our public officials are standing with the anarchists. In my opinion, **any politician calling for police reform is boldly stating that they hate America** and are serving the Council on Foreign Relations. That would include nearly all the Democrats and the majority of the Republicans. **Perhaps they should just go ahead and have it tattooed on their foreheads!**

An **aggressive campaign focused on EXPOSING THE LUNACY OF THE BLACK LIVES MATTER MOVEMENT is long overdue.** Statistics reveal that blacks kill one another as easily as if they were swatting flies and that they are doing it in large numbers. But that information is never revealed to the dumbed-down general public. Why is it that the only BLACK LIVES that matter to the protesters are the minuscule amount of black lives that are lost during encounters with law enforcement?

The following 2016 statistics are being used again to expose **the lunacy of the Black Lives Matter movement.** They are approximate but are still close to the actual numbers.

- 7,881: total number of blacks killed
- 243: total number of blacks murdered by whites
- 255: total number of blacks killed by the police (Approximately 238 of those victims were armed and dangerous. And also factor into the equation that the 17 who were not may have had health issues, mental issues, or were uncontrollable and dangerous as a result of using mind-altering drugs. So, only 17 of the 255 blacks killed by the police were unarmed and **possibly** not dangerous, but that in no way suggests that their lives were lost due to excessive force being used by the police. And further take into consideration that **those 17 had to have done something to provoke the encounter in the first place.** As the old slang saying goes, "Don't start no shit and there won't be none.")
- 7,383: TOTAL NUMBER OF BLACKS KILLED BY BLACKS
  SAY WHAT? HOLY SHIT! That bears repeating.
- 7,383: TOTAL NUMBER OF BLACKS KILLED BY BLACKS IN 2016

The statistics here expose the **total lunacy** of the Black Lives Matter movement! The ratio of blacks killed by blacks to blacks killed by the police in 2016 is **7,383 to 255.** Damn! And that ratio would be closer to **7,383 to 0** if only the senseless murders were used in the equation.

The dumbed-down citizens focus **only** on the miniscule number of black deaths that occurred during an event involving the police, and those events were almost certainly provoked by the victims. **The movement is a total scam**! The Black Lives Matter movement is intentionally and unduly focused on the wrong group; the 2016 statistic revealing that there were 7,383 blacks killed by blacks during that one-year period validate such a claim. Why is it that the only black lives that matter to the protesters are the miniscule number of black lives that are lost during encounters with the police? When our dumbed-down citizens take a knee during our national anthem, they are not kneeling in protest against or disgust at the senseless murders of the **7,383 blacks who were killed by blacks in 2016**—that reality is ignored. Instead, they are only protesting the 255 black deaths that occurred during an encounter with the police, of which all but around 15 to 20 were (possibly) unavoidable. **PEOPLE, WAKE UP!** You will also never hear that, on average, **the police kill nearly twice as many whites per year as they do blacks.**

The elite and their dumbed-down citizens portray the police as villains and accuse them of being biased, but the following statistics from 2018 prove that to be utter nonsense.

A total of 996 people were killed by the police in 2018. This is the breakdown of by ethnicity:

- White: 399
- Black: 209
- Hispanic: 148
- Other: 36
- Unknown: 204

The statistics do not indicate bias by the police. However, the following realities do show a bias against whites and the police by blacks:

- Blacks, while consisting only 13 percent of the total population, make up 42 percent of all the cop killers over the past ten years.
- In 2016, although blacks made up only 13 percent of the total population, they killed around 450 whites, while whites only killed 243 blacks. That is close to a 2 to 1 ratio, which is astounding considering that there are a lot more whites in this country than blacks.

The statistics indicate that blacks have a much higher level of disregard for human life (both black and white) than whites do, and that is why, on a percentage basis, more blacks are killed by the police than whites. Thus, **that reality** is where the dumbed-down citizens should be focusing all their anger and attention. **BLACK REFORM** should be a top priority. And it would be if we had a competent Congress, but that is not the case. The majority of our Congress members have the mentality of disobedient children and irresponsible parents and continue to throw fuel on the fire by demanding **POLICE REFORM** and calling for disbanding the police. **Goddamn, our Congress is sick!** To make matters even worse, some of the top military brass have broadcast that they have no intention of stepping in once the police have been nullified, which of course only emboldens the anarchists—and even appears to be intended to do so. **I can only interpret the military's stance as being a declaration of their support for the elite and their efforts to destroy America.**

I will end on this topic by giving my sincere thanks to the brave, self-sacrificing, and unjustly battered law enforcement officials who risk their own lives to protect ours. Thank you so much for everything that you do. And I say to any member of city and state government and our US Congress who are calling for POLICE REFORM and defunding and disbanding the police: You are a F*ING IDIOT!**

Abortion

Life begins at conception, period! It does not matter what stage of development the child is in; it is a living, evolving human life. Mayor Pete, however, argues that life begins with the first breath. How idiotic! I will repeat: LIFE BEGINS AT CONCEPTION. An early-stage baby receiving oxygen and nutrients through the mother's umbilical cord in no way invalidates the fact that the baby is indeed a living human life, even doing things inside the womb that it would do outside the womb, such as sucking its thumbs. Abortion is, therefore, murder AT ANY STAGE, period. The libs argue that it is "their body, their choice," but I argue that the body growing in their wombs is not their body; it is a separate body, a separate human life, which neither they nor anyone else have the right to destroy.

It should be of concern that **liberals use stages of development as justification for the termination of a human life.** Most states allow abortion up to six weeks into the pregnancy (it is still murder at any stage), but others allow late-term abortions and have even supported legislation allowing the termination (that is, murder) of a full-term baby within a given time frame before delivery. The thought processes of these types of people could eventually lead to the acceptance of terminating an infant or toddler up to a certain age. That may appear to be unimaginable, but their acceptance of late-term abortions and, worse yet, of full-term fetuses indicates that such a thing is certainly within the realm of possibility. And I would go on to speculate that their sick minds could also accept terminating the handicapped and putting a limit on how long an adult should be allowed to live, which is exactly what the elite desire.

Democratic Alabama Congresswoman Rolanda Hollis Proposed a Bill Forcing All Men to Have Vasectomies at Age 50; Elizabeth Warren Believes That Men Should Be Allowed to Compete in Women's Sports

Alabama Congresswoman Rolanda Hollis has authored a bill that would require every man to undergo a vasectomy at age fifty or after the birth of his third biological child, whichever comes first. And Elizabeth Warren is urging Arizona representatives to reject what she refers to as a cruel bill banning males from female sports. Welcome to the America of the CFR and the Bilderberg Group!

Global Liberal Lunacy and the European Union

In 1992, David Rockefeller thanked the *Washington Post*, the *New York Times*, *Time* magazine, and others for their decades of silence because it allowed him and his fellow elites the time they needed to develop **their plan for the world.** Well, their mentality and their plan for the world is on full display in **the European**

Union. European nations opted early on to concede to the UN and Bilderberg Group, and on November 1, 1993, the European Union was born. One bloc of the world government was now in place, and for over twenty-five years the Bilderberg Group puppets **have been legislating their plan for the world into reality**. And a disturbing plan it is!

In 2008, Tkach Serhiy Fedorovich, a Ukrainian citizen who worked as a criminal investigator, was convicted of killing thirty-seven girls and women, ages 8–18. He raped them while they were alive and also performed sex acts with their dead bodies. The public demanded the death penalty, but **the European Union does not allow the death penalty,** so he was sentenced to life in prison instead. This was not because there was not sufficient evidence to warrant a death sentence; he was very boastful and defiant about what he did, in fact. **The real issue is that the Bilderberg Group's plan for the world does not allow murderers to be murdered.** Of course, it *is* still okay to kill an innocent child in its mother's womb! Sadly, the elite-controlled American courts have the same ideology. And do not let yourselves think that Brexit is the beginning of the end for the European Union. The elite are using everything at their disposal to thwart that effort. The British government is loaded with the elite's embedded puppets—just as ours is.

The Digital Tax Equates to World Government Authorities Transferring Money from Our Hands to Their Hands

France recently approved a 3 percent tax on the revenues that companies earn from providing digital services to French users. Some of the companies impacted by the tax include Amazon, Google, Facebook, and other providers with at least $844 million in annual revenues. Trump has responded by threatening to enforce up to 100 percent tariffs on a variety of French products. Of course, a reasonable mind would only see this as an appropriate response, but we are not dealing with reasonable minds; we are dealing with liberal, socialist, world-government minds. Thus, President of France Emmanuel Macron and the other world-government EU officials have threatened to respond in-kind to Trump's counterattack. An analogy to this would be a neighbor stealing a tomato from your garden and telling you that if you take it back, he will return and take two more. The liberal, socialist mind is truly warped!

European officials are advocating for a global consensus on the digital tax because it would most assuredly create a huge revenue stream for the world government, and that is exactly what this is all about. Of course, the goal is to get the United States on board, and that would certainly be the case if anyone other than a Trump resides in the Oval Office. It is a virtual certainty that the tax would be steadily increased over time, further impoverishing the communist elite's slaves.

The Carbon Border Tax

> If you tell a lie long enough and keep repeating it, people will eventually come to believe it. The lie can be maintained only for such time as the State can shield the people from the political, economic and/or military consequences of the lie. It thus becomes vitally important for the state to use all of its powers to repress dissent, for the truth is the mortal enemy of the lie, and thus by extension, the truth is the greatest enemy of the State.
>
> If you repeat a lie often enough it becomes the truth.
>
> The truth is the greatest enemy of the State.
> —Joseph Goebbels, Adolf Hitler's close associate and devoted follower

The European Commission is proposing a carbon border tax that will put heavy tariffs all products imported from nations not enforcing the same level of environmental protection measures as the European Union. Products from nations not adhering to the United Nations Agenda for the twenty-first century polices will be heavily taxed. We see here that the elite continue to use every possible method and approach to fully implement their New World Order.

The European Court of Justice is Forcing Everyone to Have Insurance for Their Golf Carts, Riding Lawn Mowers, Four-Wheelers, and Other Utility Vehicles

This will actually become mandatory a few months from now. Owners not having insurance on any of these types of vehicles will be **arrested for using them on their private property.**

This is the same type of world government lunacy being put into law all across America by the Council on Foreign Relations-embedded puppets serving the Bilderberg Group.

CHAPTER 17
The USMCA: America Held Hostage

**Democrats are Demanding Inclusions to the USMCA—
Inclusions That Will Lead Us into the Creation of the
CFR/Bilderberg Group's North American Union**

At the time of this writing, Democrats are holding out on signing an important, job-creating international trade agreement, the United States-Mexico-Canada Agreement (USMCA), over three main issues: (1) reduction or elimination of the exclusivity period (the period of time that shields new biological drugs from competition from generic brands), (2) enforcement on environmental concerns, and (3) labor protections. I have several points to make on each of these issues.

- The exclusivity period for biological drugs—The period under the USMCA would be ten years. It is currently eight years in Canada and twelve years in the United States, and there is no exclusivity period in Mexico. Eliminating the exclusivity period would discourage drug companies from developing new drugs. Why would they go through all the time and expense involved with research and development only to have their drugs reproduced more cheaply by competitors? Instead, they should be granted the exemption period for a reasonable amount of time. Perhaps it should be something in between the three nations' current exemption periods, which range from zero to twelve years.
- Environmental protections—I have no concern about carbon dioxide and will explain why in a succeeding chapter,

211

but toxic dumping is another story. If their hand is forced on the matter by the need for trade with the United States, then that benefits mankind. But my concern is that this issue is really more about continental integration than it is about the environment.

- Labor protections—The huge wage difference for workers between the US and Mexico allows the goods from the Mexican manufacturers to be sold at a steep discount relative to the same goods being sold in America. Pelosi and company are demanding labor law changes in Mexico to help level the economic playing field and improve working conditions, going as far as wanting to have US and Canadian representatives involved with Mexican labor disputes. **This reeks of the elite!** A Mexican trade group commented on the suggestion, saying that the "sovereignty of Mexico is not negotiable." Good for them. I believe that G. W. Bush's buddy Vincente Fox may have seen things differently. The Democrats' solution amounts to forcing a sovereign nation to restructure its entire system. This just amounts to more extortion! While I agree that Mexico is a total disaster, we have no right to dictate policy to them or any other sovereign nation. Placing tariffs on products produced in Mexico by AMERICAN-OWNED COMPANIES and sold in the United States is an acceptable option. American-owned companies establish facilities in Mexico and other low-wage countries to avoid paying the higher American wages. The American citizens owning these companies should have an obligation and loyalty to the nation that they hold citizenship in—that is real patriotism—and they should consider it their duty to serve their nation. Products from **all American-owned companies** manufactured in and exported to the US from other countries should be tariffed based on a schedule that would make the prices of those products comparable to similar goods produced in the US. But goods produced by the Mexican or other foreign-owned companies should not be subject to tariffs at all. They are sovereign nations, and their exports are priced according to their existing structures—that is the true definition of free trade. And this includes China. The only products coming from China that should be subject to tariffs are those being produced by American-owned companies taking advantage of another nation's structure at the expense of the American workers. The cheaper products imported from foreign-owned companies are not and have never have been the problem. The American-owned companies exporting products manufactured in foreign nations into the United States are the problem since they are directly responsible for the loss of well-paying jobs in America. The focus should be on them; they are effectively dictating policy to sovereign nations, which is simply wrong on every level and will only serve to alienate our trade partners.

USMCA Update

The USMCA has been signed by President Trump, but it is not the agreement originally presented to him. The Democrat-revised version signed by Trump integrates three governments and mimics what those twenty-eight European nations did in 1993 with the formation of the EU. The original USMCA would have been great for America, and most importantly, posed no threat to our sovereignty. However, the version preferred by the elite that Trump actually signed acts as a segue into the NAU and Security and Prosperity Partnership (SPP). As signed, the agreement will create jobs but at a great cost. I am convinced that **Trump's (trusted) advisors** were well aware that the revised agreement was a means to finally fully implement the elite's long-desired NAU and SPP (which will create the second bloc of the elite's one-world government) and tricked him into signing it. Prior to the signing, Tom DeWeese, who is an authority on Agenda 21, the President's Council on Sustainable Development (PCSD), and the elite's world government agenda, **expressed his concerns on a conference call with two high-level White House policy experts** whom he educated about the massive revisions to the agreement.

They admitted to not being aware of the changes (a statement that may not be true), but there is no way of knowing whether the concerns expressed by DeWeese were relayed to the president.

The following article, retrieved from the American Policy Center (http://americanpolicy.org), details the many issues with the revised USMCA. It is reprinted here with permission.

What the Democrats Did to the USMCA

This Is Not the Agreement President Trump Negotiated

By Tom DeWeese

As Richard Haass, the president of the Council on Foreign Relations, pointed out on Twitter, "USMCA is NAFTA plus TPP plus a few tweaks." Trump was exactly right when he said NAFTA and TPP were terrible, sovereignty-undermining agreements. Combined, they are even worse. With the Democrats' additions, they are even WORSE. This deal is a disaster, and Americans will eventually find out. Hopefully we can alert the president before it is too late.

This USMCA is very similar to "free trade" agreements being pursued or having been approved around the world to advance regional governments that undermine sovereignty. The European Union, which began as the European Coal and Steel Community, followed by the European Free Trade Agreement, is the premier example. Similar schemes are being pursued to advance the African Union, the Eurasian Union, and other sovereignty-shredding unions in different regions of the world.

However, President Trump has a perfect opportunity to squash this assault on US sovereignty by blaming Democrats for loading the USMCA up with "poison pills." This comes from House Democrats' "fact sheet" about their additions to USMCA: "Taken in whole, these substantial changes House Democrats secured are a *true transformation* of the original United States-Mexico-Canada Agreement."

First, as requested, here are some of the worst provisions in the USMCA as far as sovereignty goes (citations included refer to the text of the USMCA):

- USMCA creates the USMCA Free Trade Commission that will be the international executive bureaucracy overseeing this all, a first step toward an EU Commission-style body over North America, with the power to propose amendments to the USMCA. It usurps many powers from Congress, including power over tariffs, which Article 1, Section 8 assigns to Congress. This is very similar to the TPP Free Trade Commission that sparked so much opposition to that agreement (chap. 30, pp. 30-1, 30-2, 30-3, and 30-4).

- Multiple highly controversial international agreements, such as the United Nations Convention on the Law of the Sea (UNCLOS), that have not been ratified by the US Senate are cited as authoritative in the USMCA. UNCLOS, which gives the UN jurisdiction over basically all oceans, is mentioned in chapter 1 and chapter 24 of the USMCA as if it were already binding, declaring that the parties "shall" base their fishing policies on best practices as defined in international instruments, with UNCLOS being cited as one of several that are applicable (chap. 24, p. 24-14).

- North American protections for homosexuality and transgenderism are in chap. 23 (pp. 23-6, 23-9, and 23-10) prohibiting "discrimination." This is a radical measure that they could not get through. See the text at https://ustr.gov/sites/default/files/files____/agreements/FTA/USMCA/Text/23-Labor.pdf

- The implementing legislation approves $1.5 billion for the North American Development Bank, which was first created under NAFTA. This bank is working to integrate the United States with Mexico and Canada—very similar to how European banks worked to advance European integration, culminating in the European Union. The North American Competitiveness Committee is to be established (see chap. 26). Article 26.1, section 5 states, "The Competitiveness Committee shall…discuss effective approaches and develop information-sharing activities to support a competitive environment in North America that facilitates trade and investment between the Parties, *and promotes economic integration and development within the free trade area*" (chap. 26, p. 26-1; emphasis added).

- USMCA purports to be above US and state law. It will force Congress to change US laws to be in line with USMCA, just as Congress obeyed orders to repeal country of origin labeling (COOL) in response to a WTO ruling. If you read the implementing legislation, section 102 goes on to explain, "Nothing in this Act shall be construed—(A) to amend or modify any law of the United States, or (B) to limit any authority conferred under any law of the United States, *unless specifically provided for in this Act*" (emphasis added). Of course, the bill contains numerous provisions that will require modifying US law. The same section also stated, "No State law, or the application thereof, may be declared invalid as to any person or circumstance on the ground that the provision or application is inconsistent with the USMCA, *except in an action brought by the United States for the purpose of declaring such law or application invalid*" (emphasis added). In other words, the US government will be able to force state governments to change their laws in order to comply with USMCA. This turns federalism upside down. It makes states subservient to the US government, which itself is made subservient to USMCA under this deal.

Poison Added in by Democrats that Trump Can Use to Quash USMCA

Here are some key words from the Democrats' own fact sheet that could be used by Trump. Taken as a whole, these substantial changes House Democrats secured are a true transformation of the original United States-Mexico-Canada Agreement:

- Democrats added "stronger enforcement" and "stronger rules" provisions—provisions that could be used against the US for allegedly violating USMCA or the rulings of the entities created under USMCA.
- At the signing of the Democrats' amendments, Mexican Senator Ricardo Monreal admitted, "It will now be easier to establish panels of regional jurisdiction, or with regional jurisdiction, composed of judges from both countries that address all types of differences that may arise on any subject covered by the treaty." Mexican judges will be ruling on American issues, with jurisdiction over Americans.
- "House Democrats established a new and enhanced labor-specific enforcement mechanism."
- Stronger environmental rules that will bind all three countries, including establishing a "presumption" that an environmental issue affects trade. That means Mexico or Canada or a USMCA-created institution could come after the US or a state under these provisions, and the presumption would be that USMCA-created institutions have jurisdiction and enforcement powers over the matter.

At the signing ceremony, Canadian Deputy Prime Minister Chrystia Freeland, touting the "progressive agreement," said: "When this agreement is enacted, NAFTA will not only be preserved, it will be updated, improved, and modernized for the 21st century." With the Democrats' modifications, **USMCA PRESERVES NAFTA**.

There are seven additional "multilateral environmental agreements" added into USMCA by Democrats (also attached as a pdf above), and it seems they added language allowing them to add more of these deals into USMCA after Trump leaves office. "Pursuant to Article 34.3 (Amendments), the Parties may agree in writing to modify paragraph 1 to include...any other environmental or conservation agreement."

On the changes, Nancy Pelosi said USMCA was now "infinitely better than what was initially proposed by the administration."

Chairman of the House Ways and Means Committee, Representative Richard Neal (D-MA), said: "Over the intense period of these negotiations with the administration, I repeatedly emphasized the USMCA will deserve a vote because it's an agreement that Democrats shaped."

Rep. Suzanne Bonamici (D-OR), who managed negotiations for changes to the environmental chapter of the USMCA, explained: "We incorporate several multilateral environmental agreements. We have an interagency committee to assess and monitor. This is going to be best trade agreement for the environment."

Republicans are also seeing this. Senator Pat Toomey (R-PA) told Politico about the USMCA after Democrat changes: "It's *clearly moved way to the left*, which is why you had a celebratory press conference by all the Democratic leadership in the House" (emphasis added). Later, speaking on Fox, Toomey said, "This negotiated agreement has made more concessions to the left, to the Democrats, to organized labor, than they've ever gotten on any other trade agreement."

Prepared by Alex Newman

* * *

Maybe Council on Foreign Relations President Richard N. Haass Should Be Delivering the State of the Union Address!

It is painfully obvious that the majority of our US representatives are ignoring the desires of our elected president and have chosen instead to serve **CFR president Richard N. Haass.** If Trump's negotiating team truly had America's best interest at heart, **the poison added to the revised USMCA agreement preferred by President Haass** should have been rejected by them—but it was not. **Shame on**

all of them; they have *knowingly* damned America! The **USMCA dream team** includes the following:

- Robert Lighthizer, US trade representative, is the team leader and a **member of the CFR.** (In-essence, the CFR is a self-created government operating within our government that many of our trusted US representatives have pledged their allegiance to).
- Larry Kudlow is the director of the National Economic Council and a **CFR member.**
- Peter Navarro is the assistant to the president and director of trade and manufacturing policy.
- John Melle is the assistant US trade representative and career bureaucrat **who has praised NAFTA.**
- C. J. Mahoney is the deputy US trade representative and legal advisor.
- Gregg Doud is the chief agricultural negotiator and trade representative.
- Jamieson Greer is the chief of staff to the US trade representative.
- Jared Kushner is the senior advisor to President Trump and White House innovations director. In 2019, **Kushner attended the Bilderberg Conference in Montreux, Switzerland from May 30 to June 2.**

I Don't Trust Any of Them!

The USMCA dream team were all well aware of the damning consequences of the Democrat-revised **(and CFR President Richard N. Haass-preferred)** version of the agreement but made no attempt to change it. Our *Republican* legislators, who were eager to sign it, also made no such attempts. **Can you say "CONSPIRACY"?**

The communist elite have covered all the bases. The agreement, as originally presented to Trump, was great for America, but the Democrat-revised version that he signed is a huge victory for the CFR and the Bilderberg Group. Even though it will create jobs, it will also pretty much finalize the NAU and SPP, which are stepping-stones to the elite's one-world government. Trump has been surrounded by enemies from day one and is viewed as a mere figurehead by them. I consider the majority of our government officials to be self-serving actors and actresses only concerned with serving Council on Foreign Relations President Richard N. Haass.

CHAPTER 18
Climate Change

> If you tell a lie long enough and keep repeating it, people will eventually come to believe it. The lie can be maintained only for such time as the State can shield the people from the political, economic and/or military consequences of the lie. It thus becomes vitally important for the state to use all of its powers to repress dissent, for the truth is the mortal enemy of the lie, and thus by extension, the truth is the greatest enemy of the State.
>
> If you repeat a lie often enough it becomes the truth.
>
> The truth is the greatest enemy of the State.
> —Joseph Goebbels, Adolf Hitler's close
> associate and devoted follower

The intent of this book is to raise awareness—awareness that we are being fed lies on a variety of topics, which the communist elite needs to do to implement their agenda. This propaganda comes from multiple sources, including but not limited to the media, elected officials, religious leaders, schoolteachers, and college professors. Hopefully, what I have revealed thus far has intrigued people enough to start thinking for themselves. I am not saying that the people buying into the elite's bullshit are ignorant, but I am implying that they are overly credulous, that is, gullible.

"Credulous" describes a person who accepts something willingly and without much in the way of supporting facts. A prime example of this is the mothers of young children that showed up at Senator Dianne Feinstein's office demanding that she take immediate and drastic action on climate change. Their concerns were in part based on rhetoric spewing from a twenty-nine-year-old female bartender's mouth. This bartender, however, was recently elected to the US Congress, representing New York's Fourteenth Congressional District.

I wonder if these ladies, who have fallen hook, line, and sinker for what a bartender/activist is advocating, have ever given thought to the fact that their source, Alexandra Ocasio-Cortez, has absolutely no credentials on the subject of climate change. Credulous people are easy targets for the elite, and these women, along with the bartender/activist/socialist congresswoman, are prime examples of credulous people. And sadly, there are a whole lot more just like them. The majority of Americans have no knowledge of the Bilderberg Group and their agenda. It is not that they are bad people; they are just misinformed and uninformed. The Bilderberg Group's ownership of nearly all media outlets allows them to misinform a broad audience. So, I truly hope that all those who are now aware will attempt to bring that same awareness to others.

I have been personally aware of the Bilderberg Group's agenda since I was a young teen. During the 1970s, my father would speak of the group and their agenda and also provide me with reading material. By correlating the events with this reading material, I became convinced at an early age that this so-called conspiracy theory was actually conspiracy fact. It was practically unmentionable in the 70s because it was so well concealed, but now it is as if they are not even trying to hide it. Yet people still do not seem to be able to figure it out, which is not entirely their fault since the group's propaganda and misinformation are being broadcast on such a large scale (so large that it amounts to brainwashing).

Bringing awareness to the communist elite and their public base (the CFR) has to be a priority for anyone concerned by their activities. Only then will we be able to challenge them. Chapters 1–3 of this book indicate that our elected representatives are most certainly well aware of the elite and their agenda. But why are they not speaking out? That is easy to answer: Because they are either serving the group or they fear the group. Either way, we lose because mum's the word on this topic.

Awareness of their misinformation campaign should raise suspicion and create skepticism about everything we have been told by their sources. I believe that the people's overdue recognition of what the mainstream media really is (a propaganda tool used by the communist elite to promote and encourage acceptance of their **one-world, corporate-controlled, unelected government**) will finally spark them into action. And even if that action is nothing more than bringing awareness to others, we are all obligated to do just that. **We owe it to President Donald J. Trump, ourselves, and our nation.**

Consider the following two quotations:

> A taste of the ideas going the rounds in Obama circles is offered by a recent report from the Managing Global Insecurity Project, whose small US advisory group includes John Podesta, the man heading Mr. Obama's transition team, and Strobe Talbott, the president of the Brookings Institute, from which Ms. Rice has emerged. The MGI report argues for the creation of a UN high commissioner for counter-terrorist activity, a legally binding climate-change agreement negotiated under the auspices of the UN, and the creation of a fifty-thousand-strong UN peacekeeping force. Once countries have pledged troops to this reserve army, the UN will have first call upon them. (*Financial Times*, December 8, 2008)
>
> Today, America would be outraged if UN troops entered Los Angeles to restore order [referring to the 1991 LA riots]. Tomorrow they will be grateful! This is especially true if they were told that there was an outside threat from beyond, whether rear or promulgated, that threatened our very existence. It is then that all peoples of the world will plead to deliver them from this evil.

The one thing every man fears is the unknown. When presented with this scenario, individual rights will be willingly relinquished for the guarantee of their well-being granted to them by the world government. (Henry Kissinger, national security advisor and secretary of state under President Richard Nixon)

How sick! It appears as if Henry Kissinger, who was a national security advisor and secretary of state for the UNITED STATES OF AMERICA, was and still is advocating for a scheme that will SCARE people to the point that they would willingly relinquish their individual rights and freedoms by believing that the creation of a one-world government is necessary to save planet earth and humanity.

The present window of opportunity, during which a truly peaceful and independent world order might be built, will not be open for too long. We are on the verge of a global transformation. **All we need now is the right major crisis, and the nations will accept the New World Order.**

—David Rockefeller

The elite are desperate to implement the New World Order and have been **using the human-created climate change hoax as "the right major crisis,"** but that scheme was moving too slowly. As a result, they did the following:

- manufacture a global pandemic and then launch a misinformation campaign to convince the public that Trump's actions to contain the virus were inadequate,
- also manufacture fake statistics showing that the most loved and adored US president in the history of our nation was losing to a mentally compromised elitist who wants to destroy America, and

- rig the 2020 election with multiple mechanisms to remove a sitting president who was challenging them.

And we will soon be hearing about yet another scare tactic. The recently "leaked" UFO videos, which can be easily found on the internet, taken from the cockpits of US military aircraft suggest that what government officials have been concealing, for at least since aviation began, will at some point be disclosed and used to convince all citizens of the world that a one-world government, complete with a one-world army, must be created and accepted. This is because such an army and the government that supports it would offer the best-case scenario for guaranteeing the survival of the human race.

There is overwhelming evidence that we are being observed by superior beings from another realm (this will be discussed in great detail in succeeding chapters), but it is simply insane to think that we could challenge them in any way. If they decided to destroy the human race, the simple release of a pathogen or toxin would be the most likely means. We can in no way challenge them; we are at their mercy. The point that I am trying to make is that their existence is *not* a valid reason for the creation and acceptance of the elite's unelected and **unchallengeable** one-world government.

If those challenging the theory of human-created climate change were given equal opportunity to present their case, the major crisis scheme, proposed by Kissinger and Rockefeller and also encouraged by those serving the communist elite, would fall flat on its face. But the public will *never* be allowed to hear the other side since the elite own and control the media outlets, including the Trump-critical hosts on talk shows. So, please get out of the credulous camp. Stop allowing yourselves to be influenced and even brainwashed by the elite's New World Order propaganda, and start thinking for yourselves.

The credulous twenty-nine-year-old bartender believes that human activity is responsible for climate change and has brought planet earth to the brink of destruction—so much so that if we do not take **the drastic measures proposed by the President's Council on Sustainable Development** over the next ten-year period, we will be doomed. Not taking these actions, they tell us, will create irreversible damage.

Let me give my thoughts on that. **The UN and the Bilderberg Group have a timetable. Full implementation of their WORLD GOVERNMENT is running behind schedule,** in part due to the election of Donald J. Trump. Their desperation is escalating, which calls for escalating **scare tactics**, including the ten-year doomsday prediction being broadcast by the genius AOC. The human-created climate change hoax was manufactured to fast-track the beginning of the elite's **New World Order**. But the scheme was not moving fast enough, so they supercharged the beginning of their New World Order by blessing the world with COVID-19.

They desperately desire a **CARBON TAX** that would provide the resources for funding their world government. The carbon tax would give world government authorities the right to enter our homes in order to validate that they are in compliance with **United Nations Agenda for the twenty-first Century** policies. In this way, they are using the **human-created climate change scheme** as a means to achieve their goal of controlling every aspect of our lives.

Their agenda is not about saving planet earth; it is about controlling planet earth! They desire government dependents because those who are dependent on their government will support their government and willingly relinquish their rights, freedoms, and liberties in return for **handouts they will not be able to survive without.** The millions of jobs that will be lost as a result of the **green energy acts** being made into law by the **union-hero Democrats** will be lost forever. Boilermakers, pipefitters, ironworkers, the UAW, sheet metal workers, coal miners, truck drivers, and the service employees who keep fossil fuel power plants operating will all become government dependents, and their retirement benefits and pensions will be slashed.

HAARP and Beyond: Our Climate is Being Manipulated

The High Frequency Auroral Research Program (HAARP) was an ionospheric research program jointly **funded by the US Air Force,**

US Navy, University of Alaska Fairbanks and **Defense Advanced Research Projects Agency (DARPA).** Ionospheric research instruments (IRIs) were used to temporarily excite a limited area of the ionosphere for the purpose of analysis and investigation of the potential for enhancing radio communication and surveillance. HAARP was completed in 2007 and permanently shut down at the end of 2014, but the **manipulation of the ionosphere** continues with **more sophisticated IRIs.**

Conspiracy

A conspiracy is defined as "a secret plan by a group to do something unlawful or harmful, often political in nature." I believe that the human-created climate change hoax is a **conspiracy** designed to convince the masses that the creation and *acceptance* of an all-powerful one-world government are necessary to save the human race. Bullshit! One of my favorite websites is **GeoEngineering Watch** (http://geoengineeringwatch.org). This site is dedicated to exposing the active and top-secret agenda of engineered climate. Intelligently presented articles on the site provide **overwhelming evidence that IRIs have been used to manipulate and engineer the earth's climate**. A group conspiring to strip all nations of their sovereignty and create an all-powerful, corporate-controlled one-world government would need multiple schemes to accomplish that; climate change is just one of the many they are using.

The elite has convinced the general public that planet earth is doomed unless nearly all human-created CO_2 emissions are stopped. They are using their embedded CFR puppets to implement laws, rules, and, regulations that not only **circumvent the US Constitution** but also eliminate millions of well-paying jobs—and there is a reason for that. They desire obedient government dependents who will have no choice but to support the only source of revenue available to them. Millions are willfully surrendering their rights, freedoms, and liberties as a result of the fear created by the elite. The elite need to convince the masses that human-created CO_2 emissions must be eliminated. The **President's Council on Sustainable**

Development was not created to save planet earth—**it was created to implement a New World Order!** A conspiracy? Absolutely!

Think about this: Of every 85,000 molecules of gas in the atmosphere, 33 are CO_2. Only one molecule of CO_2 among those 33 is of human origin, while the other 32 are of natural origin. Natural origin means originating from the natural decay of organic materials, emissions from volcanoes, and the like. We could significantly reduce human-created CO_2 emissions, but emissions from natural origins will still exist and far exceed those from human activities.

Many thought-provoking articles posted on the **GeoEngineering Watch** website expose this conspiracy further. In the next section, I have reprinted, with permission, an article appearing on this site.

Air Force Bombshell: Admits They Can Control Weather—HAARP

By Susan Duclos

While HAARP and weather control has been called a conspiracy theory by the mainstream media and government officials, during a Senate hearing on Wednesday, David Walker, deputy assistant secretary of the Air Force for science, technology and engineering, dropped a bombshell in answer to a question asked by Senator Lisa Murkowski in relation to dismantling of the $300 million High Frequency Active Auroral Research Program in Gakona this summer.

Walker said this "is not an area that we have any need for in the future" and it would not be a good use of Air Force research funds to keep HAARP going. "We're moving on to other ways of managing the ionosphere, which the HAARP was really designed to do," he said. **"To inject energy into the ionosphere to be able to actually control it. But that work has been completed."**

Many believe HAARP was created and has been used for weather control, with enough juice to trigger hurricanes, tornados, and earthquakes, and comments such as this bring about the question of whether conspiracy theorists are more on target than anyone has admitted to date.

This is not the first time a public official has acknowledged that HAARP and weather control is not only possible but has been and continues to be used as a "superweapon," as evidenced by a statement in 1997 by former US defense secretary William Cohen, where he said,

> Others [terrorists] are engaging even in an eco-type of terrorism whereby they can alter the climate, set off earthquakes, volcanoes remotely through the use of electromagnetic waves... So, there are plenty of ingenious minds out there that are at work finding ways in which they can wreak terror upon other nations... It's real, and that's the reason why we have to intensify our counter-terrorism efforts.

Is it still just a conspiracy theory if the public officials admit it is true?

* * *

Wikipedia defines **terrorism** as "acts reaching more than the immediate target victims and also directed at targets consisting of a larger spectrum of society and **acts committed by non-state actors** or by undercover personnel serving on the behalf of their **respective governments."** (The relevant governments here can be assumed to be the **elite!**) Merriam Webster defines terrorism as "the systematic use of terror especially **as a means of coercion."**

The former US secretary of defense William Cohen claims that some are even engaging in an "eco-type" **terrorism** whereby **they can alter the climate** and set off earthquakes and volcanoes remotely with **electromagnetic waves**, and for that reason we need to intensify our **counterterrorism** efforts. Cohen believes that our climate is being manipulated in a **terrorist act** by one nation against another. I agree with him that **our climate is being manipulated**, but not by, say, one nation desiring to destroy another's economy.

Instead, I believe that the actors here are the ELITE who have to create a compelling case for the creation of their desired one-world government. Mr. Cohen is right; we should intensify our counter-terrorism efforts. And those efforts should be directly focused on the Bilderberg Group and their public base, the CFR!

These so-called research projects are **jointly funded by the US Air Force, the US Navy and the Defense Advanced Research Projects Agency (DARPA).** Keep that fact in mind when you consider these words from former Senator Daniel Inouye: "**There exists a shadowy government** with its own air force, its own navy, its own fundraising mechanism, and the ability to pursue its own ideas of the national interests, **free from all the checks and balances**, and free from the law itself." In a similar vein, we have these words from James Dale Davidson:

> As my beautiful wife puts it, elected officials only ostensibly run the visible government, as outlined in Civics 101. She says they are merely Muppets **who do the bidding of the Deep State, the people George W. Bush referred to as "the deciders"**—a fascinating phrase from a former president who was twice elected by voters who naively assumed that Mr. Bush would be the "decider" so long as he inhabited the Oval Office. (James Dale Davidson, *The Breaking Point: Profit from the Coming Money Cataclysm*, pp. 236–237)

Many have concerns or at least suspicions about the true intentions and uses of these ionosphere-manipulating instruments.

A Russian military journal wrote that ionospheric testing would **"trigger a cascade of electrons that could flip earth's magnetic poles."**

The Alaska State Legislature and the European Parliament held hearings about HAARP, with the latter citing environmental concerns as a reason for doing so.

Physicist Bernard Eastlund claims that HAARP includes technology, based on his own patents, that has the capability to modify weather and neutralize satellites. Eastland is in favor of funding research into weather modification and control that could reduce the impact of severe weather. If the technology can be used to reduce the impact of severe weather, **then it most assuredly could also be used to increase the impact of severe weather.** That would work out pretty well for a group trying to convince the masses that human activities are responsible for all manner of changing and severe weather patterns!

Wildfires

Nick Begich Jr., the son of late US Representative Nick Begich and brother of former US Senator Mark Begich, authored the book *Angels Don't Play This HAARP.* He claims there that HAARP activities could trigger earthquakes and **turn the upper atmosphere into a giant lens** such that "the sky would literally appear to burn." He also maintains a website where he argues that HAARP is actually a mind-control device.

Specific areas can be targeted by HAARP. It is within the realm of possibility that the wildfires in Brazil, Australia, and California are a result of the manipulation of the ionosphere. Bear in mind that **the ionospheric research instruments (IRIs) being used today are far superior to the outdated HAARP technology.** So, taking into considering what the outdated HAARP instrument was capable of and the fact that the rate of advancement in technology are DOUBLING approximately every nine months, the possibilities are limitless.

GeoEngineering Watch has several resources on this topic. Here, an excerpt from Dane Wigington's article "Global Weather Modification Assault Causing Climate Chaos and Environmental Catastrophe" explains the threat of weather manipulation:

Is this really possible? Available science as well as observed weather events and jet stream "anomalies" say absolutely yes. HAARP is the acronym for a massively powerful "ionosphere heater" facility located in Alaska. This is a huge and extremely powerful antenna array that is capable of transmitting as much as three million watts of power into the ionosphere. This triggers an electrical chain reaction, which then causes a "bulge" in the atmosphere, which in turn can alter the course of the jet stream. Such alterations can in turn "steer" weather systems. By such manipulation, storm fronts can be combined and worsened into "frankenstorms" or broken apart and dispersed. There are thought to be nearly one hundred large, ground-based "ionosphere heaters" around the globe, some held by China and Russia. It has also become evident in recent years that "weather warfare" is already a lethal global reality. The potential of these frequency transmitter facilities is enhanced by the spraying of our skies. The saturation of the atmosphere with metal particulates makes the atmosphere more "conductive." This in turn increases the capabilities of the ionosphere heaters.

The article goes on to argue that we are being poisoned by the metal particulates when they fall back to earth.

GeoEngineering Watch

The value of GeoEngineering Watch and the man responsible for it cannot be overstated. In my opinion, we all owe Dane Wigington a great debt of gratitude and should support the man in any way that we can. The material presented on GeoEngineering Watch will even have the Green New Dealers second-guessing what they have been led to believe. **It is critical that we support Dane Wigington!** I suggest that everyone visit geoengineering.org and encourage others to visit the site and donate as well. **Donating to GeoEngineering Watch will ensure that we will continue to have a source for such forbidden knowledge well into the future.**

The President's Council on Sustainable Development is being used to implement a world government. The elite are killing two birds with one stone. They are manipulating our climate to justify **the unification of all the world's sovereign governments** and creating loyal government dependents all in one fell swoop. And it gets worse. People who will be barely existing on the government handouts will be doling out a good portion of them just to pay their **outrageous green energy** utility bills and fuel their vehicles. **The elite are truly creating a nation and even world of slaves.**

Read What They Don't Want Us to Read

I highly suggest to all who are seeking the truth, to purchase and carefully review one or all four of the climate-themed books that I have recommend.

> *Understanding the Global Warming Hoax* by Leo Johnson, retired physicist

> *Inconvenient Facts* by Gregory Wrightstone, geologist who has been investigating the earth's processes for more than thirty-five years

> *Climate Bogeyman* by M. S. King, Rutgers University graduate, private investigative journalist, and researcher

> *Climate Change: The Facts*, edited by Alan Moran, manager of Regulation Economics, former director of the deregulation unit at the Institute of Public Affairs, former director of the Australian Office of Regulation Review, and former deputy

secretary of energy in the Victorian Department
of Minerals and Energy

This last book, *Climate Change: The Facts*, first published in
2015 by Stockade Books, is a real must-read. It is a volume of essays
with twenty-three contributors, all with impressive credentials:

John Abott, senior research fellow at Central
Queensland University

J. Scott Armstrong, University of Pennsylvania;
Ehrenberg-Bass Institute, University of South
Australia

Andrew Bolt, columnist with the *Herald Sun,
Daily Telegraph,* and the *Advertiser* and host of
Sky News Australia's *The Bolt Report*

Robert M. Carter, emeritus fellow and science
policy advisor at the Institute of Public Affairs,
science advisor at the Science and Public Policy
Institute, chief science advisor for the International Climate Science Coalition, and former
professor and head of the School of Earth Sciences at James Cook University

Rupert Darwall, author of *The Age of Global
Warming: A History*, has written for the *Wall
Street Journal* and the *Financial Times*

James Delingpole, executive editor for the Lon-
don branch of Breitbart News, author of *Water-
melons: How Environmentalists are Killing the
Planet, Destroying the Economy and Stealing your
Children's Future* (published in Australia as *Killing the Earth to Save It*)

Christopher Essex, chairman of the Permanent Monitoring Panel—Climatology for the World Federation of Scientists and professor and associate chair in the Department of Applied Mathematics, University of Western Ontario

Stewart W. Franks, chair of Environmental Engineering, University of Tasmania

Kesten C. Green, senior research associate of the Ehrenberg-Bass Institute, University of South Australia, and senior lecturer at University of South Australia

Donna Laframboise, journalist, author of *The Delinquent Teenager Who Was Mistaken for the World's Top Climate Expert*, and former member of the board of directors of the Canadian Civil Liberties Association (1993–2001)

Nigel Lawson, former British Conservative politician, journalist, member of the House of Lords, and author of *An Appeal to Reason: A Cool Look at Global Warming*

Bernie Lewin, author of climate change blog Enthusiasm, Skepticism and Science (http://enthusiasmscepticismscience.wordpress.com)

Richard S. Lindzen, atmospheric physicist, former professor of meteorology at Massachusetts Institute of Technology (1983–2013), distinguished senior fellow at the Center for the Study of Science at the Cato Institute, lead author of the chapter "Physical Climate Processes and

Feedbacks" in the IPCC's *Third Assessment Report* (2001)

Jennifer Marohasy, adjunct research fellow in the Centre for Plant and Water Science at Central Queensland University, foundation member of the Australian Environment Foundation, former senior fellow at the Institute of Public Affairs (2004–2009), and author of *Myth and the Murray: Measuring the Real State of the River Environment*

Ross McKitrick, professor of economics at University of Guelph, coauthor of *Taken by Storm: The Troubled Science, Policy and Politics of Global Warming*, and author of *Economic Analysis of Environmental Policy*

Patrick J. Michaels, director of the Center for the Study of Science at the Cato Institute, research professor of environmental sciences at University of Virginia (1980–2007), and author of *Shattered Consensus: The True State of Global Warming and Climate Coup: Global Warming's Invasion of Our Government and Our Lives*

Jo Nova, science writer with columns published in *The Spectator* and *The Australian* and author of *The Sceptic's Handbook*

Garth W. Paltridge, emeritus professor and honorary research fellow at the Institute of Antarctic and Southern Ocean Studies at the University of Tasmania, visiting fellow at Australian National University and fellow of the Australian Academy of Science, former chief research scientist with the

CSIRO Division of Atmospheric Research, former CEO of the Antarctic Cooperative Research Centre, and author of *The Climate Caper: Facts and Fallacies of Global Warming*

Ian Plimer, emeritus professor of earth sciences at the University of Melbourne, professor of mining geology at the University of Adelaide, and author of *Not for Greens*

Willie Soon, independent scientist

Mark Steyn, political commentator and author of many books, including *After America: Get Ready for Armageddon* and *America Alone: The End of the World as We Know It*

Anthony Watts, holder of the American Meteorology Society Seal of Approval (retired), radio meteorologist, and author of "Is the US Surface Temperature Record Reliable?"

This will be considered totally insane by liberals, but I choose to put my faith in those with respectable credentials versus a twenty-nine-year-old bartender, the elite-owned and elite-controlled media anchors and journalists, or the liberals' most recent climate change spokesperson, sixteen-year-old Swedish activist Greta Thunberg. I could have included many quotes and facts from the books mentioned above but opted not to because such bits and pieces could be too easily picked apart by those selling the human-created climate change hoax. So, I want give just one small example from an excerpt from chapter 1 of *Climate Change the Facts* by Ian Plimer, whose qualifications were noted above: "Only one molecule of CO_2 of every 85,000 in the atmosphere is of human origin, while 32 CO_2 molecules of every 85,000 in the atmosphere are of natural origin" (pp. 11–12).

That tells me that if all CO2-creating human activity were eliminated from planet earth, there would still be thirty-two times more CO2 in the atmosphere from nature than what has been generated by humans. Pilmer also reveals here that **the main greenhouse gas is water vapor, not CO2.** CO2 has a short residence time in the atmosphere **and is naturally sequestered into the oceans, living beings, or rocks in less than a decade.** CO2 is used by plants and actually causes a greening of the planet. Warming is occurring, to be sure, but **it is not a result of human activity. Eliminating all human-created CO2 will not stop arctic ice from melting, but what it will do is create a great number of obedient government dependents.** I will say no more on the subject here. Instead, I want to encourage all readers to review the suggested material in order to have a thorough and truthful understanding of the subject. The elite own and control nearly all media outlets, meaning you have to think for yourselves and educate yourselves.

People Are So Ignorant

Time magazine (a product of the elite) has chosen sixteen-year-old activist Greta Thunberg as their Person of the Year for 2019. She has no more knowledge on the topic of earth's climate than the twenty-nine-year-old bartender but, somehow, is now revered by the liberals and the elite as being earth's savior. **Is she receiving this great wisdom from her Barbie dolls?** I am going to have to go with **Ian Plimer and company!**

I would suggest that those who think like Lindsey Graham, Matt Gaetz, Lamar Alexander, and Leonardo DiCaprio review the recommended material, but I sincerely doubt that they would be interested in what the *real* experts have to say.

CHAPTER 19
The International Brotherhood of Boilermakers, Right to Work, and Public Service Unions

I was a proud member of the Boilermakers union for thirty-five years. I started my four-year apprenticeship with Local # 363 out of Belleville, Illinois in March 1977 and retired in December 2012. The average citizen has no idea what a boilermaker is or does and just how vital they are to the industrial world. A partial list of the services these skilled craftsmen provide include the following:

- Boiler fabrication, erection, and maintenance
- Pressure vessel construction, installation, and maintenance
- Tank fabrication, installation, and maintenance (any and all, including large city water towers)
- Ductwork fabrication, installation, and maintenance (often weighing over one hundred tons)
- Fabrication, installation, and maintenance of emissions control systems for power plants, chemical plants, refineries, steel mills, foundries, and more
- Smokestack fabrication, erection, and maintenance
- Nuclear reactor fabrication, erection, and maintenance

These activities do not even begin to cover all the services that these highly skilled craftsmen provide. They do it right while performing the work safely and in a timely manner. Their welders and riggers are second to none! And that is not just an opinion; it's a fact.

Boilermakers, more often than not, have to deal with harsh working conditions, including extreme heat and cold, exposure to chemicals and toxins, extreme heights (the Kennecott Smokestack located near the Great Salt Lake in Utah is 1,215 feet tall, for example), asbestos, and all manner of dust and fumes containing all kinds of chemicals and toxins. What is more, the jobs do not shut down when there is ice and snow. The work carries on, miserable though it may be. These workers overcome the obstacles and forge ahead. Boilermakers are indeed a special breed and are worth every penny they are paid.

I decided to include this chapter in this volume because I care deeply about this organization and its members, and it disturbs me that they, more so than any other craft, are a direct casualty of the **Democrat-sponsored green energy acts** that are rapidly being put into force nationwide.

Now that we are aware of the elite's existence and of their agenda, it is crystal clear that many have aligned themselves with them and their plains. Union hero President Bill Clinton set everything into motion in 1993 with Executive Order 12852, which created the President's Council on Sustainable Development. (This was effectively the original title for the Green New Deal). Its creation is meant to strip away America's sovereignty and marked the beginning of the end for the fossil fuel industry and all other industries related to fossil fuels.

The following paragraphs have been reprinted from The Agenda 21 Course by Eileen DeRolf. The entire ten-lesson course can be viewed online or in chapters 4–13 of this book. According to DeRolf,

> The President's Council on Sustainable Development contained twelve cabinet secretaries. Six of them belonged to the Nature Conservancy, the Sierra Club, the World Resources Institute, or the National Wildlife Federation.

These same groups, called nongovernmental organizations (NGOs), worked directly with the United Nations to craft Agenda 21, and now were in a key position to put Agenda 21 policies into every single agency in the US federal government. This means every federal agency, the Department of Education, the Department of Homeland Security, the EPA, are all currently using your tax dollars to undercut our sovereignty and steal our property rights bit by bit.

The United Nations and the non-governmental organizations that do the "heavy lifting" for the UN have been very clever in the ways they have chosen to get people around the world and in the US to accept "sustainable development policies."...

NAFTA was touted as a way to make the US more competitive with Asia and Europe by combining the economic strength of the US with that of Canada and Mexico. Instead, NAFTA caused US jobs to go overseas, real wages in the US to drop, an increase in our trade deficit, and an enrichment of select corporations. In other words, NAFTA redistributed American wealth overseas. Further, it was designed to blur our national borders and weaken our sovereignty. Can you say "North American Union"?...

Last but not least, certain policies, like NAFTA, entered into by our federal government can damage the free market on a global level, weaken our sovereignty, and hasten a One World Order.

The President's Council on Sustainable Development uses the environment, and especially climate change, as sellable propaganda aimed at tricking the masses into accepting the communist elite's

New World Order. We have learned from Mr. Estulin (via Lendman's review article, included in chapters 1 and 2 of this work), along with the prominent individuals quoted in chapter 3, that the elite and their world government agenda are a reality and that the blueprint for this scheme is Agenda 21 and PCSD. Also, they indicate to us that none of this is the humanity-saving environmental agenda that it has been touted as.

Bill Clinton turbocharged Agenda 21 from the very start of his presidency with the creation of the President's Council on Sustainable Development. After Clinton came establishment-darling G. W. Bush, who was succeeded by the fossil-fuel grim reaper Barrack Obama. But it was G. H. W. Bush (Mr. World Government himself) who kicked everything off in 1992 by signing an agreement to Agenda 21 at the Rio de Janeiro Earth Summit. The Bilderberg Group has had a hell of a run! I do hope that the boilermakers reading this are paying attention because the Green New Deal Democrats elected to office (with the help of union donations and votes) will continue to support the elite and their agenda. Importantly, that agenda intends to eliminate the facilities that provide work opportunities for boilermakers. If this continues, you lose the means to provide for your families. Wages, health insurance, pensions, and savings plans are already being lost, and it might only get worse from here.

Power plants, steel mills, chemical plants, coal and ore mines, refineries, foundries, paper mills, and rail and trucking services providing well-paying jobs have all been targeted for elimination. It is unlikely that the affected employees would or will be able to secure another job that could provide something comparable to the wages and benefits previously earned—and that is if they are fortunate enough to secure a job at all. This is just another elite objective: Create more government dependents who will be grateful for the handouts and therefore accepting and supportive of the all-powerful government.

The UN world government agencies influence the creation of other like-minded agencies in nations all around the world. In the United States, they work hand in hand with the **CFR and their embedded government puppets to create agencies that are neces-**

sary for the elite to fulfill their plans. Franklin D. Roosevelt, Lyndon B. Johnson, G. H. W. Bush, Clinton, G. W. Bush, and Obama were all key players in this scheme.

Democratic presidential candidate Michael Bloomberg (the former liberal New York mayor who banned retailers and restaurants from selling sugary beverages larger than sixteen ounces) has pledged to donate five hundred million dollars to a new campaign to close every coal-fired power plant in the United States and halt the use of natural gas. This initiative, Beyond Carbon, is designed to eliminate coal by focusing on state and local governments, **bypassing Washington**. Any action challenging Bloomberg's agenda from Trump and the antiestablishment Republicans would be unlikely given that Bloomberg's fellow, **like-minded Democrats control all the chambers** and would thwart any effort to stop it. Beyond Carbon's lobbying efforts will target environmental groups, state legislators, city councils, and public utility commissioners. More than 280 coal plants have already been closed or have announced impending closure since 2010. That only leaves 241 facilities, which the campaign will aim to close by 2030.

The Illinois CFR/Bilderberg Group Puppets

Illinois boilermakers representing Local 363, Local 60, and Local 1 should be aware that important legislation strongly supported by the Democrats controlling Illinois is likely to pass in the very near future. The proposed legislation is HB3624/SB2132, the Clean Energy Jobs Act. Obviously, this is Illinois' contribution to Bloomberg's Beyond Carbon campaign and goes way past what even the most liberal-leaning states are proposing. According to the bill, 25 percent of the power provided by utility companies for all retail customers will have to come from renewable sources by 2025, with 45 percent by 2030, and the total elimination of coal plants by 2050. But Boilermaker Local 363, Local 60, and Local 1 will be slain well before 2050 because the utilities will have no choice but to abandon coal and natural gas long before that. And you can bet that the CFR-loyal Democrats representing this CFR-controlled state will continue to attack, from multiple fronts, any and all facilities connected to fossil fuels—the very facilities that boilermakers depend on for their survival.

The governor of Illinois is J. B. Pritzker. **The Pritzker family is one of the wealthiest in the country and has been near the top of the Forbes America's Richest Families list since 1982.** J. B. Pritzker's net worth currently stands at $3.4 billion (give or take). His sister, Penny Pritzker, was the secretary of commerce during the Obama administration.

To see what kind of person we are dealing with here, consider that the Chicago Sun-Times reported that J. B. Pritzker rendered uninhabitable a mansion he purchased next to his primary residence by removing the toilets. After that, he appealed his property tax assessment with claims that the *new* home next to his residence was uninhabitable. The county assessor apparently agreed with this and reduced the value of the home from $6.25 million to $1.1 million. This gave Pritzker a property tax reduction of around $230,000 per year.

That is a comforting revelation! In essence, Cook County handed over $230,000 of tax revenue that could have been used to benefit of the residents to a man worth over three billion dollars. Of course, leading up to the 2016 election, the Boilermakers International president endorsed this noble man along with every Democrat on the ticket. Fittingly, the local Boilermaker lodges representing Illinois followed suit. HB3624/SB2132, proposed by the Democrats and supported by union hero J.B. Pritzker, will most assuredly eliminate nearly all the remaining work covered by the Boilermaker union members in Illinois in a very short period of time.

Union Representatives Are Supporting the New World Order Agenda

International Brotherhood of Boilermakers President Newton B. Jones, who began his tenure in 2003, touts the use of carbon capture, utilization, and storage (CCUS) as a bridge to a clean energy future. However, his and our pleas for help only fall on deaf ears.

Why? **Because the ears in control are establishment-loyal Democrat ears.** Carbon capture technology has been an option since 1977. Charles Jones, Newt's predecessor and father, should have recognized its potential as a strong job creator for the boilermakers from the beginning and advocated for its acceptance and implementation.

One might plausibly to say that they were ignorant of the elites and their agenda—at least until 1993. That year, their existence and intentions were put on full display with the creation of Clinton's President's Council on Sustainable Development (that is, the Green New Deal). An observant union representative or any representative of those dependent on the fossil fuel industry should have immediately recognized the potential threat and launched a full-scale campaign to expose the danger and those responsible for it. Clinton and all the Democrats representing the communist elite should have been voted out of office. **Yet the Boilermaker union officials and their members continued to support (and still do!) their own slayers.** Had the Boilermaker union officials made their members aware of the threat and identified their **true enemies**, their membership would currently stand at record highs, existing coal-fired units would be fitted with CCUS units running at full capacity, and new power stations using supercritical steam generators equipped with CCUS technology would be under construction all across our nation. Currently there are NONE!

Knowledge of just how dire things really are for the boilermakers could quickly cause things to devolve into all-out panic. In an attempt to prolong the inevitable, Mr. Jones offers false hope by claiming that he is exploring what options may be available to boilermakers in the green energy sector. THAT IS JUST RIDICULOUS! Jurisdictions are not going to be reallocated, and the tradespeople involved in the green energy sector are not going to relinquish their work to the boilermakers or anyone else. Boilermakers service the fossil fuel industry, period! So, why is Mr. Jones even giving air to these false expectations? Well, the very generous amount of money padding his bulging pockets may offer an explanation. Sourced from a Kansas City Star article by Judy Thomas, here is a breakdown of recent compensation paid out to Boilermaker union officials and their employees:

- Newt Jones received $756,973 in 2016 (combined salary and expenses).
- Total earnings for the top seven officers was about $3.5 million in 2016.
- Sixteen staffers had total incomes exceeding $200,000 in 2016.

Over a five-year period, the union officials dished out

- $22,000 for Kansas City Chiefs tickets,
- $173,000 for Washington Redskins tickets, and
- $90,000 for Kansas City Royals tickets.

And in 2016, they spent

- $320,511 on a construction division conference at the Hilton Marco Island and
- $343,879 on an industrial-sector operations conference at the Mirage Hotel and Casino in Las Vegas.

There is the motive right there! Obviously, Newton Jones and company have it pretty good! How does he justify this amount of money being disbursed to him and the other officials? His job certainly beats climbing around in a slimy tray tower or crawling through a fly-ash-filled economizer. Maybe his compensation should be more in line with what the members are surviving on!

Union officials have known that boilermakers were going to steadily lose man-hours since the creation of the President's Council on Sustainable Development in 1993, but mum's the word due to their loyalty to the Democratic Party. They could have exposed the elite and their **human-created climate-change hoax** but chose to play politics instead. It does not matter to them; they live like royalty and will continue to even when the people they collect dues from are starving. Mr. Jones will ride that horse until it is dead.

Consider the following excerpt from the HuffPost article "Construction Union Leaders Endorse Joe Biden Ahead of Final Debate":

> Top officials at the International Brotherhood of Boilermakers, a building trades union, endorsed Democratic presidential nominee Joe Biden on Thursday, adding momentum to the Biden campaign's outreach to organized labor in the final weeks of the election.
>
> Newton Jones, international president of the Boilermakers; William Creeden, international secretary-treasurer; Lawrence McManamon, international vice president, Great Lakes; and J. Tom Baca, international vice president, Western states, each sent the Biden campaign a letter offering their official endorsement of Biden and Sen. Kamala Harris (D-CA), the Democratic vice presidential nominee.
>
> "As you are all too aware, this is an unprecedented time in our country where differences of opinion have escalated to extreme divides, even among friends and family and among the brothers and sisters of the Boilermakers union," Jones wrote in his letter. "Now, more than ever, we must find a way to re-unify our nation. I look to you and Senator Harris to be the leaders who will do just that; so that we, as a nation, can move forward once again to a strong and promising future.

A strong and promising future? They endorse an administration that wants to fast-track the Green New Deal…and this suggests a strong and promising future? Maybe for some but certainly not for the boilermakers! Every dues-paying boilermaker should be outraged over this endorsement. Jones, Creeden, McManamon, and Baca are paid ridiculous salaries for one reason and one reason alone: to secure man-hours for their members, not to act as moral bastions who choose uniting the nation over securing man-hours for their members. Boilermakers are *begging* for work, and these four idiots endorse candidates that are fossil-fuel slayers! They should be held accountable, but members know that will not happen. Replacing these four men would be comparable to the citizens of North Korea replacing Supreme Leader Kim Jong Un. Apparently, the elite's desires supersede those of dues-paying members for this union's leadership. They are a disgrace!

The Boilermaker Pension Plan Has Become Equivalent to a Ponzi Scheme

Boilermaker union members are being forced to make unacceptably high contributions in order to keep the pension plan funded. This situation has gotten to the point where **the pension plan is now resembling a Ponzi scheme**. Steadily declining man-hours, which are *absolutely* the result of the clean air acts precipitated by the creation of Clinton's PCSD, will assure that required pension contributions will continue to increase until they reach levels that members are simply unwilling or unable to accept. The result will be a reduction of the benefits being paid to retirees and also a near guarantee that active members will not be able to retire due to the trivial pension that may or may not be available to them. Democrat-sponsored clean air acts being put into effect across the country are **a DEATH WARRANT for all those dependent on the fossil fuel industry! Democrats do not want to consider CCUS as a bridge. They want wind, they want solar, and they want them yesterday. And, of course and as always, they desire a one-world, corporate-controlled socialist and communist government.** If you have digested the revelations in this book thus far, you must understand that **the elite's agenda is not really about their deep concern for humanity; it is all about controlling humanity.** The clean air agenda's scare tactics are just a scheme used to gain support from the uninformed and the credulous.

The Elite Prey on the Credulous

Idiots claim and believe that we only have ten years left to stop climate change or it will be irreversible. THAT IS COMPLETELY FALSE! If that were true, we would all be gasping for air outdoors, types of plants that have been thriving for ages would be struggling, crops would be scarce and dying in the fields, winters and summers would be intolerable, and fish would be dying in the lakes, rivers, and oceans. Climate change occurs over thousands of years and at a very slow pace, so the only way that an individual human could actually experience climate change would be if their lifespan were thousands of years. The slow pace of change presents a roadblock for those trying to convince the public that earth will be doomed in a few short years unless we immediately implement Agenda 21. To circumvent this problem, **they are manipulating our climate with IMIs to convince the public that the drastic and nature-defying climate changes being artificially engineered by them are the result of human activity** (again, I highly recommend visiting http://geoengineeringwatch.org). Agenda 21 is not about saving planet earth and humanity; it is all about controlling planet earth and humanity.

Consider that only one molecule of every eighty-five thousand in the atmosphere is CO_2 of human origin, while thirty-two molecules of every eighty-five thousand in the atmosphere is CO_2 of natural origin. This statistic shows that the trivial contribution from human activity, even with all the fossil fuel power plants running at full throttle, does not even come close to that from natural sources. The human-created threat touted by the elite is not really a threat at all. When and if we ever get to that ten-year countdown, it will be quite obvious to all inhabiting planet earth that things are dire. Climate change is real, the permafrost melting in Siberia is proof of that, **but it is not a result of human activity. It is a combination of a natural cycle and intentional manipulation!**

Americans have no choice but to listen to or read the elite's world government propaganda because they own and control nearly every media outlet in the world. It has to be said that this is a strategy that works—if people hear the same propaganda over and over and over again, they tend to believe it. There *appears* to be no bias because they are all saying the same thing. However, there certainly is bias because, in reality, THEY ARE ALL ONE! What a brilliant strategy. We criticize communist nations for having state-censored media, but that is exactly what is currently occurring in the United States. Of course, we are not being censored by our elected government. In fact, the reality is even worse: We are being censored by the communist elite, the unelected government. America and the world have been brainwashed by these tyrant bastards. The elite control America's money, media, corporations, universities, unions, and politicians. America has been taken without a single shot being fired. George Orwell's 1984 has become a reality.

Politicians Serve Only Themselves (Union Officials Included)

Have you ever wondered why someone possessing personal wealth of several millions, or in Pritzker's case, billions, would seek a position in government that pays a fraction of their potential earnings in the private sector? Many forfeit these government salaries, which is a noble gesture (or at least appears to be), but it still does not answer why they make these ostensibly great personal sacrifices. Are we to believe that they make such sacrifices out of concern for the people they represent? Maybe not—these are businesspeople, not monks. They do not make personal sacrifices **(Donald Trump excluded)!** They got where they are by serving number one, and their priority will continue to be serving number one. So, it would appear that they seek these positions for a reason—and it certainly is not serving the best interests of the common people.

Politicians desiring power and wealth would sell their nation, their countrymen, and their children for the right price. The Bilderberg Group is a small cadre of the wealthiest and most powerful people in the world who can fulfill those politicians' desires, but of course, they want something in return. They need help implementing their one-world government. The CFR is the elite's public base, tasked with identifying the self-servers and grooming them for positions in our government. That, it turns out, is exactly why we are seeing all these Agenda 21 policies being given the force of law all across America. Around 1,500 fossil fuel steam generators are currently being constructed or scheduled to be constructed all around the world. Quite suspiciously, however, there is nothing on the books in the United States of America. The communist elite have a stranglehold on America. Our country is being taken right from under our feet, and we are giving it up without a fight. **Maybe we should be called "the United States of the Bilderberg Group."**

The communist elite need to be in control of governorships, but they also need representatives from all levels of government on board—federal, state, county, and city. Only then can the Bilderberg Group succeed. Well, they have assembled a real dream team in Illinois! **This dream team wants to destroy boilermakers, autoworkers, ironworkers, pipefitters, coal mines, fossil fuel power plants, steel mills, foundries, chemical plants, and refineries.** And the dream team was elected courtesy of the very people they are setting out to massacre. A boilermaker or anyone dependent on the fossil fuel industry casting a vote for a Democrat is the equivalent of putting a loaded gun to their head and pulling the trigger. **J.B. Pritzker and his Democrat allies all across our nation have declared war on a large segment of the American workforce.**

The AFL-CIO Support World Government

Yes, one of the biggest labor unions supports world government. You will never hear this from your union leaders! Why? The Bilderberg Group wields enormous power and wealth, and people desire to be aligned with that power and wealth, obviously for personal gain. It is just human nature, a sad but true reality. Unfortunately, it is naive to believe that union officials would not sell out their dues-paying members. The AFL-CIO launched a campaign to assist workers with immigration, executive action, and citizenship assistance named

"We Rise!" The initiative helps the millions of immigrants who do not qualify for any immediate form of relief, that is, illegals. The AFL-CIO and their affiliates want to offer mutual aid and defense to union members. In my estimation, the AFL-CIO, led by Richard Trumka, by proxy, is encouraging illegal immigration into the United States. The union and their great leader are using unions as a backdoor for illegal entry into the United States. **Well, that is certainly supportive of the elite's open border, North American Union agenda!** The elite have people embedded everywhere. Isn't it comforting to know that a portion of your contributions to the AFL-CIO is being used to encourage illegal immigration and provide jobs for illegal immigrants? Jobs that would be gratefully appreciated by taxpaying American citizens are being filled by illegal immigrants due to the help of Richard Trumka and the AFL-CIO. Can you say "**conspiracy**"?

Newt Jones and the other union officials whose members are being impacted by this job-destroying world government scam have been aware of the elite's agenda and its players since **union hero Bill Clinton created the President's Council on Sustainable Development in 1993!** But none have ever revealed this fact to their members. Why? **Mr. Jones should be exposing the elite's agenda and telling his members to vote *exclusively* Republican because that is truly the only shot at survival the boilermaker union and its members have.** But he is most certainly not doing that. He is handling it by suggesting scenarios that are not even within the realm of possibility. Further, as an attempt to keep the Boilermaker plans funded, he advocates for increasing membership rolls. Why would anyone want to start a career in a dying trade? There has got to be an incentive! **But there is no hope or incentive as long as the Democrats are in power.** BOILERMAKERS, you are losing man-hours by the day courtesy of the world government Democrats that you continue to vote into office. Your craft is dying and it is dying fast. **The window of opportunity to reverse course will be closed permanently if the Green New Deal Democrats are not taken out completely in 2020.**

SB 54 Equals Socialism

Having been a member of a union for thirty-five years, I am well aware of union mentality. Voicing support for a Republican is considered taboo because they often do not support legislation that is seen as favorable to unions. Since I am a reasonable person, I always take into consideration both sides of the argument. As an example, consider California's passage of SB 54. In short, the legislation uses the guise of safety as a means to force refineries to use union labor; they can camouflage it nine ways to hell, but that is exactly what this bill all about. Legislation like this is why union members throw all their support in with the Democrats, overlooking all the insane socialist and world government policies that the Democratic Party supports and represents. But minds of reason should not support something that is **so obviously un-American**, even though they may benefit from it. It is frightening to me, and should be frightening to all who value freedom, that our government is mandating to *privately-owned* companies whom they can and cannot hire. We have become the equivalent of a third-world nation!

I ask union members to think about this matter more clearly. Legislation like SB 54 is used by Democrats as bait to lure support from unions. While it is true that SB 54 will secure some fossil fuel-related jobs for union members, the celebration will be short-lived because the clean-air bills being put into law by Democrats across our entire nation will eliminate ALL those jobs, both union and nonunion, in the very near future. So, the trade-off is a loss of epic proportions, not just for the unions but for all that are dependent on these fossil fuel-related jobs. Further, consider that funds allocated for job-creating infrastructure projects (look at Illinois recently) is used by the ruling parties as a selling tactic—"Look what we did for you!" they seem to be saying. These infrastructure projects create jobs, and the Democrat communists running Illinois will surely use the projects to lure votes in 2020, but funding for infrastructure projects is also a priority for the Republicans. **With them, at least, we will have the jobs but will not have the elite's communist New World Order shoved down our throats.** I just hope the voting populace is smart

253

enough to *finally* figure out what's going on. But there remains a bit of a quandary: Our elections are rigged.

Prevailing Wage and Right to Work

My plea to any and all union and nonunion workers who depend on the fossil fuel industry for their very existence and do not want to become government dependent is this: Put some real thought into your vote. The prevailing wage and right-to-work laws can be used as an example of Democrat mentality. Union members do not want the states to have right-to-work laws. But their focus should be targeted at the prevailing wage laws supported by the Democrats. Prevailing wage laws force companies to pay union-negotiated wages to nonunion members. Unions in states with prevailing wage laws but no right-to-work laws are allowed to collect dues from workers receiving the union-negotiated wages—that is only right. Union members pay dues for the purpose of being represented, and negotiating wages is part of that representation. Therefore, anyone benefitting from that representation should pay for that representation. Prevailing wage laws were never about creating better wages and conditions for nonunion workers; they were the brainchild of the Democrats for the purpose of creating another revenue stream for themselves. Companies pushed back by advocating for the right-to-work laws. Right-to-work laws exempt nonunion workers who are receiving union-negotiated wages from being forced to pay dues to the unions that negotiated those wages. This is wrong, but had the prevailing wage laws never been passed, there never would have been an issue! Eliminating prevailing wage laws will jettison the reason right-to-work laws were ever introduced in the first place.

In essence, the Democrats created the whole right-to-work mess. Union members should start thinking for themselves because their union officials have socialist mentalities and are often self-serving and narrow-minded. Sadly, they still strive to indoctrinate their members into supporting policies that, at base, are furthering the advance of socialism and communism.

Public Service Unions

When companies negotiate wages and benefits with unions, the companies are negotiating over company money. That, however, is not the case with public service employees. Their wages and benefits are paid by the government with taxpayer money. Unfortunately, for the taxpayers, this creates an opportunity for politicians to use wages and benefits as a means to secure votes for themselves and their party. They speak of these public employees as if they were the original disciples of Christ, promising them all they desire. They tell them that they are underpaid, overworked, and unappreciated, which of course resonates with them. So, these sometimes-unreasonable demands for compensation are first made by politicians. It is wrong for either party to use taxpayer dollars to secure votes, but that is exactly what the Democrats have done and will continue to do. They have secured this large voting bloc by promising and then delivering our taxpayer dollars to them. I am not saying that public service employees do not deserve a decent salary—everyone does. But it is wrong that they have been given a type of leverage that no other group in America has.

The leverage given to public sector unions by the Democrats is rewarded by campaign contributions and votes. All of the party's socialist, communist, and world government lunacy is of no concern to these folks; it is just human nature that they look out for themselves. This shortsightedness, however, has disastrous results: The United States of America is one step closer to becoming the North American Union, and then it is on to the one-world government. These union members are not bad people, but they are not going to bite the hand that feeds them—even if that means forfeiting their rights and freedoms and ours along with them.

Somehow, someway, this leverage must be taken away! Only then will this huge voting bloc be able to make an unbiased decision when casting their votes. I will only add here that the *exclusive* leverage given to the public service employees by the Democrats is also detrimental to all those dependent on the fossil fuel-related jobs. This is because **public service employees are a huge voting**

bloc, and they only vote for Green New Deal Democrats, who are massacring the fossil fuel-dependent group. Thus, public service employees are direct contributors to the demise of all workers that rely on the fossil fuel industry.

CHAPTER 20
The Media and Educators, the Elite's Indoctrinators

Indoctrination 1. To instruct in a body of doctrine or principles. 2. To imbue with a partisan or ideological point of view: children who had been indoctrinated against their parents' values.
—http://thefreedictionary.com

If you indoctrinate someone, you teach that person a one-sided view of something and ignore or dismiss opinions that do not agree with your view. Cults, political entities, and even fans of particular sports teams are often said to indoctrinate their followers.
—https://vocabulary.com/
dictionary/indoctrinate

If people are indoctrinated, they are taught a particular belief with the aim that they will reject other beliefs.
—https://collinsdictionary.com/
dictionary/english/indoctrinate

Indoctrinate definition, to instruct in a doctrine, principle, ideology, etc., especially to imbue with a specific partisan or biased belief or point of view.

—https://dictionary.com/browse/indoctrinate

In March 1915, the J.P. Morgan interests, the steel, shipbuilding, and powder interests and their subsidiary organizations, got together twelve men high up in the newspaper world and employed them to select the most influential newspapers in the United States and sufficient numbers of them **to control generally the policy of the daily press**... They found it was only necessary to **purchase the control** of twenty-five of the greatest papers. An agreement was reached; **the policy of the papers was bought,** to be paid for by the month; an editor was furnished for each paper to properly supervise and edit information regarding the questions of the preparedness, militarism, financial policies, and other things of national and international nature **considered vital to the interests of their purchasers.**

—Oscar Callaway, US congressman
representing Texas (1911–1917)

If you tell a lie long enough and keep repeating it, people will eventually come to believe it. The lie can be maintained only for such time as the State can shield the people from the political, economic and/or military consequences of the lie. It thus becomes vitally important for the state to use all of its powers to repress dissent, for the truth is the mortal enemy of the lie, and thus by extension, the truth is the greatest enemy of the State.

If you repeat a lie often enough, it becomes the truth.

The bigger the lie, the more it will be believed.

The truth is the greatest enemy of the State.
—Joseph Goebbels, Adolf Hitler's close associate and devoted follower

Our job is to give people not what they want, but what we decide they ought to have.
—Richard Salant, CBS News president (1961–1964 and 1966–1979)

CBS and other media giants control everything we see, hear, and read through television, radio, newspapers, magazines, books, films, and large portions of the internet. Their top officials and some journalists attend Bilderberg meetings—on a condition that they report nothing.
—Stephen Lendman, in his review of Daniel Estulin's book *The True Story of the Bilderberg Group*

The real menace of our republic is **the invisible government,** which like a giant octopus sprawls its slimy legs over our cities, states, and nation. To depart from mere generalizations, let me say that at the head of this octopus are the Rockefeller Standard Oil interests and a small group of powerful banking houses generally referred to as international bankers. **The little coterie of powerful international bankers virally run the United States government for their own selfish purposes. They practically control both parties,** write political platforms, make catspaws [a person used unwittingly or unwillingly by another to accomplish the other's own purpose] of party leaders, use the leading men of private organizations, and resort to every device to place in nomination for high public office only such candidates as will be amenable to the dictates of corrupt big business. **These international bankers and the Rockefeller Standard Oil interests control the majority of the newspapers and magazines in this country,** they use columns of these papers to club into submission or drive out of office public officials who refuse to do the bidding of the powerful corrupt cliques which compose **the invisible government.** It operates under cover of a self-created screen and seizes our executive officers, legislative bodies, schools, courts, newspapers, and every agency created for the public protection.

—John Francis Hylan, New York City mayor (1918–1925), in a speech in 1922

The Rothschild cabal have infiltrated your government, your media, your banking institutions. They are no longer content with committing atrocities in the Middle East; they are now doing it on their own soil [Europe], desperate to complete the plan for a one-world government, world army, complete with a world central bank.

—Vladimir Putin, Russian president, comment made to a Kremlin tour group in 2017

* * *

Of course, the quotations above refer to international bankers, that is, the communist elite who are identified as the Bilderberg Group as of May 29, 1954. The quotes explain why nearly every magazine, newspaper, search engine, radio and television news broadcast, internet article, and so-called talk-show comics are broadcasting anti-American propaganda. The international bankers have been buying up every form of media for over the past one hundred years and now have almost absolute control over everything we hear, read, and see. **Even comedians and social media are being censored.**

Changing channels is no solution because they are all broadcasting the same anti-American propaganda. This is part of their strategy! Having ownership or at least control of all the media outlets has given the elite the ability to brainwash the general public. When people hear the same thing over and over and over again on every radio and television station and read the same ideas printed over and over and over again in nearly every magazine and newspaper, they believe what they are being fed because the same thing appears in nearly every outlet. Unfortunately, because of this bombardment, they assume that it must be true! This amounts to brainwashing. We criticize communist governments for censoring their media, but that is exactly what is currently happening in the United States. **We are most certainly being censored, just not by the elected government—the communist elite are doing it**. They have taken control of nearly all the outlets and are using them to create a **New World Order**.

Even Corporate Retailers Are Censoring and Indoctrinating

The big, **corporate** retailers are refusing to market any product or merchandise that challenges the elite's narrative. For example, they will market the Black Lives Matter merchandise just fine but will not even consider marketing White Lives Matter or Police Lives Matter products. None of us are supposed to challenge *any* narrative pitched by the elite, and those of us that do are portrayed as being hateful and racist. It is obvious that big corporations are walking hand in hand with the elite and that America is becoming a corporatocracy. Just look at the definition of the word per Wikipedia:

"Corporatocracy is a term used to describe an economic and political system controlled by corporations or corporate interests, as opposed to the people's interests."

"Corporatocracy: A society or system that is governed or controlled by corporations."

The elite-owned and elite-controlled media (i.e., the mainstream media) use every tool at their disposal to brainwash the citizens of all nations.

It does not matter if you are watching the news or the liberal, so-called comics and talk show hosts, such as Jimmy Fallon, Jimmy Kimmel, Stephen Colbert, John Oliver, Trevor Noah, Seth Meyers, Bill Maher, or Samantha Bee. They are all spewing the elite's anti-American propaganda, which is intended to divide America. Every action taken by our antiestablishment president is mocked and ridiculed along with anyone supporting him and his anti-elite agenda. The networks are not interested in employing unbiased anchors or talk show hosts; they only hire activists or people willing to say or do anything for a paycheck. The best advice I can give is to just tune them out.

There are some antiestablishment media sources, but they do not get much exposure because they do not have the luxury of the limitless funds that the mainstream media receives from the party of the communists.

People do not seem to realize that **America is under attack**— not an imagined attack but a very real one that goes unnoticed and unchallenged because it is unconventional. Consider the elite to be the invading army. They have taken control of **our elections**, our money, our media, our unions, our universities, and a good portion of our government. The communists (via the CFR) have people embedded in every branch and level of our government: the State Department, the Department of Labor, the FBI, the Department of Justice, the Secret Service, the military, the Department of Agriculture, **the courts**, cities, and states—you name it, they have got it covered. America is no longer ours; it belongs to the elite. No shots fired; they just took it! An elected government means nothing if the government and its power are only instruments to be used by the elite. **Trump is the only president we have ever had with enough guts to challenge the communist elite, but the man is surrounded by enemies on both sides of the aisle.** He needs all the support that we can give him. Concerned Americans should make exposing the elite, their allies, and their agenda a top priority. Ousting the Democrats and all the elite's embedded Republicans and replacing them with **anti-elite Republicans** is the only solution for all of us desiring to save our republic. Sadly, that is not possible as things stand because our elections are rigged.

The Real News

Media sources refusing to bow to the elite and their narrative are few and far between. But they are out there. Fox News has some great anchors who are aware of what is really happening and desperately desire to tell their viewers about it, but they cannot because if they challenge the elite-controlled narrative beyond the network's allowed limit, they will be benched or unemployed. They will not dare

- mention the Bilderberg Group or speak of their agenda;
- mention the CFR and explain to us what they are, tell us that they are deeply embedded in our government, tell us who and what they represent (communists and communism), and tell us what their agenda is;
- tell us that Julian Assange is being tortured and humiliated in the UK for revealing forbidden knowledge to a deserving public;
- tell us that the Green New Deal and UN world government policies have been and are being made into law all across America since 1993 through the President's Council on Sustainable Development;
- tell us that **CFR-embedded city council members are creating HUMAN SETTLEMENTS** by not issuing permits for single family dwellings;

- tell us that **our climate is being manipulated** by technology as required to support a controlled narrative; or
- tell us that our elections are rigged.

Fox really drank the Kool-Aid!

If you really want to know what's going on, then you should consider reading, watching, and donating to the following pro-American authors, anchors, and media outlets:

Tom DeWeese, the American Policy Center (http://americanpolicy.org). Mr. DeWeese is the absolute authority on Agenda 21 and is ready, willing, and able to give help to anyone requesting it.

Stephen Lendman (http://stephenlendman.org). Mr. Lendman is truly a noble man. I love him because he just tells it like it is. He is one of only a few who refuse to bow to the elite.

Dane Wigington, GeoEngineering Watch (http://geoengineeringwatch.org). I cannot stress enough just how vital it is to follow the GeoEngineering Watch website. Mr. Wigington provides *overwhelming* and compelling evidence that our climate is being intentionally manipulated. I believe that even the proponents of the Green New Deal will be questioning the controlled narrative after visiting Mr. Wigington's site.

Global Research (http://globalresearch.ca). Global Research is an absolute must. They provide *real news*, not the elite-controlled narrative.

Eileen DeRolf, The Agenda 21 Course (http://agenda21course.com). Eileen DeRolf and Tom

DeWeese are the authorities on Agenda 21, and their work still calls for more attention.

Rev. Irvin Baxter, End Time Ministries (http://endtime.com). Rev. Baxter is amazing and details events that, in my opinion, prove that the elite's world government agenda is a reality nearing completion.

Daniel Estulin, author. Mr. Estulin is the absolute authority on the Bilderberg Group.

Gary Franci, Next News Network (http://nextnewsnetwork.com), and YouTube

Right Side Broadcasting (http://rsbnetwork.com)

James O'Keefe, Project Veritas (http://projectveritas.com)

Tom Fitton, Judicial Watch (http://judicialwatch.org)

The Epoch Times (http://theepochtimes.com)

Jack Posobiec, One America News Network (http://oann.com)

Newsmax (http://newsmax.com)

Lou Dobbs, FOX News

Tucker Carlson, FOX News

Biz Pac Review (http://bizpacreview.com)

Big League Politics (http://bigleagepolitics.com)

If America were still the nation that our Founding Fathers created, Tom DeWeese, Eileen DeRolf, Dane Wigington, Stephen Lendman, Daniel Estulin, Irvin Baxter, and others like them would be all over the airwaves. But that is not even scarcely possible because the elite have silenced them by taking ownership and control of nearly every media outlet in America and the wider world—thus, we are forced to listen to the elite's communist propaganda. **Maybe Fox News (they still have a few anchors that are not spreading the elite's anti-American sentiment), the One America News Network, Newsmax, the Next News Network, and, The Epoch Times will consider asking them to appear as guests.**

Support Them or We May Lose Them

We should all show our appreciation to these great patriots by donating whenever possible and encouraging others to visit their sites and donate as well. Honest, unbiased, and unscripted outlets are few and far between; we have to support the few that we have. These individuals are heroes in my world. I would drop to my knees and kiss the ground they walk on.

Chapter 21
Health Insurance

Health insurance was not a concern for me while I was an active member of the Boilermakers union. Though the cost of the insurance was astronomical, it was deducted out of my paycheck and in part covered by the contractors, so I did not really notice too much. It was not great insurance, but it was good enough. However, I lost that insurance when I retired in late 2012 and had to find something that would fit my budget. I contacted an insurance broker who offered many different policies, and I chose one that worked for me. It was not nearly as good as the insurance I had with the Boilermakers union, but at least I had something.

Then the Obamacare mandate took effect in 2014, forcing everyone into an Obamacare plan. All the premiums for the Obamacare plans offered to me (by the same broker) were twice that of the plan I was forced out of. If I did not choose one of these government plans, I would be punished by having to pay what is effectively a fine. This absolutely infuriated me. I already could not stand Obama, and now he was doing this to me. I was deeply disturbed by the idea that **the United States government was being led by a freedom-stealing socialist** and that the American populace was actually embracing him and his warped socialist/elitist policies. I will *never* accept a government that infringes on our individual rights and freedoms and would choose to go to jail before allowing myself to be any part of it. Consequently, I opted not to have health insurance and just pay the fine to my socialist government.

I realized that not having any coverage is a risky proposition, so I kept exploring options. One option was the discount cards, but they are not actually considered insurance. With them, **I would still be fined by Mr. Obama as punishment for not accepting socialism**. Then I stumbled across programs called Christian health sharing plans. Technically, these are not insurance but a system for members to share medical expenses with steady monthly share amounts. I visited the Liberty Healthshare website (http://libertyhealthshare. org) with skepticism and left with optimism. The share amounts, equivalent to premiums, were well below Obamacare premiums, and the coverage was even better than what I had with the outrageous health insurance provided through the union.

Still skeptical, I called Liberty Healthshare to confirm what I was reading on the website. After assuring me that it was, I immediately went to their site, filled out the online application, and was covered within just a few days. What a relief! I no longer had to stress about unforeseen medical expenses—and for far less than what I would have had to pay for any of the Obamacare plans. And although they are not technically considered insurance **(which would put them on Obama's shame-on-you-for-not-supporting-socialism list)**, they exempted me from the Obamacare fines. You can bet that the exemption was simply an oversight by the Obama administration. Had the Democrats been made aware that there were folks receiving coverage for medical expenses outside of Obamacare, they surely would have been punished with the removal of the exemption and who knows what else.

Moreover, unlike the Obamacare plans, the share amounts are the same for *all* income groups. Obamacare premiums are determined by individual income; the more a person makes, the higher the premium. **Those with higher incomes pay significantly more for the same coverage.** This is precisely why low-income earners and government dependents enthusiastically support Obamacare. Money from the higher income groups is taken, via higher premiums and against their will, to provide the funds necessary for low cost and even free health insurance to low-income individuals and government dependents. **If anyone needs an example of SOCIALISM, Obamacare is the crown-jewel!** Using Obamacare mentality, I will give the following analogy.

Anyone with the financial resources to purchase an automobile priced at $20,000 would be forced to pay an extra $10,000 in order to make that same car affordable to those below the poverty level. Those below the poverty level would pay $10,000 for the automobile previously priced at $20,000, and anyone above the poverty level would now pay $30,000. In essence, those above the poverty level would be forced to purchase automobiles for those below it.

The Obama administration and the world government elite's implementation of Obamacare is just one of the many means used to strip us of our rights, freedoms, liberties, and sovereignty.

There is still reason for concern today. **THE OBAMACARE CORE IS STILL IN PLACE**. If the Democrats take control in 2020, Obamacare will be quickly returned to its glory. Of course, those of us using health-sharing plans will no longer be exempt from Obamacare fines. **Mr. Trump tried in vain to fully repeal Obamacare while the Republicans were in control of both chambers during 2017–2018. It should not have been a problem, but it was. Why? Because the majority of our Republican legislators serve the elite**—not all of them but still enough to stonewall anyone or anything perceived as a threat to the elites and their agenda. Obviously, the elite will benefit from socialized healthcare, **as indicated by the Republicans lack of any sincere effort to repeal Obamacare.** Naturally, this is also the reason why **no sincere attempts have been made by the Republicans to secure ADEQUATE funds for the construction of a border wall or change our ridiculous immigration laws.**

I do not believe that health insurance should be an entitlement, but I do believe that everyone should have access to **affordable health insurance**. Obviously, the Democrats believe that people above the poverty level should be forced to, in essence, buy health insurance for those at or below the poverty level. That is just un-American and, in the end, completely insane.

The problems lie on two fronts. Medical care providers and facilities are gouging insurance companies, and insurance companies are gouging their policyholders. If the government would put its focus where it belongs and take appropriate action, there would not be a crisis. **Trump is trying, but the CFR-embedded puppets continue to run cover for the elite.**

I believe that many supporting Obamacare would have opted for a health-sharing plan had they been aware of the existence of such options. For those currently covered by an insurance company and those uninsured who need affordable health insurance coverage, I highly recommend that you consider a health-sharing plan. They offer good coverage at a price that anyone should be able to manage. Overall, health-sharing plans blow conventional plans away. There are no percentages with these plans. For example, if your conventional plan covers 80 percent of a $500,000 medical bill, you are stuck with a $100,000 out-of-pocket bill. In comparison, a single person enrolled with Liberty Healthshare would, at the time of this writing, only pay $1,000. Yes, I said $1,000. Dental and vision are not covered, but you can find discount dental and vision plans (I use Aetna, for example) that offer considerable savings with no waiting period.

CHAPTER 22
Our Origins and a Possible Connection to the Elite

Part One: The Megaliths

Ancient Megalithic Structures

Incredible, geometric, precisely built megalithic structures constructed with outrageously heavy stone that was most often quarried many miles from the construction sites exist all around the world. Their mere existence baffles scientists, geologists, stone masons, archaeologists, and engineers to this day. Many have attempted to explain how our ancient ancestors could have possibly achieved these fantastic feats of engineering, but none of these theories has been truly convincing. Some might be ranked as possible but not certainly probable. I have something of an obsession with this topic, so I have researched many of the attempted explanations and have concluded that none are credible. Even some of the better explanations only address the aspects of the structures that are more easily explicable but omit any part of the structures that cannot be so straightforwardly accounted for.

Giza, Egypt

Attempts to account for the existence of the Great Pyramid of Giza in Egypt are examples of a desperate scientific community trying to explain something that cannot be explained. Some possible, though unrealistic, construction theories have been offered for the Great Pyramid's core and casing. However, no one has ever presented a fitting explanation for how the precisely built granite inner chambers, consisting of stones weighing tens of thousands of pounds, were constructed and why and how they were built to precise tolerances that would be difficult to achieve even today. And *no one* knows what purpose these chambers really served; **every statement addressing the method of construction and their intended purpose is only speculation**. There is no need to build a tomb to such exact tolerances, which suggests to me that they served another purpose—a purpose that our most brilliant minds are still unable to figure out to this day.

How they sculptured the inner chamber and casing stones with such close fitment is one thing, but it goes way beyond that. How were they able to transport and hoist into position objects weighing thousands to tens of thousands of pounds each? I say "hoist" here because, in my opinion, explanations that rely on crude ramps, sleds, timber, and ropes are simply nonsense. It is also worth pointing out that the granite stones used for the inner chambers were transported over 500 miles.

At a few locations, the core stones were not jammed up tightly next to one another; some had gaps between them filled with smaller stones. However, that is relatively insignificant because these stones were stepped and only served as a base for the **highly polished and beveled Tura limestone casing stones**, which were precisely cut and fitted, providing a smooth finish that could not be climbed. To be clear, we are talking about a lot of heavy stones here—an estimated **2.3 million** individual stones were used to construct the Great Pyramid alone. Another apparently inexplicable mystery is that **the Great Pyramid has a distinct inward crease in the middle of each of its four sidewalls,** which are easily visible from the aerial views.

All kinds of people have offered theories about possible methods used by the ancients to construct the pyramids, but none have proven satisfactory. The discovery of a papyrus referencing a crew of two hundred journeying up the Nile River to transport rock from the quarry is used by some as proof that, naturally, our fellow human ancestors the ancient Egyptians built them. Though the scenarios presented for moving the blocks from the quarries to the construction site seem possible, they are nevertheless only speculation and not ultimately believable.

How were the blocks dragged or hoisted onto and off of the barges hauling them down or across the river? Keep in mind that we are not talking about a small number of stones or stones of small size. The average weight of the 2.3 million limestone blocks used for the pyramids core was five thousand pounds (note that the core stones were quarried close to the Great Pyramid). Imagining the loading and unloading of just one of these stones without machinery is mind-boggling enough, but imagining the loading and unloading of a full 2.3 million stones is beyond belief.

Indeed, how they transported the stones is just one of many unresolved questions. The pyramid stands 455 feet tall with a total of 210 stone layers, the larger blocks on the lower levels averaging 6.5–10 tons and the smaller stones used on the upper layers about 1.3 tons. How were they put into place, moved up to such heights with only simple machines and human power? And then there are the **144,000 casing stones, which were smoothly polished and precisely beveled to match the slope of the pyramid. They were placed together with an accuracy of five one-thousandths of an inch and, for those that are still extant, bonded with a mortar that is still holding to this day.** Had a huge earthquake not rocked the pyramid in AD 1303, the casing stones would most assuredly still be in place. The pyramid is also aligned with true north.

Imagining a primitive civilization having the ability to construct just one of these impressive monuments is nearly beyond belief, but eighty Egyptian pyramids have been discovered as well as many other mind-boggling structures, including obelisks, statues, the Saqqara underground labyrinth and the Karnak Temple in Luxor.

Obelisks

Obelisks are tapered monolithic pillars, with monolithic meaning made from a single stone. These ancient examples are huge, precisely tapered granite columns covered with expertly etched hiero-glyphs that exhibit the same degree of perfection as stone monuments sculptured today, which are only able to be made with the assistance of modern technology. The pyramidions (the pointy top sections) were often topped with gold or a natural gold-silver alloy called elec-trum, which was removed by archeologists or thieves through the years.

The largest is the Lateran obelisk in Italy, on land seized by the Romans from the pharaohs, standing just over 105 feet tall, and weighing over a million pounds. I do not and will never believe that a monolith weighing over one million pounds was precisely sculp-tured and raised by our ancient ancestors, period. Just for the sake of argument, let's say that they did construct it. We are to believe, then, that they expended all this effort for an ornament? Rigging procedures of the caliber required for such a feat are frequently used by highly skilled boilermakers today, but the equipment and tools used by them were not available to those credited with erecting these huge megaliths. Ropes, sleds, timbers, wagons, shovels, and ramps? I don't think so! And why were these mysterious obelisks topped with highly conductive electrum? They were constructed from granite stone, which is composed mainly of quartz. Quartz crystals are dis-tinguished by their interesting electrical properties. While they an insulator that is not conductive in itself, they also have piezoelectrical properties, meaning they can release electrical charges under certain conditions.

The idea that these skillfully crafted monuments were merely used as ornaments strains credulity. Given the properties of quartz, and also taking into consideration that the obelisks **were often capped with highly conductive materials,** it is more than likely that the obelisks are a form of highly advanced technology used by a supe-rior species. This species likely possessed an appearance very similar to our own and was coexisting with early humans. I am convinced that the obelisks are a type of technology that is so beyond the level of known science achieved thus far, that our most brilliant minds today are still incapable of fully understanding it. The same logic applies to the pyramids, or at least those exhibiting features that indicate advanced technology was used to construct them, like the precisely engineered internal chambers within the Great Pyramid of Giza. It is beyond belief that so much effort was expended just for passageways. The inner chambers of the Great Pyramid must have served a distinct technological purpose.

Saqqara, Egypt

Egypt is full of mystery. The Serapeum located in the Saqqara region is every bit as puzzling as the Great Pyramid and the obelisks. The Saqqara Serapeum is an underground labyrinth with a 382-yard-long passage lined with twenty-four side chambers carved into the bedrock. The Serapeum contains a total of twenty-five very heavy and precisely built (to a tolerance within 1 micron) sarcophagi (granite boxes) weighing seventy-thousand pounds each with perfectly matched granite lids weighing thirty-thousand pounds each. Twenty-two of the sarcophagi have-been placed into the snugly carved chambers, and three are in the isles located not far from the entrance. The lids are so precisely cut that when in place, the coffer is essentially hermetically sealed. The insides of the boxes are polished smooth and perfectly square. They were sculptured and polished above ground, some from rose granite that would have been quarried some five hundred miles from the site and some from diorite, a material even harder than granite, which would have to have been quarried six hundred miles away. After moving these stones such great distances, the builders must have then somehow lowered their huge masses into the ground.

But how? And why? The experts have it all figured out! They used ropes, sleds, timbers, ramps, wooden wedges, barges, pounding and shaping stones, relatively soft copper chisels (only wrought iron is hard enough to chip granite), and ramps? Twenty-five one-hundred-thousand-pound objects, which were even heavier prior to sculpturing, were transported five to six hundred miles, precisely sculptured with primitive tools, moved down a narrow underground passageway, and then turned and inserted snugly into chambers. No! No! No! Our ancient ancestors did not do that. Boilermakers or ironworkers could achieve the task of maneuvering the sarcophagi today, but it would still be a hell of an undertaking, requiring a lot of planning and equipment. Monorails, cranes, rollers, ramps, jacks, sleds, hoists, and more would all have to be employed to achieve the task. It just blows my mind that people at all levels of intelligence actually believe that our ancient ancestors did what they have been given credit for. Not surprisingly, many of the same minds that believe that our ancient ancestors accomplished these amazing feats also believe that the biblical character Samson got his incredible strength from his hair.

Karnak, Egypt

The Karnak temple complex is another impressive site in Egypt. Amazing temples, pylons, obelisks, and sculptures there exhibit precision that should have not been achievable at the time, casting doubt on the notion that our ancient ancestors did this sophisticated work. More likely, our human ancestors were utilized for certain tasks—but **they were not the architects**. The Ramses sculpture, along with a number of others, is **perfectly symmetrical.** How did our ancient ancestors accomplish that?

The colossal statue of the Eighteenth Dynasty pharaoh Akhenaten at East Karnak exhibits a distorted representation of the human form, a detailed yet strange human-like being. I believe that Pharaoh Akhenaten was among the visitors coexisting with early humans for a limited period of time and that he was one of the architects participating in the construction of these incredible ancient structures, built thousands of years ago. The experts (scientists, geologists, archaeologists, etc.) really do not know for sure how many thousands of years ago this must have been because rock cannot be carbon dated.

Baalbek, Lebanon

Perhaps the most interesting megaliths to me are the foundation stones used to support the Temple of Jupiter. They are believed to have been part of an earlier structure's ruins—a structure that existed many years, perhaps thousands, prior to the Temple of Jupiter being erected over it. Three of the sculpted foundation stones weigh an estimated two million pounds each and another twenty-five weigh an estimated nine hundred thousand pounds each. Three more sculpted stones still lie in a nearby quarry. The lightest is estimated to weigh 2,000,240 pounds and the other two are estimated to weigh 2,484,000 and 3,300,000 pounds. The stones still lying in the quarry are not just roughly cut pieces of stone; they have been sculpted to specific dimensions and were obviously meant to be transported and installed as part of the foundation at the temple complex as an addition to the trilithon, where similar stones were placed as long as fifteen thousand years ago. Think about it! We are to believe that, thousands of years ago, people used ropes, sleds, timbers, and ramps to maneuver stones weighing *millions of pounds*. Not even a chance! These would be easy tasks for skilled boilermakers today, but they have the advantage of lifting lugs, cranes, heavy hauling equipment, monorails, chockers, chains, slings, and sophisticated tools at their disposal.

Cusco, Peru

There are too many amazing megaliths in Peru to discuss fully and in detail, but I will mention a few here. The huge Temple Hill Fortress in Ollantaytambo has a partially constructed section of a wall consisting of six stones that were precisely sculptured to fit closely together. The architects even incorporated slip joints at the seams to allow for movement in case of an earthquake. The huge stones, weighing up to sixty-seven thousand pounds each, were quarried miles away from the top of the mountain, across the valley from the complex, transported down that mountain, moved across the long valley, and then up to the top of the steep slope to the fortress. Wow! Now imagine removing the wheels from a half-ton pickup truck and dragging it over this kind of terrain and distance. That would be quite an achievement, and the truck would only weigh around five thousand pounds.

The Temple Hill Fortress is another example of a project that was under construction by the visitors and suddenly interrupted. Work resumed at a later point in time, but the succeeding builders lacked the talent of the visitors; the successors' inferior work is easily distinguishable from that of the visitors.

The ancient stone walls at Sacsayhuaman also stand out. The huge stones that comprise it are all shapes and sizes but still **fit snugly together like a jigsaw puzzle**. There is not a person on this entire planet that can explain how the builders managed to shape and accurately fit the stones used to construct the numerous pylons, walls, and structures that exist throughout the Peruvian Andes.

Puma Punku, Bolivia

If the intricately cut stonework in Puma Punku, Bolivia does not have you scratching your head and doubting that our ancient ancestors had the ability to fabricate the magnificent monoliths there, then nothing will. The many *H*-shaped stones have a variety of identical, very detailed cuts in strange patterns. They appear to have been manufactured for some type of structure, but it is part of a sophisticated puzzle that no expert has yet figured out. An overhead view reveals an intentional geometric layout to these stones. This is just one group of stones among several that are sprawled across a huge area, each displaying intricate cuts and perfectly round holes of varying diameters.

As with other megalithic sites, it is obvious that this was a work in progress that was suddenly halted by an unknown event. Red sandstone was used—not as hard as granite but still very hard—hard enough that the precise cuts still have their sharp, detailed edges after what some archeologists have estimated to be some fifteen thousand years.

Gobekli Tepe, Turkey

Gobekli Tepe is a massive ancient stone temple that remained hidden from sight until 1994, when German archeologist Klaus

Schmidt realized that the exposed slabs of broken limestone, first observed by farmers in the 1960s, indicated more than the ancient graveyard that the farmers assumed it to be. Schmidt started excavating the site in 1996, and his work continues to this day. In my opinion, Gobekli Tepe offers the strongest case for the possibility that a superior species with an appearance very similar to our own was involved in the construction of many ancient megaliths.

Gobekli Tepe was constructed over eleven thousand years ago, predating writing, the wheel. Metallurgy, and agriculture. Yet more than two hundred pillar stones weighing from twenty-two thousand to over forty-four thousand pounds were quarried, sculptured, transported, and maneuvered into position to construct the twenty circular structures. Further, the huge pillars were fitted into sockets hewn into the bedrock and have impressive reliefs carved on them. A detailed sculpture of a crocodile was incorporated into one of the pillars on the third level. Thus far, only four of the circular structures have been excavated, but ground penetrating radar and geomagnetic surveys revealed that there are sixteen more still buried beneath the surface. Although the entire complex is spread out over twenty-two acres, only one acre has been excavated since the investigation began in 1996.

At this particular site, the quarry was relatively close, which was very seldom the case with other megaliths. Even though the stones did not have to be moved a great distance, however, they were still very large and heavy. Some quarried and sculpted pillar stones still lie in the quarry, one weighing an estimated one hundred thousand pounds. **Also, the four circular structures excavated so far have POLISHED terrazzo stone floors, so it is reasonable to assume that they all have this feature. HUH?!**

The site predates the discovery of metallurgy, so not even soft copper was available to be formed into chisels and used to shape the stone and carve the reliefs. The only tool at their disposal would have been **flintstone and rocks**. Can you imagine quarrying and sculpturing all those structures using only rocks as both hammers and chisels?

We should take a moment to review. Eleven thousand years ago, our ancient ancestors constructed twenty circular structures (complete with polished terrazzo stone floors and spreading over a twenty-two-acre area) that consist of over two hundred stone pillars weighing from twenty-two thousand to forty-four thousand pounds each that were quarried, sculptured, transported, and maneuvered into sockets that were chiseled into the bedrock with flintstones and stood upright. **I don't think so!**

On top of that, experts have determined that around ten thousand years ago our ancient ancestors deliberately backfilled the entire twenty-two-acre area for reasons no one can even begin to intelligently speculate on. The pillars stand about twenty feet tall. So, imagine backfilling a twenty-foot-deep, twenty-two-acre pit with buckets, scoops, and shovels. Filling a pit this large with the large powerful excavation equipment available today would be quite a task. But how can people sincerely believe that our ancient ancestors did this with buckets, scoops, and shovels? The notion that our ancient ancestors exhausted so much energy to fill that pit is not even within the realm of possibility! The ancients started using copper about ten thousand years ago, meaning they could have made buckets and shovels from it. However, since the wheel was not invented until 3500 BC, they could not have even had carts. The goal of the backfill was obviously to hide the site. But why and from whom? There are no realistic theories explaining how our ancient ancestors built Gobekli Tepe and then filled in the entire site. Its existence and what occurred there give credibility to the supposedly "out there" theories, suggesting that a species superior to our own could have been involved. Similar suggestions arise from the nine hundred thousand to three-million-pound stones that were quarried, sculptured, transported and maneuvered into position at the temple complex in Baalbek, Lebanon and the amazing accomplishments at the Serapeum in Saqqara, Egypt.

I believe that the monuments discussed thus far should be slap-in-the-face eye-openers for everyone because they present the strongest evidence that a species other than our own had to have been involved. I implore you to research these megaliths and think carefully and deeply about what was accomplished. It astounds me that they, along with many other amazing megaliths, are so easily considered the results of merely human endeavors—and that is if they are thought about at all. Many people do not even know that they exist or just do not care. Yet something incredible occurred thousands of years ago, and knowledge of how these amazing feats were accomplished may just lead us toward answers to some important questions about our existence. There are too many mysterious megalithic structures to discuss fully here, but the ones mentioned so far should have you thinking about these issues and desiring to learn of more.

The following are examples of manufactured structures that would have been within the realm of possibility for primitive man to achieve. However, I do not believe that such possibilities lie within the realm of probability.

Longyou Caves, China

Five huge, **artificially created caves** were discovered in 1992 by farmers investigating five ponds that had drained for no apparent reason. The floor area of each is over eleven thousand square feet, with ceiling heights of up to ninety-eight feet. **The ceiling, wall, and pillar surfaces all have a series of bands or courses spaced about twenty-four inches apart, running at an angle of about sixty degrees to the axis of the course. It appears as if some type of machinery or technology was used—and yet they are presumed to be thousands of years old.** Since there are no historical records of their existence, archeologists have no idea of just how many thousands of years ago they were fabricated. They may have existed for tens of thousands of years. **Further investigation has revealed nineteen more similar caves in the area, bringing the total to twenty-four thus far.**

Buddhist Caves, China

Caves, grottoes, shrines, statues, pillars, rooms, and rooms within rooms, all carved from solid rock—they are absolutely amazing. There are a number of these large cave complexes in the region, including the Mogao Caves of Dunhuang, China; the Longmen Grottoes in Luoyang; and the Yungang Grottoes near the city of Datong.

Equally impressive are the Buddhist grottoes in India—the Ellora, Ajanta, and Elephanta caves.

Lalibela Churches, Ethiopia

Did our ancient ancestors precisely sculpt eleven churches from solid rock in Lalibela, Ethiopia? They are truly amazing! Using the side of a mountain as a starting point for a project like this would have been advantageous, but that was not the way it was done here; the option was simply not available. They started the project at ground level and worked their way down, moving through the solid bedrock. The structures themselves are far from crude; they look like they could have been erected in modern times. **The locals claim that the ancient builders were assisted by angels.** No jackhammers, no cranes, no mechanical conveyor belts, no grinders, and no dust-collecting ducts. And what about protective gear? No safety glasses, no ear plugs, no dust masks (rags do not work so well), no hard hats, no steel-toed boots, and no face shields. The eye injuries alone would have been off the charts. What is more, **the churches are still being used to this day**.

Angkor Wat Hindu Temple, Cambodia

This amazing stone complex is **rumored to have been constructed by a divine architect.**

Borobudur Buddhist Temple, Indonesia

Borobudur is the world's largest Buddhist temple. It consists of nine stacked platforms, six square and three circular, topped by a central dome. Seventy-two open-work stupas (a hemispherical shaped object used as a place for meditation), each containing a statue of the Buddha, surround the circular platforms. Aerial views reveal that the temple has the classic shape of a pyramid.

Teotihuacan, Mexico

There are more than a thousand pyramids scattered throughout Central America. In addition, thus far, 135 have been discovered in Egypt and 240 in Sudan. Many areas around the world have pyramid-shaped mountains, inviting speculation that constructed pyramids may exist below some of them, hidden from sight by dirt and rubble accumulated over thousands and maybe even tens of thousands of years. The ancient architects used the pyramid form all around the world. Though the structures are not identical, the pyramid form is a constant.

Why this shape? The pyramid obviously had some kind of significance. Consider the structures at Teotihuacan. No one knows who built the complex for certain, but it was one of the largest urban centers in the ancient world. It encompassed an area of about eight square miles and had an estimated population of one hundred thousand people. The Avenue of the Dead runs more than two miles and consists of three major pyramid complexes: the Pyramid of the Sun, the Pyramid of the Moon and the Pyramid of the Feathered Serpent. **At some point in time, a fire occurred that was hot enough to scorch some of the stones along the Avenue of the Dead.** It takes a considerable amount of heat to scorch rock, so what did this? In 1983, archaeologists discovered unusual ceilings composed of six inches of mica placed between two layers of stone. Mica is used as a thermal insulator and is capable of withstanding extreme heat. The type of mica used would have come from Brazil, nearly four thousand miles from the site. Mica, it is worth noting, can have specific technological functions since it is an effective heat conductor but also an electric insulator.

Was the Pyramid of the Sun some type of technology that malfunctioned and resulted in a blast that was capable of scorching the stones along the Avenue of the Dead? And then there are the many (individual) artistic tiered platforms. They are beautiful, but what other purpose did they serve? Why would a people with the ability to construct something so perfect waste their time on something that has no apparent practical function? They wouldn't! These platforms had to have had some purpose or function beyond mere aesthetics. For example, they could have been receiving pads for some type of vessel or craft. The stupas used by Hindus and Buddhists for meditation could also have served a similar use.

To formulate their estimates for the age of these megaliths, archeologists rely primarily on carbon dating materials found at the sites. However, that does not tell us much because the carbon-dated material was most likely deposited by humans who stumbled across these magnificent structures and began inhabiting them, perhaps thousands of years after the actual builders abandoned them. Since rock cannot be carbon dated, the actual age of these megaliths could be much older than has usually been speculated.

Palenque, Mexico

King Pakal's sarcophagus lid depicts what appears to be the king in a cockpit. The skeptics call this a ridiculous, "out there" theory. But just look for yourselves. Look closely and you will probably realize that it actually does resemble a cockpit. There is nothing "out there" about it! I am not saying that it definitely *is* a cockpit, but it certainly does resemble one. Some 640 miles from Palenque in La Venta Tabasco, Mexico, an ancient stone carving referred to as Monument 19 has similar features.

Stonehenge

Stonehenge is an example of a megalithic structure that could have been built five thousand years ago using the speculated-on techniques. But that doesn't answer the question of why it was built at all. The thirty upright stones (sarsens) averaged a weight of twenty-five tons each and would have to have been transported over twenty miles from their source quarry. There were eighty-two stones total when the structure was still fully intact, with the weight of the small stones averaging two and a half to five tons each, and the larger stones averaging twenty-five tons each.

Just imagine being tasked with moving only one of the thirty twenty-five-ton stones twenty miles across an uneven, unpaved landscape. Engineers have suggested that the large stones could have been loaded onto wooden carts with ropes and then pulled by teams of two hundred men for a one-way trip estimated to take twelve days. Then the poor souls would have had to drag the empty carts back for another one—no mean feat since a wooden cart capable of supporting a twenty-five-ton stone would have been very heavy on its own. And they would have done this thirty times for the large stones and fifty-two more times for the smaller (but still very heavy) stones. These smaller stones are the inner bluestones, which would have been transported two hundred miles. There are so many questions:

- Why undertake such a laborious, time-consuming task? Those efforts could have been utilized for hunting and farming or building homes and cities.
- The Stonehenge complexes were skillfully arranged on the basis of celestial schedules for reasons still unknown to this day.
- Why was its location so far from the quarries? Why was it not constructed closer to them?

I chose to discuss Stonehenge because, while it would have been a hell of an undertaking for an ancient civilization, it is one of the few that would have been achievable even though the undertaking would have been arduous and taxing to the point of insanity. The Great Pyramid of Egypt, the obelisks, and other megalithic structures, however, are not so easily explained.

The Mayans and Ancient Egyptians Were Expert Astronomers, Mathematicians, and Engineers. Where Did They Get This Knowledge?

I believe that deities from a realm unknown to us were here on an assignment to observe and nothing more, but they chose to interact with humans and give our ancient ancestors forbidden knowledge. I believe that a number of megalithic structures were engineered by the deities and served a purpose clear only to them. King Pakal obviously interacted with the deities, but he and his people probably did not engineer the city.

The goal of this chapter is to provoke thought. In my opinion, the incredible feats said to have been accomplished by our ancient ancestors were not, in fact, done by them. Those accomplishments were simply out of reach for these ancient societies. But, nevertheless, the structures do exist. So, who did build these incredible works? Our ancestors from the future?

I admit that this is all going to sound a bit crazy to many, but I am going to present a thought-provoking argument for my beliefs about this matter. The Great Pyramid and the obelisks are some type of technology that was built and used by a superior species for a purpose known only to them. These beings were shuttled to earth from another planet, an alternate dimension, or the future to observe the early stages of human behavior and development but were ordered not to participate in any type of activity that would alter the course of events. Many of the huge and precisely constructed and engineered ancient megalithic structures existing around the world offer compelling evidence that a superior species inhabited the earth and was coexisting with humans thousands or maybe even tens of thousands of years ago.

The skeptics offer many cynical opinions and commentaries, suggesting that anyone questioning the ability of our ancient ancestors to construct these incredible monoliths is an idiot. I see it the other way around: I believe that they are the idiots. They focus on certain elements of a megalith or monolith that would have been possible, but they ignore the elements that were not.

The debunkers who sarcastically insinuate that anyone doubting the official line is stupid, but I would bet that the lot of them could not build a birdhouse without assistance. They are just idiots attempting to make themselves look intelligent. I would love to get an entire crew of the debunkers together and challenge them to recreate the methods and techniques that they claim were used by our ancient ancestors to accomplish what they supposedly did. If the debunkers are so confident about their theories, then they should have no problem backing them up. Maybe the History Chanel should arrange and finance a challenge for them. Ropes, sleds, wooden wedges, timbers, soft copper chisels, manpower, shovels, a trainload of Gatorade, and a team of cheerleaders should be provided to them so that they can prove that the tasks were achievable by ancient human beings. I am sure that they would appreciate the opportunity to flaunt the intelligence that they think they possess. Do not overload them; just give them three simple tasks:

1. Remove the twenty-five one-hundred-thousand-pound sarcophagi boxes from the Saqqara Serapeum.
2. At the trilithon temple complex in Lebanon, transport and maneuver into position the three quarried and sculptured stones, which weigh 2,000,240, 2,484,000, and 3,300,000 pounds, located 1,320 feet away.
3. Quarry six sixty-seven-thousand-pound granite stones from the top of the mountain that is across the valley from Ollantaytambo. Transport them down the mountain, through the long valley, and up to the top of the mountain where Ollantaytambo is located. Precisely sculpt them and the required slip joints between the stones, and then maneuver them into position.

I think we know what the outcome would be.

|||||||||||||||||||||||||||||||||||||||||||||||||||||||||||||||||||

CHAPTER 23
Our Origins and a Possible Connection to the Elite

Part Two: The Bible

While I do believe that some of the biblical figures existed and some of the events occurred historically, I also believe that many did not. A passage in the Gospel of John tells of Jesus healing a cripple next to the pool of Bethesda, even describing five porticoes (covered entrances or walkways) leading to the pool (John 5:2–9). Interestingly, archaeologists have recently found a location that fits with that description forty feet below the ground. However, even if that is the actual location being described, that in no way validates the actual occurrence of the event described in John. Religious texts should not be dismissed, but they should be questioned. I am not suggesting that God does not exist. However, some parts of the Old Testament cause me to question if it is in fact God's word or simply human words.

The Hebrew Bible was written over a long period of time, approximately between 1200 BC and 165 BC. Both the Old and New Testaments were written over a span of 1,500 years by at least forty writers. None of us were witnesses to any of these events, so how do we distinguish between fact and fiction? Much of the scriptures seem simply too bizarre to be believed and certainly not righteous. Here are some examples of God's laws and commands that seem suspect:

Numbers (King James Version)

Num. 31:7 And they warred against the Midianites **as the Lord commanded Moses; and they slew** all the males.

Num. 31:9 And the children of Israel took all the women of Midian captives and their little ones, and took the spoil of all their cattle, and all their flocks and all their goods.

Num. 31:17 **Now kill** every male among the little ones and **kill** every woman that hath known man by lying with them.

Num. 31:18 But all the women children, that have not known a man by lying with him, keep for yourselves.

Numbers: Synopsis of Commands

Num. 31:7 **Kill** all the males.

Num. 31:9 Take the women and children captive. Take their cattle, flocks, and goods.

Num. 31:17 **Kill** every living soul except the virgins.

Num. 31:18 You can have your way with the women children that are virgins.

Wow!

Deuteronomy (KJV)

Deut. 2:34 And we took all his cities at that time, **and utterly destroyed** the men and the women and the little ones of every city, we left none to remain.

Deut. 3:6 And we **utterly destroyed** them as we did unto Sihon King of Hashbon utterly destroying the men, women and children of every city.

Deut. 5:17 Thou shalt **not kill**.

Deut. 17:5 Then thou shall bring forth that man or that woman, and shall stone them with stones till they die.

Deut. 21:18–21 If a man have a stubborn and rebellious son which will not obey the voice of his father or the voice of his mother and that they have chastened him will not harken unto them: Then shall his father and his mother lay hold on him and bring him out unto the elders of his city and unto the gate of his place. And they shall say unto the elders of his city. This our son is stubborn and rebellious he will not obey our voice he is a glutton and a drunkard. And all the men of his city shall **stone him with stones that he die**; so shalt thou put evil away from among you; and all Israel will hear and fear.

Deut. 22:10 Thou shalt not plow with an ox and an ass together.

Deut. 22:23–24 If a damsel that is a virgin be betrothed unto a husband and a man find her in the city and lie with her; Then ye shall bring them both out unto the gate of the city and ye shall **stone them with stones that they die**; the damsel because she cried not, being in the city and the man because he hath humbled his neighbor's wife. So thou shalt put away evil from among you.

Deut. 23:1 He that is wounded in the stones or has his privy member cut off shall not enter into the congregation of the Lord.

Deut. 23:24 When thou comest into thy neighbor's vineyard then thou mayest eat grapes at then own pleasure; but thou shall not put any in thy vessel.

Deut. 23:25 When thou comest into the standing corn of thy neighbor, then thou mayest pluck the ears with thine hand but thou salt not move a sickle unto thy neighbor's standing corn.

Deut. 25:5 If brethren dwell together and one of them die and have no child the wife of the dead shall not marry without unto a stranger, her husband's brother shall go in unto her and take her to him to wife and perform the duty of an husband's brother unto her.

Deut. 27:23 Cursed be he that lieth with his mother in law.

Deuteronomy: Synopsis of Laws and Commands

Deut. 2:34 **Kill** all the men women and children.

Deut. 3:6 **Kill** all the men women and children.

Deut. 5:17 God's sixth commandment—**do not kill**?

Deut. 17:5 Sinners should be **stoned to death**.

Deut. 21:18–21 Disobedient children should be stoned to death by all the men in the city. (This seems a little extreme! I used to ground my kids off of video games).

Deut. 22:10 You can plow, but don't dare plow with an ox and an ass together!

Deut. 22:23–24 **Kill** cheating wives and their lovers.

Deut. 23:1 Men that have no penis and any with wounded testicles (injured or vasectomy) are not welcome in heaven.

Deut. 23:24 You can eat all of your neighbor's grapes that you desire—as long as you only do it on his property.

Deut. 23:25 You can pluck by hand and take all of your neighbor's corn that you can carry, but you are not allowed to do it with any kind of a tool.

Deut. 25:5 If you live with your brother and his wife, and he dies, then his widow is yours—whether she likes it or not.

Deut. 27:23 Men should not have sex with their mother in laws. Umm…

Ezekiel, Joshua, Samuel, and Chronicles (KJV)

Ezek. 44:9 Thus saith the Lord God; No stranger uncircumcised in heart nor **uncircumcised in flesh** shall enter into my sanctuary of any stranger that is among the children of Israel.

Josh. 6:21 And they **utterly destroyed** all that was in the city both man and woman, young and old, and ox, and sheep, and ass, with the edge of the sword.

Sam. 18:27 Wherefore arose and went he and his men and **slew** of the Philistines two hundred men; and David **brought their foreskins** and they gave them in full to the king that he might be the king's son in law. And Saul gave Michal his daughter to wife.

Chron. 14:10 And David inquired of God, saying, Shall I go up against the Philistines? wilt thou deliver them into mine hand?

Joshua, Samuel, Chronicles, and Ezekiel: Synopsis of Laws and Commands

Ezek. 44:9 **Uncircumcised men** are not welcome in heaven.

Josh. 6:21 God commands to **kill**.

Sam. 18:27 David, a man of God, **killed** two hundred men and then he and his men cut off their penis heads and presented them as an offering to King Saul. In return, King Saul offered his daughter's hand in marriage to him. (Maybe the king asked for their opponents' helmets and David misunderstood).

Chron. 14:10 David has a personal conversation with God. David asks God if he should attempt to defeat the Philistines and, if so, will God assist him and his army with **killing** them.

You can draw your own conclusions, but this is all lunacy to me. God's sixth commandment says "**Thou shalt not kill**" yet, on multiple occasions, God has apparently given direct orders to kill men, women, and children, whether in war of for some other reason. And God also commanded that disobedient children and sinners be taken to the gates of their cities and stoned to death. Such a violent act does not fit with what we believe God is and represents. Thus, I do not believe those were God's actions or directives.

Many of the stories in the Bible are partial accounts of actual events into which fabricated, **fictional dialogues** were interpolated by a group of men who were trying to mitigate the concern that a society existing without the fear of serious repercussions for undesired behavior would result in total chaos. Their logic was to convince humankind that there is an almighty entity who offers everlasting life to those who obey God's commandments—and a fiery, painful, everlasting existence in hell for all those who do not. The Bible tells us that we have a spirit, and maybe we do. But a spirit would be non-biological. How would it be possible for a non-biological existence to feel pain from fire or anything else, for that matter? Once again, I am not saying that there is not an all-powerful God. However, I am saying human beings used the existence of God as a tactic to manipulate society by instilling fear.

The Council of Nicaea and the Savior

We are told that the Council of Nicaea was responsible for reviewing and establishing the authenticity of biblical texts and determining which of them should be included in the Bible. Essentially, their goal was to establish consensus. Their tactic was similar to that used by a group of people trying to avoid being implicated in a crime. The group would have to agree on a script and stick to it because, if any of them deviated from the script, their story would fall apart. Biblical writings from the Old Testament detail very strict codes of ethics that were required of people if they desired to enter the kingdom of God after their biological death and receive everlasting life.

Obviously, as time passed, the Council of Nicaea realized that the code of ethics outlined in the Old Testament was unachievable by the majority. As a result, they had to lower the bar, otherwise only a few dozen of us would ever make it past the pearly gates. They desired to keep hope alive, so they created a savior. Jesus Christ was born. Glory be! Now we have a savior, and all he requires is that we believe that an almighty God exists and we try to live by his commandments. Beginning with the savior's creation, we no longer are required to actually live by God's commands. Just trying to do so is good enough as long as we keep the faith Jesus will wash away all our sins and forgive us—all in return for us doing nothing more than trying to be righteous and believing that there is an almighty God. I will say again: I am not saying that God does not exist, but I am saying that **some** biblical scripture may have been **manufactured** by the Council of Nicaea as part of an effort to steer society in the desired direction, thus avoiding total chaos. But the savior's arrival brings up an important question: What about all the poor souls that expired prior to his arrival? Are they just out of luck and out of hope?

Superstitions and Self-Servers

Many believe every word printed in the Bible. I am not insinuating that they are ignorant—just superstitious. So much so that they fear questioning anything in the Bible out of fear that they will be punished by God and not be allowed into heaven when their biological body expires.

Those who pray for themselves are a pathetic, self-serving lot. Professional athletes can be used as an example. It is common for them to thank God for a victory, and they even pray for victory. How truly pathetic! There are children born without limbs, people starving to death around the world, and people just struggling to survive. Yet these self-serving, **privileged idiots** pray for a touchdown! And if there is a touchdown, they drop to their knee (as they do while refusing to stand for America's national anthem), point to the sky, and thank God for answering their prayer. These idiots have the brain capacity of a newborn duck! They actually believe that God has chosen to involve himself with professional sports and has given their prayers priority over the limbless and sometimes wheelchair-bound children that we see during the Shriners and St. Jude's commercials. If they truly understood and lived by the Bible, then **all** their prayers would be focused on the less fortunate and not themselves. As long as there are people on this planet that are worse off than the professional athletes praying for touchdowns, baskets, home runs, holes in one, and goals, it is and always will be a pathetic, self-serving act. The same also applies to the wealthy, privileged celebrities advocating for socialism or communism. They pray to God, thanking him for their wealth and success, believing that God has favored them over limbless, wheelchair-confined children. What a pathetic bunch of self-serving morons!

Media Ministers

The majority of these kinds of ministers are nothing but greedy, self-serving businesspeople. I currently only watch one. I used to watch another, though, only because his political views and commentary aligned with mine. I usually would not watch past the political commentary, but one night I did, and what I witnessed dissuaded me from ever watching again.

The minister's son was pleading for donations, which is fine in itself. His tactics, however, were anything but righteous; he had a real sales pitch. "Donate at least forty dollars per month to the ministry and God will reward you!" During the segment, a man and his wife claimed that they had fallen on hard financial times and were about to lose everything due to a failing concrete business that he and his wife had established. But then they saw the minister's son (**preaching a bullshit lie**) on the ministry's show and decided to gamble. They alleged that after giving forty dollars per month to the ministries, their luck spun around 180 degrees, and their business was booming. Really? So, the Lord will grant prayers requesting touchdowns and monetary desires but not prayers requesting that missing limbs be replaced or vision restored to those whom are blind or good health restored to those with terminal illnesses. I wonder how much a person afflicted with any of those would have to donate. Would eighty dollars per month produce a miracle arm or leg? I despise these vultures! They prey on the credulous, many of whom are senior citizens on fixed incomes.

But there is one preacher that I believe is exactly what he appears to be, a man of God. That is Irvin Baxter. He is a biblical scholar and hosts the syndicated biblical prophecy television program *End of the Age*. Though biblical prophecy is all speculation and interpretation, he presents a compelling case that the biblical prophecy describing the end times aligns with events that have already occurred and are presently occurring. I sense a sincerity in him lacking in all of the others.

The next chapter will cover more of the relevant religious texts and will also discuss portions of scripture that I believe were not altered or fabricated by the Council of Nicaea.

CHAPTER 24
Our Origins and a Possible Connection to the Elite

Part Three: The Book of Ezekiel, the Book of Enoch, and the Watchers

Since I maintain that the Bible consists of both fiction and reality, I obviously do not believe everything written in the Bible. I do believe some of it, however. And I have always been fascinated with the numerous descriptions of the fiery chariots mentioned in scripture because they do not align with the idea that God and the angels are spiritual beings. **Why would spiritual beings need transportation?** The descriptions in Ezekiel are very certainly describing an eyewitness account of extremely advanced technology that was considered by Ezekiel to be a spiritual encounter.

The story is believable because, at the time it was written, there was nothing on this earth that would have even remotely resembled what Ezekiel described. Technology did not exist; there were no radios, televisions, magazines, or science fiction novels that could have planted in his mind what was described. It only stands to reason that he actually saw precisely what was described. I am including Ezekiel 1:4–28 (King James Version) in this chapter because I believe that it offers compelling evidence that our ancient ancestors witnessed some amazing technology, events, and interactions that were interpreted as spiritual encounters. The italicized text included with some of the quotations is my own commentary.

> Ezek. 1:4–7 And I looked, and, behold, a whirlwind came out of the north, a great cloud, and a fire infolding itself, and a brightness was about it, and out of the midst thereof as **the colour of amber, out of the midst of the fire**. Also out of the midst thereof came the **likeness** of four living creatures. And this was their appearance; they had the likeness of a man. And every one had four faces, and every one had four wings. And their feet were **straight feet;** and the sole of their feet was like the sole of a calf's foot: **and they sparkled like the colour of burnished brass.**

> *Could they have been robots?*

> Ezek. 1:8 And **they had the hands of a man** under their wings on their four sides; and they four had their faces and their wings.

> *"The hands of a man" could be describing robotic hands.*

> Ezek. 1:9 Their wings were joined one to another; **they turned not when they went**; they went **everyone straight forward.**

> *"They turned not and they all went straight forward." That says a lot! It had to be a mechanical device, perhaps a mechanical arm with appendages being extended and retracted from the vessel.*

> Ezek. 1:10 As for the likeness of their faces, they four had the face of a man and the face of a lion

on the right side; and they four had the face of an ox on the left side they four also had the face of an eagle.

Obviously, Ezekiel's mind was running wild during this event. It may be that there were four separate mechanical arms, each having different appendages that he convinced himself were faces. The perceptions of a man, a lion, an ox, and an eagle were created by his mind as he was trying to make some kind of sense out of what he was observing.

Ezek. 1:11–12 Thus were their faces: and their wings were stretched upward; two wings of every one were-joined one to another, and two covered their bodies. **And they went everyone straight forward**: whither the **spirit was to go, they went; and they turned not when they went.**

A bright beam of light was obviously mistaken for a spirit, and the light was attached to the mechanical arm that was moving in and out of the vessel.

Ezek. 1:13 As for the likeness of the living creatures, their appearance was **like burning coals of fire**, and **the appearance of lamps**: it went up and down among the living creatures; and the fire was bright, and out of the fire **went forth lightning**.

Bright lights and fire were moving up and down these things as they were emitting lightning. Ezekiel saw something incredible, but it was not God.

Ezek. 1:14 And the living creatures ran and returned as the appearance of a flash of lightning.

Obviously some kind of relatively advanced technology, the mechanical arms were being extended and retracted very quickly.

Ezek. 1:15–16 Now as I behold the living creatures, behold one wheel upon the earth by the living creatures, with his four faces. The appearance of the wheels and their work was unto the **colour of a beryl**: and they four had one likeness; and their appearance and their work was as it were a wheel in the middle of a wheel.

Beryl is a stone of many colors, including green, blue, yellow, red, and white. Biological living creatures do not have the characteristics described by Ezekiel but highly advanced technological creations would.

Ezek. 1:17–18 When they went, they went upon their four sides: and **they turned not** when they went. As for their rings, they were so high that they were dreadful; and **their rings were full of eyes** round about the four.

"Their rings were full of eyes" has to be a reference to windows or lights.

Ezek. 1:19 And when the living creatures went the wheels went by them: and when the **living creatures** were lifted up from the earth, the wheels were lifted up.

It is possible that the "living creatures" were actually an autonomous artificial intelligence.

Ezek. 1:20 Whither so ever the **spirit** was to go, they went, thither was their **spirit** to go; and the wheels were lifted up over against them: for the **spirit** of the **living creatures** was in the wheels.

Any kind of advanced technology was not known at the time; the only light known to them was from fire. Thus, any source of light beyond that produced from fire was believed to be a spirit.

Ezek. 1:21–23 When those went, these went; and when those stood these stood; and when those were lifted up from the earth, the wheels were lifted up over against them: for the **spirit** of the living creature was in the wheels. And the likeness of the **firmament** upon the heads of the living creatures **was as the colour of a terrible crystal**, stretched forth over their heads above. And under the **firmament** were their wings straight, the one toward the other: everyone had two, which covered on that side, their bodies.

Apparently, more than one vessel was involved.

Ezek. 1:24 And when they went, I heard **the noise of their wings like the noise of great waters**, as the voice of the Almighty, the voice of speech, as the noise of a host: when they stood, they let down their wings.

He heard the propulsion system or noise created from whatever type of technology these highly advanced visitors were using to maneuver.

Ezek. 1:25 And there was a voice from the **firmament** that was over their heads, when they stood, and had let down their wings.

I believe that the occupants of the vessel or the vessel itself conversed with Ezekiel. **Artificial intelligence will function on this level and beyond thousands of years from now.**

Ezek. 1:26 And above the firmament that was over their heads was **the likeness of a throne**, as **the appearance of a sapphire stone**: and upon the likeness of the throne was the likeness of the appearance of a man above upon it.

Ezekiel saw some type of a vessel or craft and convinced himself that anything as spectacular as what he was seeing could only be God and the throne of God.

Ezek. 1:27 And I saw the colour of amber, as the appearance of fire round about within it, from the appearance of his loins even upward, and from the appearance of his loins even downward, I saw as it were the appearance of fire, and it had the brightness round about. *Ezekiel attributed a human likeness to the vessel and was actually convinced that he was seeing almighty God.*

Ezek. 1:28 As the appearance of **a bow that is in the cloud in the day of rain**, so was the appearance of the brightness round about. This was the appearance of the likeness of the glory of the Lord. And when I saw it, I fell upon my face, and I heard a voice of one that spake.

A bright ring resembling a rainbow surrounded the vessel.

Ezekiel 2 describes a conversation between the vessel or craft believed by Ezekiel to be God. He was commanded to go into Israel and deliver God's words, which were provided to him from a rolled book that God gave to him and ordered him to eat. Yes, he was commanded to eat the book. Per the story, he ate it and the word of God was then with him.

I believe that Ezek. 1:4–28 describes actual events because, during that period, no man could have imagined what Ezekiel described without actually seeing something like it himself. The account is comparable to what we see in science fiction movies. It is possible that the occupants of the vessel or the vessel itself engaged in conversation with Ezekiel. (Thousands to hundreds of thousands of years from now, artificial intelligence will become living entities, thinking, planning, and making decisions of their own free will.) However, the specific dialogue recounted in Ezekiel 2 was created by the Council of Nicaea.

The Book of Enoch

Many people are unaware that the Book of Enoch even exists because it was not included in the traditional Bible. I believe that the Council of Nicaea excluded it because **they feared that future generations may figure out** that the events revealed in the text suggest that a superior species, which nevertheless closely resembled human beings, was conducting forbidden activities with our species.

The Council of Nicaea's and the Catholic Church's objective was to review all relevant religious texts, determine which ones delivered their desired script, and omit any that challenged the existence of a spiritual world. It is possible that they were concerned that the book of Enoch revealed knowledge of events that could expose something very different than what we have been led to believe. The Bible describes advanced technology in great detail in Ezekiel 1:4–28. Moreover, "fiery chariots" are mentioned several times in both Enoch and the Bible as a whole. I would speculate that this content was allowed to remain in the books because what it describes could be seen as divine or angelic creations.

The Watchers and giants detailed in the book of Enoch are also mentioned in the Bible but are only given brief consideration. Why? Most likely, the global effort to dismiss the true significance of the sophisticated and highly engineered megaliths is an ongoing conspiracy intended to divert attention away from the visitors/Watchers and their activities. It is also possible that other books were omitted from the Bible for the same reason.

There is overwhelming evidence that superior beings, very similar in appearance to ourselves, coexisted with our ancient ancestors. Yet this evidence continues to be mocked and dismissed. That is suspicious because there is enough evidence to support the existence of the Watchers and that they have a key role in the events I have been discussing here—events known to the Council of Nicaea, the Vatican, and world governments. A desperate effort to conceal the reality of the Watchers and the events tied to them exists to this very day.

Certain passages in the Bible refer to the angels as spiritual beings, but I believe that those references were fabricated by the Council of Nicaea as an attempt to divert attention away from scripture revealing that they were, in fact, biological. Lot ate bread with the angels, and the gay men of the city desired to rape them. These so-called angels also fornicated with women.

In essence, the Bible tells us that a superior species chose to colonize the earth with an inferior species. Why would they do that? They wouldn't! Would we create an inferior subspecies of ourselves to colonize other planets? No, that is just ridiculous! Overwhelming evidence exists suggesting that we were visited thousands of years ago by a species very similar to ours (perhaps even identical in appearance) that possessed abilities, knowledge, and skills far exceeding our own. Ezekiel 1:4–28, the megaliths, ancient art depicting technology, and the ancients' impressive knowledge of astrology, engineering, and mathematics all offer compelling evidence that such beings coexisted with our ancestors thousands of years ago. And some very credible descriptions of UFO encounters during more recent times (which will be discussed in the next chapter) indicate that they are still monitoring and possibly coexisting with us to this day.

Both the Bible and the Book of Enoch tell us that God was angered not only by fornication between the so-called angels and humans but also by the giving of forbidden knowledge to humans. We should analyze both of these aspects. Why would God have an issue with giving knowledge to an emerging species? Why would the rate at which a civilization advances be a concern for God? The fact is, it would not be unless it posed a threat or a danger. Now, before reading any further, really think about everything I have said thus far. Take it all into consideration and keep it closely in mind as you read the next several paragraphs.

Time Travelers

We know that we have evolved from a subspecies and that, over very long periods of time, our DNA has changed and will continue to do so. Imagine that time travel is realized several thousand or possibly hundreds of thousands of years into the future. Physicists theorize that forward time travel is a possibility, but according to current understandings of physics, reverse time travel is not. Einstein's theory of special relativity says that time slows down or speeds up depending on how fast an object is moving relative to something else. For instance, at the fastest speeds that have so far been achievable, it would take over thirteen million years to reach the nearest star in Orion's Belt. But if we could travel at the speed of light, it would only take 736 years to get there. Although current knowledge does not suggest that reverse time travel would ever be possible, when and if forward time travel is achieved, new discoveries in physics may reveal themselves. Such new information could lead to not only backward time travel but other advanced technology—the kind of technology that would make humans from the future appear godly to ancient humans. The evidence indicates that it is possible that our ancestors from the very distant future figured out how to travel into the past.

The Watchers were probably a select group of backward time travelers chosen to observe their ancient ancestors, but they were instructed to offer no knowledge or indulge in any type of activity that could possibly alter the future they came from. That is a possible explanation for why revealing knowledge to human beings was forbidden; in theory, altering events from an earlier time period could have catastrophic consequences for the future.

I speculate that our ancient ancestors witnessed and interacted with humans from the future who looked nearly identical in appearance but had a slightly different DNA structure due to evolution or maybe even DNA manipulation. Their DNA was close enough to produce a fetus with their slightly different ancient ancestors, but that slight difference was enough to cause mutations. This theory aligns with the events and evidence discussed here. There is ample evidence supporting the existence of biblical giants and mutants and their parents.

Giants and Mutants Were the Result of Our Ancient Ancestors Fornicating with Their Slightly Different Ancestors from the Future

The spectacular ancient megaliths provide overwhelming evidence that beings with abilities and knowledge far exceeding our own were interacting with our ancient ancestors. Their assignment was only to observe, but they reveled in being worshiped as if they were gods and took advantage of the that status. The males in particular took full advantage of the situation. They fornicated with any woman they desired, married or not. Their husbands and the chosen women gave no resistance because they were afraid to challenge any of the desires of God's so-called heavenly angels. The following biblical verses from Judges (from the King James Version) describe how Samson was conceived and suggest that a superior species visited our planet thousands of years ago and fornicated with our ancient ancestors.

> Judg. 13:2–3 And there was a certain man of Zorah, of the families of the Danites, whose name was Manoah; and his wife was barren, and bare not. And the **Angel of the Lord** appeared unto the woman, and said unto her, Behold now,

thou art barren and barest not: but **shall conceive,** and bear a son.

Judg. 13:6 Then the woman came and told her husband, saying, **A man of God came unto me** and his countenance was like the countenance of an, very terrible: but I ask him not whence he was, **neither told me his name**.

Judg. 13:20 For it came to pass, **when the flame went up toward heaven from off the altar, that the angel of the Lord ascended in flame of the altar.** And Manoah and his wife looked on it and fell to their faces to the ground.

The biblical account of Samson's conception indicates that his father was a biological being very similar to us but with a slightly different DNA structure who lusted for and impregnated *a married woman* from our species because he was horny and he could. What the event amounts to is rape! **Samson's conception was not planned; it was the result of lust.** The beings referred to as God's heavenly angels and the Watchers were most likely a superior biological species who were visiting planet Earth (or an earlier time period on Earth) on assignment and were given strict orders by their superiors to not interact with our species. The story of Samson's conception clearly indicates that they ignored those orders. I believe that Samson was a genuine historical figure and that his great strength was the result of a mutation that occurred from two slightly different biological species interbreeding. The story of his hair being the source of his strength, however, was obviously fabricated by the Council of Nicaea.

The First Book of Enoch: The Book of Watchers

The following passages are from the R. H. Charles version of 1 Enoch, published in 1923. I believe these passages support my belief that a superior species interacted with our own thousands of years ago. The bolding of some phrases is my own.

> And it came to pass when the children of men had multiplied that in those days were born unto them beautiful and comely daughters. **And the angels, the children of the heaven, saw and lusted after them**, and said to one another: "Come, let us chose us wives from among the children of men and beget us children." And Semjaza, who was their leader, said unto them: "I and said to one another I fear ye will not indeed agree to this deed, and I alone shall have to pay the penalty of this **great sin**." And they all answered him and said: "Let us all swear an oath, and all bind ourselves by mutual imprecations not to abandon this plan but to do this thing." Then sware they all together and bound themselves by mutual imprecations upon it. And they were in all two hundred; who descended in the days of Jared on the summit of Mount Hermon, and they called it Mount Herman, because they had sworn and bound themselves by mutual imprecations upon it. And these are the names of their leaders: Semiazaz, their leader, Araklba, Rameel, Kokabiel, Tamiel, Ramiel, Danel, Ezeqeel, Baraqijal, Asael, Armaros, Batarel, Ananel, Zaqiel, Samsapeel, Satarel, Turel, Jomjael, Sariel. These are the chiefs of tens.
>
> And all the others together with them took unto themselves wives and each chose for himself one, and **they began to go in to them and to defile themselves with them, and they taught them charms and enchantments, and the cutting of roots, and made them acquainted with the plants. And they became pregnant,** and

they bare **great giants**, whose height was three
thousand ells.* And when men could no longer
sustain them, the giants turned against them
and devoured mankind. And they began to sin
against birds, and beasts, and reptiles, and fish,
and to devour one another's flesh, and drink the
blood. Then the earth laid accusation against the
lawless ones (1 Enoch 6–7).

The angels had to have been made aware that mutations would
occur, but they clearly did not care; the women looked good and
gave no resistance, and the time travelers were lustful. They enjoyed
their status in this ancient world and chose not to return to their own
time. It can be assumed that females from the future were also a part
of the group. The time travelers were probably allowed to fornicate
with each other, but any offspring would eventually be shuttled back
to the future with their parents.

Our ancestors from the future were angered and concerned
because the time traveler's (that is, the angel's) activities were dangerous and reckless and had to be stopped. Apart from the forbidden fornication, they were also revealing forbidden knowledge to our
ancient ancestors—knowledge that could produce dire consequences
by altering the evolution of mankind. This could have the speculative
outcome of fundamentally changing or even completely annihilating
the time branch or period that the travelers originally came from.

---

* A biblical cubit/ell equates to eighteen inches; thus, three thousand times
eighteen inches would equate to four thousand five hundred feet tall. The height
of the giants being stated as three thousand cubits may have been fabricated by
the Council of Nicaea as an effort to divert from the reality of the actual height
of the mutants being twelve to fifteen feet. People would consider the existence
of mutants with a height of twelve to fifteen-feet to be within the realm of
possibility so the Bibles creators exaggerated descriptions of the mutants or
giants so that they would appear to be just fictional characters.

The Cover-Up

It has been reported that many huge skeletal remains have been discovered at locations all around the world—only to be taken away by authorities and never seen again. Sardinia, Italy has one such site where such activity is rumored to be occurring now. The Smithsonian Institution has been accused of being involved with the cover-up in the United States. This organization was founded in 1846 and is an extension of the United States government, with congressional members sitting on its board of regents. Reports of the Smithsonian involvement with the cover-up date back to the early 1900s. It is claimed that Smithsonian representatives mysteriously show up at ancient burial sites whenever reports of giant skeletons being found in them began to circulate. In every case, they took the skeletons, which are then never seen or mentioned again. It has also been claimed that these representatives or agents purchase giant skeletons excavated by private citizens. Some of the skulls are reported to have two rows of teeth and very large jaws. So, it appears as though the conspiracy to hide the existence of an extinct race of giants started near the early 1900s and continues to this day around the world. As to why, in my opinion, the controlled narrative has three objectives:

1. Dismiss and mock any person or argument challenging the controlled narrative that our ancient ancestors had the ability to construct megaliths that would require tools, equipment, and engineering skills not available to them.
2. Conceal any evidence supporting the existence of now extinct hybrids or mutants that were produced as a result of slightly different humans from the future fornicating with their ancient ancestors and the hybrids fornicating with each other.
3. Dismiss and mock any and all reports of UFOs regardless of the evidence and the credibility of the witnesses.

Obviously, world authorities are hiding something so incredible that the creation and implementation of a **controlled narrative** was considered necessary to mitigate the predictable panic reaction from the public.

For further reading on this topic, please consider *The Encyclopedia of Ancient Giants* by Fritz Zimmerman and *The Ancient Giants Who Ruled America* by Richard J. Dewhurst.

Forbidden Knowledge and So-Called Mythology

It is illogical to believe that sophisticated megaliths were created thousands of years ago by primitive humans but also that the structures are so complicated that contemporary experts are still scratching their heads, trying to figure out how they were built. There had to have been interaction with a superior species. Religious or not, one cannot deny that the unexplainable, sophisticated megaliths exist and that advanced knowledge of math, astrology, and engineering had to have been involved in their construction. Had our ancient ancestors achieved this on their own, we would currently be living in a world like we see in the science fiction movies. Thus, I have no doubt that a superior species interacted with our ancient human ancestors.

The First Book of Enoch: The Book of Watchers

The following passages are from the R. H. Charles version of 1 Enoch. They explain how our ancient ancestors acquired knowledge previously unknown to them. Again, the bolding is my own addition to the text.

> And Azazel **taught men** to make swords, and knives, and shields, and breastplates, and made known to them the metals (of the earth) and the art of working them, and bracelets, and ornaments, and the use of antimony, and the beautifying of the eyelids, and all kinds of costly stones, and all colouring tinctures. And there arose much godlessness, and they committed fortification, and they were led astray, and became corrupt in

all their ways. Semjaza **taught** enchantments, and root-cuttings, Armaros the resolving of enchantments, Baraqijal (taught) astrology, Kokabel the constellations, Ezeqeel the knowledge of the clouds, (Araqiel the signs of the earth, Shamsiel the signs of the sun), and Sariel the course of the moon. And as men perished, they cried, and their cry went up to heaven (1 Enoch 8:1–3).

This verse describes what the "good angels" were reporting to God:

Thou seest what Azazel hath done, **who hath taught** all unrighteousness on earth and reveled the eternal secrets which were [preserved] in heaven, which men were striving to learn (1 Enoch 9:6).

Greek Mythology?

Others from the same time period as those rouge time travelers had to mitigate the threat created by the time travelers or else risk disrupting history. Thus, they determined that, in addition to killing off the rouge time travelers and their offspring, it was also necessary to alter historical events and even fabricate events that never actually occurred. Reality was distorted by presenting actual events and people as spiritual or mythological. **So-called mythological characters and events may not be fictional but rather truly historical.**

It is possible, and I believe even probable, that the so-called Greek gods were actually visitors, the Watchers, from the future who possessed superior minds and abilities. Because of this, they were granted deity status by ancient human beings. The ruins of ancient structures include huge and sophisticatedly engineered temples that would have been out of reach for our species to construct at that time, some of which are still functional and fully intact to this day. It is obvious that much effort was put into the construction of these

313

monuments and that they had to have been erected by an extraordinary species. The controlled narrative tells us that the ancient Greek writings are ultimately fiction and, therefore, are classified as mythology. But I believe that idea was manufactured by the powers that be and was designed to divert attention away from what actually occurred.

The controlled narrative tells us that the sophisticated megalithic structures were built by our ancient ancestors, but that theory does not hold water for the following reasons:

- It is highly unlikely that they possessed the knowledge and engineering skills required to erect such sophisticated structures.
- They did not have the tools and equipment that would have been required for the project.
- Why would our ancient ancestors exert the great effort required to construct the sophisticated structures for FICTIONAL CHARACTERS? That is just ridiculous to me! There are no temples for Superman, Batman, or Wonder Woman!

The structures had to have been built by a species possessing extraordinary knowledge and abilities—a superior species that was stranded in that time period and forced to work and create without the benefits of their sophisticated technology available to them. That would explain how the mysterious megaliths were constructed during a time when their erection would not have been achievable by our ancient ancestors.

Historical events and realities have been manipulated and altered to conceal what really occurred. Sophisticated ancient temple ruins created for the so-called mythological Greek and Roman gods exist to this day. Physical evidence suggests that **the so-called ancient Greek mythology may, in fact, have been reality and is actually Greek history.** The following material details some of the so-called mythological deities and the extraordinary temples and monuments erected in honor of them:

- The Temple of Jupiter was dedicated to Jupiter (or Zeus to the Greeks) and his companion deities Juno and Minerva. Zeus was the god of sky and thunder. Pluto and Poseidon were his brothers and his sister was Ceres. Zeus and his brother both **possessed a powerful and deadly device,** often referred to as a thunderbolt or trident, **which was capable of shaking the earth and shattering any object.**
- The Greek Parthenon was dedicated to the goddess Athena. She was credited with having many **deity-like** attributes and values, including wisdom, courage, inspiration, civilization, law and justice, strategic warfare, mathematics, strength, strategy, the arts, crafts, and skill.
- The Odeon of Herodes Atticus is a stone theater megalith in Athens, Greece. Herodes Atticus, another name for Herod the Great, built the structure in memory of his wife, Aspasia Annia Regilla. Atticus claimed lineage to the Greek god Zeus and the so-called mythological Greek kings Theseus, Cecrops, and Aeacus.
- The Temple of Hera was solely dedicated to the Greek goddess Hera. A marble head of Hera was discovered along with a statue of Hermes. The statues are now displayed in the archaeological museum at Olympia. Hera was one of the twelve Olympians as well as the sister and wife of Zeus. She was also the daughter of the Titans Cronus and Rhea.
- The Temple of Artemis has a metope (a rectangular area just above the columns) decorated with carvings of Achilles and Memnon. Artemis was the daughter of Zeus and Leto and the twin sister of Apollo. She was the goddess of hunting, wild nature, and chastity.
- The Great Theater of Epidaurus was large enough to provide seating for thirteen to fourteen thousand people. A variety of events were hosted there, one of which was worshiping the god of medicine, Asclepius. Asclepius, the son

of Apollo and Coronis and god of medicine, was considered a hero.

- The Temple of Apollo was dedicated to one of the most important gods. Apollo was the son of Zeus and the Titan Leto. Apollo was said to be an immortal and powerful god with many special powers, including the ability to see into the future, manipulate light, and heal as well as cause illness and disease. The temple's architects were Trophonius and Agamedes, who were most certainly also products of the deity lineage (that is, they were time travelers) as well.
- The Stoa of Attalos is an architectural marvel that was constructed by King Attalos of Pergamon as a gift to Athens in return for the education he received there. The original building, dating to before Christ, was reconstructed in 1952–1956 and looks today much as it did in 150 BC. King Attalos was considered to be a champion over the beasts and giants. Obviously, he battled and defeated the hybrids, mutants, or giants created by the "sons of God" (time travelers) who fornicated with the "daughters of men" (a species of human slightly different from themselves).
- Temple of Hephaestus was constructed of Parian and Pentelic marble and was dedicated to Hephaestus, the god of craftsmanship, the art of sculpture, metal-working, forges, and fire, and also to Theseus, a hero. **Amazingly, 2,435 years after its construction, it stands today just as appeared in 415 BC.** The images of this structure truly boggle the mind. Modern skyscrapers and other similarly intricately engineered buildings would have long-since crumbled over this span of time. His parents were Zeus and Hera, and he was married to Aphrodite. **He was a smiting god, making all the weapons** for Olympus and acting as blacksmith for the gods. It is important to note here that this set of facts could not line up more perfectly with the biblical story of the Watchers. They were rouge time travelers who relished their godlike status—so much so that they chose to stay and refused to stop their dangerous activities.

- The Erechtheion was built by Mnesicies, and Phidias was the sculpture and stonemason. It was dedicated to both Athena and Poseidon (who is Neptune in Roman "mythology"). **Poseidon wielded a powerful device, a trident** that was said to have been forged by the cyclopes. The cyclopes themselves were possibly a product of the hybrids fornicating with other hybrids. Ancient artifacts depicting the trident survive to this day. **Coins found from the sixth century BC depict Poseidon wielding the trident, and pottery from around the fifth century depicts Poseidon killing the giant Polybotes with the trident.** These depictions are not of a farmer with his pitchfork; they are showing real technology. **Ancient writings describe Poseidon creating a salt-water spring after striking the ground with his trident.** They also give an account of him **using it to split a rock in order to dislodge a foe from it.** Wow! That certainly sounds like technology to me.

People who think as I do are considered credulous by the skeptics, but everything presented thus far debunks the skeptics. Detailed stories and events, coins, statues, and extant ruins of brilliantly engineered temples all point to REALITY—not mythology.

In my opinion, Homer's Iliad, which describes a portion of the Trojan War, is also an actual account of historical events. Homer never referred to the story as mythological or fictional. Others who did not even live in a time close to his have made such claims, not Homer.

The Anunnaki

I will not go into great detail here because that could entail another whole book. However, I will give a little bit of food for thought here. The Anunnaki were a group of deities described in ancient Sumerian texts that have been dated to as early as 4500 BC. Some believe that the existence of the Anunnaki may well date back tens of thousands of years. My research indicates that they were most likely the first group of Watchers to arrive in ancient times.

The Epic of Gilgamesh is regarded as the earliest surviving great work of literature yet found. Gilgamesh was obviously a hybrid, which is indicated by ancient depictions of his huge stature. One such depiction shows him holding, with only one arm, a full-grown male lion by the neck as if it were a house cat. The Epic of Gilgamesh is another ancient piece of literature often identified as fiction or mythology by people who lived far removed from when and where it was originally written.

In 2003, while working in Iraq, a group of German archaeologists equipped with sophisticated ground-penetrating imaging equipment located what appears to be the tomb of King Gilgamesh as it is described in *The Epic of Gilgamesh*. The location corresponds with the story, and the images correspond with the descriptions provided there. Although the site has not yet been excavated, it could reveal physical evidence of a historical reality in the same way that the ancient Greek and Roman temples, the pyramids, and so many other mind-boggling megaliths do.

The Great Flood

Although I would argue that the story of Noah's ark is a complete fabrication, I nevertheless believe that the great flood was an actual event and that it was manufactured by our ancestors from the future. A species capable of time travel would surely also be capable of controlling the weather. We are capable of doing that now, after all. The time travelers committed unforgiveable crimes—crimes that, as I argued above, could potentially wipe out their own future society. **The Watchers were not banished from heaven; they were banished from the future time period from which they came.**

Allowing them to continue their activities, for obvious reasons, was not an option. They had to be destroyed. The decision was made to kill them all and start over. The Bible tells us that Noah, his three sons, and their wives were chosen to repopulate the earth. Maybe so, but being tasked with building a huge boat capable of housing two of every animal species on earth and feeding them for 150 days would be quite an accomplishment—an extremely unrealistic accomplishment. How did he convince the lions, tigers, bears, elephants, hippos, two-toed sloths, deadly snakes, and alligators to come along for the trip? And can you imagine the smell? It would have been terrible on the first day, but the voyage lasted 150 days. Speaking of which, how did they feed all those animals for 150 days? Why were they not just picked up in a fiery chariot, like Elisha, and taken up to reside in heaven until the waters retreated? I will tell you exactly why. Because that part of the story was fabricated just like many other biblical events. Many ancient texts describe a great flood, but there is no mention of Noah and his ark—that is a fairytale.

The flood killed the majority of human beings, but some surely survived. They probably had advance warning of what was coming and prepared shelters, such as the ancient, artificially created Longyou caves in China and the underground cities found throughout Turkey. Some of these underground complexes had the capacity to house more than sixty thousand people and animals.

Walking Among Us

Government whistleblowers claim that superior beings are walking among us today, and that certainly could be true. If we are indeed dealing with our ancestors from the future, it is possible that their physical appearance has not deviated all that much from ours. If that is the case, then they would blend in well. Enough may have survived to carry on their linage, and might have made themselves and their true identities known to select world authorities. They would be great assets if the assumption that their mental capabilities are far superior to ours is correct.

But what if they have an agenda to rule the world? Those from their linage relished having a godly status—so much so that they defied commands from their superiors and ignored the seriousness of their actions. If they were capable of that, they would be capable of anything!

Here is something to think about! David Rockefeller had many titles. He was chairman and chief executive of Chase Manhattan Bank, a CFR member and chairman, Trilateral Commission chairman, and a Bilderberg Group member and advisor. The Rockefeller family has always staunchly supported the United Nations and a one-world government.

David Rockefeller said in from June 1992,

> We are grateful to **the *Washington Post*, the *New York Times*, *Time* magazine** and other great publications whose directors have attended our meetings and respected their promises of discretion for almost forty years. It would have been impossible for us to develop **OUR PLAN FOR THE WORLD** if we had been subject to the bright lights of publicity during those years. But the work is now much more sophisticated and prepared to march towards a world government. **The supranational sovereignty of an intellectual elite and world bankers is surely preferable to the national auto-determination practiced in past centuries.**

In essence, Rockefeller was saying that sovereign governments have to be eliminated, and a group of "intellectual elites" should be given total authority over all nations of the world. And that is exactly what the Bilderberg Group is all about.

Further, the *Washington Post*, the *New York Times*, and *Time* magazine were all praised by a man representing a group that wants to eliminate the sovereignty of all nations. How interesting! We know that the elite own or control nearly every media outlet in the world, but Rockefeller directly and openly offered up the names of these three, just three of the many that are constantly attacking and mocking our antiestablishment, anti-world government president and advocating for world government policy. Dignitaries, including elected officials from around the world, attend Bilderberg Group meetings and are **sworn to secrecy**. I will not explain why because we know why. The group yields enormous influence and power, and many dignitaries are obviously putting the group's desires before their own sovereign nations. The group has been given a superior or even **godlike** status by these dignitaries. So much so that they have been surrendering their nations' rights, freedoms, and liberties to them by complying with the United Nations Agenda for the twenty-first century. Why are elected officials and other dignitaries from all over the world so obsessed with serving the Bilderberg Group? It is as if they are worshiping and serving a species that possesses minds and abilities superior to their own.

So why is there no physical proof of the advanced technological devices used thousands of years ago to construct the megaliths? It can be assumed that they were allowed to bring some advanced technology with them. It can also be assumed that every piece was trackable and recovered before the flood or perhaps after. They had to be and obviously were very fearful of altering the course of events. Many megalithic monuments could be used to argue that advanced knowledge and technology existed when, by all mainstream accounts, it should not have, but the ancient megaliths and monuments at Baalbek offer strong enough evidence all on their own.

The next part of "Our Origins" will discuss UFOs.

CHAPTER 25
Our Origins and a Possible Connection to the Elite

Part Four: Agenda 21, Hidden Dimensions, Time Rifts, and UFOs

Writings, drawings, and carvings dating all the way back to the Stone Age describe and depict advanced technology. What is more, the many reported and investigated UFO sightings and encounters provide compelling evidence that these ancient depictions are not fabrications. It is obvious that government officials, the Vatican, and even the media have been tasked with concealing the existence of the highly advanced vessels and their occupants. Nevertheless, it is my conviction that their existence is as certain as the conspiracy to cover up their existence.

The United Nations Agenda for the Twenty-First Century

If the rouge time travelers, the Watchers, are real, it is possible that they have an agenda to rule the world and have convinced key world officials that planet earth is destined for doom unless all authority is relinquished to them—**enter Agenda 21**. Agenda 21 is a disturbing document! It is absolutely a blueprint designed to strip all nations of their sovereignty and force them to surrender all of their authority to a single world-governing body, the elite, and **the human-created climate change hoax is being used as a sales tactic**. Though not officially ratified by independent nations, they are enforcing Agenda 21 by their own actions. President Bill Clinton set everything into high gear almost immediately after taking office in 1993 with the creation of the President's Council on Sustainable Development in Executive Order 12852. **The President's Council on Sustainable Development is essentially Agenda 21 with a different title.**

Everything about Agenda 21 is disturbing, but I am only going to touch on the Biodiversity Treaty here. The Biodiversity Treaty encourages and allows for private property to be incrementally taken or stolen from private landowners, which is disturbing. And the council's Wildlands Project is just a camouflaged version of the Biodiversity Treaty.

The Wildlands Project is designed to gain control of over 50 percent of the rural land in the US and then return it to the condition that predates Columbus' arrival. In short, people will be corralled into the human settlements that are being created now, and that should terrify everyone. The Biodiversity Treaty and Wildlands Project call for the creation of core areas, buffer zones, and human settlements. The core areas and the buffer zones will be dedicated to carnivores. They are currently being acquired by methodically forcing people off the desired lands and into human settlements. As incredible as this all may seem, it is actually a plan that is being implemented not just in the United States but all around the world.

If you doubt what I am saying here, just search on the internet for the **biodiversity map**, and you will see the reality for yourselves. A mind-blowing 50 percent or more of rural lands are supposed to be freed of human activity in order to establish protected areas for predators, such as wolves, cougars, and grizzly bears. That is very suspicious! **It is almost as if they are creating a zoo in which humans are to be included and controlled along with the other animals.** Why is over 50 percent of all the rural land in America in the process of being designated as off-limits to humans and used only as sanctuaries for dangerous animals—animals that could provide food for humans? Why are the carnivores who only view us as a meal being given preferred status over humans? Something very strange is happening.

In a growing number of places, it is becoming increasingly difficult to acquire building permits or approval for desirable single-family home subdivisions. How difficult depends on the number and status of CFR or Bilderberg operatives holding power in a given location. The most common reason given for these denials is social injustice. The argument says that because certain groups cannot afford the single-family dwellings, then no one should be allowed to have them. Of course, that aligns neatly with socialism, but I believe it is also being used as a cover for the elite's creation of human settlements—more proof that the so-called conspiracy theory is, in reality, conspiracy fact.

I urge those who are concerned or desire to learn more about what is going on behind closed doors to follow Tom DeWeese at the American Policy Center (http://americanpolicy.org) and Eileen DeRolf at the Agenda 21 Course (http://agenda21course.com). The names and locations of past and current events provided on the sites reveal that our trusted authorities are willingly surrendering our rights, freedoms, and America to a powerful group of international bankers.

Hidden Dimensions and Time Rifts

Per Wikipedia, "The multiverse is a hypothetical group of universes. Together, these universes comprise everything that exists: the entirety of space, time, matter, energy, information, and the physical laws and constants that describe them. The different universes within the multiverse are called 'parallel universes,' 'other universes,' 'alternate universes,' or 'many worlds.'"

UFOs have been observed traveling great distances, moving from a standing stop to another stopping point in a split second and then repeating the same type of maneuver multiple times before disappearing from sight. I actually witnessed such an event as a child in the 1960s. My father took me with him to visit a relative, and while they conversed in the yard, I gazed up at the crystal-clear sky. It was around 8:00 p.m. when a bright red ball appeared out of nowhere. Then three more appeared, and they were all making bizarre zigzag maneuvers, traveling great distances from a dead stop to another dead stop, all in the blink of an eye. I was a little rattled because I was seeing something that just did not make any sense, so I interrupted my father's conversation and pointed to the sky. He and our relative immediately looked up at the sky and said, "What the hell is that?" The zig zag maneuvers continued for a short period, and then they all appeared to merge before simply disappearing. The whole event only lasted a few minutes, but it remains in my mind today as vivid as it did when it occurred.

Intergalactic and interdimensional space exploration are not realistic with conventional propulsion. That would be the case even if we had technology to move at the speed of light. The three brightest stars in Orion's Belt are referred to as the Three Kings or the Three Sisters. I mention Orion's Belt because the three main pyramids at the Giza plateau in Egypt and the three main pyramids at the Teotihuacan temple complex in Mexico correlate with the relative positions of the three brightest stars in the Orion constellation. Why? There must be a reason! It could be that time travelers from the future are showing us where we are eventually going. Or it could be that visitors from there are showing us where they are from. That being said, a trip to the nearest star in the Orion constellation would take 736 years to achieve when traveling at the speed of light. Hence, intergalactic space voyages using this method are not realistic. Our visitors are using something much more efficient.

It is possible that intergalactic and interdimensional travel are as simple to them as stepping from one room to another is for us.

Since it would not be possible for any biological species to survive the g-forces produced during the maneuvers described here, it is reasonable to assume that these vessels are operated by self-sufficient artificial intelligences that are capable of thinking and making decisions for themselves on a level comparable to or beyond human beings. This is likely the case for at least some of the vessels, but there are credible reports of humans being taken aboard vessels occupied by biological beings doing the same types of maneuvers. So, what's going on?

In an article on prominent physicists' thoughts on the possibility of traveling to parallel universes, several expressed positive reactions: "Theoretical physicist Michio Kaku believes that our universe will end up in a 'big freeze,' and that technology can one day allow us to travel between universes" The big freeze is a hypothetical distant future in which the universe keeps expanding and eventually all thermodynamic energy is uniformly distributed. The article continues, "Neil DeGrasse Tyson, on the other hand, says that if you come from 'a universe with higher dimensions, **then it could be as easy to move between dimensions as stepping from one room to another**" (https://futurism.com/physicists-weigh-in-could-we-ever-travel-to-a-parallel-universe).

Astronomers believe there are at least **one hundred billion galaxies** in the observable universe. And scientists estimate that our single galaxy, the Milky Way, may consist of over one hundred billion solar systems, revealing that galaxies, even individually, are huge beyond imagination. But a universe dwarfs a galaxy, and it is possible that our universe is surrounded by other, independent universes. Enoch describes the existence of ten heavens, which suggests that the writer was being taken on not only intergalactic travels but also inter-dimensional travel. I find it interesting that Enoch describes the ten heavens considering that it is only during recent times that astrophysicists have suggested the possibility of alternate universes. Further, his detailed accounts suggest that the journeys from one heaven to another were accomplished quickly.

Neil DeGrasse Tyson: **"It could be as easy as stepping from one room to another."**

No biological being could survive the g-forces created by the zigzag maneuvers being witnessed. The maneuvers are being done by something other than the propulsion that has been assumed to be in use. It may be that, with their incredibly advanced technology, they are shifting in and out of a dimension that we cannot see; thus, the g-force would be taken out of the equation. For some reason, we can see them shifting back and forth between the dimensions, but we cannot see the dimension that they are coming from. Another possibility is that we are able to see them manipulating time rifts.

How they might be doing all this is a mystery, but their existence is a reality.

Credible UFO Encounters

Anyone interested in really researching this phenomenon is probably well aware that world authorities, including the Vatican, are involved in a conspiracy to hide the existence of otherworldly beings. The majority of the debunkers and skeptics are **products of the establishment** and should not be taken seriously; no amount of evidence would ever be enough for them. Their goal is to mock anyone that dare think for themselves, and their only intention is to sell the **controlled narrative**. The mainstream media either ignores the encounters or makes a mockery of them no matter how credible the account may be. But who now owns and controls nearly every media outlet in the world? That would be the elite, who seek an all-powerful one-world government and a New World Order.

No Need to Look beyond Planet Earth for Intelligent Otherworldly Species—They Are Here!

I am going to include in this chapter reports of encounters that, in my opinion, cannot be disputed. They say that a picture is worth a thousand word, and I agree—but a video is even better. The US government declassified three in 2019, which I will detail in what follows, and they can be viewed with a quick internet search. Interviews with the pilots involved are also in circulation. Though the videos present more than enough footage to prove that the vessels are real, people involved with the encounters claim that government officials are in possession of much more material that has not been released.

First is the "Gimbal UFO" video of a 2015 incident. It is actual US military footage captured from the cockpit of a Navy fighter jet and was declassified in 2019. The audio between the pilots mentions a whole fleet of the objects, which the video reveals are shaped like saucers. Audio of the pilots reveals that they were amazed and excited by what they saw.

The USS Roosevelt "Go Fast UFO" video from a 2015 incident (also referenced to as the "FLIR1" video) is next. Just one object is mentioned by the pilots, but they are amazed by the "impossible" aeronautics it displays.

In the USS Nimitz's 2004 UFO incident, the actual pilots who witnessed the encounter have come forward and participated in public interviews. Footage from the cockpit is also available on the web. There were ten objects in all, with an estimated size of ten feet by forty feet and an oval shape resembling that of a Tic Tac candy. The objects would drop from an altitude of twenty-eight thousand feet to a dead stop on the ocean's surface in a split second and then ascend back to twenty-eight thousand feet in the same timeframe.

These could have only been living, **self-functioning machines**, as the g-forces would have turned any biological creature into mush. Many similar reports have been made over many years, and they all describe aeronautics that defy what our most brilliant minds think they understand about physics. **The search for intelligent species from other realms need not to go beyond planet Earth**—they are here. Though the public has only been allowed to view the three videos mentioned, it would be naive for anyone to think that only these three exist. These three videos standing on their own should be enough to convince anyone that a **CONTROLLED NARRATIVE** intended to suppress the truth exists.

Actual military video captured highly advanced, unidentified vessels performing zigzag and hairpin maneuvers at incredible speeds. These objects were seen descending from a dead stop at twenty-eight thousand feet above the ocean's surface to just a few feet above it in a split second! We have no technology that comes close to what they filmed. On top of that, our most brilliant physicists claim that what the vessels are doing should not even be possible. And yet they have it on film. No noise, no fire, and no vapor trails—these entities are light years ahead of us. I believe that their technology even goes beyond what we see in Star Wars.

I will include a few more credible reports, none of which have physical evidence (or at least physical evidence the general public is allowed to know about). However, they are credible due to the circumstances and the people involved. The unclassified videos were presented first as an attempt to give credibility to the events that do not have video corroboration. While many do have pictures and videos, the authorities have confiscated and denied the existence of the material. I could write a whole book on UFOs, but this book is not about just UFOs. It is intended to expose a cover-up and an agenda. I believe that the alien and UFO encounters may have a connection with the lunacy outlined in Agenda 21. The authorities' obvious attempts to dismiss, mock, distort, and hide the details of every event, including those providing compelling and overwhelming evidence (the three videos were leaked and not voluntarily released), indicate that they may be surrendering our planet to superior entities from another realm. Multiple factions may be involved and competing with one another for the control of planet earth, and it is possible that world leaders have agreed to a controlled surrender of the planet to one of the factions. It is likely that Agenda 21 is being implemented to fulfill one of their demands. It could be that our environment, as is, is intolerable to their species. Maybe the Green New Deal and Agenda 21 are being implemented to alter the current earthly environment because that is what is required for a superior species desiring to inhabit our planet.

Agenda 21 is a total scam! It has nothing to do with saving planet earth; it is *only* about controlling planet earth. **In essence, it is about turning us into slaves**. Why are our world authorities surrendering to a particular group? It could be that the chosen species desires to make us their slaves. Perhaps Agenda 21 is being implemented to put in place a government and infrastructure they desire and require to take control of every aspect of our lives. The deal may have been made in exchange for protection from an opposing species that also wants to take control of planet earth. Regardless of what is really happening, it is quite obvious that world authorities are leading us to a one-world government. Though it would seem as if we could never stop or even challenge the superior entities from these outer realms, we can and must try. Stopping Agenda 21 may be one method of achieving that for this reason: If our climate is intolerable to their species, we should keep it that way. Now, more UFO encounters.

The Rendlesham Forest Incident

In December 1980, a small craft landed just outside RAF Woodbridge, which was being used by the US Air Force. Lieutenant Colonel Charles I. Halt and Sergeant Jim Penniston observed broken branches above the landing site and along the vessel's path. Sgt. Penniston claims to have touched the vessel, and upon doing so, received visions of binary code, which he had no understanding of but became embedded in his mind long enough to write down when he returned to the base. Experts in binary code determined that these notes could be translated as "exploration of humanity continuous for planetary advance eyes of your eyes origin year 8100."

A series of longitudinal coordinates were also found in the binary code. (Of interest is that Einstein claimed he received his theory of relativity in a similar manner. He said that it somehow seemed to be downloaded into his mind out of nowhere.) Radiation was detected at the site, and three indentations were pressed into the soil from the landing gear. Sgt. Penniston also claims to have observed hieroglyphs on the vessel and sketched them on a pad as he was observing them. That is nearly as good as a picture; the man did not just create the bizarre images in his head. Of course, the authorities tried to cover up the whole event, as they do with all of them. However, years after the event, an employee working for the British Ministry of Defense, Nick Pope, ordered a new investigation that revealed that what authorities classified as "of no significance" was indeed very significant. Though the British Government has claimed to have declassified its UFO files, Nick Pope, who served twenty-one years with the British Ministry of Defense, claims that eighteen have been forever hidden from public knowledge. Considering that the British government allowed the "spectacular" Rendlesham Forest incident to be made public (thank you, Nick Pope), one can assume that the eighteen hidden cases are even more spectacular.

The Phoenix Lights

On March 13, 1997, thousands of people witnessed two enormous low-flying, boomerang-shaped vessels flying over Phoenix, Arizona. They were black, made no sound, and had five huge circular areas (seeming to be lights) underneath them. The then Arizona governor, Fife Symington, made a mockery of the event, angering the thousands who witnessed it. Years later, it was disclosed that he knew for certain that the sightings were genuine because he actually witnessed one of the vessels himself. Former governor Symington, who is a retired Air Force captain and has been a pilot most of his adult life, was watching the evening news with his family when they broke in with the sightings of the first vessel. So, he decided to drive to the location since it was nearby. He parked and, almost immediately after getting out of his car, witnessed the second vessel gliding directly above his head. Mr. Symington said that he had never seen anything like that in his life, and he referred to the vessel as being "otherworldly." He did not say why he mocked the events while serving as governor, but it can be reasonably assumed that he was directed to by a higher authority. I have watched interviews with eyewitnesses, and they are adamant that what they saw could have only been otherworldly vessels. These witnesses are angered that they are being told by authorities that it was all a figment of their imaginations.

Many reports describe this same type of vessel. Many pictures and videos are said to exist, but you and I will never be allowed to see them. Authorities will continue to force the concealment of any solid evidence. Witnesses that have seen these triangle craft at other times were located in the following areas:

- Belgium, 1989–1992
- Illinois, 2000, 4:00 a.m. in the cities of Highland, Dupo, Lebanon, Shiloh, Summerfield, Millstadt, and O'Fallon. That is my home area. Damn, I wished I could have seen that!
- Tinley Park and Oak Forest, Illinois, 2004–2006
- Texas, 2008 and 2014
- Kansas, 2008 and 2014

O'Hare International Airport in Chicago, Illinois

A disc-shaped object hovered over gate seventeen for at least five minutes before shooting straight up at an incredible speed, leaving a perfect hole in the dense clouds above. The FAA refused to investigate the incident even though it was observed by a large number of credible witnesses. Transcripts of the event are available via a web search or the "Secret Access UFOs on the Record" video.

Anchorage, Alaska

On November 18, 1986, a Japanese pilot was followed for fifty-five minutes (and some 350 miles) by an acorn-shaped object as big as three aircraft carriers. The vessel had many lights, and smaller vessels were coming and going from what he described as nozzles in the big vessel. The radar tower in Anchorage detected the object and tracked it throughout the entire flight. The pilot and his copilot were terrified that the object was going to collide with their plane, and those monitoring in the tower were also concerned. As a precautionary measure, the pilot was instructed to make a 180-degree turn and return to Anchorage, but the object followed his turn and tailed him all the way back to Anchorage. All the involved parties were interrogated by authorities, and they confiscated all of the data (recordings, radar, etc.), maintaining possession to this day. The CIA claims that the event never happened.

The Japanese pilot was stripped of his flying license by Japanese authorities and never allowed to fly again. This is a great example of just how desperate authorities from around the world are to conceal the existence of otherworldly beings. Coupling that with the New World Order agenda should raise concerns. An experienced pilot and copilot were stripped of their livelihoods because they witnessed something the authorities are desperate to hide from the public. Actions such as this are meant to mitigate the risk of exposing the public to something they are not supposed to know and send a message. And that message is: Keep your mouths shut.

I could go on forever with the UFO encounters, but I have included just enough to expose the reality of the coverup. The reason for the coverup is not known for certain, but it can be assumed that world authorities are in agreement that admitting the existence of superior otherworldly beings (who, if they desired, could claim ownership of Earth in an instant) would, at the very least, create extreme anxiety. Furthermore, it is reasonable to assume that there are many species of these superior beings competing for the control of planet Earth, as indicated by the following recorded events.

The Nuremberg Event of 1561

The Nuremberg event was a mass sighting of celestial phenomena. Witnesses described an aerial battle involving many flying ships. Immediately following the event, local artist Hans Glaser produced a broadsheet, offering a woodcut engraving of the scene and a detailed description of what was witnessed. Again, all of this can easily be found on the internet. The text reads,

> In the morning of April 14, 1561, at daybreak, between 4 and 5 a.m., **a dreadful apparition occurred on the sun**, and then this was seen in Nuremberg in the city, before the gates and in the country—by many men and women. At first there appeared in the middle of the sun **two blood-red semicircular arcs,** just like the moon in its last quarter. And in the sun, above and below and on both sides, the color was blood, there stood **a round ball of partly dull, partly black ferrous color.** Likewise there stood on both sides and as a torus about the sun such **blood-red ones and other balls in large number, about three in a line and four in a square, also some alone. In between these globes there were visible a few blood-red crosses, between which there were blood-red strips, becoming thicker to the rear**

and in the front malleable like the rods of reed-grass, which were intermingled, among them two big rods, one on the right, the other to the left, and within the small and big rods there were three, also four and more globes. These all started to fight among themselves, so that the globes, which were first in the sun, flew out to the ones standing on both sides, thereafter, the globes standing outside the sun, in the small and large rods, flew into the sun. Besides the globes flew back and forth among themselves and fought vehemently with each other for over an hour. And when the conflict in and again out of the sun was most intense, they became fatigued to such an extent that they all, as said above, fell from the sun down upon the earth "as if they all burned" and they then wasted away on the earth with immense smoke. After all this there was something like a black spear, very long and thick, sighted; the shaft pointed to the east, the point pointed west. Whatever such signs mean, God alone knows. Although we have seen, shortly one after another, many kinds of signs on the heaven, which are sent to us by the almighty God, to bring us to repentance, we still are, unfortunately, so ungrateful that we despise such high signs and miracles of God. Or we speak of them with ridicule and discard them to the wind, in order that God may send us a frightening punishment on account of our ungratefulness. After all, the God-fearing will by no means discard these signs, but will take it to heart as a warning of their merciful Father in heaven, will mend their lives and faithfully beg God, that He may avert His wrath, including the well-deserved punishment, on us, so that we may temporarily here and perpetually there, live as his children. For it, may God grant us his help, Amen. By Hans Glaser, letter-painter of Nuremberg.

The Events of 1566 in Basel, Switzerland

In a 1566 newspaper article, Samuel Apiarius and Samuel Coccius describe the following:

> It happened in 1566 three times, on 27 and 28 of July, and on August 7, against the sunrise and sunset; we saw strange shapes in the sky above Basel.
>
> During the year 1566, on the 27th of July, after the sun had shone warm on the clear, bright skies, and then around 9 pm, it suddenly took a different shape and color. First, the sun lost all its radiance and luster, and it was no bigger than the full moon, and finally it seemed to weep tears of blood and the air behind him went dark. And he was seen by all the people of the city and countryside. In much the same way also the moon, which has already been almost full and has shone through the night, assuming an almost blood-red color in the sky. The next day, Sunday, the sun rose at about six o'clock and slept with the same appearance it had when it was lying before. He lit the houses, streets and around as if everything was blood-red and fiery. At the dawn of August 7, we saw large black spheres coming and going with great speed and precipitation before the sun and chattered as if they led a fight. Many of them were fiery red and, soon crumbled and then extinguished.

I believe that the four events actually occurred and that the witnesses were observing aerial battles between rival, superior otherworldly beings competing for the control of planet Earth. It is also possible that the battles are ongoing and our ancestors from the future are involved. If humans from a time period **well into the future** achieved time travel, then it is reasonable to assume that other species—who may be quite different from our own—have the technology as well. If that is true, then humans from the future would have to protect planet Earth through the ages. For, if a non-human species desired to control or colonize our planet themselves, it would be achievable and much easier to do by making an offensive move prior to humans attaining technology and weaponry that might equal their own. That would explain the rumors of astronauts reporting huge spacecraft on the far side of the moon. They could be human sentinels from the future. Also, UFOs are frequently seen entering and exiting our oceans and flying over Antarctica. It could be that Antarctica, the moon, and our oceans are all being used by our ancestors from the future, the Watchers, as sentinel bases. Some have claimed that the Roswell incident involved a species that was very distinct from our own. Could they have been rivals and were shot down by the sentinels?

Does this all sound crazy to you? **Watch the three leaked military videos. They present a compelling case for the existence of these superior beings from other realms** and reveal that they are conducting activities in our solar system and on our planet. As indicated by the findings detailed in this book, overwhelming evidence suggests that they have been here working for their own ends for a long, long time.

Every report or encounter is mocked and dismissed regardless of the credibility of those involved—and not just by the United States. Obviously, authorities representing nations from all around the world are in consensus that the threat posed by the potential disclosure is so severe that it has to be kept from public knowledge. We can only speculate why. But consider the BIPARTISAN denial of Agenda 21 by our elected officials. Elite darlings Mitch McConnell and Lindsey Graham dismiss it as a nonbinding agreement **despite the fact that**

they both know damn good and well that it is being implemented in the United States at breakneck speed through the President's Council on Sustainable Development.

The Elite's Itinerary

The elites want to install a corporate-controlled, unelected, all-powerful one-world government by first creating blocs of nations. Currently, there are 195 individual nations, each of which has their own sovereign governments, but the elites have been conspiring to eliminate all but seven of the 195 governments by combining them into blocs prior to combining the remaining seven governments into their own **one-world government**. The EU is the first bloc of nations created by the elite, and the **North American Union** (NAU/SPP) will be the second. It can be assumed that, when the United States falls, the nations required to create the remaining five blocs will be soon to follow.

The Bilderberg Group created the Council on Foreign Relations as a unit to infiltrate our government. They groom self-serving, aspiring politicians for positions in government, both elected and unelected, that can be utilized to serve the elite. Their most recent assault on America comes in the form of the Democrat-revised USMCA. It was a great agreement prior to the revisions but is now a terrible, sovereignty-stealing one. The agreement was obviously revised per Bilderberg Group instructions, as it integrates the United States, Canadian, and Mexican governments—in essence, creating the North American Union. **Please take note that the establishment Republicans were all on board with signing the revised agreement as well. TRUMP WAS TRUMPED BY HIS TRUSTED ADVISORS!**

The Book of Revelation—Time Travel?

As disclosed previously in this book, a number of ancient texts are combinations of both reality and fiction. I do not believe, for example, that God created Adam from the dust of the earth and breathed life into his nostrils or that Aphrodite brought a marble statue, Galatea, to life as described in Ovid's *Metamorphosis*, but I do believe in the end-time prophecies described in the Book of Revelation because they line up so perfectly with past and current events. Time travel would explain how it was possible to describe events detailed in the Bible before they happened in our timeline. The superior beings behind the New World Order agenda may be the fallen angels or Watchers or their lineage, and the second coming of Christ may be a reference to a time when our superior ancestors from the future will return to eliminate them and put a stop to their agenda. I believe that the spiritual and religious content was fabricated by the Council of Nicaea, the Vatican, and possibly the time travelers themselves to create a means of keeping the human race from utterly destroying itself.

CHAPTER 26
The Georgia Guidestones, COVID-19, and the New World Order

The Georgia Guidestones are a stone monument constructed in 1980 in Elbert County, Georgia. They were built by the Elberton Granite Finishing Company at the request of a man claiming to be representing "a small group of loyal Americans." The mysterious man chose to remain anonymous, using the pseudonym Robert C. Christian for the transaction. The Georgia Guidestones, as we will see, are linked to the United Nations Agenda for the 21st Century.

The monument consists of base stones, a vertical center stone, four vertical stones surrounding it, and a capstone connecting all five of them. The overall height of the monument is nineteen feet, three inches, and the total weight of all the granite stones combined, some 951 cubic feet, is 237,746 pounds.

The eight sides of the four vertical stones surrounding the center stone are engraved with a set of ten guidelines or principles in eight different languages, one language on each side. The languages are English, Spanish, Swahili, Hindu, Hebrew, Arabic, traditional Chinese, and Russian. The guidelines or principles are as follows:

Maintain humanity under 500,000,000 in perpetual balance with nature.

Guide reproduction wisely-improving fitness and diversity.

Unite humanity with a living new language.

Rule passion—faith—tradition—and all things with tempered reason.

Protect people and nations with fair laws and just courts.

Let all nations rule internally resolving external disputes in a world court.

Avoid petty laws and useless officials.

Balance personal rights with social duties.

Prize truth—beauty—love—seeking harmony with the infinite.

Be not a cancer on the earth—Leave room for nature—leave room for nature

My Analysis of the Ten Guidelines/Principles

"Maintain humanity under 500,000,000 in perpetual balance with nature."

World population currently stands at approximately **7.6 billion** but **the small group of loyal Americans responsible for the monument want it reduced to and maintained at under 500,000,000.** Damn! This small group of loyal Americans desire the elimination of over seven billion human beings from planet earth. Who is this self-described small group of loyal-Americans? Could it be Watchers? Agenda 21, the Green New Deal, core zones, buffer zones, food shelters, human settlements, pandemics, the elimination of fossil fuels, and a new world order...something very strange is happening!

"Guide reproduction wisely-improving fitness and diversity."

Their first guideline suggests **genocide to the tune of over seven billion people**. It is obvious that their second guideline is referring to a time following the genocide.

Many of the upper class favor a **massive reduction of our population**. In 1998, CNN founder Ted Turner pledged to give more than $1 billion to the United Nations to be spent for the implementation of large-scale population reduction.

According to Turner, "A total world population of 250–300 million people, **a 95 percent decline from present levels**, would be ideal."

David Rockefeller: "The negative impact of population growth on all of our planetary ecosystems is becoming appallingly evident."

Bill Maher, HBO personality: "I'm pro-choice, I'm for assisted-suicide, I'm for regular-suicide, I'm for whatever gets the freeway moving—that's what I'm for. It's too crowded, the planet is too crowded **and we need to promote death**."

Margaret Sanger, Planned Parenthood founder: "The most merciful thing that the large family does to one of its infant members is **to kill it**."

David Brower, the first executive director of the Sierra Club: "**Childbearing should be a punishable crime against society, unless the parents hold a government license... All potential parents should be required to use contraceptive chemicals**, the government issuing antidotes to citizens chosen for childbearing." Note that the Sierra Club is a product of the Clinton Administration and has used court action several times to stop the border wall.

I am not implying that Ted Turner, David Rockefeller, Bill Maher, Margaret Sanger, or David Brower have been involved with any kind of a plot. I am only revealing what they said. But back to the Georgia Guidestones...

"Unite humanity with a living new language."

Apparently, the small group of loyal Americans have created a new universal language to be used by all those still living after the genocide. And that also means that a new form of writing will be necessary, maybe hieroglyphics similar to what was observed by Sgt. Penniston during the Rendlesham Forest incident in 1980.

"Rule passion—faith—tradition—and all things with tempered reason."

Really? The small group of loyal Americans say this after suggesting what appears to be a *planned* massive genocide?

"Protect people and nations with fair laws and just courts."

No comment.

"Let all nations rule internally resolving external disputes in a world court."

No comment.

"Avoid petty laws and useless officials."

I am all in on that one!

"Balance personal rights with social duties."

No comment.

"Prize truth—beauty—love—seeking harmony with the infinite."

And genocide? Just propaganda! The small group of loyal Americans are portraying themselves as righteous, which of course is precisely the opposite of what they truly are.

"Be not a cancer on the earth—leave room for nature—leave room for nature."

That room is being created now via Agenda 21. Our representatives have been creating the core zones, buffer zones, food plots, and **human settlements** across the entire United States. **City officials around the nation are refusing to grant building permits for single-family dwellings.**

An explanatory tablet at the site includes a passage that reads, "Let these be guidestones to an **age of reason**." And the sponsors are identified as a small group of Americans who **seek the age of reason**. The monument also has astronomical features. The center column has a hole drilled through it at an angle that aligns with the North Star, and a carved slot aligns with solstices and equinoxes. The capstone has a 7/8-inch hole that allows the sun's rays to pass through at noon each day, shining a beam of light on the center stone and indicating the day of the year. **Why the astronomical features**—features that are also common to numerous ancient megalithic monuments? Are the **Watchers** responsible for the Georgia Guidestones?

I find it of interest that many Georgia dignitaries are contriving to remove Donald Trump, the elite's greatest threat, from the White House.

The Great Depression and COVID-19

When I think about COVID-19, **the Georgia Guidestones come to mind**. Is it possible that COVID-19 is the beginning of a calculated mass genocide? The virus has unique characteristics, and it is possible that **patients that have recovered can be reinfected**. Interesting! That indicates that the virus can come in waves and continue to **reduce population** until a successful treatment is available. I cannot help but wonder whether another mysterious virus will appear following the successful treatment of COVID-19. The next pandemic or pandemics may already exist, residing in test tubes on lab shelves just waiting to be released? Considering everything revealed in this book, I have concluded that the existence of the Georgia Guidestones and their inscription reveals a disturbing agenda.

COVID-19 has created a global economic disaster that will probably end up being worse than the **contrived** stock market crash of 1929, which led America into the Great Depression. People find it hard to accept that there are others who could have such nefarious and amoral intentions. But such people do exist and have the ability to manipulate governments, the environment, the world's economy, and more. Sadly, I believe that we are all at their mercy, and the problem there is that they have no mercy. Everything this small yet very powerful group does is only to benefit themselves. Ample evidence suggests that the elite-contrived the stock market crash of 1929 led to the Great Depression. Many people lost everything and were never able to recoup; a great many of them even committed suicide. Now, if the elite were capable of that, then they would be capable of just about anything. Ponder on the following quotations:

> **The depression was the calculated** shearing of the public by the world money powers, triggered by the planned sudden shortage of call money in the New York money market… **The one-world government leaders and their ever-close bankers** have now acquired full control of the money and credit machinery of the US via the creation of the **Federal Reserve Bank.**
> —Curtis Dall, Franklin Delano Roosevelt's son-in-law, in *F. D. R.: My Exploited Father-in-Law*

> **It was a carefully contrived occurrence. International bankers sought to bring about a condition of despair** so that they might emerge the **rulers of us all.**
> —Louis McFadden, US congressman representing Pennsylvania (1915–1935), commenting on the stock market crash of 1929

THE GLOBAL CONSPIRACY EXPOSED

*The COVID-19 virus is bringing about a **condition of despair.***

This present window of opportunity, during which a truly peaceful and interdependent world order might be built, will not be open for too long. We are on the verge of a global transformation. **All we need now is the right major crisis, and the nations will accept the New World Order.**

—David Rockefeller

Bankrupting every nation in the world by destroying their economies and confining them to their homes under the pretense of a (manufactured) pandemic just might do it.

Today, America would be outraged if UN troops entered Los Angeles to restore order [referring to the 1991 LA riots]. Tomorrow they will be grateful! This is especially true if they were told that there was an outside threat from beyond, whether rear or promulgated, that threatened our very existence. **It is then that all peoples of the world will plead to deliver them from this evil.** The one thing every man fears is the unknown. **When presented with this scenario, individual rights will be willingly relinquished** for the guarantee of their well-being granted to them by the **world government.**

—Henry Kissinger

It is no secret that population reduction is a major goal of the communist elite, so it is reasonable to assume that the Georgia Guidestones are somehow connected to them. The information revealed in this book suggests that the monument was not just put there on a whim; it exists for a reason. The self-described small group of loyal Americans seeking what they refer to as a new age of reason have revealed that the new age of reason will only allow five hundred million people to exist on **their planet** at any one given point of time. That and the fact that the monument exists at all suggest that it is a real agenda.

So why is a population reduction of 95 percent desired by this group? That is easy to answer. They will control all the money, and the five hundred million allowed to live on **their planet** will basically only exist to serve them. This small group thinks big; they are not content with just ruling nations—they want to rule the entire world. That may all seem crazy, but all the curious events and everything else revealed in this book should at least have you wondering.

COVID-19 Was Manufactured to Fast-Track the Beginning of the Communist Elite's New World Order and Remove a Sitting President from Office

Just consider the timing of the virus. The communists realized that Trump had a clear path to victory and had to be stopped. The elite and their indoctrinators, the media, knew that the only way to prevent a landslide victory against the communists was to manufacture a global pandemic and then use it to support their manufactured polls claiming that Trump mishandled the virus. The narrative that Trump mismanaged the virus was used as an attempt to convince the public that Trump really lost what was a rigged election. The communist elite absolutely rigged the election, and both parties supported this move. Why both parties supported it will be explained in the next chapter.

I am convinced that the global pandemic was contrived and is being utilized by the elite to fast-track the beginning of their **communist New World Order.** The elite want the New World Order to begin immediately but could not announce that to the public because it would cause outrage. So, they manufactured a scheme that would *covertly* allow them to achieve their goals. The pandemic has successfully transformed free and independent societies into the submissive, obedient societies desired by the elite, and they intend to keep it that way. It all happened in the blink of an eye!

Those planning and orchestrating the New World Order have operatives embedded in every branch and at every level of our government. During an interview in 2020, Chicago Mayor Lori Lightfoot made the following statement while discussing how the city government should be run: "Pick people to run the agencies that are **pledging allegiance to the New World Order and good governance,** and the inspector general should do spot audits to ensure that there is compliance."

Sorry, Mayor Lightfoot, I only pledge allegiance to the United States of America!

Some argue that the virus cannot be eradicated, and that is true, but it is also true that no virus can be utterly eradicated; multiple strains of the flu have been around for thousands of years. The elite will continue to manufacture false statistics related to COVID-19 in order to justify and retain control over those who are now their submissive and obedient world government citizens. Even if interventions are discovered that can successfully treat the virus, do not expect life to revert back to how it was. Citizens from every nation around the world have fallen hook, line, and sinker for the COVID-19 scheme, thus surrendering themselves to the elite, their masters. The elite achieved their objective by using COVID-19. People have accepted the government controlling every aspect of their lives, and the elite will keep that in play even after the virus is no longer a threat.

COVID-19 and Tracking Chips

The elite desire total control of **their planet,** and **implanting tracking chips in their citizens will expand that control**. COVID-19 has given them an excuse to do what has been on their bucket list for decades. They are suggesting that the tracking chips are necessary to control the current global pandemic (or any that may arise in the future) by being able to track those who have been vaccinated. And who knows what they may add to the vaccine. Will they sterilize us as they did with the unknowing masses in third-world nations receiving the polio vaccine? Perhaps they will inject us with something to accelerate the aging process.

The elite argue that implanting tracking chips now will serve to protect us from another pandemic, should it arise in the future, because we will be ready if such an event occur should occur. Of course, that is utter bullshit. The tracking chips will give the elite the ability to monitor every facet of our lives, which is the true intention of the tracking chips. I am not really a religious man, but I do find it interesting that all of these things have been prophesized in the Bible. Just saying!

COVID-19 is a dream come true for the elite—A ZERO-GROWTH SOCIETY, LOYAL GOVERNMENT DEPENDENTS, POPULATION REDUCTION, REMOVAL OF THE ONLY PRESIDENT TO EVER CHALLENGE THEIR AGENDA and TRACKING CHIPS are all being achieved in one fell swoop.

The manufactured and exaggerated pandemic has shown that the majority of the population can be indoctrinated to believe anything. This has to be repeated over and over and over again. (Please consider what I have just said when you hear the elite's indoctrinators preaching their human-created climate change bullshit.)

If you **indoctrinate someone, you teach that person a one-sided view of something and ignore or dismiss opinions that don't agree with your view.** Cults, political entities, and even fans of particular sports teams are often said to indoctrinate their followers.

Again, as Joseph Goebbels once said,

> **If you tell a lie long enough and keep repeating it, people will eventually come to believe it.** The lie can be maintained only for such time as the State can shield the people from the political, economic and/or military consequences of the lie. It thus becomes vitally important for the state to use all of its powers to repress dissent, for the truth is the mortal enemy of the lie, and thus by extension, **the truth is the greatest enemy of the State.**

CHAPTER 27
Various Topics

The Proud Boys

Per Wikipedia, "the Proud Boys is a far-right neo-fascist organization that admits only men as members and promotes and engages in political violence."

This book just would not be complete without a shout-out to the Proud Boys. The Proud Boys is a group of badass, America-loving patriots who attend the elite's organized, America-hating protests as counter-protesters. They attend to support law enforcement and stand against the elite's terrorist armies. We all need to support them. Their website is http://officialproudboys.com. They have some great merchandise, but it cannot be purchased at this time. See this explanation from their website:

> We've now been banned by the following vendors/payment processors:
>
> Amazon
> Chase
> NMI
> PayPal
> Shopify
> Square
> Stripe
> TeeSpring

We're currently in the process of being setup with a new payment processor.

We apologize for the inconvenience. We'll be back and bigger than ever before! If you have a question regarding your order or would like to know when the site is back up, please contact support.

Really think about what this indicates. The aforementioned vendors and payment processors have banned an America-loving organization but have no problem with the elite's America-hating terrorist armies and their marketing and merchandise. The Proud Boys are just one of many organizations banned by vendors and payment processors for no other reason than rejecting the elite's America-destroying agenda. Any person or group challenging the **communist elite's terrorist armies** are labeled as haters by their controlled media outlets, vendors, and payment processors. They have effectively brainwashed Americans into believing that challenging any aspect of the elite's America-hating narrative make them bad people; they are labeled as haters. Well, if despising the elite and their efforts to totally destroy America make me a hater, then I will proudly accept that title.

Update: The elite have shut down the Proud Boys website.

The Oath Keepers

The Oath Keepers (http://oathkeepers.org) are another badass, great, pro-American organization that is fighting to reclaim our republic from the communist elite who have taken it. Not surprisingly, Twitter has banned accounts associated with them for violating its policy on violent extremist groups. The following descriptions on Wikipedia highlight the anti-American bias being shoved down our throats

"Oath Keepers is an anti-government American far-right organization associated with the militia movement."

"The Proud Boys is a far-right neo-fascist organization that admits only men as members and promotes and engages in political violence."

"Black Lives Matter is a political and social movement."

Well, that is quite a contrast. I hope that you are all seeing the pattern here. Any and all groups fighting to reclaim our republic are labeled as violent extremists, but the groups representing the elite are labeled as poor innocent victims. It is OK with the owners of the mainstream media and social media that the so-called American-loving, innocent victims are rioting, looting, vandalizing, shutting down roads, highways, and businesses, and setting police on fire. **Support the Oath Keepers and the Proud Boys!**

Update: The elite have shut down the Oath Keepers website.

The Second Amendment and the Real Reason Our Government is So Desperate to Eliminate Our Right to Bear Arms

"The Second Amendment provides US citizens the right to bear arms… Having just used guns and other arms to ward off the English, the amendment was originally created to give citizens the opportunity to fight back against a tyrannical federal government" (https://www.livescience.com/26485-second-amendment.html).

In reality, the United States no longer exists. Citizens are being indoctrinated with United Nations and New World Order propaganda that starts from preschool and continues throughout our entire lives from educators, the media, the entertainment industry, professional athletes, and government officials. What is more, a duly elected president was denied reelection by a rigged election in 2020.

It is all part of a coup crafted by the international bankers, that is, the communist elite, over a hundred years ago.

The Second Amendment was originally created to give citizens the ability to fight back against a tyrannical federal government, and the current state of affairs in America strongly suggests that the country has reached that critical juncture.

Now, I want to make it crystal clear that I am not advocating taking up arms against anyone; I am only explaining to the people why our government is so eager to strip us of our Second Amendment rights.

Our government is aware that a growing number of Americans have become informed about its involvement with the elite's coup. That makes the powers that be nervous because, as more and more Americans become aware of the coup, a movement to stop it will surely evolve. Our government realizes that the public's awareness of rigged elections may prompt a revolution in which that invoking its Second Amendment rights has now become the only option. So, the government will work at break-neck speed to keep that from happening. They realize that they are few in number and would be targeted by Americans trying to reclaim the republic. Their numbers are quite small. On the federal level, there are 435 congressman and 100 senators. In comparison, there are 72 million Americans who own registered firearms. They also realize that local and state government officials—city council members, mayor's, congressmen, senators, judges, lawyers, governors, and anyone connected to the America-hating Council on Foreign Relations—as well as the elite's indoctrinators—schoolteachers and news anchors—corporate retailers (corporate retailers are censoring big-time now), payment processors, media owners (including social media), and talk show hosts serving the elite would also be targets. They are all poisoning American minds due to their demented desire to serve the America-hating elite. Our treasonous government realizes that it is all coming to a head and that the only option they have is to take our firearms—an action that would render American citizens defenseless against their totalitarian government.

Update: Bilderberg Joe desires to strip gun manufacturers of protection from lawsuits. He actually said that God called out to him and asked for this—apparently, he believes the elite are God. What's next? Will food manufacturers that use sugar in their products be liable for every person who develops diabetes?

Boycotts Equal Extorsion

Boycotts are defined as "a punitive ban that forbids relations with certain groups, cooperation with a policy, or the handling of goods."

On top of kicking, screaming, destroying property, setting police on fire, and shutting down businesses, roads, highways, and schools (with strikes), liberals and anarchists, both with the mentality of preschoolers, use boycotts to force business owners away from supporting any movements or beliefs that run contrary to their own. Sadly, many of the business owners are forced to bow down to these disobedient children or risk losing revenue. Thus, pro-American businesses are no longer allowed to voice their support for America while the America-hating businesses standing with the **anarchists** can say or do anything they desire.

McCarthyism

McCarthyism was an aggressive campaign carried out under Senator Joseph McCarthy during the mid-1940s and 1950s against alleged communists and their activities in the US government and other American institutions. McCarthy was a great patriot and was deeply disturbed by the large-scale subversion and treason occurring in our government and other institutions, like colleges and universities, the entertainment industry, and the media. Senator Prescott Sheldon Bush (G. H. W.'s father), his CFR allies, and the media made a mockery out of McCarthy for his accusations. They pretty much destroyed the man.

During the mid-1950s, the SCOTUS, led by ultra-liberal Republican chief justice Earl Warren, made a series of rulings that helped bring an end to McCarthyism, using the premise that it created heightened political repression.

The McCarthy investigations targeted those who were advocating **altering the form of government of the United States by unconstitutional means**. Thousands were investigated, including government employees, entertainment industry employees, studio owners, media owners and personalities, governing boards of universities, and labor-union activists. Some lost their jobs, went to prison, or were blacklisted. The communist-packed courts realized that McCarthyism was advocating for the repression of communism and had to be stopped. In essence, **the Warren Court** supported the communist invasion of America that started in 1921, the same year the CFR was created, with their rulings meant to stop the **anti-communist movement**. McCarthyism temporarily disrupted the communist invasion, but SCOTUS, led by Chief Justice Earl Warren, helped revive the invasion. And it continues to this very day.

McCarthy was taken down for attempting to expose and dislodge anti-American communists from our government and other institutions. That is exactly what President Donald J. Trump is attempting to do—and why both **communist-embedded parties** are so desperate to see him removed from the White House and **replaced with a Council on Foreign Relations communist puppet**.

The communist elite have taken ownership or control of nearly every institution in America. The entertainment industry, our universities, professional sports teams, and the media are all packed with America-hating communists. During the 1940s and 1950s, people involved with these industries were shunned for identifying as a communist and struggled to find employment, but now it has become a requirement.

The Communist Elite and Their Allies Are Erasing the Existence of a Free and Representative Republic

The following statement is one of the most important made in this book, so please read it carefully.

All of the anti-American movements have been contrived by the elite and are designed to create total anarchy in America. They are meant to create a hatred for our Founding Fathers and the great nation they created. They hate everything about America. Why? Because a truly free society of people who are aware of what our Founding Fathers did and understand why it is so important to preserve it cannot be tolerated by a group desiring to take our rights, freedoms, and liberties and control our every action. Our children know nothing of our Founding Fathers because the elite have taken control of our schools and forbid them to reveal the significance of the Founding Fathers and what they did.

The Black Lives Matter movement covers multiple bases for the elite, two of which are disarming America and brainwashing the masses into accepting the elite's agenda to **totally erase America's history**.

It is vitally important to understand the elite's intention here. They want to totally erase America's history by removing Confederate monuments, renaming military facilities named after Confederates, and prohibiting our children from learning about our great Founding Fathers and the significance of what they did because **knowledge of just how great America "once was" would encourage future generations to fight to reclaim that past existence**. Thus, the elite must erase all evidence that a nation as great and truly free as America ever existed. Therefore, the elite have been and are creating a dumbed-down society (through multiple mechanisms but mainly the media) that is willingly relinquishing its rights, freedoms, and liberties to a group of greedy, power-hungry, controlling international bankers who are creating a United States where only two classes will exist, the very rich and the poor, and where anarchy will be the new norm (it already is).

Those covertly serving (I say "covertly," but most are no longer even attempting to hide it) the elite are not really all that difficult to identify. Those who support erasing America's history are using the guise of bringing America together as a mechanism to destroy it. Of course, all Democrats stand with the elite, so there is no need to mention their names. However, I will mention some of the many

Republicans who have indicated that they are OK with erasing America's history. We should take their stance into consideration when it is time to go to the polls. Maybe someday we will have fair elections that matter again. In any case, the names are as follows:

> Mitch McConnell, Republican Senate majority leader from Kentucky
> Kevin McCarthy, Republican House minority leader from California
> John Thune, Republican Senate majority whip from South Dakota
> James Inhofe, Republican senator from Oklahoma
> John Cornyn, Republican senator from Texas
> David Perdue, Republican senator from Georgia
> Joni Ernst, Republican senator from Iowa
> John Neely Kennedy, Republican senator from Louisiana
> Marco Rubio, Republican senator from Florida
> Mitt Romney, Republican senator from Utah
> Chuck Grassley, Republican senator from Iowa
> Mike Rounds, Republican senator from South Dakota
> Mark Lankford, Republican senator from Oklahoma
> Roy Blunt, Republican senator from Missouri

Now, bear in mind that the aforementioned legislators (and all those supportive of erasing America's history not mentioned here) know damn good and well that renaming the military bases and removing monuments has nothing to do with uniting America and everything to do with erasing America's history. They are all apparently okay with removing the Confederate monuments in Georgia but have no problem with allowing the Georgia Guidestones to stand. Instances like this are why I no longer donate to the Republican Party.

The numerous members of our Congress and high-ranking military officials wanting to rename military bases are ignoring our commander-in-chief's desire not to. And that suggests to me that they are giving the desires of an **unelected government's** president priority over those of our duly elected president.

Per Wikipedia, "The president of the United States is the commander-in-chief of the United States Armed Forces and as such exercises supreme operational command over all national military forces of the United States... The president and the secretary of defense, collectively, form the National Command Authority."

Chapters 1–3 of this book argue that the Council on Foreign Relations has many of their handpicked people embedded in the military and the State Department, so it only stands to reason that many of them also support the erasure of America's history.

The Federal Reserve

The Federal Reserve was created on December 23, 1913 when President Woodrow Wilson signed the Federal Reserve Act into law. Shortly afterwards, he made the following statement:

> I am a most unhappy man. I have unwittingly ruined my country. A great industrial nation is controlled by its system of credit. Our system of credit is concentrated. **The growth of the nation, therefore, and all our activities are in the hands of a few men. We have come to be one of the worst ruled, one of the most completely controlled and dominant governments in the civilized world. No longer a government by free opinion, no longer a government by conviction and the vote of the majority, but a government by the opinion and duress of a small group of dominant men.**

Wilson's statement explains three things:

- why the Federal Reserve chairman ignores the desires of the duly elected president of the United States,

- why our Council on Foreign Relations-serving treasonous Republicans will never support a Trump-preferred nominee for a position on the Federal Reserve Board, and
- why our treasonous Congress will never allow the Federal Reserve to be audited.

The Dominican Republic-Central Free Trade Agreement (DR-CAFTA)

In his review of Daniel Estulin's *The True Story of the Bilderberg Group*, Stephen Lendman states, "In June and July 2005, the Dominican Republic-Central America Free Trade Agreement (DR-CAFTA) passed the Senate and the House, establishing corporate-approved trade rules **to further impoverish the region and move a step closer to continental integration.**"

And now the real reason for the influx of immigrants at our southern border has been revealed—the situation was manufactured by our Congress. The covert North American Union agenda is very real, and DR-CAFTA is just another cog in the wheel created by the elites and legislated by their embedded puppets as another mechanism meant to strip America of its sovereignty. They are trying to convert the country from a representative republic into a servile, corporate-controlled nation ruled by the United Nations socialists.

We Are All Victims of a Coup d' État

Per Wikipedia, "a coup or coup d'état is the removal of an existing government from power through non-legal, often coercive means typically, it is an unconstitutional seizure of power by a political faction, the military, or a dictator."

The Executive Departments

The executive departments are the administration arms of the President of the United States. The heads of the departments are nominated by the President and need to be confirmed by the Senate.

Once the nominees are confirmed, they are obligated to serve at the pleasure of the president, **who can remove them at any time without the approval of the Senate.**

The DOJ and the FBI are two of the fifteen executive departments. The DOJ is headed by William Barr and the FBI is headed by Christopher Wray. It is quite obvious that Wray and Barr are not fulfilling their obligation to serve President Donald J. Trump. Both are guilty of concealing vital information that should be shared with the president in full. But that has not been the case. People who have been committing treasonous acts against the United States of America are being protected. WHY? This book reveals why! Because the communist elite control the departments and our entire government. Wray and Barr have totally disrespected our commander-in-chief and should not only be removed from their positions but also held in contempt. President Trump has the authority to remove them without approval from the Senate, and he speaks about doing so but still does not. Why? Obviously, someone is overruling him!

The Military

Military officials continue to disrespect our commander-in-chief just as DOJ and the FBI officials have. The communist riots, orchestrated by the communist elite, continue to be supported by communist mayors and governors (the radical left title distracts from what they truly are—communists—so we should start calling them communists). In response, Trump pushed for military intervention using the Insurrection Act. Per Wikipedia, "The Insurrection Act of 1807 is a United States federal law that empowers the President of the United States to deploy US military and federalized National Guard troops within the United States in particular circumstances, **such as to suppress civil disorder, insurrection and rebellion.**"

President Trump had every right to order the military to intervene, as the communist mayors and governors were ignoring and actually supporting the civil unrest. But several communist senators opposed intervention on the grounds that citizens' First Amendment Rights would be violated, and of course, Defense Secretary Mark

Esper and Joint Chiefs Chairman Mark Miley agreed. That is CON-TEMPT! They have no business second guessing their commanding officer, President Donald J. Trump, or worse yet, disobeying his commands. Trump is up against a communist-controlled government (communists currently hold the majority in our Congress) who have been undermining his every effort to take back America from the communist elite.

The president has plenary power to command and control all military personnel, launch, direct and supervise military operations, order or authorize the deployment of troops, unilaterally launch nuclear weapons, and set military policy with the Department of Defense and the Department of Homeland Security.

Though the communist majority running our government are staunchly opposed to using the Insurrection Act to quell the communist invasion, they would use it in a heartbeat to quell Trump-loving American patriots fighting to remove the communists from our government and our land. Exactly that will happen if a communist president should take the White House.

It is quite obvious that the communist elite are deeply embedded in the Pentagon, which is evidenced by the military brass **refusing to acknowledge our duly elected President as their commander-in-chief**. Considering this, it is reasonable to assume that the military will stand with the communist elite in the event that an almost certain uprising moves against them. Such an uprising would be spurred by angry patriots having their votes thrown out in **the rigged election**.

Martial Law

Joint Chiefs Chairman Mark Miley has overstepped his authority yet again by reaching out to the communist Democrats. He desperately wants to protect the communist rioters from a powerful military on the grounds that their First Amendment rights would be violated. He is not a stupid man; he knows exactly what they are—scary. Miley's actions indicate who the military will stand with should war break out between loyal Americans and the communists running our government. In essence, the military has already revealed their stance in their attempts to stop President Trump from invoking martial law. Martial law invoked under President Trump would be an attempt to save America; martial law invoked under a communist president would be an attempt to destroy America. Either way, it is none of Miley's business. CONTEMPT!

Due Process and Appellate Rights

The communist elite removed Donald Trump from the White House and **replaced him with a stooge** who will serve them. The 2020 election was rigged, and there is ample evidence to support this conclusion. Yet *none* of the courts are interested in reviewing the suits. Citizens demanding election integrity have not been given the due process and appellate rights that they are entitled to.

Isn't fair treatment in the judicial system part of due process? The courts have dismissed nearly all of the suits without so much as even glancing at the evidence. Moreover, appellate rights are granted, but they can only appeal a lower court's decision to not hear the suits in the first place. Thus, there is no due process, and the appellate rights are a joke. By the way, this is exactly how the judiciaries operate in the communist nations. We were all concerned that the Democrats would pack the courts to ensure that they get what they want, but the SCOTUS decision to not give citizens demanding election integrity due process tells me court-packing will not be necessary. The nine justices currently occupying the high court are going to work out just fine for them.

QAnon

QAnon has been described as a far-right conspiracy theory that details a supposed secret plot by the elite against President Donald J. Trump and his supporters (that is, anyone desiring to save our republic). The cabal behind the secret plot to destroy and take control of America are accused of being power-thirsty pedophiles involved with sex trafficking and even cannibalism. Pedophilia and cannibalism: Does Epstein come to mind? Is that what the 500 million of OUR SPECIES who will be allowed to coexist with the superior species going to be used for? Government officials from both parties are denouncing QAnon, and the FBI has labeled QAnon a potential domestic terrorist threat. Think about that. It appears to me that they are diverting attention away from a sinister reality in order to protect it.

Republican congressmen Lindsey Graham, Kevin McCarthy, and Adam Kinzinger have stated that there is no place for QAnon in the Republican Party, but what they should be saying is there is no place for pedophilia or TREASON against a sitting president in the Republican Party. In my opinion, any elected official claiming that such an obviously true conspiracy is fiction may be involved with the conspiracy and should be scrutinized by the voters. Well, damn, that is going to be a problem because 2020 has revealed that the elections are rigged.

Why are Lindsey Graham, Kevin McCarthy and Adam Kinzinger up in arms and mocking a group that is attempting to expose such an obvious conspiracy—a conspiracy that is meant to remove a sitting president from office, keep him from being reelected, and also hide the possibility that some members of our Congress engage in sex trafficking and pedophilia? And why would QAnon be labeled a potential domestic terrorist threat by the FBI? The only threat that QAnon presents is to those involved with the alleged activities, and it is obvious that the FBI has their backs. Expectedly, Graham, McCarthy, and Kinzinger tell us that there is no agenda to remove Trump from the White House, while every living soul in America knows goddamn good and well that there is, and it started before Trump ever took office. The desire to silence QAnon extends to nearly all of Congress.

On October 2, 2020, all but eighteen members of Congress voted in favor of House Resolution 1154. This bill condemns QAnon and rejects the so-called unfounded conspiracy theories it promotes. Once again, the conspiracy theories that QAnon promotes appear to be conspiracy fact. Our government's desperate attempt to condemn QAnon seems to be implying something. Members of Congress from both parties are involved with the activities alleged by QAnon and conspired to remove Trump from the White House. In August 2020, Facebook removed hundreds of QAnon groups from its site. And Mike Pence recently canceled a fundraiser hosted by a couple (a couple who has donated $220,000 to the Trump' campaign) that publicly supports QAnon—that action alone is enough to convince me that Mike Pence cannot be trusted by the Trump base. **Trump and his base HAVE NO PARTY!**

Did Epstein Commit Suicide? Not Even a Chance!

Had Jeffrey Epstein ever made it to the courtroom, the numerous prominent people involved with the disgraceful behavior occurring on Epstein's island (and beyond) would have been revealed to their adoring public. Thus, Epstein had to go. Think about it: Given the seriousness of the allegations, Epstein would have had top level security, including constant surveillance, which would have made it impossible for him to be killed by anyone, himself included.

It is believed that many high-ranking politicians, dignitaries, wealthy individuals, professional athletes, and nearly all of Hollywood are associated with the cabal and are aligned with their desire to transform America from a representative republic into a servile nation of people controlled by a group who serve ONLY themselves and those supportive of them. QAnon is an attempt to bring the American-hating cabal and all those serving it to justice (good luck with that!). The titles *The Storm* and *The Great Awakening* refer to a time when the elite, America's most dangerous ENEMY, are finally brought to justice. I believe that the supposed plot is not supposed at all—it is a reality. Just think about the insane amount of money privileged celebrities donated to stop Trump from being reelected. They were donating massive amounts of money in an effort to save their careers and keep themselves from being sent to prison.

Our elected officials (from both parties) desperate efforts to denounce QAnon and their reluctance to acknowledge that the 2020 election was rigged coupled with their refusal to make any attempt to overturn it implicates them so very clearly. They have some major skeletons in their closets and have gone to great extremes to keep those skeletons from being revealed. They denounce and mock QAnon because QAnon would reveal those skeletons. It represents the greatest threat ever to their secrets and lies. QAnon is such a threat that a scheme was contrived to remove a sitting president from office. Trump was attempting to spoil their party and had to go. The election was rigged, now the sex-trafficking, under the table deals with corporations and rouge nations, pedophilia, and drug deals and drug use can continue unchallenged. Let the good times roll!

Bilderberg Joe Has Everything Going the Elite's Way

- Open borders are leading to continental integration, that is, to the North American Union. Goodbye, United States of America!
- They are shutting down the fossil fuel industry. Goodbye, well-paying jobs; hello, Agenda 21 and the New World Order! This is not the earth-saving climate change agenda the elite are touting it to be. Instead, it is an agenda meant to give a small group of international bankers total control over every institution and every human being on this planet (as discussed in chapters 1–13).
- Extending lockdowns for the manufactured global pandemic means creating a zero-growth society (discussed in chapter 1) and a subservient, obedient society that willfully relinquishes its rights, freedoms, and liberties in return for the government handouts that have become their only source of income. Worse yet, the majority of these government stipends will have to be used to pay for our outrageous green energy bills and fueling our vehicles.
- They push for the demonization of all males.
- They allow any and all to vote, including the deceased. If that does not produce the desired results, they will manipulate the numbers until the elite's stooges have enough votes to secure a win.

THE GLOBAL CONSPIRACY EXPOSED

- They ignore and even advocate for the complete censorship of any content considered to pose a threat to the elite, their New World Order, and one-world government.
- They are rejoining all of the UN world government organizations. Nationalism is out the window, and our corporate-controlled dictatorship is allowing the elite-controlled UN to make decisions for what used to be we the people's republic.
- Creating a single class by confiscating the majority of income earned after $400,000, a.k.a. wealth redistribution.
- They use extortion to repeal anti-elite legislation, destroy anti-elite companies, and indoctrinate the entire nation to embrace communism. Thus, they are allowing and even advocating that the communist-owned and communist-dominated corporations, entertainment industry, professional sports industry, media, and schools become the ones that really govern the country.

The Elite Are a Deadly Cancer That Has Infected Our Entire Nation

They have taken control of every institution in America, including but not limited to

- professional sports,
- the entertainment industry,
- schools (the elite's indoctrination starts from preschool and continues all the way through college),
- corporations,
- the media, and
- every branch of government at every level, from city to federal.

With the possible exception of JFK, Trump was the only president to challenge the elite and their public base, the Council on Foreign Relations, since they started vetting and choosing our legislators, judges, executive branch heads, and many other positions in 1921. Thus, Trump had to go. They removed our duly elected president and seated THEIR president in his place. I just hope that we can all unite and rally behind President Trump and his family. All of us have got to work together and come up with a way to take back our nation.

Donate ONLY to Donald J. Trump at http://donaldjtrump.com. All the other PACs are almost certainly fronts for the Council on Foreign Relations, and those asking for donations should be considered false prophets.

Trump "Save America" Donations—Be Mindful

Here are some observations you should seriously consider before donating to the Republican Party or any political action committee representing them.

- Both parties serve the elite and are well aware of their America-destroying agenda—an agenda with specific deadlines.
- Both parties knew that the elite wanted a global reset in 2021 and that the only way to accomplish that in a timely manner would be a global pandemic—and then one magically appears.
- The RNC, more often than not, glorifies the establishment incumbents and vilifies the antiestablishment challengers. They assure us that the elite-serving Republicans will always have the majority and with it the ability to cancel out the anti-elite Republicans.
- Republicans knew why the global pandemic was manufactured and that the elite would use it to justify using easily manipulated mail-in voting—yet they did nothing. They made no attempt to stop the rigging of the 2020 election or overturn it after the fact.
- The Republican majority, while led by McConnell and Ryan during 2016–2018, was tasked by the elite with nullifying any actions taken by Trump that could be a problem

for their New World Order/one-world government agenda, and that's exactly what they did!

- Both parties conspired to create the endless bullshit accusations and hearings during 2018–2020 in order to tie Trump's hands for another two years. McCarthy's win over Jordan for speaker was predictable given that the position is voted on by the Republican House members, the vast majority of whom are serving the Bilderberg Group's public base, the Council on Foreign Relations.

- The Republicans absolutely knew that the elite were desperate to meet a specific timeline and that Trump had to go. Their actions and inaction prove that they are walking hand in hand with the elite.

- Every Republican senator stabbed Trump and his base in the back by not challenging the electors. The only Republican senator to challenge was Josh Hawley, and his actions were a joke because he only challenged one state (old "One-State" Hawley). If he were as concerned as he made himself out to be, he would have mounted a challenge in all contested states. It was all a charade! The Republican House members put on a show—that's all it was, just a show. They realized that the Trump base was not buying into their bullshit; thus, they attempted to cover up their betrayal in an attempt to salvage the 2022 and 2024 elections.

Bear in mind that the Republicans made no sincere attempt to save Trump or our republic. We are all receiving emails and physical mailings from political action committees that are aligning themselves with the Republican Party. They are representing the Republican Party, but the Republican Party does not represent Trump, his base, or America. There are a number of good America-loving patriots identifying as Republicans, but those poor souls are mocked and ridiculed by the elite-serving Republican majority, for example, Marjorie Taylor Greene. The PACs are talking the talk, but that's all it is—just talk. Those endorsing the PACs were only pretend allies to Trump, at least until the day they exposed their loyalty to the elite. DON'T TRUST ANY OF THEM! Donate only to Donald J. Trump at http://donaldjtrump.com. One hundred percent of the donations will go to anti-elite Republicans.

> **All we need now is the right major crisis, and the nations will accept the New World Order.**
> —David Rockefeller

David Rockefeller said in from June 1992,

> We are grateful to **the *Washington Post*, the *New York Times*, *Time* magazine** and other great publications whose directors have attended our meetings and respected their promises of discretion for almost forty years. It would have been impossible for us to develop **OUR PLAN FOR THE WORLD** if we had been subject to the bright lights of publicity during those years. But the work is now much more sophisticated and prepared to march towards a world government. **The supranational sovereignty of an intellectual elite and world bankers is surely preferable to the national auto-determination practiced in past centuries.**

The Rothschild cabal have infiltrated your government, your media, your banking institutions. They are no longer content with committing atrocities in the Middle East; they are now doing it on their own soil [Europe], desperate to complete the plan for a one-world government, world army, complete with a world central bank.

> —Vladimir Putin

Countless people…will hate the new world order…and will die protesting against it.

—H. G. Wells

If we are to guard against ignorance and remain free, it is the responsibility of every American to be informed.

—Thomas Jefferson

Manufactured pandemics, forced to eat only what they desire us to eat, told how to think and conduct ourselves, RIGGED ELECTIONS, the elimination of law enforcement, human settlements, manufactured social unrest, a military defying the duly elected president of the United States and servile to the elite, a zero-growth society, lockdowns, CLIMATE MANIPULATION, crisis creation, and censorship and indoctrination on a grand scale. **WELCOME TO THE NEW WORLD ORDER!**

About the Author

The author is the proud father of six children and proud grandfather of ten, worked in the industrial construction field for thirty-six years as a boilermaker, and is an antiestablishment Republican. He also is an avid reader who has had a long-standing fascination with mysterious phenomena, UFOs, and ancient megaliths.

CPSIA information can be obtained
at www.ICGtesting.com
Printed in the USA
LVHW091210170921
698064LV00001B/1